More Precious Than Gold

LYNN DEAN

Cover art by Lynnette Bonner of Indie Cover Designs

All verses and references are taken from the *Holy Bible*, King James Version.

ISBN: 1545151822
ISBN-13: 978-1545151822

FOR DADDY

Who likes to watch people
and loves history because it tells their stories,
who demonstrates God's love in wonderful ways,
and who introduced me to Elizabethtown.

Happy Birthday

I love you

IN APPRECIATION

It takes more than one person to write a book! So many people have encouraged me along the journey. There's always the fear of leaving someone out, but to all and to these I am deeply grateful:

To my husband, Tom, for encouraging me at all times and to my daughter, Katelyn, and my son, David, for being my first readers, technical advisors, and cheering squad.

To my mom (who wrote down my first story), my dad, and my sister who lovingly pressed for "the next chapter, please."

Kim for her encouragement.

Dr. and Mrs. J. Rush Pierce for a delightful afternoon and a great education in the lore of the Red River and Moreno valleys. Their publications (*Mountain Wildflowers of Northern New Mexico*, *Red River Mining District Gold Mines*, *Historic Buildings in Red River City*, and *The Big Ditch*) were invaluable resources.

The Mutz family who own and operate the Elizabethtown Museum at the site of the old town.

Rayetta Trujillo, Colfax Co. Clerk, who supplied a copy of the original plat.

The staff of the St. James Hotel in Cimarron, NM for taking time to give an amateur historian a tour and information about Clay Allison.

Anne and Ron Skrabanek for information on cattle, and Lynn Squire for her input on horses and how heifers give birth. Any errors are mine, not theirs.

Alvin G. Davis, founder of the National Cowboy Symposium & Celebration in Lubbock, TX, and his wife, Barbara, for their excellent information and for preserving western culture in modern times.

The librarians of Baylor University's Texas Collection who put me in touch with numerous original source documents.

Aaron David at the Federal Archives Center in Fort Worth and Bill at the Waco-McLennan Co. Library genealogy department, who helped me discover "who done it," who got them off, who looked the other way, who stood for justice, and most importantly Tony

McCrary, the victim, whose crime was likely nothing more than being in the wrong place at the wrong time.

To my critique partners—Debra Shirley, Fay Lamb, K. Sue Morgan, Linda Strawn, Lynn Squire, and Melinda Evaul who patiently read and re-read the manuscript, offering countless suggestions for improvement.

And to my first readers, who cheered me on, caught typos, and cried in all the right places.

Greatly rejoice,
though now for a season ye are in heaviness through manifold temptations: that the trial of your faith,
being much **more precious than gold** that perisheth,
though it be tried with fire,
might be found unto praise and honour and glory
at the appearing of Jesus Christ.

I Peter 1:6-7

Prologue
Waco, Texas—February, 1867

Torches bobbed above the crowd gathered around the jailhouse. The flickering light cast unnatural shadows beneath the oaks on the courthouse lawn, animating the underside of the arching boughs. Like hellish fingers they seemed to hold the mob in their grip.

Eliza Gentry slipped her hand into the crook of her father's arm, her breath forming clouds as they hurried through the starless night. At six foot six, Papa's long legs covered a lot of ground, but she managed to keep up—one of the rare advantages, she supposed, of inheriting her height from him.

With the passing of each city block, the sounds of the uproar grew louder and more distinct, punctuated now and again by angry shouts.

"You got no call to hold those men. Turn 'em loose, you carpetbagger, afore we fetch 'em out ourselves!"

"Go on home, Yanks, while you can still leave standing!"

Judging from the ensuing swells of approval, the threats expressed the general sentiment of those gathered, though only a few were brave or foolish enough to speak out, surrounded as they were by cavalry. Most folks in Waco were good church-going people—the type who disapproved of the use of liquor—but this group was drunk on hate.

Torchlight contorted the features of many familiar faces. The grocer and the proprietors of several shops Eliza frequented. The school's headmaster and a handful of older students. Women who attended the fine ladies' teas and Bible studies at Papa's church. Respectable citizens clamoring alongside the commoner residents—barmen and drunks, drifters and prostitutes—people who pretended not to notice one another by daylight. Tonight rage lent them a grotesque similarity that transcended social status.

Papa quickened his pace, and Eliza tightened her grip on his sleeve. She could see the federal soldiers now, standing at rigid attention, rifles at the ready across their chests. As her foot left the hard-packed street, a shadowed figure broke from the mob and lunged for one of the infantrymen who guarded the barred door.

The soldier's eyes widened in surprise. As if by instinct, he took a step backward before determination hardened his jaw.

A shot rang out as he fired into the air, the report echoing in the cold night air.

Eliza flinched.

For the space of a collective gasp, a shocked silence fell over the scene. The only sound was the startled squawk of thousands of blackbirds rudely awakened from their roosting places in the courthouse trees, then the rush of wings as they flew in search of safer havens.

The crowd seemed to erupt just as the birds had. With cries of protest they surged forward, and skittish horses moved to intervene.

Papa dropped Eliza's hand and broke into a run. Diving into the crowd, the swelling human tide carried him forward even before he began to stroke, swimming through a sea of people, pushing aside anyone who stood in his way.

Eliza hitched up her skirts and ran after him, reaching the fringe of the mob just as Papa reached the jailhouse door. Peering over the heads of the men in front of her, she hugged her arms about her chest and shoved her hands beneath them to stop their shaking. She fixed Papa in her gaze as if she could somehow protect him by doing so.

Taking a position between two soldiers, Papa faced the aggressors and raised both hands as if in benediction. "Brothers!" His voice carried easily from years of practice projecting from the pulpit. "Brothers!" he said again, and this time his booming voice seemed to penetrate the frenzy and turn the tide.

Eliza's heart swelled with pride just like it did every Sunday she could remember.

"This is not the way civilized people handle disagreements."

No one could argue with that. After four years of civil war and two bitter years of occupation, Southerners were acutely aware of the consequences of passionate disagreement. But the passion remained. The government's efforts to enforce restoration had only succeeded in forcing the issues beneath the surface. There they festered like an uncleansed wound. Now and again the abscess of old hatreds ruptured into unimaginable atrocities.

"What's he going on about? Trying to stop a lynching?"

"No. Trying to convince them a fair trial is in order." Intent on watching Papa, Eliza had barely noticed the cowboys who pressed in behind her. "They're holding a landowner and a doctor. These people want them released."

Five pairs of eyebrows sprang up. "The prisoner's a doctor? What'd he do?" The tallest—a handsome fellow despite a layer of trail dust—acted as spokesman.

How could she explain the horrible deed in mixed company? She groped for words before deciding to put the crime in terms cattlemen would understand. "He gelded a boy."

The men gulped in collective sympathy before the spokesman said, "Why?"

Why, indeed. Assumptions. Accusations based on prejudice. She had no wish to rehash the details, but the cowboys stared at her in silent expectation. Outsiders, obviously. Everyone in town knew the ugly facts.

Frustrated, Eliza rattled off the essentials, tossing the words over her shoulder without taking her gaze from Papa. "The Freedmen's Bureau sent Lt. Manning to investigate this incident as well as the murder of a former slave. When the local judge refused to try the murder, he realized this case would never receive a fair hearing, so he made the arrests himself pending further instructions."

"Oh." Heads nodded. "The boy's Black."

A furious pulse roared in her ears. "What difference does that make?" she snapped. "The boy had a name. Tony. He had hopes—a future—his whole life before him, and now it's..." She started to say "gone," but Tony's future was worse than gone. It was empty.

The men stared, uncomprehending. Without comment they sauntered closer to the commotion.

A sick feeling twisted her stomach. The whole sordid situation should have caused her to weep, and before the war it would have.

When had she stopped crying? Three years ago? Four? The year her own dreams died. When, like this boy, she fell victim to a fight she had no part in. Crying changed nothing. Every day was a struggle to reconcile the faith of her childhood to the empty life that had been thrust upon her. Empathy should have helped her pray for the boy, but her prayers hadn't seemed to change much, either. She'd quit asking God for anything about the same time the tears stopped.

Her loss, like Tony's, was pointless. No one could avenge the wrong. Nothing could repair it. This crowd was not interested in truth or justice, only in defending their own prejudice. How could educated men praise God on Sunday and harbor the potential for such evil in their hearts? What was a shade of skin compared with the blackness of men's souls?

"It ain't right!" One stubborn voice rose from the crowd. "You oughtn't to punish a man for sterilizin' vermin!"

Eliza tasted the bitterness in his words, and bile rose in her throat as she confronted the depth of wickedness surrounding her. These people had been her friends, her fellow church members. Had the whole world gone mad, or just her corner of it?

"Go home." Papa's tone was stern—like a judge pronouncing sentence. His eyes flashed with righteous fury, but the fire was quickly quenched by welling tears. "Y'all go on home, now." Eliza heard the brokenness of his heart in the breaking of his voice.

Though disgruntled murmurs made it clear that their hearts had not changed, the crowd began to dissolve grudgingly back into the shadows of the night. As they passed, no one looked at her. No one spoke. One woman, a deacon's wife, spared her a quick glance and the hint of an awkward smile, but she looked down again when her husband gave her arm a yank and glared his disapproval. In a matter of minutes, Eliza stood alone beneath the towering oaks, dark now that the torches were gone. The taste of coal oil smoke lingered on the night air.

In the light that remained by the jailhouse, Papa spoke with the guards.

Eliza did not approach them. It would be inappropriate to eavesdrop on men's business, but in the still night she couldn't help hearing snatches of conversation.

"I appreciate your cooperation." One sergeant spoke on behalf of the federal soldiers.

What he called cooperation most folks were likely to term

sympathizing with the enemy.

Papa tugged at his stiff collar. "They're good people, mostly. This situation's just got them riled up."

Papa didn't like the Yankee occupation any better than anyone else did—and with good reason—but he was determined to obey the governing authorities. To him it was a matter of religious integrity. God was sovereign, and whomever He set over the affairs of men must be obeyed, even if obedience required sacrifice.

Eliza had always found obedience to be something of a sacrifice. When she was a child, she often exercised an independent spirit, and Mama did not hesitated to swat her backside with a switch whenever she got sassy. "Spare the rod; spoil the child," she'd say, and Eliza's strong will ensured that the fruit trees around the parsonage received regular pruning. But Papa believed that all differences could be settled through cooperation and understanding. He preferred to reason with Eliza, patiently listening to her frustrations and explaining why certain rules were necessary. Many times, she'd wished he would just spank her and get it over with, but he insisted that any lasting change must come from the inside—from the heart.

It was surely the same now. No lasting change could be enforced by government troops until the hearts of men were changed and filled with compassion for one another. From the looks of things lately, they had a long way to go.

At last Papa shook hands with the officer in charge and turned to look for her, squinting as his eyes adjusted to the dark. His face was weary, etched with furrows of unspeakable sorrow, but a smile touched his eyes when he saw Eliza.

Eliza smiled back. "You were wonderful. I'm so proud of you."

"We're a good team," he said. He tucked her hand once again into the crook of his arm, warm and safe, and gave it a pat.

They walked home in silence. How many hours had Eliza spent studying Greek and Latin with him in his pleasant library? Yet the two of them seldom needed words of any language to communicate. Eliza reveled in the feel of his arm beneath her hand. Solid. Unshakeable. That was Papa.

ꕥ

An oil lamp on the parlor table cast a welcoming glow across the porch of their modest parsonage. When they rushed out at the first cry of alarm, Eliza had not paused even long enough to retract the wick, but now she was glad of it. The cheerful light promised peace inside.

Papa held the door as she entered. The latch gave a reassuring click as the door closed behind them, and Eliza turned to hang her shawl on its hook. Despite whatever happened outside, all was well within.

The expression on Papa's face made her blood run cold. His eyes were fixed on the stair hall behind her. Turning again, she saw a figure emerge from the shadows and recognized the man whose warped and bitter words had sickened her a quarter hour before. He was a good head shorter than she was and had a dull, weaselly look about him. Papa towered over him, but a six-shooter was a great equalizer of angry little men.

"Put your gun down and be on your way. There's nothing here you want." Papa opened the door and stepped aside so as not to bar the man's escape.

"You got that straight, you miser'ble traitor. There ain't nuthin' here I want." The man lurched a bit, as if inebriated, waving his gun around to indicate the parsonage and everything in it before pointing the muzzle again in their direction. "I don't want you, and don't nobody want her!" He sneered at Eliza, his words piercing as surely as any bullet, causing an explosion of painful memories. How could old wounds still cause such anguish?

Eliza had barely time to register the muzzle flash before the revolver's discharge deafened her. The concussion wave hit like an invisible thrust, turning her insides to quivering jelly. She screamed, but could not hear her own voice—only the ringing echo of the pistol blast. By instinct her hand went to her belly, but she felt no pain. She stared at the gunman who stared back at her, eyes wide, then looked down in disbelief at his shaking hand.

His lips moved. "Oh, Lord! I've shot the preacher!"

He threw the gun to the parlor floor as if it were a snake that bit him. Bolting past her, he jumped the steps and disappeared into the night in the time it took Papa to slide slowly down the wall of the parsonage entry, leaving a red streak on the wallpaper behind him.

Eliza snatched her shawl from the hall tree and pressed it to Papa's wounds, cradling his head in her lap. She felt the door creak open, squeezing them against the wall. Stifling a cry she leaned forward to shield him with her body.

It was only a neighbor. "I heard a shot. Do you ... oh, Lord! I'll get help." His words seemed to come from a great distance.

An eternity passed before he returned with a doctor in tow, but it was a wonder he found a physician at all, with one in jail and another in hiding as an accomplice. Who knew where the sympathies of the town's other physicians lay? Eliza didn't ask, and she didn't care at that point. Stanching the flow of blood was of paramount importance.

When it seemed safe to lift the bloody compresses, the doctor studied Papa's wounds, his face grave. "The bullet passed through just below the shoulder. It's a wonder it missed the bone."

Or his heart.

"There's still a risk of infection, though. Help me get him upstairs."

Between the three of them and Papa's own feeble efforts, they managed to half carry the patient to his room. Papa groaned considerably as they settled him on his bed, though they made every effort to handle him gently. Eliza fumbled for a match and struck a light while the men pulled off Papa's boots.

The doctor rummaged in his bag. When Eliza saw that he withdrew a vial of laudanum, she nodded to the neighbor. "Thank you for your help. He should rest easier soon."

With promises to check in on them in the morning, the man left.

Eliza's relief was short lived, though. Papa waved the bottle away. Stubborn man. The doctor shrugged and pulled out another vial.

The tang of alcohol burned her nose as liberal amounts splashed over the entry and exit wounds, sterilizing them.

Papa sucked in a sharp breath and moaned. A fine sweat broke out along his upper lip and forehead, and his face turned pale in the lamplight. His eyelids fluttered and drifted shut, and his weight sagged against her.

Eliza looked away, biting her lip, but kept her arms firm about his shoulders, holding him upright while the doctor packed his wounds with bandages and wrapped his ribs in several yards of rolled muslin.

At last he dropped his scissors into the black satchel that lay open on the lamp table. "He should rest more comfortably now, but he'll be weak from the loss of blood," he said, snapping the bag shut. "It's been a long night." He stretched before taking up the medical bag. "I'm going home."

Eliza eased Papa back against the pillows. Was that it then? Was that all that could be done?

Whatever his political leanings, the doctor gave her hand a compassionate pat. "Watch him through the night. I'll be back tomorrow."

Eliza walked with him as far as the door of the bed chamber.

"Stay with him. I'll see myself out."

She heard his weary steps on the stair treads then a creak as the front door opened and closed again. Holding her breath, Eliza listened for the comforting rattle of the latch, but it never came. Pressed small against the door jamb, she listened to the silence as her blood rushed loud in her ears. Every imagined whisper reminded her that the gunman was still at large, still bigoted, still angry—him and a host of others, and now there was no man to protect her. A cold hand of fear lay heavy between her shoulder blades, urging her to bolt down the dark staircase and secure the lock, but a greater fear froze her where she stood.

She mentally cataloged all the small sounds in the shadows below, hardly daring to breathe, then crept to a straight-backed chair beside the bedstead and sank into it. A twist of the lamp stem lowered the wick to a dim glow. With as much composure as she could muster, Eliza watched Papa's chest rise and fall steadily. Solid. Unshakeable.

Her mind rambled as she settled in for the long night watch—back to her coming-out party ten years ago. Papa thought such things were silly, but Mama was the daughter of local aristocrats, and Eliza longed for once not to feel different from the other girls—the ones she towered over, the ones whose papas preached no controversial sermons. And so at sixteen she had her introduction into polite society, though afterwards that society politely ignored her for the most part. Her friends were courted and married in short order, but no one spoke for her.

Until Grayson, a young seminarian who came to apprentice with Papa. The three of them studied scripture together; then the two of them studied alone, first in the pleasant parlor and then on long walks beside the Brazos River. When war broke out between the states, Grayson went with all the other young men. He left Eliza with such sweet words, telling her he cherished their time together—cherished her—and begged her to wait for his return. "Come magnify the Lord with me, and let us exalt His name together." No proposal could have pleased her more. But Grayson never came home. Part of Eliza died, as well, that sad Christmas when she received his commander's letter. She devoted herself to relief work with Mama, burying her pain in the solace of service.

Mama. How she missed her! She was Papa's helpmate in every way, and Eliza found comfort in assisting as she ministered to the sick, both slave and free. But Mama was not like Papa and Eliza. She was tiny and fragile. In the last year of the war, worn and thin from hard work and deprivation, she caught a fever from one of the children and quickly succumbed. Union troops blockaded the harbors, blocking the simple medicines that could have saved her.

Eliza exhaled a ragged breath. The grief of all she'd lost threatened to choke her. *Not Papa, too.* He was all she had left. She pressed a handkerchief to her lips.

Papa stirred slightly, and Eliza jumped to her feet. She grabbed a cloth from the edge of the basin and poured cool water from the pitcher to dampen it, wringing it out before she pressed the compress gently to his brow.

His eyes flickered open. He stared up at her for a moment before he seemed to realize where he was and remember how he came to be there. "Think I'll live?"

"Yes! Oh, yes, you must." Eliza's most desperate hope took the form of an answer before she noticed the smile lines tugging at the corners of his mouth.

He patted her arm, still trying to take care of her even as she cared for him. "There's a letter on the bureau." He gestured weakly.

"Don't worry with it now, Papa. You can read it later."

"I've read it," he said, his voice thin and strained. "I want you to read it."

Eliza fetched the correspondence. Even in the dim light she recognized her aunt's familiar handwriting. She hesitated, but Papa urged her on with a nod. Resuming her seat beside the bed, she pulled the scented paper from the envelope and began to read.

Dear Rutherford, dear Eliza,

I know I need not tell you of our difficulties in the wake of the war. When Earl did not return with his regiment, Rufus was lost in grief. I find that I can no longer bear these familiar surroundings where every room and every scene remind me of our great loss.

After much searching of our souls, Rufus and I feel our best chance to begin a new life lies in a new place. They've discovered gold in New Mexico territory, and we aim to go there. Rufus has no prospects for mining, but the men who do will need food and clothing, lumber and supplies. We will close our store here and set up shop north of Ft. Union and Cimarron.

You have faced losses of your own—first Eliza's intended and then my sister—and I know the carpetbaggers are a burden to you there. Julia misses her brother dearly. She would welcome a cousin, and I'm sure the territory could use a man of God. Won't you consider joining us as soon as you may?

Warmest regards, Charlotte

Eliza dropped the letter into her lap. "Papa, you must be joking. You're in no condition to travel. We have no money, and your people need you. Tonight proved that. They need godly men to lead them back to peace."

Papa's eyes had drifted shut while she read. "Not safe."

Eliza bent close to hear his voice. The lingering scents of gunpowder, alcohol, and blood confirmed his words. "When have you ever cared for your safety? God holds you in the palm of His hand."

"I don't care for my safety. I care for yours."

He would leave his ministry to protect her? She could not ask such a sacrifice. "He holds me, too. Our work is here."

"My work is here, but there is no future here for you."

What was he suggesting? "My future is with you."

"No, Eliza. I am not afraid, but God showed me tonight how fleeting my life is. He could require it of me at any moment, and then who would care for you?" She drew breath to object, but he put up a hand to stay her. "You need a husband, Eliza, and a home of your own. It's God's plan."

"Not always. Look at Anna, the prophetess who saw Christ. She served God in the temple."

"...after her young husband died."

Eliza turned her face and stared out the window toward the street. She could not tell if the wavy glass or welling tears distorted her reflection in the dark panes. "I've had my love."

She folded the letter and slid it into the envelope once more, then laid it back on the bureau.

Papa watched her return with sadness in his eyes. Sadness was often in his eyes these days, but he always smiled when Eliza smiled at him, as she did now.

She bent to kiss his cheek.

"'Entreat me not to leave you,'" she said and turned out the light.

Chapter 1—February 1870

"Things are looking up." Papa wiped his lips and pushed his chair back.

Eliza scowled as she reached for his plate. "How can you say that?" Receiving no immediate answer, she headed for the warming kitchen, returning directly with pie and coffee. It was good to serve coffee again instead of the bitter chicory they'd made do with for years, and there was sugar now for pie, but those improvements were hardly newsworthy.

Papa picked up his newspaper, scanning the headlines as she set a cup before him. "Business is good with the cattle drives coming through town. The new suspension bridge is 'a bridge into our future' they say." He summarized the editor's opinion before adding his own. "Folks have begun to forget the war and set the past behind them."

"You wouldn't know it to look at your congregation." She smirked, hands on her hips. "When that federal officer came for Easter services, no one would sit within three pews of him."

Papa waved off the incident. "That was last year. The animosities can't last forever. Now that the amendments have passed, Texas will be welcomed into the union again, like all the other states."

He was obviously working up to something—trying to put a bright face on a situation they both knew was far from over. Eliza waited.

Papa tested his coffee and signaled for sugar. "I got another letter from Charlotte."

So that was it. He'd been trying to sweeten her up.

"Mmm?" was the most enthusiastic response she could muster. Every time the subject came up, she hoped it would be the last she heard of it.

Her cool response didn't daunt him. "It's old news by now—mail's slow from the frontier—but she says they're happy in Elizabethtown. Julia is married." Papa paused for her reaction, but she refused to exhibit one. He plunged on with optimism. "Their store is a great success. She asks again if we will come."

His polite prodding left a sour taste in her mouth, since she knew he had no intention of going himself. Eliza squared her chin. Her height wasn't the only thing she'd inherited from her father. She could be stubborn, too. "Papa, we've discussed this before. I am happy with you. Things are safer now. Besides, there's no way to get there from here." She'd memorized a list of objections for these not infrequent occasions and began to tick each one off on her fingers. "The cattle drives come through Waco because the railroads don't, and those trails all head north. The stage routes to California run too far south, and they're too expensive anyway. We don't own a wagon, so unless you plan for us to go on horseback..." She paused only when she had to draw breath.

Papa took advantage of the gap. "I talked to the Major yesterday." He plopped two cubes into his cup as he dropped this most recent bit of information. He'd cooperated with the officer in charge of federal forces garrisoned in Waco since the riot three years before, but his tone told her this conversation was different.

Eliza froze with the sugar bowl in her hand.

"Some of the troops are transferring to Fort Union in New Mexico territory. A few of the officers are taking their families. It would be an appropriate travel arrangement for a lady, and you'd be protected." He stirred his drink with casual deliberation.

Eliza scrunched up her face and tried to look implacable. She couldn't help it.

"Don't look at me like that, young lady." For all her stubbornness, Papa had been practicing recalcitrance longer. "There's money enough for a stage from Fort Union to Cimarron, and I can write Uncle Rufus to meet you there. Charlotte says he makes the trip once a month for supplies." He tapped his spoon twice against the rim of the cup and rested it on the saucer as he rested his argument.

Eliza set down the sugar bowl with enough force to jar the lid. "Why must I go if you will not?"

"Because this is the time to travel—after the snows and before the heat. Perhaps I will join you, when the situation here is resolved, but that could be next year or even longer." His expression became tender. "You're twenty-eight, my dear. Time is passing, and your opportunities are passing with it. There are few men of your age left here after the war." Kindness kept him from saying that those who returned whole had married others.

"I won't be any different there than here. I'll still be nearly six feet tall. Men seem to find that intimidating for some reason." She winked. She cared for Papa too much to mention that his outspoken political views were likely more to blame for the wide berth most folks gave her.

"It is entirely my fault, my dear."

Eliza hoped he referred to his own towering height—something that couldn't be construed as anyone's fault but God's. She doggedly continued to play the game, determined to protect him from guilt. "How could I blame you? You cannot change your frame."

"Not that."

Eliza caught her breath and prepared to argue, but his next comment caught her off guard.

"It was the Greek."

"I beg your pardon?"

"It was the Greek. Women who speak three languages are considered formidable intellects. I should have stopped with Latin." He tipped his cup in mock salute then winked back, and she laughed in spite of herself. "So you'll go?"

She acknowledged defeat with a sigh. "I will obey your wishes."

Papa smiled over the rim of his cup, but when he put it down his face was sober. "Now that that's settled, why do you not want to go?"

Had he not heard her at all these three years? "We've been over and over my reasons."

"We've been over and over your list of objections. I would like to understand your true reasons." His eyes were soft, open to see things from her perspective.

"You're all I've got left." ...in more ways than he knew, but she couldn't tell him that. Papa's faith seemed as solid and unshakeable as he was. She could not bear to disappoint him.

"The whole truth, please, Eliza."

How could he see through her like that? Like she was glass. Most days, nothing was clear to her anymore. Unshed tears choked her. No words came. Eliza shrugged, her hands flopping lamely by her sides.

And then Papa was there, embracing her as if she were a small child—something she hadn't been in a very long time. He stroked her hair with strong hands. "I ask why, too, sometimes." His deep voice rumbled through her.

"It's more than that." Her voice emerged as a hoarse whisper.

He waited as she struggled to find words.

"I know there's a reason. There has to be or 'we are of all men most miserable.'" She searched his face for signs of understanding. "But I was so sure I knew God's will for me. I've studied His Word—in three languages, no less. I prayed. I waited and worked while I waited. All I ever wanted was to serve God with my life. I thought He'd sent the answer to my prayers." Sharp tones of resentment edged into her voice, but she didn't care.

"And it feels unfair."

She nodded. "But more even than that. If serving the church and marrying a godly man isn't in God's will for me, then what is? And if a future with you and Mama and Grayson wasn't His answer after all my praying, how can I know what to do with my life?" A sob shuddered like an echo in her chest though the well of tears had long since run dry. "I don't know what to do. There's no light for my path, Papa. It's all just dark, and when I pray there are no answers."

Papa was silent. No glib advice, at least. Her grief was deep, her faith broken beyond patching. "Eliza, will you trust me?"

A sigh tore through her. "As I told you, Papa, you're all I've got left."

He gripped her hands. "I still want you to go."

As his words stabbed at her hopes, she marveled that they found anything left still capable of feeling pain. But they did. How could he ask this? She stared at him, unbelieving.

Papa caressed her cheek. "Sometimes, Eliza, God gives us a light for our path. Sometimes only a lamp for our feet. I do not know His path for you, but I feel strongly that this is the next right step." He paused, searching her eyes, before he spoke again. "I would see you happy. Will you trust me?"

Her voice was hollow as she answered. "I will obey your wishes."

ᘛᘚ

The next few weeks were a flurry of activity. The ladies of the church were kind enough to fete her with a farewell tea, or perhaps they simply wanted to part on good terms. No matter. Eliza would have wished to say goodbye in any case.

She was resigned to her going, numb with exhaustion from her preparations. She tried not to think of a life without Papa, without their quiet afternoons of study, without serving the people of his church. If she could just stay busy...

Papa wrote to Uncle Rufus and Aunt Charlotte, informing them of Eliza's planned arrival the third Friday of April. He entrusted the post to the first group of soldiers leaving Waco for Fort Union. They promised to see to its delivery to Elizabethtown via the next surveying expedition. Due to the rapid growth of the region, the territorial legislature was creating a new county, and Elizabethtown was to be county seat. Messengers went out from the fort with far more regularity than standard mail, so chances were good that the letter would be delivered. If not, Eliza would deal with that when she got there.

She carefully washed, starched, ironed, and folded the various articles of her wardrobe and packed them into Mama's old Jenny Lind stagecoach trunk. She took one last look at her keepsakes—the treasures that had been her trousseau—and locked them away in her dome-topped hope chest. Papa could bring it later; she had no need of it now. Since she was going as the guest of others, it was important to be considerate of their limited space. There was room for necessities only. Her favorite sunbonnets would pack flat, and she planned to wear her best Sunday hat and every petticoat she owned to save room in the trunk. As she did every morning while dressing, Eliza gave thanks that hoop skirts had passed out of fashion on the frontier. She'd always found them cumbersome, and they would be impossible to pack.

Her belongings were ready, but her heart was not. When Captain Price brought the wagon around for her trunk, the reality of her going hit her full force. The captain stowed her trunk on top of his family's baggage. While he secured it with ropes, Papa helped her onto the buckboard and climbed up beside her. She turned for one last look at the parsonage and fought the urge to climb right back out the other side of the wagon and run back to her haven. She could not tear her gaze from the parlor window, framed in honeysuckle, until they turned the corner and it was lost to view. Gone. The memory of it would have to last her.

Papa rode with them back to the captain's home where a small, dark-headed woman waited on the porch with two tow-haired toddlers and a babe in arms. Eliza could well imagine that the woman would be grateful for assistance with the children, and it made her feel less of a burden.

Captain Price made the introductions. Mrs. Price was pleasant enough, though she seemed as jittery about the journey as Eliza felt. Such a trip would be a daunting prospect even under ideal circumstances, but with Indian unrest and small children in tow, travel was a fearsome undertaking.

The dew was already off the grass. Time to be underway.

Papa shook hands with Captain Price and bowed to Mrs. Price. He thanked them again and tousled the toddlers' hair. Then he turned to Eliza.

Papa often said that fear expressed a lack of faith. If he was afraid now, he would not speak of it, but his eyes spoke volumes, and Eliza understood full well. "God bless all your endeavors, my dear. You are the pride of my life, and you will always be at home in my heart."

Tears clouded Eliza's view of his dear face. She pressed her lips together and clenched her jaw, waiting for the moment when she would be able to speak without betraying emotion. That moment never came, so she merely grasped his hands between her two and kissed him gently on both cheeks. She didn't dare to look in his eyes as he helped her into the wagon once more.

Mrs. Price sat in the center of the buckboard, and Captain Price handed the baby up. He swung the other children into the wagon bed and climbed up to take the reins.

"All in? Gee-up!" He clucked his cheek and jostled the driving lines, and they were off.

Eliza clung to Papa's hand until the last moment—as if a flood threatened to rip her from him. Until this moment she had not fully considered what it would mean to journey with these foreigners—the ones who swept across boundaries like a raging river, bringing the destruction that now uprooted her, a devastation God allowed. The current was carrying her away. She turned so that she could see Papa as long as she might.

He stood in the road with his arms raised in silent blessing.

ꕥ

The Brazos River was wide and full after the spring rains. Captain Price paid a toll to cross at the new bridge.

Eliza peered down the side of the wagon as the metal-rimmed wheels bumped and rumbled over the slats. Between the heavy timbers the river swirled away beneath them, the waters churned to a muddy froth. Hundreds—perhaps a thousand head—of cattle struggled to cross the ford. The water was deep, the current swift. The frantic animals balked and bawled, raising a ruckus. Cowboys on horseback splashed in and out along the frenzied fringe of the herd, hemming them in on either side, driving them forward with shouts punctuated by the crack of a whip.

There could be no conversation with her traveling companions above such a din, and Eliza was glad of it. She couldn't think of a thing to say. What could she possibly have in common with Yankees?

As they passed between the cable towers on the far side, Captain Price reined in his mules to let the herd pass.

The cattle came up from the river, wide eyed and dripping. Poor beasts—driven to a future not of their choosing.

Eliza could sympathize. Grief and loss were the whips that drove her—west to a market where women were scarcer—where even the rangiest heifer might hold some appeal for men who were desperate. That seemed to be Papa's hope, anyway.

As soon as she thought it, she knew it wasn't so. He only wanted her to have a chance of happiness, but she could not indulge in his delusions. She sat up straight and squared her chin, shoving the hurt of rejection deeper. Loving, longing, and losing hurt too much. She could not risk such pain again. No, she was going to appease Papa and to help in Uncle Rufus' store, but all of that was merely a diversion until she figured out what to do with her life.

Straining through mud of their own making, the cattle were preoccupied with their misery, oblivious of anyone's presence. But the cowboys stared openly—at what, she could not imagine. They weren't looking at her. No one in this town ever had.

Eliza gave Waco a backward glance, letting the brim of her hat hide her face. Aside from Papa, there was little here she would miss. The people she'd loved, the life she had known—everything was gone. There was nothing left but memories, and those she took with her.

They headed northwest, traveling up the river along the north bank where the trees were thinner, and the ground was more level. An escarpment rose up along the south bank, blocking Eliza's view of the city as they rounded a bend.

It would do no good to look back, so Eliza shaded her eyes to look forward.

Bluebonnets painted the meadows beside the river. They were early this year—a fitting farewell present. Splashes of heavenly blue stretched as far as she could see until the land merged with a sky that arched above her like a blue sponge ware bowl. The bluebonnets always bloomed first, followed by paintbrush and primroses as the spring days warmed. Black-eyed susans and Indian blanket replaced them, thriving in the stifling heat of summer. This promised to be a good year for wildflowers.

How she would miss them. Eliza stiffened her back and gripped the edge of the seat. She was going, and there was no turning back.

The mules clopped out a traveling cadence, unhurried to the point of tooth-grinding agony. It would take weeks to reach Fort Union at this rate—an interminable journey that would seem even longer in the company of strangers. And the Prices were strangers, though she knew their names—their names and the fact that they were her former enemies. Fellow humans who had, until now, been merely a category: "Those who are different." Like oil and water they shared the same space but remained separate. Had their cultures ever been 'United'? Here in close quarters Eliza began to suspect a truth that seemed painfully evident. The silence that hung over them would have been awkward except for the plausible excuse of their private preoccupations.

She cast about in her mind for something to say. At least the children did not feel like enemies. She had to allow that they were sweet. Perhaps they would provide common ground.

In the end it was Captain Price who initiated conversation. "I'm glad to be traveling before the summer heat sets in." It was strained and obvious, but it was a start.

Eliza was grateful for his attempt. "I should say so. Is it hot where y'all came from?"

She immediately wished she could retrieve the words. Would she ever learn not to say the first thing she thought? This was exactly what she'd feared—drawing a distinction between North and South, inferring that they were outsiders, and perhaps implying that their presence was not voluntary from either perspective.

If she had erred, Captain Price was gracious enough to let it pass. "It can get warm in Pennsylvania, but the heat does not set in so early as it does here, nor last so late. Still, working in my father's fields near Boalsburg there were days I thought the corn might pop while still on the stalk."

In spite of herself, Eliza laughed. Shared humor was a good beginning. "You were a farmer, then?"

"Yup. Land's been in the family for generations. My ancestors came over with William Penn," he said. His pride was understandable.

A Quaker heritage. Peace-loving people. Odd that he should be a soldier, though perhaps no stranger than that Grayson should have been one.

Grayson had volunteered to serve as chaplain for a company from Salado so that he could minister to the boys from home—childhood friends.

Would Captain Price understand that? Did he know that men like Papa and Grayson had never owned slaves? Considered slavery a moral evil? Could he possibly imagine the personal hardships she had suffered during the war and even afterward when Papa was labeled a Union sympathizer? Perhaps he could understand what it meant to be unwelcome, an outsider, but to feel so among those who had formerly been friends?

In the best of times Eliza's world had consisted of Papa and Mama and Grayson. One by one, all had been stripped away until now even Papa was lost to her. She felt utterly alone in a world where blood and hatred had become so common she was numb to them. Perhaps that was what compelled her to New Mexico territory in the end—the hope that in a new place things would be different, old animosities not ever-present, and men not so inclined to violence.

Eliza examined her heart. What part of the hatred had she brought with her? Had she carefully safeguarded a trunk of bitterness—an invisible collection of old offenses and assumptions she dragged along like so much baggage? Was that why her heart felt heavy? For all that she hated slavery and injustice of any kind, her sympathies still lay with the South. With the invasion, Captain Price and men like him had changed her world forever. What was destroyed could not be reconstructed, no matter what the government labeled this awkward process that had everyone walking on eggshells, pretending civility. She'd tried to forgive, but she could not forget. To forget the war would mean forgetting Grayson, forgetting Mama. But if she could bridge the gulf of misunderstanding with Captain Price and forgive this one man's part in all that was lost then, perhaps, she could forgive the next man, and then the next. The journey to new beginnings would be slow. Painstaking. Ponderous as the wagon wheels that creaked on mile after mile, but Eliza recognized it as progress.

The toddlers, Amos and Ada, were as bright as the brass buttons on their father's blue uniform. Eliza did her best to break the monotony of their journey by playing finger games with them in the wagon bed—cat's cradle and the like. When they stopped for lunch she showed them how to make fancy ladies with primrose skirts and bluebonnet faces. By the time Mrs. Price had set out cold meat and bread, a dozen belles danced beside the Brazos. After lunch the children romped and played in the tall grass under the watchful eye of their mother while their father watered the mules. Sitting beneath a cottonwood, listening to the gentle music of the river as it sparkled in the midday sun, Eliza drowsed.

"Load up." Captain Price shoved the lunch basket beneath the buckboard.

Eliza pulled herself up from the grass and gathered the blanket as Mrs. Price positioned the baby on her hip and beckoned her other children. A storm brewed in Amos' blue eyes as he trudged back to the wagon in manful obedience, but Ada burst into a torrent of tears.

"I not ride. I tired of wagon." She stamped her little foot and tossed her curls in defiance.

Eliza expected the captain to bark military orders at his insubordinate offspring. Instead he shifted the trunks in the wagon bed and spread the picnic blanket between them. "Come, Ada. I've built you a nest. Come and see."

The ruse worked. Both children bounded toward their father. Mrs. Price threw Eliza a wink over their heads as the Captain lifted one and then the other into the wagon bed. Ada clapped her hands and squealed with pleasure. "I'n a bird! I'n a bird!" she chirped as she hopped and flapped her arms.

"Little birds often sleep in their nests after a big meal of worms," Mrs. Price told her, passing the baby to Eliza while her husband helped her up.

"Worms!" Amos, all boy, was delighted. "Will you feed us worms,

Mama?"

Ada cast her mother a worried glance.

"Had I a worm, I'd use it to catch you a fish." She touched her finger to the children's noses, causing them to go cross-eyed before collapsing in a fit of giggles. "Tuck your heads now, baby birds. When you wake up, I'll feed you crackers."

It was a silly scene—the sort that's recalled fondly ever after at warm family gatherings, a treasured memory to those who were included. And Eliza now had a part in one Northern family's drama, if only by proximity—an observer, if not a participant. She marveled. Were they so different after all, these enemies of hers? Were they not fathers, mothers, children—families?

The wagon jolted as Captain Price released the brake, and Eliza's heart took a jolt as well. There would be no family in her future, despite Papa's hopes. The bullet that killed Grayson shattered those dreams. When he died, those hopes died with him.

A familiar tightness seized her throat, and she blinked back tears. They did no good. She'd cried them all. Nothing remained but to accept, with as much grace as she could muster, the fate sealed for her by some faceless soldier—a man who could not be much like Captain Price, but whose uniform was also Union blue.

Eliza turned from the scene and retied the strings of her bonnet, studying a cloud that hovered above the northern horizon. It was nothing—just the dust of a distant trail drive—but it provided an excuse for her burning eyes.

Chapter 2

It wasn't true what folks said about misery loving company. Eliza could barely stand the company of her own thoughts; she had no intention of airing her troubles. Learning to exchange pleasantries with Yankees was one thing. Exposing her grief was quite another.

Every time she thought about Captain Price in his blue uniform, her stomach twisted. Her misery wasn't his fault. Logic argued that while Captain Price had been involved in the war, only one man killed Grayson, and odds were it wasn't him. Still, for him the war was over. Eliza feared that for her it would go on forever. The invisible scars—the aching loss of Grayson and Mama and cousin Earl—never seemed to heal. How could the Prices understand the constant, throbbing pain she lived with, the personal battle she waged daily with bitterness and self-pity?

Frankly, it was beginning to make her a little crazy, too. It must be wrong to feel so angry at the unfairness of life, so indifferent about living any more of it. God, Himself, must be tired of her complaining. Clearly, hers was a private war. She was going to have to find some way to escape her grief alone.

They crossed the Clear Fork of the Brazos and headed north to Fort Griffith where Captain Price had business with the commandant. While he helped Mrs. Price and Ada from the wagon, Amos clambered down by himself and was off to "see the soldiers." Eliza caught him by one wrist as he flew past. They had business elsewhere. She kept a tight grip on the little wriggler as they headed for the sutler's store.

Mrs. Price placed her order for the items they needed to restock. "Dried beef, dried beans, dried corn..."

Sometimes it seemed like the only thing that wasn't dry was the baby. A damp warmth worked its way through the layers of calico and muslin as Eliza bounced the little one on her hip. Lip curled, she glanced down to confirm her suspicions. The infant shoved a fist between its swollen gums and grinned up at her. Poor thing. At least it had stopped mewling for the moment.

The unfamiliar quiet caught its mother's attention. "... and canned milk."

Little Ada popped a thumb into her mouth and twisted a handful of her mother's skirts as Mrs. Price counted out payment for their provisions. Eliza scanned the store for Amos, who had wandered off as soon as she dropped his hand. There. By the surveying equipment. She handed the baby back to its mother and went after the errant youngster.

"This way, please." She made her voice cheerful and inviting as she took his hand, but Amos was not so easily enticed. He grappled for the display, throwing all his small weight into a lunge for freedom.

A box of pencils cascaded from the shelf, and a surveyor's notebook plopped to the floor with a smack that turned heads.

Eliza scrambled to collect the items and return them to the shelf, but her hand lingered on the cloth binding of the notebook. A journal. Writing would give her something to do—someplace for her thoughts to dwell instead of on her own misfortunes. Snatching it up along with a pencil, she hustled to the counter with Amos in tow and paid the man from her meager funds. No matter. Those few precious pennies would purchase peace of mind.

That was the idea, anyway, but she realized the flaw in her plan soon enough. What was there to write about? Each day was filled with tedious, mind-numbing sameness.

'Grass and sky.'

'Grass and sky.'

And then, when she thought the journey could not be more wearisome, 'Rain.'

More grass. More sky

In addition to the things that weren't worth writing about, there were things she could not write about.

Her desperate need for a bath.

The constant whining cry of the baby, miserable with a rash. Captain Price had rigged a wash barrel to the side of the wagon. Every day a score of diapers accumulated in the churning water. Every night after supper Mrs. Price rinsed and wrung them by hand and laid them on the prairie grass to dry. But they were never truly clean, and the poor child was never truly dry.

It seemed they each had their private miseries. If she could not unburden her soul into the pages of the journal, perhaps she could escape her own torments by assisting others. Mrs. Price was about her age. She might yet become a diversion, if not a true friend.

"Let me help." Eliza gritted her teeth and plunged her hand into the murky water of the wash barrel. Relationship required sacrifice.

Mrs. Price rewarded her with a tired, thin-lipped, but genuine smile. "You wouldn't know any secret remedies for diaper rash, would you?" Rinse water dripped from her fingertips and splashed on her apron as she brushed back a strand of fallen hair with her forearm. "Something the Southern women do?"

Cornstarch? Lard? Browned flour? Strong tea? Eliza sifted through every home remedy she'd heard. Which had Mrs. Price not already tried?

"Oh, never mind." Mrs. Price sighed. "You don't have children. Sorry I asked." She twisted a diaper, folded it double, and wrung it again before shaking out the wrinkles and laying it on the tall grass. Then she paused, stretching her arms, and groaned. "Look at my hands," she said, holding them over the water.

Eliza tried not to take offense at the first comment by focusing on the second. "It's the water that makes them red..."

"No, they're brown! Look how the sun has darkened my skin." Mrs. Price studied her flesh as if it were a tragedy of great consequence. "I suppose women down here are used to it, but I never shall be."

Eliza studied her own sun-browned hands. For years she had done laundry outdoors, worked beside Mama in the garden, even cooked outside when the summer heat made the kitchen insufferable. How she wished that brown skin was something she could spare time to worry about. She'd never had that luxury.

She'd been foolish to think that Mrs. Price could ever understand her life. They had less in common than Eliza had with the women back home. She was unusually strong, unfashionably educated ... and single. "Don't nobody want her." The gunman's taunt returned to haunt her. It was true. She did not fit in with her sisters, nor was she the type of woman men seemed to prefer. And now she was alone. Eliza shook off the slight. It was a good thing, then, that she could be independent.

Ʂ

Once they passed Fort Griffin the terrain became rougher, the land drier. Day after day the wagon wheels rattled over the rocky ground. The mules' plodding hooves beat a steady, mesmerizing rhythm. Eliza drowsed on the hard seat but woke when she started to sway. She must not sleep. The ground was hard and a long way down.

"Whoa." Captain Price drew back the reins.

Squinting into the late afternoon sun, Eliza looked out over an arroyo—a dry, sandy riverbed with steep banks as tall as a man's shoulder. Her heart sank. Already they'd encountered several rain-swollen streams that forced them to travel miles out of their way to ford. Though this stream held no water, it was yet another obstacle to their progress.

"This one's not marked on the map. We'll have to unhitch."

No one said anything as Captain Price jumped down and unhitched the lead mule. He would ride up the stream bed in search of a place where the bank was less deep or less steep.

Eliza hoped he would find such a spot within a reasonable distance. If not, he would have to double back and search in the other direction. She held out her hand to block the sun and measure its height above the horizon. They had only three hours of good light.

"I'll be back within the hour." Captain Price kissed his wife and babies then unstrapped his gun belt and laid his revolver on the wagon seat.

The women stared down at it then at each other, and Eliza's mouth went dry.

He took up his rifle, mounted the mule and rode north, his silhouette growing smaller and smaller until the horizon swallowed him.

Eliza gauged the sun's descent. One finger's breadth. Two.

When Amos and Ada grew restless in the wagon bed, Eliza

climbed down from the wagon and helped them to the ground, watching as they collected pebbles. Still she watched the sun, a full hand lower now, but Captain Price had not returned. She glanced up to Mrs. Price, who scanned the plains from her seat, and raised a questioning brow.

Mrs. Price shook her head ever so slightly. She would say nothing to alarm the children, but she clutched the baby tight to her chest.

A shot rang out to the north, then another—the reports carrying on the breeze.

Eliza started.

Mrs. Price's eyes were wide and fearful. The baby began to squeal in her grasp.

Eliza called the children and lifted them back into the wagon.

The revolver lay at eye level on the buckboard—hot steel glinting in the west Texas sun.

Eliza gulped down terror then, as if it were nothing at all, she took up the gun and held it to her side. She tested its weight, half hiding it in the folds of her skirt. Her hand curled around the grip, and her index finger found the trigger. She sucked in a shaky breath and forced herself to breathe it out calmly before walking back to the north side of the wagon to stand between the children and the gunshots.

"Do you see anything?" she asked without taking her eyes from the horizon.

"No. Not yet." Mrs. Price's words were clipped, her voice strained. For the space of several minutes Eliza hardly dared to breathe, then, "Wait ..."

Eliza saw it. The silhouette of a lone rider. Could she shoot him? Oh, yes. Before she'd let harm come to this family, she knew she could, though that certainty surprised her. She set her feet and brought her arms up, one hand bracing the other. Shutting one eye, she set the rider in her sights. Her thumb eased back the hammer, and the cylinder advanced and locked with a metallic click.

There was a scrabble in the wagon bed behind her then Ada squealed, "Daddy!"

Eliza jumped and eased her finger away from the trigger, hazarding a glance over her shoulder. Mrs. Price shielded her eyes and peered intently before a slow smile replaced the tension in her face. Eliza turned again to see Captain Price, now recognizable upon his mule, holding a brace of jackrabbits aloft. Her knees wobbled with relief.

Within minutes he was with them, and Eliza was only too glad to return his pistol.

"Would you have shot me?" He teased her as he buckled the gun belt around his hips.

She squared her chin and nodded once.

"Good," he said. "To refuse to take up arms in one's own defense is sometimes noble, but to fail to do so in the defense of others is cowardice of the lowest sort." He stroked his daughter's fair head. "There's a crossing about four miles north. The bank is low on this side, and the west bank has washed out where the riverbed bends. We should be able to ease the wagon down the east bank on slats, and then I can shovel the washed area into a ramp." He hitched up his mule.

The wagon turned and creaked forward again. Slow. Plodding.

They found the place. The riverbed was broad here, and the spreading waters had not cut as deeply into the earth.

Everyone dismounted. Eliza felt a bit like Moses, walking across the riverbed on dry ground, leading Amos and Ada as Mrs. Price followed with the babe. Captain Price coaxed the mules down the low, loose bank of the arroyo, across the sandy bottom, and back up the other side. It was a slow business.

They reached the west bank just as the sun sank. They could go no further. They would camp here and start again tomorrow.

After tucking the children into their pallet in the wagon bed, Eliza drew a slip of paper from the back of her Bible. She sketched a calendar on the last page of her journal and began to transfer tally marks from the slip—a record of their journey. When she left Waco and all the weeks stretched before her, time seemed ample. Now she chewed the end of her pencil, wondering if she would still arrive in Cimarron in time to meet Uncle Rufus. There was no way to contact him and no way to predict the obstacles they might yet encounter. She needed to give serious thought to an alternate plan, but if there was anything she had in abundance, it was time to think.

The bluebonnets grew scarce as they pressed north. How far she was from anything that looked like home. Eliza felt more desperate than ever to reach the familiar arms of her family in New Mexico territory. They followed the White Fork of the Brazos as far as it would take them then made for Fort Bascom on the Canadian River.

The entire garrison at Fort Bascom was being transferred to Fort Union, and a small contingent was detached to escort them. Though Eliza thanked God for their protection thus far, she was nonetheless grateful that their party would be larger on the last leg of their trip. With wry irony she acknowledged that God had chosen to use these blue-clad soldiers to protect her. Something about thankfulness felt good—or at least not bad. She would have to try that more often.

Two days out of Fort Bascom, they finally encountered something Eliza could write about in her journal—Indians. Navajo, thankfully, rather than the more warlike Comanche or Apache who raided this region. For a moment she was tempted to leave that bit of information out. It would have made the entry more exciting. Instead she noted that in facing a common danger, her former enemies became her allies. It was difficult to admit, even in writing.

As she penciled the last period by firelight, Captain Price came to light a straw for his pipe. The glow of their dying campfire faded just past the ring of wagons, but the vast expanse of dry prairie grasses rustled in the wind beyond the bounds of sight. Above them the stars twinkled like distant candles. They listened to the coyotes in companionable silence. Somewhere out there, the Navajo and the Comanche and the Apache made their camps around other fires.

"Like ships in an ocean of grass." The captain put words to Eliza's thoughts.

"A vast ocean, indeed," she said, hugging her knees to her chest. "The plains seem even bigger at night—miles and miles of nothing. No landmarks. No maps. How do you know where we are and where we're going?"

"We follow the rivers, and when those give out we follow the stars."

"Like the wise men?" How she wished God would lead her as clearly.

"Not quite. The sun and the stars rise and set in predictable patterns to show us east and west, north and south. We line up the wagon tongues to point toward the North Star every night and set the sun behind our right shoulder each morning."

"And how is that different?"

"Some stars don't follow the expected pattern. See there?" He pointed with the stem of his pipe to one brilliant luminary, low in the west. "You can't miss them. The ancients called them wanderers, but they have patterns of their own. They cross paths with the others, and when they do, some say it has meaning. Something about the way the stars aligned convinced the wise men they'd seen a sign."

If even heathen magi could discern His will, why couldn't she?

They fell silent again. At last the captain inverted his pipe and knocked it against his palm. He ground the ashes beneath his boot. "Well, good night," he said and wandered toward the wagon where his family lay waiting.

But Eliza lingered, pondering the sky alone.

ꕥ

March was gone, along with the first week of April, when they first caught sight of purple ridges lying low along the western horizon—varying in hue from lavender to violet by distance. The high plains, which had seemed barren and endless, yielded at last a full view of the Rocky Mountains. Again Eliza had something worth writing about, but her words failed to express such grandeur. To think that God created this! The streams they followed now were full of water, running fresh and clean through green meadows. Here and there patches of snow were still visible, but there were also wildflowers in profusion. *He maketh me to lie down in green pastures; He leadeth me beside the still waters. He restoreth my soul.*

Oh, that He would restore her soul. Eliza knew she should be grateful. She could be grateful. For providence. For beauty. Who would not? But the lush landscape was a stark contrast to what she felt inside. Dry. Barren. The praises she quoted from memory seemed dutiful and distant. Someone else's words, not hers.

She hadn't talked much to God since ... how long? Mama's death? Grayson's? Long enough that she couldn't remember. She wasn't angry with Him, exactly. Was that even allowed? Praying just hadn't seemed to do any good—not when it came to her most heartfelt requests. If she'd been a heathen, she wouldn't have counted on God to do anything for her in the first place. Somehow it hurt worse to know that He could, but chose not to.

Eliza had agreed to come west in search of the plans God had for her—the ones His Word promised would give her a future and a hope, but she had no delusions that her future included a family of her own. She wasn't interested in replacing the people she'd lost. What she wanted was a purpose for living, people to love and serve, and a little distance from her grief. She studied the calendar in the back of her journal. Each tally mark brought her closer to the day she was to meet Uncle Rufus, closer to the day when she would be among people like herself.

It took twelve days for the wagons to reach Fort Union. Only one day remained.

She said her goodbyes to the Prices at supper. "Will you miss us?" Amos asked, and she assured him she would. She hugged the children and shook hands with the captain and his wife to show her thanks. The gestures were sincere. She was truly grateful for their escort. In time, she might even come to feel at ease in their presence, but it would take longer than a few weeks to unlearn years of distrust.

The first morning after their arrival, she set out to inquire about the availability of a stage to Cimarron. Though it was early, the fort was already alive with activity. Men stood at morning formation on the parade ground as Eliza strode the length of the officers' quarters, a row of identical buildings lined up like a regiment of brick soldiers at the edge of the drill field. Between the columns of the deep porches, she gazed past the patch of lawn to the mountains beyond. Somewhere just over those peaks lay Elizabethtown. One more day, and she would be with family—at home with people who thought as she did. She paused for a moment to watch a bird of prey soar on the updrafts. If only she could fly over the intervening ridges ... but a fast stage was her best option. As she resumed her mission, her footsteps rang out firm and confident on the weathered planks—a satisfying sound that bespoke more confidence than she felt. Thoroughly lost, she crossed several more porches before she found a door with a sign indicating the commander's office.

Her knock brought a sharp reply. "Enter."

A sergeant, several years younger than herself, sat behind an oak desk facing the door. His face registered surprise when Eliza entered. Jumping to his feet he came around the desk to offer a chair. "How may I help you, ma'am?"

"I'd like to speak with the commander of the fort." Eliza hoped she had chosen the proper title. It was the highest she could think of.

"Major General Sheridan, ma'am?" His increased surprise was only exceeded by her own.

General Sheridan. Eliza sucked in a sharp breath. His very name was horrifying. Sheridan commanded the Union's Third Division at Chickamauga where Grayson was killed. He was among the last men she would wish to see. His were the very men responsible for her loss. Eliza's face burned. Obviously she had committed a serious blunder by even requesting to speak to a high-ranking officer about a personal matter. "...or anyone who could assist me in securing passage to Cimarron. It is vitally important that I arrive there tomorrow." She stammered at first, but struggled to maintain a tone that would convey her urgency.

The sergeant relaxed. "Oh, well, most anyone could help you with that, ma'am. I could let you talk to Major Evans." It was gracious of him to ignore her mistake.

Eliza tried to appear calm and reasonable. "I hate to bother him if it's unnecessary."

"Ain't much to it, ma'am. There's a stage comin' in from Mora this evenin'. You just be out front at daybreak tomorrow and hop on." He grinned at her, and she couldn't help smiling back.

Here was another Yankee she could learn to like.

ꕥ

At daybreak on the third Friday of April, Eliza stood on the porch in front of the commander's office, waiting. The stage had arrived just before sunset the evening before, and Eliza spoke to its driver about loading her trunk. It meant she had to sleep in her petticoat, but she'd done so many times on the trail. So many nights on hard ground; so many early mornings. Even a government issue cot was a welcome change. She'd slept deeply, but the night had not been nearly long enough. She was stifling a yawn behind her gloved hand when she heard the thump of military boots at the other end of the porch. It was the young sergeant, and Eliza guessed that he had seen her with her mouth gaping as he, too, was suppressing an enormous yawn. They shared embarrassed smiles before the young man unlocked the office door.

Eliza soon heard more footsteps, but these were light and quick. Turning, she saw a tiny slip of a girl approaching—a life-sized incarnation of one of the flowery belles she'd made for Ada. The girl wore a primrose pink confection, all ruffles and lace. Wherever she was from, hoopskirts were still in fashion. Myriads of blonde ringlets bounced with every step, and she carried an elaborate bonnet with pink satin streamers. Eliza entertained the wicked yet fervent hope that the girl would not stop, but she did.

"Good mornin'!" She sounded entirely too cheerful. "I'm Millie

Morrell." She stuck out a dainty hand. "Come to catch the stage to Cimarron this morning."

As if I hadn't guessed. Eliza had the good grace, for once, not to say what she was thinking.

"You goin', too?"

No, I always rise early to linger at men's office doors.

It didn't seem to bother Millie in the least that Eliza had yet to speak. She talked right on. "We'll be friends, then—traveling companions! What's your name?"

Did the girl never pause for breath? "Eliza. Eliza Gentry." She accepted the proffered fingertips and scolded herself for her unchristian attitude.

Millie barely came up to her shoulder, not that either of them could help it. But she was exactly the sort of girl men seemed always to prefer.

As if in confirmation, the young sergeant emerged from the office with a chair. He beamed ridiculously at the dainty belle, and Millie beamed back, blushing adorably.

Only after Millie was seated did he turn to Eliza. "I can fetch another one for you, if you like, ma'am."

Eliza tried to accept his offer at face value, but it struck her as an afterthought. She dismissed the gesture with a raised hand. "The stage will be here soon."

Already the clop of hooves and the crunch of gravel beneath iron-rimmed wheels announced its arrival. Six brown horses rounded the corner from the livery pulling a Concord stagecoach. Eliza forgot her disgruntled thoughts when she caught sight of the shiny red paint and bright yellow wheels. The horses tossed their manes, in high spirits to be off while the day was cool and fresh.

The young sergeant fairly jumped to assist Miss Millie as she clambered onto the stage. He turned to offer Eliza the same courtesy, but something about his foolish grin made her think that he had no intention of washing Millie's touch from his hand for the rest of the day. Shaking her head, Eliza gathered her skirts and stooped to enter the roomy interior.

When she settled into the cushioned seat, a sigh of comfort dispelled much of her irritability, and she determined not to allow anything to diminish her gratitude for this luxurious provision. *Why, there's even room for Millie's hoopskirts.* Immediately she repented of the naughty thought and resolved to be more gracious.

Eliza peeked out the side window to reassure herself that her trunk was loaded on the back. It was. Right there under the mail bags, along with three others. *Must be Millie's.* She grinned. That thought wasn't really naughty—just fact.

The driver slapped the reins, and they were off.

Millie was off and running, too, narrating the entire experience and asking a string of questions without waiting for the answers.

Eliza sighed. She had, indeed, many reasons to be thankful. She could start by being grateful that a stagecoach traveled more quickly than a loaded wagon.

By mid morning, she'd taken to peering out the window as if in response to Millie's incessant cries of, "Oh! Looky there!" In that way Eliza could enjoy the scenery without obviously ignoring her companion. That was how she came to see one of the mailbags fall off and go bounding down the slope toward a creek as they rounded one particularly sharp curve. She tried to signal the driver, but he took no notice. It was probably a lost cause, anyway. It was a long, steep drop to the creek, and letters fluttered to rest all along the slope.

Millie chattered on, completely oblivious.

By noon, Eliza seriously considered asking to ride on top. She truly tried to discipline her thoughts and exhibit a more charitable spirit, but Millie's shrill giggles hurt her ears. Why did men seem to be captivated by such twittering birds?

When they finally reached Cimarron, Eliza's prayers of gratitude were entirely sincere.

The driver unloaded Eliza's small trunk and Millie's three large ones before carrying the mailbags—or what was left of them—into the Barlow & Sanderson stage stop.

Eliza pressed a clenched fist to her waist as a sudden thought caused her stomach to lurch. She sincerely hoped that Papa's letter to Uncle Rufus had not met a similar fate.

Anxiously watching for any sign of Uncle Rufus, Eliza couldn't help noticing the tall, slim cowboy approaching the boardwalk in front of the stage stop. She smiled at him above the blonde head of her companion, and he winked in return, raising one finger to his lips. The twinkle in his eye, his mischievous grin, and the pleasure of a shared secret caused her heart to trip over her hopes. She smoothed the butterscotch plaid of her traveling dress to hide her amusement.

"I'm sure your uncle will send someone for you if he doesn't come himself." Millie chattered as she had almost continually since they left Fort Union, apparently under the impression that Eliza would find her platitudes encouraging.

Lands' sakes, this girl could talk water back uphill! But Eliza had to admit that any feminine presence was a comfort in these wild, new surroundings.

Millie was oblivious to the cowboy's approach until he jumped with both boots onto the boardwalk, rattling the weathered joists and causing a bang like a shotgun blast. The dainty belle seemed to fly, like a flushed quail, into a flurry of feathers. Her eyes were framed in white, and a fragile hand flapped at her throat like a broken wing. She whirled with a rustle of petticoats, blonde curls flying, and stamped her little foot.

The cowboy hooted with the success of his prank. His laughter sounded like church bells, inviting anyone who heard to join in.

Eliza laughed aloud. She couldn't help it.

He snatched the dusty hat from his head and slapped it across his thigh, then dropped it as his dainty victim flew toward him, squealing.

"Zeke! Oh, Zeke, you nearly scared me half to death!" She pounded on his chest with small fists.

The handsome cowboy wrapped his arms around her and spun her until her skirts flew.

"Put me down!" When he relented, she beamed up at him adoringly. "Eliza, I want you to meet Zeke, ..." Eliza guessed the rest before she said it. "...my fiancé."

Not anyone coming for her, then, obviously. She tried not to look crestfallen.

"Pleased to meetcha, ma'am." Zeke inclined his head before retrieving his dusty Stetson and placing it back on his straw-colored thatch. A nudge of his thumb set it at a rakish angle. "Ain't she jest all purty, pink, and precious?" He gazed at Millie as if she were strawberry taffy.

They chatted for a few moments, and Zeke was kind enough to offer her a ride if she was going their way. He'd left his wagon down the street when he came to town earlier, "hoping for the chance to surprise my Millie." They were headed for the Moreno Valley where Zeke had the beginnings of a ranch, but it was clear they were hungering for time alone.

So was she. Eliza declined the offer.

Zeke shook her hand, Millie kissed her cheek, and they were gone.

Eliza sat down on a bench beside the door to wait. Alone.

Chapter 3

Over the next hour, Eliza glanced anxiously in the direction of every sound of approaching steps or hoof beats, but Uncle Rufus did not appear. When the shadows grew long on the street, she drew out her pocket and dumped a handful of coins into her lap. She counted them carefully then poked at them, counting them again, hoping she had miscounted the first time. The meager amount remained unchanged. With a sigh, she scooped up the coins and poured them back into their pouch, dropping it discretely down her waistband as she stood and straightened her skirts.

Several wagons had gone up the dirt street empty and come down again loaded with dry goods, indicating the direction of the general store. A short walk confirmed her guess. She entered the store and waited her turn behind three other customers. Cimarron was a busy place. Eliza tried not to fidget while she waited for the round-faced proprietor to turn his attention to her.

At last he looked in her direction, raising bushy eyebrows toward his receding hairline to indicate that she was next.

"I was to meet my uncle here today. Rufus MacMannus. Has he been here?"

The man shook his head. "No, ma'am, but I been expectin' him," he said, revealing the absence of several molars. "He comes in 'bout once a month when the weather's good to trade furs and restock his store in E-Town. When he di'n't show last week, I thought sure to see him today, but he ain't come in."

Eliza tried not to imagine the worst. "Might he come tomorrow, do you think?"

"Aw, no ma'am, I don't reckon. Rufus is religious, y' know? He wouldn't want to be doin' business on the Lord's day."

"But this is only Friday..." Eliza tried to follow the man's line of reasoning.

"Yup, 'at's right, but it's a full day's ride back up the canyon with a loaded wagon. Ol' Rufus always comes on Thursday or Friday so's he kin git back up to the valley afore the Sabbath. If he ain't come by now, he ain't comin' this week."

Eliza's hopes dropped like a rock into the pit of her stomach. She thanked the proprietor and left her name, asking him to contact her through the stage company if he heard any news. As she walked back to the stage stop, the scant weight of the coins in her pocket swung against her hip. She analyzed her options. If she was frugal, she might have enough money to stay at a boarding house until next Friday; but while it was likely that Uncle Rufus would come soon, there was no guarantee that it would be this week. She thought again of the missing mail bag. He might not even know she was waiting for him. Perhaps there was a stage line that could carry her to Elizabethtown.

As she stepped into the stage office, a middle-aged man in a vest and armband glanced up from his ledger. The office was empty except for one other man—tall and rather dapper—who was intent upon reading the wanted posters tacked to one wall. Eliza read the list of routes and fares posted above the ticket desk and felt her hopes rise again slightly. The stage line ran from Springfield, Missouri to Santa Fe, making a side trip through Elizabethtown. The posted prices for a full-fare ticket in either direction were high, but for a ride just the short distance to the next stop she might have enough. She stepped up to the ticket counter to inquire about booking passage to Elizabethtown on the next stage.

"Yes'm. Stage from Santa Fe takes the mountain branch to Springfield once't month. That's the one you just came in on."

"And it stops next in Elizabethtown?"

"Yup. 'At's right."

Relief flooded her. "I'd like a ticket, please."

"Yes'm, and it'd be my pleasure to sell you one. Stage'll be back through here..." the ticket agent ran an ink-stained finger down his schedule, "...three weeks from next Thursday."

"Three weeks?" Eliza felt dizzy.

"Well, yes ma'am. Like I said, stage runs once't month. The one you came in on left as soon as they watered the horses. Next one'll be through here..."

She gripped the edge of the counter as the room began to spin.

The agent jumped to his feet. "Ma'am? Do you need some water?"

Eliza closed her eyes and breathed a prayer of desperation, willing herself not to give in to rising panic. *Lord, show me the way.*

"May I help you, ma'am?" The man's voice startled her, though he sounded almost shy.

Looking up, Eliza gazed into the deep blue eyes of the handsome stranger who was the only other customer in the shop. He certainly looked like an answer to prayer, and his soft southern accent was like a warm breeze from home. "I ... ah ... no, thank you, sir. I was just trying to find a way to Elizabethtown." Eliza peered at his face, trying not to be obvious. He seemed familiar somehow, but no...

"I live in the other direction—up towards Raton." The man was staring at her intently. "I could escort you, though, if you're in need."

"That's very kind of you, but I—" Eliza was touched by his magnanimous offer, but it would not be appropriate to be on the road, unaccompanied, with a man she did not know.

"Have we met?" His voice interrupted her thoughts.

"I don't think so," she said. "I just arrived this afternoon."

"I haven't been here that long, myself. Name's Allison, Clay Allison." He stuck out his hand in polite greeting, and Eliza accepted it. His touch was gentle. "I come from Tennessee, but I've been working cattle around the Brazos River in Texas since the war."

Eliza's eyes flew open. "I'm from Waco. My Papa's a pastor there. I wonder if you ever visited his church?" Perhaps she and Mr. Allison were acquainted, after all.

Clay Allison's expression abruptly lost its warmth, though he remained genteel. "No, I don't think so." All of a sudden he seemed in a hurry to be on his way. "I wish you well, ma'am."

His abrupt change was puzzling. Eliza stared after him as he left and disappeared into a building across the road.

"Lucien Maxwell's dining room and lodgings is two blocks up toward the river if you're interested, ma'am. 'Course there's also the National Hotel one block back o' here." These new bits of information offered by the stage master were the last drops that filled Eliza's mind to overflowing. Her muddled thoughts whirled with the pros and cons of various options. It would be best to grapple with one decision at a time, she determined. It had been a long time since breakfast. At the mention of food, her empty stomach prompted her to tend to that necessity first. Perhaps with a full stomach, the next decisions wouldn't be so daunting.

As Eliza started for the door, she nearly ran headlong into Zeke, who was looking back over his shoulder.

Reflexively, he grasped her arms to avoid a collision.

Eliza caught her breath in surprise. "I thought you and Millie left."

"Not this late in the day," he said. "I just toted her trunk over to the hotel and got her set up for the night. I aim to sleep with my wagon so's I can leave it loaded. Livery stable's just out back a'here, sorta catty-corner from the plaza. We'll leave first thing tomorrow." He eyed Eliza perceptively. "You want to reconsider that ride? I gotta run Millie into Elizabethtown, anyways. It wouldn't be proper to have her staying out at the ranch with me before the weddin' and all. I'd be happy to take you along."

"Oh, yes! Thank you!" Eliza clasped her hands just beneath her chin as if thanking God for this new providence, though she thought with amusement that Zeke talked almost as much as Millie, when he could get a word in edgewise. It might make for an interesting trip, but she had few other options. "My uncle was to meet me here, but he seems to have been detained."

"Who's yer uncle?"

"Rufus MacMannus. He has a store in Elizabethtown. Do you know him?"

"I seen his place. Been in a time or two," Zeke drawled. He looked concerned, but said nothing discouraging. "You'd be welcome to join Millie and me fer supper," he offered, and though Eliza had been relieved to part company with them earlier in the afternoon, she couldn't remember a time when she was more glad to see anyone.

Zeke called for her trunk and slung it easily over his shoulder.

Eliza was surprised that such a skinny weed should display such strength. Knowing he had already carried Millie's trunks, she apologized for the weight of her own.

Zeke shrugged it off with a grin. "Ain't no more work than tossing calves or hay bales."

As they set out, the doors of the building across the street swung wide, and two men staggered out, each with a bottle in hand. A tinkling piano tune and bawdy laughter spilled through the doors with them, and Eliza caught a glimpse of a large gambling hall with a bar running down one side. Judging from the manner of dress—or undress—of the women inside, it seemed obvious they were there for the use and pleasure of the male customers.

Her forehead felt tight where her eyebrows pinched together. There were such establishments back in Waco, of course, but she'd never gotten comfortable with the idea.

Still glancing over her shoulder, she followed Zeke as he walked the short block to the hotel. They reached it just as a red sun touched the mountaintops. Eliza wasn't sure she liked the idea of spending the night so close to a saloon. The ticket agent had mentioned other accommodations closer to the river. "Is the hotel less expensive than Maxwell's?" she asked, keenly aware of the light weight of her coin purse.

"I'm not sure, ma'am." Eliza was amused to see that he blushed. "But Mr. Maxwell's ain't no fittin' place fer a lady. The hotel's 'round here."

Eliza had grave misgivings about staying in such a place, but Zeke seemed unconcerned. If he had entrusted Millie there for the night, she reasoned, he must consider it safe.

Sure enough, the reception parlor of the hotel was tastefully decorated and respectable looking. Zeke rang a little bell on the desk, and a matronly woman bustled in to assist them. Millie traipsed down the stairs moments later and was exuberant to see Eliza again.

Zeke already knew the rates since he had just gotten Millie settled. He relayed the information now to Eliza. "You want a room of your own, or would you just as soon bunk in with Millie?"

Millie was obviously in favor of having a roommate and chattered encouragements end-to-end, tempting Eliza to ask for a private room, but her practicality won out. It would be safer and less expensive to stay with Millie. Surely the girl didn't talk in her sleep.

Since she had saved expenses by sharing a room, Eliza was able to enjoy her meal in the dining room with a clear conscience. Her steak came with a plate of beans, biscuits to sop up the gravy, and enough coffee to fill in the chinks. An hour later, full and in a much brighter frame of mind, Eliza thanked Zeke again and bade him a good night before climbing the stairs with Millie.

Cotton sheets never felt so good.

ꕤ

As it turned out, Millie did talk in her sleep. She also thrashed and kicked off the covers, but her disturbance to Eliza's rest was nothing compared to the noise from the saloon and gambling hall that traveled easily on the night air. The music and laughter continued until the small hours of the night when gunshots startled them both awake. Millie fell asleep again almost immediately, but Eliza lay awake for what seemed like hours, staring at a papered ceiling that reflected the glow of a full moon.

She was troubled by the memory of Clay Allison entering the saloon. He seemed so mannerly—so nice—and it had been so comforting to meet someone from home, even if she had not known him there. The sound of crashing glass prompted a prayer for his safety. If he worked cattle here in New Mexico territory, perhaps Zeke was acquainted with him. She would have to remember to ask him.

The crow of a rooster awakened Eliza, though she did not remember falling asleep. She stretched and climbed from the bed, not at all rested. Her head felt heavy, and she was sore all over. Rubbing her stiff neck, she groped her way slowly to the wash table and poured water into the basin. She splashed some on her face and used a rag to freshen up, then checked her reflection in a mirror hanging on the wall behind the pitcher. She found a brush in her trunk and returned to the mirror to stroke her hair vigorously before twisting it up into a bun. A few quick pinches brought color to her cheeks, but she did not feel any more prepared to face the day than she had before. No matter. By tonight she would be in Elizabethtown with Uncle Rufus, Aunt Charlotte, and Julia, and all would be well.

Zeke joined Millie and Eliza for a breakfast of eggs, steak, beans, and biscuits before excusing himself to load up their trunks and hitch up the horses. Eliza had time for one more cup of coffee before he returned with the wagon. She wrapped her fingers around the china cup, letting its warmth soak into her cold hands. She yawned and hoped its steaming contents would help her wake up.

As they rolled down the main street of town, Eliza hugged her shawl tight around her shoulders to ward off the morning chill. Though a bright sun promised a fair day, she could see her breath on the air at this early hour.

The only sign of life was a sleepy store owner sweeping the dust from the hard-packed earth in front of his door. The wagon crossed a silvery stream bordered by scrubby trees and turned west at the end of town. The sun on the water caused a mist to rise. Eliza glanced back at the dozen or so buildings scattered like dice up the gentle slope of the foothills. Adobe walls glowed golden pink in the early sunlight. Cimarron was quiet this morning, its inhabitants likely sleeping off a night of carousing.

They followed the little river and headed straight for the mountains, which seemed to rise ever higher out of the earth as they approached. Eliza wondered how they would get the wagon up and over such heights to Elizabethtown on the other side, but just as they reached what seemed to be an impenetrable cliff, a narrow canyon opened before them.

Zeke stopped the wagon at a little cabin at the canyon entrance. A man emerged, and Zeke matter-of-factly handed him a number of bills. Without a word, the man jerked his chin in the direction of the canyon, and Zeke climbed silently back into the wagon.

"Toll road," he said once they were underway again. "Mr. Maxwell owns all the land around Cimarron—all the land in New Mexico territory, purt' near, or at least it seems that way. Cimarron Canyon is narrow, and the trees growed right down to the river's edge. Mr. Maxwell had his men cut the forest back so's a wagon could pass, but then thieves took to hidin' in the shadows, robbin' everybody that came through. Got to where folks was scared to travel, so Mr. Maxwell posted guards and started charging tolls to use the canyon road. It's safer now, and somehow Mr. Maxwell managed to line his pockets in the bargain." He shrugged it off as an inevitable fact of life. "Man's a pure genius for makin' money, Mr. Maxwell is."

If there was any place in the world more beautiful than Cimarron Canyon, Eliza had not seen it. The wagon ruts followed a rushing stream, full from the runoff of melting snow that poured from the white topped mountains. The icy water made blithe, earthy music as it flowed over moss-covered rocks, winding its way down to the mouth of the canyon. High above them the wind in the massive pines played a tenor harmony to the stream's sprightly melody. Fallen needles and pinecones carpeted the forest floor and sunlight streamed in golden shafts through breaks in the verdant ceiling. Here and there, clumps of aspen were setting forth pale green leaves that flickered in the dancing beams of light. Eliza drew in her breath as every turn brought a change of scenery, painted by the very hand of God against a backdrop of towering stone walls. It was easier, now, to praise Him—to thank Him for bringing her here to this peaceful wilderness—a pleasant passage through her impenetrable grief and onto higher planes beyond. Surely these mountains held the balm her heart required.

They rode in silence for some time, listening to the sounds of the forest. Even Millie was silent as they basked in the beauty of their surroundings.

Eliza sighed. "You know what I'm looking forward to?" Millie raised a quizzical brow, but did not break her silence as Eliza continued. "Seeing Julia again."

"Your cousin?"

Eliza nodded. "She's about four years younger than I. We were seldom together except for holidays, but I so enjoyed her on those occasions." She paused. "I had no brothers or sisters, so Julia and her brother, Earl, were especially dear to me."

"Is she much like you?" Millie seemed eager enough to let Eliza carry the conversation for now. Perhaps she had talked herself out at last.

Eliza considered the best way to answer her question. "Yes and no. Our mothers were sisters, so we do favor in some ways, but Julia is tiny like Mama and Aunt Charlotte. In every other way though—all the things that are important—we have much in common. Julia has a head for figures and a natural gift for organization. She was born to be a storekeeper's daughter. She's practical—a good cook, too. Even during the war, she could make a feast out of nothing, it seemed to me." Eliza smiled as she thought back to happy times and family gatherings and looked forward to more.

ꕤ

They climbed for hours and came at last to another toll cabin at the top of the canyon. Zeke touched the brim of his hat to salute Mr. Maxwell's man as they passed.

The horses followed a curve in the road around to the left as they rounded a dome of rock. Eliza and Millie sucked in their breaths in unison as the lower basin of a high valley opened in a sweeping vista before them.

Zeke stopped the wagon. "The Moreno Valley. My place ... our place, I mean ... is right down yonder." His voice was husky with awe and pride as he pointed toward the west where his and Millie's future home lay nestled between the folds of the far ridge.

They sat for a full minute, the three of them, taking in the view.

Millie leaned forward, as if an extra twelve inches would help her see her future better. Then she squealed and hugged Zeke's arm.

Eliza reined in a twinge of envy. Millie knew exactly where she was going and who she was going there with. In a way, Eliza did, too. She was going to Uncle Rufus and Aunt Charlotte's store in Elizabethtown, but it wasn't the same, somehow. Up until now, it had seemed like enough, but the old hollow feeling returned when she thought of marriage and families. Would the home she'd have with her aunt and uncle be enough? Could she stay busy enough to feel like her life had purpose, even without Grayson—without children?

Never doubt the Lord's goodness. She heard Papa's voice in memory. *His will is ever directed to His children's good.*

She willed herself to believe that it was true. She accepted it on faith. But 'faith is the assurance of things unseen,' she countered, and 'hope deferred makes the heart sick.' What she had seen in the last nine years was enough grief to convince her that there was no guarantee of happiness in life. She and the Lord seemed to have different definitions of what constituted "good." Still, there was hope. Around the next bend, or the next, there was always hope.

Zeke clucked and jostled the reins, and the horses, glad to be on the homeward stretch, leaned forward in their harnesses.

As they curved back to the right, Eliza craned her neck to see around the bend in that direction, anxious for a glimpse of Elizabethtown in the upper valley. What she saw made her throat go dry.

Millie cried out in alarm, and Zeke sprang into action, tying off the reins and leaping from the wagon.

In front of them a rig lay on its side, the horses still harnessed.

Zeke threw back a canvas tarp in the bed of his wagon and pulled out a rifle before he ran to investigate. He disappeared behind the overturned wagon, then reappeared quickly and signaled for help. "It's your Uncle Rufus," he hollered back to them. "Come help me git this contraption off him!"

Already Zeke was dragging a fallen tree to use as a lever. Millie showed pluck Eliza would never have guessed she possessed, running without hesitation to the restless horses and gathering their fallen reins. She spoke to them gently and stroked their manes, distracting and calming them, while Zeke placed one end of the slender tree trunk beneath the wagon and positioned the trunk across a large boulder. He circled around to the other end and began to pull downward with his full weight while Eliza ran to Uncle Rufus.

She lifted his head and slid her two hands under his shoulders so that she could pull him free of the wagon as soon as its weight was off him.

For what seemed like a long time, nothing happened. Then, with a terrible creak, the wagon shifted and teetered precariously on its wheel rims before rocking and landing with a crash back on four wheels. The horses shied and side stepped, showing the whites of their eyes.

Eliza heaved mightily, and Uncle Rufus groaned in pain—a welcome sign that he was still alive and regaining consciousness.

Millie took one look at his bloody legs and ran quickly down to the stream. Eliza saw her hoist her lacy, ruffled skirts and tear long strips from the hem of her petticoat. These she soaked in the cool stream before running back to begin gently cleaning Uncle Rufus' wounds while Eliza stroked his bald head and whispered words of comfort interspersed with fervent prayers. She could feel a frightful knot just behind his left ear.

Eliza scanned the vicinity as she worked.

"It's okay," Zeke said reassuringly. "There ain't nobody here. Whoever done this is long gone."

"It's not that." Eliza caught a glimpse of smooth wood among some rocks further up the slope. Scrambling up, she lifted a pair of crutches—one broken. "Uncle Rufus has a bad hip. Mule kicked him when I was a little girl." She returned to the wrecked wagon and checked to make sure her uncle was still insensible before continuing in a low voice. "What kind of place is this? Who would pistol whip a crippled man and steal from him?"

Millie gasped, and Zeke shook his head. One side of his mouth twisted in disgust, but he did not seem particularly surprised.

Eliza recalled how quickly he had retrieved his rifle.

Taking the crutches from her, Zeke used the broken pieces to splint Rufus' legs with more strips from Millie's petticoats. "Just in case," he said.

He returned his rifle to his wagon and came back with the tarp, which he folded double around the undamaged crutch. Eliza helped rock Uncle Rufus to one side and then the other as Zeke and Millie eased the canvas beneath him to make a sling, then Eliza helped Zeke lift the injured man into the bed of his wagon. Millie held Rufus' horses while Zeke brought his wagon around to the front. He tethered Rufus' horses to the back of his rig. "You think you could drive this team?" he asked, and both Eliza and Millie nodded. "That's my girl," he said to Millie. "Eliza, we need you in back with your uncle."

With no further words, he lifted Millie onto the buckboard of Rufus' wagon and helped Eliza into its bed where she braced her back against the wooden sides and lifted Uncle Rufus' poor bruised head into her lap. Her attention was trained on her uncle as the wagons began to move forward. With each bump and jostle, he groaned, and always Millie would look back with tears of compassion in worried eyes.

Eliza continued to murmur prayers and comforts, pressing one cool, moist cloth to the lump on his head and dabbing his brow with another. It was strange how quickly she returned to the habits of her youth in times of trouble. Praying was natural. It made her feel better—less helpless—even if she still wasn't sure God was listening. But maybe He was. Uncle Rufus' eyes opened and squinted against the light of day.

He began to struggle and mumble feverishly. "Bandits!"

"Shhh…" Eliza sought to calm him, but that one word explained a great deal. Uncle Rufus and Aunt Charlotte must have received Papa's letter, and her uncle was coming to meet her as planned. He would have left the morning before, bringing a long winter's profits to buy supplies to restock his store. Now it was gone. Any furs he had brought to trade were gone as well. The wagon was empty when they found him, and she guessed that his pockets were, too. If his legs were broken, it would be weeks or months before he could think of making another trip to Cimarron, but without stock to sell and profits to invest, his hopes were ruined anyway.

Uncle Rufus moaned again as he lapsed back into unconsciousness.

"Zeke, how far is it to Elizabethtown?"

"'Bout five miles from here." Zeke's voice carried over the squeak of wheels and harnesses.

For whatever good it would do, Eliza resumed praying.

Chapter 4

When Eliza first caught sight of Elizabethtown sprawled across a rise on the western bank of Moreno Creek, she could not tell if it was the altitude or anticipation that left her breathless. At the time of Aunt Charlotte's first letter only three years ago, gold fever had just begun to lure adventurers to the slopes of Baldy Mountain. Elizabethtown was nothing more than a tent camp surrounding a single store. Now it was the largest settlement in New Mexico territory, boasting nearly seven thousand residents.

She'd thanked the Lord for Zeke and Millie so many times today she'd lost count, but she thanked Him again when she saw the grid of streets lined with saloons, hotels, shops and cabins. She had no idea which of the hundreds of gray wooden buildings housed her uncle's general store, but Zeke drove straight to it with Rufus' wagon in tow. A painted sign on the false front above the tin-roofed porch read "MacMannus General Store." Eliza winced at the poignant memory it evoked. The sign above Uncle Rufus' old store read "MacMannus & Son."

They caused quite a stir coming into town with two wagons in tandem. It could only mean there'd been trouble. People stopped to stare and speculate.

Eliza recognized Aunt Charlotte as she emerged from a shop just off Washington Street, shielding her eyes to peer at the wagons. At first her aunt's expression registered only curiosity, but when they drew close enough for her to recognize Rufus' horses and rig, she hitched her skirts up and began to run.

When she reached the wagon, she searched Eliza's face anxiously then stared at the still form of her husband, laid out bruised and bloody on the wagon bed. Her complexion paled above the black lace of her collar. "Oh, Lord! Please don't take him!"

Her piteous wails pierced Eliza's heart. Tears of sympathy stung her eyes. She laid a comforting hand on her aunt's shoulder. "He's alive, Aunt Charlotte, thanks to Zeke and Millie here. He even talked to us a little on the way down the mountain."

Charlotte searched Eliza's face once more as if trying to decide whether to accept the hope extended, then nodded and gulped back any further sobs.

Zeke climbed from his wagon and joined several townsmen lifting Rufus out. "He'll rest better once we git him inside, ma'am."

The gentle directive gave Aunt Charlotte a task to accomplish. She flew into action, opening the door to the mercantile and moving goods aside to create a path wide enough for the men to pass, carrying Rufus on the canvas between them.

They carried the injured man to a small room at the back of the store—the family's living quarters. A bedstead stood in one corner. Aunt Charlotte was already turning back the quilt and plumping the pillows. The men eased Rufus onto the straw tick mattress, taking care to move his injured legs as carefully as possible when they shifted him off the canvas. As soon as they had him settled, one said, "I'll run fer Hiram," and left at a quick pace.

Seizing onto the hope of another encouragement, Eliza turned to her aunt. "Is Hiram your doctor?"

"We have no doctor in Elizabethtown."

Eliza's heart fell.

"Hiram's a carpenter. He works down at the saw mill." A rough-looking man wearing baggy trousers with a single suspender spoke matter-of-factly. "He's done a heap of doctorin'. He kin feel out broken bones and splint 'em up like busted chair legs. He kin make crutches." Eliza's hopes began to rise again until she heard the man's final words. "He kin also build a casket, if one's needed." Her face must have reflected her horror, for the man quickly added, "Speaking only gen'rally, of course."

Zeke glared at the man, yanked off his hat, and hit him with it. He jerked his thumb in the direction of the door, and the men filed out awkwardly.

Eliza watched in stunned silence.

Now it was her aunt's turn to extend comfort. She patted Eliza's arm. "He'll mend."

"Oh, Aunt Charlotte! I've only just arrived, and already I've brought you trouble."

"Whatever do you mean by that, child?" Her aunt rinsed out a bloody compress and reapplied it to the knot on Uncle Rufus' head. Her gentle hands—so like Mama's—were red from work and stiff with age.

"Uncle Rufus was robbed on his way to meet me." The connection seemed obvious.

"Nonsense. We asked you to come. Rufus would have gone to Cimarron yesterday in any event to buy supplies. If you had not happened upon him this afternoon on your way here, I would not have missed him until this evening when he did not return. He would have lain there for several more hours at least. We might not have found him in the dark. The way I see it, you've already been a great blessing to us." She tossed the ruined water out the side door and poured more to rinse the basin.

When Hiram arrived, Zeke brought him to the back room. The carpenter nodded briskly to the two ladies before beginning his examinations. With skilled hands he felt the length of Rufus' splinted legs, pressing gently from several angles.

Uncle Rufus groaned and roused.

They all watched in silence as the man finished his work.

Finally Hiram straightened and addressed them. "You can take those off now," he said, indicating the splints. "The bones aren't busted—just bruised and maybe some sprains, from the look o' that swelling."

Eliza released a breath she hadn't realized she was holding.

"I'll make him another crutch to take the place o' that busted one, but he don't need to be on them much for at least the next month."

Uncle Rufus groaned in dismay at this news and tried to rise.

Zeke put a hand to his chest to stop him, and the injured man fell back against the pillows, defeated.

Aunt Charlotte's expression was compassionate but firm. "It's going to be all right, Rufus. We have Eliza here now. She can help out in the store until you're up and about."

Eliza smiled and nodded, eager to be useful.

Aunt Charlotte thanked Hiram, and Zeke left to show him out.

When they were alone, Uncle Rufus turned to his wife with a pleading expression in his eyes. Eliza had not seen her uncle in the four years since Earl died. It struck her now that he seemed to have aged at least ten years in that time, and another five since this afternoon. She had never seen such a look of despair in any man's countenance.

"I've ruined us." His voice was a tragic moan as he raised a shaking hand to wipe his face.

"I don't see how you figure that." Aunt Charlotte seemed to have recovered from her initial shock. She spoke now with spirited pluck.

"Our money's gone. All of it. We got nothing much to sell and no way to buy more."

"God will provide. The main thing is you're safe."

"I'm not much good to you, Lottie—a useless cripple." Uncle Rufus let his hand fall, listless.

It pained Eliza to hear her uncle speak this way, not that she blamed him for feeling as he did. Life was hard—difficult enough to make even strong men grow weary. Sensing their need for privacy, she gathered Zeke's canvas in her arms and carried it out to the front porch to fold it. She'd be within earshot if Aunt Charlotte needed her.

ᘓᘐᘏ

Zeke had already unhitched the horses, put the wagon in the barn, and carried in Eliza's trunk.

She thanked him and Millie again profusely, and they reluctantly took their leave, satisfied that Rufus was resting in good hands. In an attempt to make herself useful, Eliza found a broom and began to sweep the porch. She'd swept it twice before her aunt joined her.

Closing the door softly behind her, Aunt Charlotte settled into a willow rocker. She leaned back and shut her eyes, letting out a breath that sounded like a weary sigh.

Eliza came to her and offered her hands. "It'll be all right, truly, Aunt Charlotte."

"I know," her aunt said simply. Aunt Charlotte took Eliza's two hands and kissed them before resting her cheek against them. "I'm glad you're here."

"I'm glad I can help. And surely Julia will come, too, as soon as we can get word to her of her father's accident." The prospect of seeing her cousin again and meeting Julia's new husband was like a sturdy candle glowing brightly at the end of a dark passage, but when her aunt looked up at her with tear-filled eyes, a sense of foreboding snuffed her hopes.

Aunt Charlotte glanced at the door. "Julia cannot come, dear," she said in a low voice.

There was more. She could tell. Eliza hardly dared to breathe until she heard the rest.

"Julia is no longer with us."

Eliza grappled for some acceptable meaning to the words she was hearing.

"She passed away last September."

Eliza felt as if the earth had crumbled and dropped away from beneath her feet, plunging her into a black, bottomless void of grief. Her mind clawed for something solid to cling to. It was all she could do to choke out one word. "How?"

"When I wrote you at the beginning of September, Julia's husband had just brought her down to us. His claim is way up the Red River on Bitter Creek. Julia was expecting their first child, and he didn't want to risk her going into labor so far from help. He brought her in her eighth month, before there was risk of early snow, then went back to his claim to close up for the winter, expecting to join us before the baby came." She paused, rubbing a thumb across sore knuckles. "But the baby came early—barely a week after he left," she continued with downcast eyes. "There was no doctor..." Aunt Charlotte's voice trailed off at this point, but there was no need to say more.

"And the baby?" Eliza had to ask, though she had already guessed the answer.

Aunt Charlotte shook her head. Her chin began to quiver. "It was a boy. He was beautiful and perfect, but too small to survive without his mama." Tears washed her cheeks, and Eliza tasted the salt on her own lips. "They died the same day. We buried them together on that rise there." Eliza followed her gaze to a tidy fenced cemetery on a low hill just north of town. "It seemed fitting. Julia had so longed to hold him."

The cemetery seemed unusually large for a town so new.

"Will you take me to her?"

Her aunt nodded and rose from her rocker.

Together they walked the puddled path to the graveyard just as the sun slipped behind the trees. The hill had a lonesome feel, isolated from the bustling town by something other than the wire fence that surrounded it—something intangible.

Aunt Charlotte opened the picket gate and shut it again behind them as if closing them into some holy place, quiet and serene.

The air seemed sweeter here, the evening breeze scented with the fragrance of pine. Eliza wasn't sure if she felt the change or simply became more observant.

Aunt Charlotte led the way to a patch of ground raked clean and outlined with smooth stones. The wooden marker still looked new.

Eliza read the inscription in the fading light. "Julia Craig. Beloved wife of Jacob. Born 13 February 1845. Died 9 September 1869. Aged 24 years." Then below: "and infant son, Earl."

They had named Julia's baby after her brother. Both gone. Eliza put her hand to her mouth to stifle her sobs as she read the last line. "The Lord giveth, and the Lord taketh away. Blessed be the name of the Lord."

❧

Supper was a simple meal of soup and biscuits in the little room at the back of the store. The savory aroma was tempting, but Eliza could barely swallow for the lump in her throat. She put on a brave face for Uncle Rufus and tried to think of something cheerful to say.

"Papa sends his love." Obvious, but safe.

Aunt Charlotte murmured a pleasant, "Hmm."

Uncle Rufus, propped up in the bed, barely grunted an acknowledgment.

She'd have to do better than that. Eliza groped for other tidbits of news from home, trying to avoid weightier topics. It was like picking her way around the fresh, crumbling edge of a gaping hole in the earth, desperately afraid of falling in and at the same time studiously trying to ignore its presence. A horrible thought occurred to her. Were the crumbling edges the remains of her faith—that once firm foundation she had built her life upon? Did Uncle Rufus feel that too?

She tried again to fill the aching silence. "The town is bigger than I expected." She forced her words to sound casual and optimistic.

Uncle Rufus looked up for the first time. "Gold fever." He shook his head and ladled up another spoonful of broth. "It's a sickness.

Seven thousand men all hoping the means to a better life lies in these hills."

"Have they found much?" Eliza had to admit that the prospect of discovering gold was exciting. Hope feeds the soul as surely as food nourishes the body. Maybe that was what Uncle Rufus needed—a ray of hope. Even she had come west in hopes of finding a better life than the one she'd left.

"They've found quite a bit." Aunt Charlotte was quick to enter this bright opening in the conversation.

Uncle Rufus shrugged. "Problem is getting it out of the rock and out of this valley." His voice was still laced with a tone of discouragement, but he continued—interested, at least, if only in making her aware of the hardships. "It ain't as easy as panning for dust and nuggets. That's just how you find where the gold has washed loose."

He waved his spoon as he lectured. It was almost comical, but Eliza dared not smile for fear he would stop and return to his brooding. She settled herself to listen, glad that she was no longer the only one carrying the conversation.

"These crazy gold diggers decided to give nature a boost. Them two hollers that run up Mount Baldy over there—Grouse Gulch and Humbug—is mostly dry. There ain't enough water in Moreno Creek to supply the placer boxes, and that's slow, anyhow." He jerked his thumb toward the front of the store, as if they could see the mountain from where they sat. "Last year Lucien Maxwell, what owns this grant, hired out an engineer. Smart fella. He crossed this ridge behind us into the next valley and tapped water from the Red River."

"He stole a river?" Water rights were no joking matter back home in Texas.

"Borrowed it, mostly, and brung it over here. Julia's husband was on the work crew."

"Did they bring the river through the mountain? They can't have gone over."

"Actually, in a couple places, they pumped the water uphill in huge pipes. There's stretches where they ran them pipes over deep valleys on wooden trestles eighty feet high." Her uncle seemed to enjoy Eliza's round-eyed attention. "But mostly they went around—more'n forty miles north down that valley and back around here. They call it The Big Ditch, and they use the water to blast away the side of that mountain out yonder."

Eliza shook her head in amazement. "There must be a good deal of gold to make it worth so much trouble."

"There is, but it ain't all prime quality ore."

Eliza's brow furrowed as she pondered that.

"They take the rock samples to the assayer's office to see how much gold there is in it. Then they gotta figure a way to get tons and tons of rock outta this here valley."

"It's a long way to Cimarron, and about as far to Taos," Aunt Charlotte said.

"Can they go north?"

"No roads. Just the work trails they used for the Ditch."

Eliza tried to picture just how remote this valley was. She wanted to ask her uncle more questions, but he seemed suddenly tired.

"All in all, most of 'em find just about enough to break even..." Uncle Rufus set his empty bowl on a shelf beside the bed and laid back against the pillows, trying to ease into a comfortable position. "...enough to keep the dream of a better life just out of reach." His face looked pinched and gray. "One of these days reality will knock them over the head, too, and they'll wake up."

Eliza pursed her lips. So much for her attempt to cheer him up.

Aunt Charlotte said nothing. She just rose to collect the dishes, tenderly kissing her husband's forehead before she blew out the lamp.

As Eliza and Aunt Charlotte washed the dishes, the only sound was the clink of pottery. The hard, painful realities Uncle Rufus spoke of lurked in the silence, and nothing she said could make them go away.

Afterward, they climbed the narrow stairs behind the sales counter. At the top a large storage area filled the space under the roof above the store, but a door to their left led to an attic bedroom over the living quarters—a room which had obviously been Julia's. Eliza recognized the quilt on the low rope bed. It was the one she and Julia slept under as children. Her sweeping gaze lit upon one painful reminder and then another as Aunt Charlotte tried to make the room comfortable for her. A framed scene Julia sketched while Eliza and Earl fished one summer day. The doilies Julia made the year Mama taught them both to crochet. The lace-edged pillowcases Eliza helped her pack into the chest of treasures they each saved for their future homes. She swallowed hard, choking down her grief. If her aunt did not finish and leave soon, she would break down entirely.

Aunt Charlotte arranged an extra blanket at the foot of the bed and fluffed the pillows. "There's a pitcher of fresh water on the wash stand. Can you think of anything else you need?"

Only to be alone, but she could not say so. "I'm sure I'll be fine." Eliza took the pillow from her aunt and patted her hand. "I can see to myself. Why don't you check on Uncle Rufus? It's been a long day."

Charlotte squeezed Eliza's hand and kissed her cheek. Her aunt's sad eyes would have broken her heart if it hadn't already lain in pieces.

Alone again, Eliza looked out the window in the back gable, over Aunt Charlotte's dormant kitchen garden, and north up the Moreno Valley. The moonlight outlined a soft black ridge feathered with pines against a velvet blue sky. Over that ridge lay a lonely cabin, made warm and pretty by Julia's hands—a home meant to welcome a child who would never see it. Tears flowed at last as memories streamed through Eliza's mind—reminiscences of happy Christmases and long summer visits with Earl and Julia in the carefree days before the war. Secret confidences whispered in the dark beneath this very coverlet. Plans of what they'd be and do when they grew up and had families of their own. And what was left? Julia was gone along with her baby and Earl and Mama and Grayson. At least they were together in a happier place. Did God allow such senseless tragedy to make men long for heaven? Eliza had never felt so lonely.

It was hard to breathe. The attic was warm and stuffy from the heat of the woodstove below. Eliza opened the window just a crack before sliding into bed. Her cheeks were hot with tears, but nothing could ease the icy grip of grief upon her heart, as cold as the night air in these mountains once the sun had left the sky. She stared at the ceiling. *Dear Lord, You promised not to lay on us more burdens than we can bear, but I am not strong enough to bear more. You promised to work all things together for our good, but I cannot escape the sorrow that surrounds me.* Her prayer seemed to stop at the sloping boards above her.

I will lift up mine eyes unto the hills, from whence cometh my help. My help comes from the Lord. The words of the familiar Psalm should have brought comfort. Instead, they seemed to mock the shredded remnants of her faith. She'd come west in hopes of finding a better life here in the mountains, but her only hope—the source of healing for her hurting heart—lay not in the mountains but in the Maker of the mountains. Did she really trust Him? It was one thing to trust Him for heaven, but another to trust Him in life. She'd never expected that the sun of His blessings would always shine, but she had wandered in this cold, black night for so long. Could she trust His plan even if it meant more pain? It was well and good to sing that He was worthy of any sacrifice until she was called upon to make them. Was He worth more to her than loved ones, plans, and dreams? Her soul felt naked. Everything was stripped away—everything but the one essential question, *Do you love Me more than these?*

Eliza lay still in the close attic, listening, desperate to hear some answer to her anguished prayers. Instead she heard only the lonesome sound of wind in the pines up on the ridge and the muffled sounds of weeping that rose through the floorboards from the room below. She was not the only one who had experienced great grief. Perhaps that was part of God's purpose in bringing her here—not to escape, but to provide comfort to others, to heal as she ministered healing.

She cried herself to sleep anyway—soaking her pillow with all the tears she hadn't been able to shed for years. She could not hold them back any longer.

Chapter 5

Sunday morning dawned bright and clear. The world always looked brighter in the morning. Nothing could stop that promise of new beginnings. Though she often felt like a hypocrite at worship, Sunday mornings were still special, because they began a new week as well. And today was Easter Sunday—the epitome of new beginnings.

Opening her trunk, Eliza hurried to shake out her dresses and hang them on pegs behind the door. Her folded items could remain in the trunk at the foot of the bed, but she left the lid up so they could air after the long trip. She picked out her next-best dress and hoped it would suffice. She'd seen a church on the way to the cemetery, but knew nothing more about it. Aunt Charlotte would know.

Coffee was brewing. Tendrils of its tempting aroma beckoned her, promising warmth and comfort, and Eliza followed her nose down the stairs.

Aunt Charlotte bent over the woodstove, poking up the fire.

Eliza was pleased to see Rufus sitting up in bed, propped with down pillows. "You're looking better than yesterday."

He lifted a mug. "Feeling better, too. Lottie already fixed me up with some tea."

The stove door squeaked as Aunt Charlotte closed it and gave the handle a twist before she began to rattle among the cast iron pans for a skillet. "You could find some eggs in the yard for our breakfast, if you're willing."

Eliza found a basket near the side door. Stepping out, she breathed deeply. The cloud of her breath surprised her. It did not feel so cold, now that the sun was shining. She gazed again for a moment at the ridge beyond the yard, dusky blue this morning beneath a pink sky. She could never view life in Elizabethtown as mundane as long as that ridge lay just beyond.

A couple dozen hens were already distracted, scratching, making it an easy matter to rob their nests. There were far more eggs than three people could eat, but the rest would be good for the store.

"The air is different here," she said, stepping again into the warm room. "Cool and crisp. It'll make for a nice walk to church."

Uncle Rufus barely looked up from his mug. "No church this morning. No preacher."

Her uncle could not have known the consternation his few words caused. What was Easter morning without worship? Especially for a preacher's daughter. Seven thousand souls with no pastor on Easter? A total sense of isolation swallowed her.

Her face must have betrayed her disappointment. Aunt Charlotte spoke up quickly. "We'll have a time of worship here, then there'll be a church service this afternoon when the circuit rider arrives."

Eliza swallowed her disappointment. This was different, but many things would be different here. She might as well get used to that.

After breakfast Uncle Rufus read from the twenty-fourth chapter of Luke while Aunt Charlotte kneaded sourdough and set a dozen loaves to rise on a warming shelf above the stove.

"Fetch me my fiddle, girl, and I'll play us something fitting," Uncle Rufus said, pointing.

Eliza found the instrument in its case under the bed. He played a medley of hymns while the bread rose. Eliza found time to write a letter to Papa, letting him know of her safe arrival. She didn't know when she'd have an opportunity to send it, but she prayed for him as she wrote. At that very moment, he would be preaching back home. Aunt Charlotte slipped the loaves into the oven and kept careful watch to make sure they didn't fall. They took turns sharing favorite passages of scripture to encourage one another.

The sweet smell of baking bread filled the room. Heartwarming. Eliza helped her aunt remove the golden loaves. They coaxed them from the pans and set them back on the shelf to cool. Aunt Charlotte saved out two loaves. One she set on the table; the other she wrapped in a bit of muslin tied up with string. "For the preacher," she said simply, and set the soup on to warm for lunch.

Eliza was struck by the blend of work and worship. For her, worship had always been a time set apart from the rest of the week. Here, it was all wrapped up in a single stream of life.

The church bell began to ring just as Eliza set the last washed dish to drain on the sideboard. Its sound carried brilliantly on the thin mountain air.

"He's here," her uncle announced, and Eliza knew he meant the preacher had come. "Take off your apron, Lottie, and go on along, the two of you. I'm full and comfortable and ready for a rest. I'll do fine until you get back."

Aunt Charlotte studied him only a moment before deciding he was well enough to be left alone. Then with deft hands she removed her apron and took up the loaf of bread.

Eliza was relieved to know that she would not have to attend the service alone. Meeting new people was always easier with someone who could make introductions.

They walked again a portion of the path they took last evening. Eliza glanced north to the cemetery, peaceful on its little rise, before they entered the welcoming doors of the small church and took a place on the back bench.

She looked around the rustic wooden interior, unimproved even by a coat of paint, and was glad that someone had thought to bring an arrangement of pine boughs to grace the altar. There were no flowers yet in the alpine meadows, even though Easter came late this year. Winter lingered long in the high valleys.

The congregation was small, Eliza thought, for a town this size. She had seen no other church, yet scarcely more than a handful of worshippers gathered. There were perhaps ten families in attendance, each with a string of children spit and polished for the occasion. Zeke sat straight and proud on a bench by the window with Millie by his side. A few single men—prospectors, from the look of them, and mostly young—made up the rest of the assembly. One man, strikingly tall, sat alone on the front row, his head bowed in prayer. Eliza took note and wondered what brought him here.

The preacher took as his text Matthew 6: 19-21—"Lay not up for yourselves treasures upon earth." An odd choice for Easter. Was that where everybody else was? Panning for gold and working for a living on the Lord's day? Elizabethtown was a very different sort of place. In Waco even scalawags came to church on Sunday, no matter who they cheated the rest of the week. Eliza always thought it was the best place for them to be. Maybe they'd hear something that would make a difference. But then again, if they'd heard it every Sunday of their lives to no avail, perhaps they cared more about the pretense of propriety. She had an odd feeling that everyone who showed up for church in Elizabethtown had made a deliberate effort to be there.

They sang a final hymn *a capella*, and the preacher prayed a blessing on them before moving to greet the faithful at the door.

Aunt Charlotte pressed her loaf of sourdough into the circuit rider's arms as she introduced Eliza to him, then to everyone else as they filed past in turn.

Apparently it had been many weeks since the pastor last visited Elizabethtown. He asked about several in the congregation who had been sick.

Zeke lingered, eagerly seizing the first opportunity to introduce "his Millie" to the preacher and Aunt Charlotte and to ask how Rufus was after his "accident."

Aunt Charlotte gave a report and recounted the events for the pastor, only she didn't call it an accident. She called it what it was—a robbery—and the minister accepted the news as if it were nothing out of the ordinary. If Eliza had come to New Mexico in search of peace, she'd plainly picked the wrong place.

The conversation drifted to news of people she did not know, and Eliza let her attention wander. She noticed the tall, rugged-looking man on the front row as he rose and walked to the altar to lift the jar of greenery. He brought it with him as he made his way down the center aisle toward them.

When he drew near, Aunt Charlotte turned as if to make his introduction. Instead, they stared at one another for an awkward moment before she said, "Eliza, I'd like you to meet Jake."

The man nodded in polite greeting, but his eyes never left Eliza's face.

She tried to meet his steady gaze, but there was pain in his eyes—so much pain that it threatened to engulf her, as well. She could not bear it. She looked away, staring at her hands. Even then she felt him watching her. If he wasn't going to speak, she hoped he would take his leave soon.

"Eliza is my niece, Julia's cousin," Aunt Charlotte continued. Another awkward pause, then, "Would you care to join us for dinner? Rufus is laid up, but he'd love to see you."

Eliza's head snapped up.

At least the man was no longer staring. Jake's brows knit with alarm and concern, but he nodded his acceptance of the invitation. "I need to make a stop first."

"Of course."

Charlotte continued to chat with the pastor, Zeke, and Millie as Jake carried his greenery to the cemetery hill. Eliza watched him go, back straight, shoulders square. He cast a long shadow.

"Preacher, when you reckon you'll be back through?" Zeke asked, with an effort to appear casual.

The circuit rider smiled. Anyone who saw Zeke's bashful expression and Millie's beaming blush could guess the obvious goal of that question.

"Well, now, I hadn't thought to be back before mid-May." The preacher paused for a moment, watching the dismay on the two young faces before continuing. "But I do believe the first of May would be a fine time for a wedding."

They made a few hasty plans before Zeke and Millie set off in the direction of the boarding house.

The circuit rider tucked Aunt Charlotte's sourdough loaf in his saddlebag then mounted up for the next leg of his journey.

Scanning the hill for their invited guest, Eliza caught sight of Jake as he walked slowly to Julia's grave and set the evergreens beside the wooden marker.

Jake.

Jacob Craig.

The realization struck Eliza at last. His back was turned, but she saw that it was bent with sorrow, as if a burden of grief weighed on his shoulders. His head remained bowed for a long moment until at last he looked up, up toward the ridge and beyond.

I will lift up mine eyes unto the hills.

Eliza imagined she could hear his thoughts—thoughts she had so recently shared. But his help did not lie in those mountains either. There was no hope over the next ridge—only a lonely cabin.

Jake's face was composed as he returned to them, but his gaze returned to Eliza's face.

She understood now, but it did nothing to alleviate her discomfort. She looked like Julia. Darker, much taller, but the resemblance was there. Her cheeks warmed, and Jake looked away.

Aunt Charlotte called out to Uncle Rufus as soon as she entered the store, announcing their guest and giving him time, Eliza supposed, to prepare for the meeting.

Jake looked around him as they passed the sparse rows of shelves. By the time he ducked to enter the back room, both Jake and Rufus seemed prepared for a moment that was awkward—painful, but inevitable.

Reluctant to intrude, Eliza stood at a respectful distance.

"Glad you came." Uncle Rufus leaned forward and offered his hand.

Jake accepted it with a firm grasp. "Sorry you're laid up." He didn't press for details.

"Blasted thieves. Knocked me in the head and dumped my rig up on the pass when I was going for supplies Friday."

"What all did they get?"

"Everything." Rufus said it now with a good deal more resigned acceptance than he had been able to muster last night.

"What're you going to do about stock for the spring?" Jake's eyes had missed nothing.

"Don't know, yet. Lottie says the Lord will provide, but He's gonna have to, 'cause I'll be switched if I can see my way outta this mess. I'm stuck here for the next month 'til my legs heal up, Hiram says." He gave the quilt that lay over him a frustrated smack.

Jake pulled a rush-seated chair up beside the bed and sat eye to eye with his father-in-law, but for a long time he just rested his elbows on his knees, watching his hands as his fingers worked around the brim of his hat. Finally, he took a deep breath and began. "You know, after losing Julia and the baby, I didn't have the heart to stay here. I felt like it was my fault."

"Wasn't anything you could'a done even if you'd a'been here," Uncle Rufus said. His voice was thick and husky, warm with forgiveness, but Eliza noticed that he stared out the window as if he couldn't trust himself to look at the man who shared his grief.

"Not that." Jake took another deep breath and let it out slowly. "Julia died having my child." His face was so awash with sorrow that Eliza wondered how he could hold back tears, but he managed. She saw his jaw clench with the effort.

Aunt Charlotte had been busying herself at the stove, but now she turned to stare, saying nothing.

Drawing a ragged breath, Jake swallowed hard. "I didn't have the heart to go home, either. I built that cabin for a family. It was empty, you know?"

Uncle Rufus nodded brusquely, but the gesture seemed to give Jake the strength to go on.

"I had the old shanty up by my mine—the one that I used when I first came into the valley. Figured I could work out of there, but I had no heart for digging, either."

Uncle Rufus nodded again and waited.

No one said anything, just letting Jake work it out.

"Couldn't work. Couldn't eat. Couldn't sleep. So I walked." His shoulders lifted in a shrug. "I walked alone out in the woods. I walked out there, and I talked to God. I talked to Him a lot." Jake looked down at his hands, grinned crookedly, and huffed. "But I finally got hungry."

Aunt Charlotte began to laugh, but it was not mirth. She pressed her hand to her mouth to quiet the sound so Jake would continue.

He looked at her quickly, then back at Rufus. These words were for him, apparently—a peace offering between men. "Life's got to go on—even if you don't particularly want it to." He shrugged again. "I shot some rabbits. Then I got a buck, and then I set out a few traps. I caught beaver and even a bear." He smirked when Eliza jumped at that last bit.

She had not thought about the wild animals that would come with a wild new territory.

"The meat froze quick up there, but once I thawed it, I had to use it up, and it was more than I could eat. So I smoked it. And I tanned the hides."

Jake paused, and Uncle Rufus studied his face. "You offering to sell me your meat to stock my store?"

"No." Jake looked the older man square in the eye. "I've got no use for so much. I want to give you the meat ... and the furs."

"I can't buy them, and I can't take them to Cimarron to trade for at least a month."

"You can't, but I can."

"It's too much." Uncle Rufus started to protest, but Jake talked right on.

"We're family—at least we were, and I'd still like to be. I'll take the furs to Cimarron this week and get what I can for them. You make up a list of the stock you need while I go back up to Bitter Creek, and I'll pick it up on my way back down. Would you trust me with your wagon?"

"I trusted you with my daughter, didn't I?" Uncle Rufus' voice was rough with embarrassment.

Jake seemed to misread his tone. Eliza saw the look of guilt and remorse that flickered over his features before he looked down at his hands again. "I'll take better care of the wagon," he said, his voice gravelly.

"That's not what I meant!" Uncle Rufus' red face showed that he realized his blunder instantly.

Aunt Charlotte cast him an understanding look as she came to stand behind Jake's chair. She placed her hands gently on his shoulders, and Jake rested his head against her arm. "We'll have the list ready."

Uncle Rufus eyed Jake for a short moment, reading his earnest expression, before offering his hand. "We've gotta work with what we got left. Might as well go for broke."

Chapter 6

Jake spent the night in the hayloft above Uncle Rufus' wagon barn.

Though Eliza rose at first light to gather eggs for an early breakfast, Jake was already mucking out the stalls by lantern light when she stepped outside. A single star still shone in the paling sky. The cold made her cheeks tingle, but in the morning quiet she could hear Moreno Creek rushing with runoff from the spring thaw. The horses looked up from a mound of fresh hay and huffed a greeting before returning to their munching.

Jake looked up, too. "'Mornin'." He hung the pitchfork on its peg and clenched one leather glove in his teeth to pull it off. "I was just finishing up." He cupped his hands to warm them by the lantern for a moment before blowing out the flame.

As he sauntered toward her, his smile warmed her like the sunrise. Without warning, something stirred within her—something she hadn't felt since Grayson. As if some frozen place inside of her began to thaw. Eliza reminded herself that Jake was her cousin's widower. An attraction to him would be most unseemly. He was still in mourning for Julia. It was a good thing that her cold-reddened cheeks would hide her blush.

"Let me break the ice for you." With a practiced motion, he broke the thin crust on the washbowl with his elbow. A towel hung from a twig hook lashed to the porch post. Jake grabbed it and held it out to her. "You can go first."

Eliza stared skeptically at the icy water, then gazed at him as if he were daft, one eyebrow raised.

Jake chuckled. "What's the matter? A mite cold for you?"

That smile again. It made her think things she shouldn't. No wonder he'd won Julia over. "I ... um ... need to get the eggs for Aunt Charlotte." She finished lamely, holding up the basket as evidence before scurrying around the corner to the hen coop.

His soft laughter was soon lost in splashing.

Get a hold on yourself, Eliza. So he's friendly. You needn't act desperate. She took a calming breath and resolved to be cordial, but nothing more.

ꕥ

After an early breakfast, Jake saddled up the team and left by the north road.

Eliza helped Aunt Charlotte clear the dishes then went up to air her linens. From the gable window, she could just see the horses as they disappeared around a bend of Moreno Creek, Jake riding one and leading the other two. She lingered for a guilty moment before turning her energy to better purpose, plumping the down pillows with more vigor than necessary.

She rummaged in her trunk and found a bandana to tie back her hair then spent the next hour wiping down the store's shelves while they were empty. After that she helped Aunt Charlotte carry down the last of the provisions from the storage loft. With some careful arranging, they managed to make the shelves look as full as possible before they opened the door for the day's business.

Aunt Charlotte gave Eliza a quick introduction to the ledgers and accounting procedures. When the first customer arrived, Eliza excused herself to take charge of the sourdough in the kitchen, chatting with Uncle Rufus as she kneaded the sponge.

"Did Jake decide against taking your wagon after all?"

"Oh, he'll take it to Cimarron but not to Bitter Creek. That trail into the Red River valley ain't what you'd call a road. You'd be hard put to git a wagon through in summer, and the pass through the road canyon will still be full of snow this time of year."

With the back of a flour-covered hand, Eliza swiped at a wisp of hair that slipped out of the bandana. "Are these mountains so high as that? I wouldn't be surprised if you could see all the way to California from the other side."

Uncle Rufus chuckled. "Nowhere near. The Rocky Mountains are like a cat with two tails. This here's the eastern range—the Sangre de Cristos. Ain't nothin' the other side of that ridge but another valley, and the other side of that is desert with Taos to the south and Colorado on up north of us."

Eliza stretched her thoughts beyond the mountains and deserts, trying to reach with her imagination as far as the great ocean that lay beyond the western territory. She could not encompass it and felt small and insignificant for the attempt, like the plodding mules that brought her this far in her journey. An obscure verse echoed in memory—part and parcel for preachers' progeny. *'Lord, my heart is not haughty, nor mine eyes lofty; neither should I exercise myself in great matters, or in things too high for me.'* When she got right down to it, she held control over very little in life. Why did she wear herself out trying? With wry irony, another question came on the heels of the first. Why struggle so to decide whether to place complete trust in God for all things? What choice was there? Better to turn her attention to the things she could actually do something about. It was little enough in the grand scheme of things.

A list of mundane tasks filled her morning—new only because she performed them in a fresh context. The satisfaction she derived in completing each one took her by surprise. Busyness kept idle thoughts at bay—the ones her mind reenacted in a vain attempt to discover some happier ending to her story. And useful work returned some small sense of the control she craved.

After a rush of customers at lunch, they began to take inventory. When Aunt Charlotte waited on customers or tended to Uncle Rufus, she worked alone, but somehow she was not lonely.

When evening came they presented their list to Rufus. Eliza put a kettle of water on the stove to warm while they prioritized the items they needed most. "Better put flour near the top. I heard the scoop hit the bottom of the barrel when I measured for tomorrow's bread."

The kettle began to sing. Eliza poured the boiling water to warm a pail frigid from the well and headed upstairs, glad for the excuse to retire early. In the warm attic room she scrubbed off a layer of grime, luxuriating in the raw, tingling cleanness of the skin beneath. The warm rag soothed her sore muscles, and she congratulated herself on what they'd accomplished. Tomorrow held the comforting promise of predictability, and all the tomorrows after that would be the same.

She'd managed not to dwell on her losses for most of one day. If only she'd done as well avoiding thoughts of Jake.

Eliza fell into bed, exhausted, and thought of nothing at all. Sleep dragged her eyelids down before she even had time to pray.

ꕥ

On Tuesday Eliza began to help with customers. She recognized some of the faces she'd seen at church on Sunday along with many new ones.

Her aunt seemed to know everyone in town by name. They came for her fresh eggs and bread and seemed not to notice the meager stock on the shelves. Before noon Aunt Charlotte took another baking of sourdough out of the oven. The smell of homemade bread seemed to draw a crowd of hungry men around lunchtime—so many it took both women to wait on them all.

Eliza's head spun with the many newly-learned business skills she was using all at once.

Aunt Charlotte smiled encouragement as she passed. "You're doing fine, dear." She wrapped up orders, took money, and made change with ease that came from experience. A store full of customers was a blessing, not a problem. Her aunt probably timed her baking to create opportunities to be blessed with business.

Afternoon customers kept Eliza so busy she didn't hear the horses return an hour before closing time.

"Where do you want this?"

She gasped when Jake entered with an enormous bundle wrapped in canvas. Aunt Charlotte gratified him with a smile and directed him to the back stairs. The savory tang of spiced, smoked meat blended with the aroma of sourdough. Eliza's mouth watered.

"We'll eat soon," Aunt Charlotte said as Jake came in with a second load, but he declined the offer with a quick shake of his head.

"I started before first light and made good time this morning. If I hitch up and leave now, I can make it to the head of the canyon by nightfall." He took the stairs to the loft two at a time.

"Where will you sleep?" Aunt Charlotte hollered up after him.

Jake was down again in an instant. "By the toll house," he said.

Aunt Charlotte looked anxious. Rufus' robbery was fresh on everyone's mind.

Jake squeezed her shoulder. "Don't worry. I'll be safe enough."

He helped himself to a box of rifle shells, and the door slammed behind him.

Seizing a sudden inspiration, Eliza climbed to the storage room, untied the canvas wrapping, and tore off a handful of smoked venison. She was three steps down when she remembered her letter to Papa and turned again to retrieve it from her room. Downstairs again, she cut two hunks of sourdough from a loaf in the back room and arranged the meat between them. By the time Jake deposited the last load in the loft, she had the hasty meal snugly wrapped in brown paper.

"God speed," she said, handing him the package along with her letter home.

"I covet your prayers," he replied, and with a tip of his hat he was off.

Business was brisk again on Wednesday. With each gratifying sale, Eliza could not help noticing that the shelves were that much emptier. Jake's trip was dangerous but essential, and she was grateful that he would soon return with more supplies. Beyond that she was grateful that he cared enough to take the risk.

Each night, feeling exhausted but useful, Eliza drank in the view of the ridge as she raised the gable window to let in the cool night air. She smiled as the irony sunk in. Maybe their help had come from beyond those mountains.

ꕥ

On Thursday morning, Eliza came downstairs and reached for the egg basket that hung beside the door to the barnyard. Her daily routine was becoming comfortably familiar. Back in Waco she found fulfillment in her ministry role in Papa's church, but the tangible results of her labors at the end of a day in Uncle Rufus' store were new and satisfying. Her heart lifted as her hand raised the latch.

"Eliza, don't gather today from the last two nests."

She wondered at Aunt Charlotte's instruction, but did not question it. Each nest had one egg this morning, still warm from the hens' setting. Eliza gave them a quick wipe in her apron pocket before depositing them carefully in the basket. As always she took a moment to glance at the ridge, but today she looked the other direction as well and said a prayer for Jake's safe return.

"I'm starting a brood of chicks for Zeke and Millie," Aunt

Charlotte explained as Eliza set the egg basket on the kitchen table. "That'll make a nice wedding present, don't you think?"

Eliza agreed and was surprised at the tears that sprang to her eyes. This was how a Christian community was supposed to be—everyone helping everyone else, even without being asked. Folks were like that back home during the war. Somehow, the harder times got, the more people reached out to one another.

Until Papa stood up with the officer from the Freedmen's Bureau.

Until they were branded as Yankee sympathizers.

After that, most folks continued to smile politely and make small talk, but there was only coldness behind it. It was as if their hearts had turned to stone, their smiles fixed in place like those of unfeeling statues. Their words were like pebbles thrown at Papa and Eliza. Belonging was extended only to those who were the same; Papa and Eliza were different now. Papa was still head of the church, but they were no longer a part of it.

Eliza had grown accustomed to separateness. She didn't realize how much she'd missed being included in a community until now. Somehow that realization colored her attitude as she waited on people throughout the day. Each new person who came through their door was no longer simply Uncle Rufus' customer or Aunt Charlotte's friend. They were Eliza's new friends. She was a part of a community again, and it felt wonderful.

The day passed quickly. Before it seemed possible, Jake returned from Cimarron. Through the shop's open door, Eliza saw the horses pull the loaded wagon past the store and into the wagon barn. Standing behind the sales counter with her back to the side door, Eliza could hear him unhitching and putting the horses into their stalls. When he came through the door, he was smiling broadly. They'd have to wait until the close of business to see what he'd been able to trade for, but Eliza could tell he was pleased with his bargaining.

Aunt Charlotte wrote up the last sale of the day and followed the customer to the front of the store. "Have a pleasant evening," she called. Then she hung a sign on the door and closed it behind them. She looked like a kid at Christmas when she turned back to Jake and Eliza, rubbing her hands in expectation. "Now then! Let's see what you've brought us!"

"Aren't we going to eat first?" Jake teased. "I've worked up a powerful hunger."

"You didn't pull that wagon—the horses did, and they're eating now." Aunt Charlotte returned his jest. "If you want to eat, you'd better start unloading."

Jake threw his head back and laughed.

"Don't leave me out of the fun in there." Uncle Rufus hollered from the back room, and Eliza ran to tie back the curtain that separated the living quarters from the shop. Uncle Rufus sat bolt upright so he could see everything they brought in.

Eliza followed Jake into the barn to help carry in the boxes and bundles. Jake jumped easily into the wagon bed and gently handed down each item, saving the bulkier crates for himself. There were candles and coal oil, canned goods, yard goods, and work gloves. They tipped each box so Uncle Rufus could see the contents before depositing their treasures on the counter for Aunt Charlotte to unpack and record in her ledger.

At the last, Eliza began to place goods on the shelves while Jake made a half dozen trips to the barn, returning each time laboring with a large wooden barrel. Aunt Charlotte pointed out a spot beside the counter, and Eliza helped him roll the barrels into position against the wall. There were two barrels of wheat flour and two of dried beans. The fifth barrel contained corn meal and the sixth, salt crackers. On his last trip he brought in a somewhat smaller barrel.

Aunt Charlotte raised a quizzical brow, and when Jake said, "Pickles!" she clapped her hands in glee.

"Mailed your letter, too," Jake said, turning to Eliza.

She had forgotten about the letter, but she was glad that he had not.

"You got all this in trade for a few furs?" With a sweep of her hand Aunt Charlotte indicated the full shelves as she eyed Jake skeptically.

"More than a few, I guess. I had the rest of the smoked meat to trade, too." He shrugged off the implied allegation with a humble grin. "I'm a decent shot." When Charlotte looked satisfied with the answer, he added, "Now can I eat?"

With high spirits they drew the curtain on a store that was definitely back in operation.

While Eliza and Aunt Charlotte made a stew from soaked jerky, potatoes, and onions, Jake brought the ledger so that Uncle Rufus could review the stock figures. Eliza's heart warmed as she watched the two men work—not family, not business partners, but very much a team.

When the meal was ready, Jake helped them pull the table closer to the bedside so that Uncle Rufus could more easily be a part of the conversation.

"I don't know what we'd a' done without you." Uncle Rufus had said the same thing so many times she'd lost count, but each time he sounded more sincere than the last.

Jake ducked his head, deflecting the praise. "'Each according to his gift.' But I did have time to do a bit of thinking along the way." He paused to savor a bite. "There's still a good deal of snow up in the higher elevations—enough that I probably wouldn't be able to work my claim until next month anyway. And you're going to be holed up a bit with your legs for that time." He paused again, this time to study the faces around the table and gauge the reception of the idea he was warming up to. "I'm offering to stay for the month. I can sleep in the barn and tend to the horses so Charlotte won't have to. I can tote and carry around the shop, too."

Jake sat back in his chair, waiting as the others considered his offer.

If the decision were Eliza's to make, there would be no question. But of course she couldn't say that—shouldn't say that. She smiled a demure smile and waited, biting her cheek to prevent herself from shouting, "Yes!"

Aunt Charlotte and Uncle Rufus looked at each other the way folks long-married do—talking with their eyes. At last Uncle Rufus spoke for them all. "We'd like that, Jake."

Once again the warmth of belonging soaked into the cold loneliness that had filled Eliza's heart. This was a family—albeit an unusual one—and she was a part. It felt mighty good.

ꕥ

Friday passed quietly. Eliza had time during the morning to slip up to the loft with the hand scales and make up one-pound parcels of the dried meat. She marked the brown paper wrappers to indicate squirrel, rabbit, venison, and bear, and Aunt Charlotte priced them accordingly.

That afternoon, just after the lunchtime customers left, Eliza came down the stairs to see four buffalo soldiers entering the store.

Their horses were loosely tethered to the porch rail, and the men looked nervously around them, making sure the store was empty. Eliza wondered if they were afraid they might need to make a hasty retreat.

"Come on in." Jake welcomed them.

The men straightened and approached the counter with more confidence.

"Y'all got any of that bread left? We could smell it from the road east of town and folla'd our noses to this store here." The spokesman for the group was lean and fit. His skin was the color of strong coffee, and his eyes had a keen, intelligent gleam. His military cap rested atop nappy black curls, from which the Indians derived the nickname for these special troops.

"You're in luck. I have one loaf left," Aunt Charlotte said. "It'd make a nice lunch for the trail, with some left over for your fire tonight."

"Yes, ma'am. That'd be nice. We'll take it and go, ma'am."

"Shall I wrap it up for you?" Eliza saw no reason to give any different level of service than she would offer any other paying customer. When the man nodded, she added, "Would you like some smoked meat to go with it?" She quoted the prices for the various types.

The soldiers conferred and dug in their pockets for a bit before the spokesman replied. "Yes, ma'am. Thank you, ma'am. We'll take some of that rabbit."

The youngest of the soldiers didn't look like he could be more than eighteen years old. He watched as Eliza sliced the bread and wrapped the meat, and once she smiled when she saw out of the corner of her eye that he licked his lips.

She remembered how the fresh air and sunshine whetted her appetite when she was on the trail west.

They paid for their food, thanked Aunt Charlotte again, and left the store, stopping only long enough to tuck their meal into one of the saddlebags.

Jake followed the men as far as the door.

Eliza had the distinct impression that he was watching to see them safely on their way.

They rode along the outskirts of town and headed north up the road toward the ridge.

"Wonder where they're headed?" Eliza remembered seeing

buffalo soldiers among many others while she was at Fort Union, but she had been there too short a time to be familiar with their mission.

"No telling, but it's a shame they couldn't even stop long enough to eat," Aunt Charlotte said. Many of their lunch customers sat on the porch to enjoy their meal.

The bell that hung on the door tinkled as Jake leaned against it. "Might be in a hurry to be on their way, or they might not trust the kind of reception they'd have if they stayed," he said.

"I thought I'd left that kind of hate behind when I came here," Eliza said, shaking her head. "Once a man's free, who can fault him for doing any honest work he can to better himself?"

"Plenty do." Jake shielded his eyes as the sound of their hoof beats faded into the distance. "You know, for some, the war's not really over."

Eliza knew that better than he could ever imagine, but she made no response. Turning, she dusted a jar she'd already dusted and set it back on the shelf. She wasn't in the mood to pursue the topic. She'd had her fill of the talk of hate and war. Maybe, just maybe, hard work could help her forget that, too.

ꕥ

Eliza's first Saturday in the mercantile was busier than all the other days combined. The store was so crowded there was hardly room to turn around. As the weather warmed, more men were preparing to return to their claims, and they all needed provisions. Aunt Charlotte filled orders with efficiency, Eliza totaled the sales and tied up the bundles, and Jake carried the items out to waiting carts and saddlebags. Eliza lost count of how many pounds of smoked meat they sold along with the shovels, buckets and gold pans, but the profits were considerable. Men suffering from gold fever took time for little else, and they didn't mind spending now what they felt sure of earning later. Uncle Rufus was less optimistic—or at least more practical. Other stores might offer unlimited credit, but he and Aunt Charlotte enforced a strict "cash only" policy.

Millie dropped by to take a look at the yard goods and sewing notions. "I been stitchin' all week in my room," she said.

Poor dear. She'd likely been lonely, being new in town and with Zeke out on his ranch. She'd have a heap of talking to catch up on by now. Eliza had learned to appreciate Millie's talkative nature, and she could sympathize with the girl's yearning for friendly conversation, but she was still very busy this morning. She gave a quick nod to indicate that she was listening as she logged another sale.

Millie followed her as she fronted some canned goods on their shelf, still chattering amiably. "Mama sent a stack of fabric with me—cotton for sheets and dishtowels and the like. I've been hemming it up and adding some trim work while I wait. Got nothin' better to do, but May will be here soon enough." She blushed with pleasure at the mention of her upcoming marriage. "Y'all got any colored thread?" She switched topics seamlessly. "I'm flat outta red. Sure thought I'd brought plenty. I packed everything else..."

That explained the three large trunks. Eliza experienced a twinge of shame as she led Millie to the case of embroidery floss. The girl had likely brought her entire trousseau with her as well as all her wedding gifts.

"...'ceptin' my little cow." Millie giggled.

Eliza paused long enough to raise one eyebrow.

"Daddy gave Zeke money for a shorthorn when he came out with all his ol' range cows last spring. Said we'd be needing milk for a family eventually, and longhorns ain't much for milk," she explained, blushing again.

Millie decided on a packet of red thread and one of blue.

Aunt Charlotte totaled her purchases. "Here's your change, dear, but don't you leave without promising me that you and Zeke will come for Sunday dinner."

"We'll do just that," Millie promised, beaming at the prospect of an outing.

She hadn't been gone an hour when Zeke rode in. Eliza never thought to see such a sober expression on the sanguine cowboy's face. "I need Jake," he said without preamble.

The two men conversed on the front porch in hushed tones then Jake disappeared into the barn. Moments later he led his horse out to the hitching post. His rifle was strapped to the saddle.

He came back through the store and grabbed a box of shells off the shelf behind the counter before poking his head through the dividing curtain to apprise Uncle Rufus of the situation. "Gotta go kill a cat."

Eliza's eyes widened when she heard his terse tone.

"Mountain lion got after Zeke's cattle this morning." He turned to face Eliza. "It shouldn't take more than a day to track it, since the trail's fresh. Can you and Charlotte handle things until I get back?"

"I reckon."

Her answer seemed to amuse him. "Yes, I 'reckon' you can, too." He turned to go.

"Jake..." When he faced her again, she tried to keep the worry from her voice as she asked, "just how good a shot are you, exactly?" If a mountain lion was anything like the cougars back home, they hunted silently and could spring suddenly. A man might not have time to get off more than one shot. "Are you very good? Truly?"

He spared her a grin as he adjusted his hat. "I reckon." Then he was gone.

Chapter 7

When Zeke and Jake returned at sundown, Jake had the limp body of a huge cat slung across the horn of his saddle. Zeke was pulling his wagon.

Odd, Eliza thought.

The horses seemed skittish as they turned the rig in the street and backed it up to Uncle Rufus' barn. Horses didn't like the smell of cat or of blood. The light was failing as the men unloaded whatever was in Zeke's rig.

Eliza hurried to light a lantern and left by the side door to meet them. The barn door squeaked on its hinges as she opened it.

"Don't come in here." Jake's voice was strong and protective. "It's bad."

As if in answer to his words, a pitiful bawl came from the stall nearest the door.

"I've tended wounds before," Eliza protested. "I don't faint at the sight of blood." She was through the door before anyone could stop her, though she wondered why they brought a wounded cow here instead of butchering it on the range.

Jake had moved both horses into one large stall and secured the wounded animal in the smaller pen.

Eliza immediately recognized that this was no longhorn. This was a milk cow, close to calving. The poor creature lay on her side on a mound of fresh hay, panting, her eyes wide and white-rimmed with pain and fright. One eye rolled to watch Eliza as she approached slowly and stroked the heifer's soft muzzle before laying a hand on her bulging side. The tracks of the lion's claws were clearly visible on the animal's flank, stirring Eliza's compassion for the helpless beast, but beneath her hand the stirrings of life moved her still more.

"I ought to have shot her and put her out of her misery," Zeke said, "but I just can't bring myself to do it."

"This is Millie's heifer?" Eliza already knew the answer.

Zeke nodded. His expression was doleful. "I had to go all the way to Mora to find a shorthorn in this country. It pains me to see her hurting like that, but I hate to lose her." He chewed his lip, uncomfortable with either option. "She'd be an easy mark on the open range, crippled an' all, but if she can't stand up, she'll die, anyways."

Eliza realized Jake's interest in the matter when he put in, "Lord knows we need milk cows out here." Was he thinking of his and Julia's son?

"Zeke, sell me this cow." It was a statement rather than a request. Zeke blinked at Eliza in confusion, and Jake was squinting at her skeptically, but neither offered any arguments, so she talked faster. "Let me take care of her. I can dress these wounds to ease the pain and keep the chance of infection down." Eliza rushed on, desperate to convince them. "There's nothing wrong with that calf. It deserves a chance to be born. Its mama may not be strong enough to make it on the open range, but she'll do fine around here. She'll give milk for the store, and we can have butter, too, once she gets her baby weaned. And you can have the calf to give Millie." She caught the gleam of admiration in Jake's eyes and knew her idea was workable. His smile encouraged her. "I've seen all the dying I can stomach for a good while."

Zeke nodded slowly as the possibility sunk in. "It's worth a try."

"How much do you want for her?"

The cowpoke reckoned in his head for a minute before naming a reasonable price.

She could do this. This would give her an opportunity to return a service to those who had done so much for her. Eliza dashed up the stairs to her loft and returned, breathless, with her coin purse. It contained all that was left of the money she'd brought with her, but she had no other need for it now that the Lord had seen her safely to a new home.

Jake and Zeke were in the kitchen, explaining the plan to Aunt

Charlotte and Uncle Rufus, who seemed amused at Eliza's grit.

She dumped the contents of the pouch onto the table and counted out the amount, then scooped it up and dropped it into Zeke's outstretched palm.

He stared at it, counting, then looked again at Eliza, still amazed.

"So do we have a deal, or not?" Eliza stuck out her hand.

Zeke grinned and spat into his palm, then apparently remembered that he was dealing with a lady and wiped his hand on his pants leg before accepting her grasp. "Deal."

ꟊ

Jake leaned over Eliza's shoulder as they observed the wounds closely by lamplight. The lower two cuts were mostly welts, open only at the base where the great claws caught, but the other two were deeper. The flesh of the heifer's flank gaped to reveal the muscle beneath.

Eliza covered the raw wounds with salve. She couldn't bandage them, located as they were, but the oily ointment would keep dirt out. At least the weather was still too cold for flies. When the heifer was calm, Eliza coaxed her to accept a handful of hay then looked around for a saddle blanket. If she was in shock, it would be good to keep her warm through the night.

Jake helped Eliza drape the heifer with the blanket. "Zeke's gone to visit Millie, but he'll be back to bunk in the loft with me tonight. We'll check on her again for you."

Eliza rose. "I'm glad you shot that ol' cougar." She had seen the great cat laid near the entrance, as far as possible from the livestock.

"Yup, and her litter, too, but that means there's a male still out there somewhere."

Eliza pressed her lips together, sorry about the cubs.

Jake must have seen the wave of regret reflected in her face. "I took no pleasure in it, Eliza, but it's calving season. Once that lion decided Zeke's ranch lay in her territory, she would have killed again to feed her young."

"I know," Eliza said. "Sometime's killing's necessary. A lion's a predator."

A strange look came over Jake's face as he held the door for her. "Most creatures kill for cause. Man's the only animal that hunts for sport or pleasure ... or for meanness."

ജ്ജ

When Eliza stepped out the side door to gather eggs on Sunday morning, her heart jumped into her throat, and she sent the basket flying. A cougar pelt with the head still attached stretched across the back wall of the barn, the skin of its forefeet extended as if springing.

Jake came around the corner from the direction of the well, a bucket swinging from one hand. When he saw Eliza leaning against the wall of the mercantile with her hand to her throat, he made a vain attempt to assume a sympathetic expression before he burst out laughing.

She glared at him. "It's not funny, Jacob Craig! That thing scared me out of a year's growth!"

"Zeke and I skinned it last night." He retrieved her basket and returned it with an apologetic grin. "Cougar steak is a delicacy in these parts. We can eat part today and sell the rest to the hotels in town."

It was several moments before Eliza's knees ceased quaking and her pulse slowed enough that she felt up to resuming her task. Even then her hands shook so that she had to take extra care not to drop the fragile eggs. Setting the basket on the stoop, she eyed the cougar skin warily as she nudged the barn door open.

Daylight filtered through louvered vents high up on the barn wall, and dust motes danced in the slats of sunlight.

The heifer lifted her head when Eliza entered. She'd made it through the night and showed no signs of an early labor. That was good.

Eliza lifted the saddle blanket and checked the wounds. The blood was dry, and there was no sign of infection, but the gaping flesh was still ghastly. It turned her stomach. As she left the wagon barn for the kitchen, she glanced again at the cat skin.

"Serves you right," she said, though the lion was long past hearing.

ജ്ജ

There was no church service at all that day. The circuit rider came from beyond Cimarron. It was too far to ride every week. Eliza brought Uncle Rufus his fiddle again, and he played hymns as she helped Aunt Charlotte with the morning's work. They kneaded sourdough and set the day's loaves to rise, then pared apples for a pie.

Zeke fetched Millie toward noon. They went straight to the barn. When they came in with Jake a few minutes later, Millie's eyes brimmed with tears, but she bit her lip and put up a brave front.

"I reckon she'll be all right, don't you?"

Aunt Charlotte and Eliza both assured her that the heifer's chances seemed better this morning.

"I can't thank you enough for taking care of her. I'll come and help you with her every day."

Zeke shifted uncomfortably. "You ain't mad that I sold her, are you, Millie? I ain't got a barn built yet—just an enclosure. Fence won't keep a lion out."

Millie obviously saw the sense in what he said. "Shorthorns don't have much means of defense, I don't guess. Maybe we can get a shed up by the time her calf's weaned, you think?"

Aunt Charlotte laid out a spread while Jake helped Uncle Rufus to the table. A week after the robbery his bruises were healing well. He felt good enough to complain about his confinement—"Downright crotchety," Aunt Charlotte said—and it took all three of them to insist that he stay put.

Thinking of the dramatic blessings she had seen in the short time since her arrival, Eliza added a hearty "amen" to Uncle Rufus' prayer of thanks.

Aunt Charlotte forked thick slabs of steak onto each tin plate. "Seems to me we're coming out on the good end of this deal, Zeke. We'll have milk and cougar meat to sell, and all we have to do is mind a little heifer. How about if we barter you for some of the supplies you'll be needing?"

"That'd be mighty nice, ma'am" Zeke said, "but Jake shot the cat." He paused to cut a mouthful of lion steak. "I was glad, too, 'cause it was gettin' dark, and we was way out on the Palo Flechado Pass along the back road to Taos." He shivered. "That's a spooky place, that is."

Somehow Eliza was not surprised that Zeke was superstitious, but Jake, too, seemed to suppress a shudder. She looked at him quizzically.

"Ran into an innkeeper up there. Charles Kennedy."

"Got himself an Indian wife and a half-breed son," Zeke interjected, "but I'm scareder of him than of them."

"He offered us to stay overnight." Jake scowled and shook his head. "That man makes my skin crawl. I can't say why, but I'd rather take my chances with the wild critters than spend the night in his cabin."

"Me, too!" Zeke said as he stabbed another slab of meat with his knife.

Aunt Charlotte turned the conversation to a more pleasant topic. "Millie, you'll have to tell us if you need any help before the wedding, since your folks can't be with you." When Millie nodded thanks she added, "How'd you meet ol' Zeke here, anyway? Are y'all from the same hometown?"

Millie stole a glance at Zeke and blushed as she always did when she looked at him. "No, ma'am. Not exactly."

"Millie's from Lou'siana; I'm from around Jefferson," Zeke supplied, though Eliza thought that bit of information made the explanation less clear than before.

Millie apparently shared her opinion and pursed her lips in exasperation before offering a more enlightening answer. "My daddy raised cotton outside of Shreveport. Growing up I had everything a little girl could want—pretty dresses and even a pony. Mama had the most wonderful garden." Her eyes glowed for a moment as she reminisced, but soon they grew dark. "The war ruined him. Northern mills wouldn't buy Southern cotton. The Confederate Army needed cloth, but not raw cotton, so there was no market at home. No one had money to buy it, anyway. He tried shipping his bales to England through Jamaica, but the harbors were all blockaded. Those bales sat on the docks in New Orleans until the rains came and rotted them. Then the Yankees came through and burned us out, and that ended any hope of startin' over."

Jake shifted in his chair.

Eliza took note and saw that Aunt Charlotte did, too, but Millie seemed too engrossed in her story to notice.

"Fortunately, Mama had a brother who raised cotton in east Texas. We packed what we could and sold the rest to buy passage on a steamboat to Jefferson. My Uncle Henry made a place for us and said he was grateful for the help, the slaves bein' free and all, but I think Daddy knew he was croppin' for shares. When I think how hard he worked to save enough for my passage out here and that silly cow out there..." Tears filled her eyes, and one escaped down a rounded cheek to trickle toward her quivering chin.

Zeke quietly pressed his handkerchief into her palm.

Eliza once again felt ashamed of her first impression of the girl. *She's been through as much as I have, Lord, and she's not lived nearly as many years.*

Millie drew in a fortifying breath and squared her chin. "Still and all, there's no great loss without some gain. If I hadn't come to Texas, I'd 'a' never met my Zeke." She gazed at him again with dewy eyes, but this time Eliza didn't think she was silly.

"You were lucky!" Zeke winked at her. "You nearly missed me!" He took up the tale. "I was too young to join up for the war, which was a relief to my ma, but I was itchin' to be a man first chance I got, I guess."

Eliza struggled to stifle her surprise. How old was he? Toward the end, the South ran short of able-bodied men and signed up anyone willing above the age of sixteen, and some younger if they could lie convincingly. Any way she figured it, he could be no more than twenty now. He looked older, though. Capable. Like he'd done a lot of living in those few years. Unconsciously, her hand reached to touch her own face.

"When this new territory opened up, I signed on with a cattleman who was relocating his operation to Cimarron. Anyone who was willing to help him drive his cattle out here, he'd give 'em a start on a herd of their own, and land was practically free for the taking."

The mention of Cimarron nudged Eliza's memory. "Oh! I've been meaning to ask you. That man we met in the stage office at Cimarron—Clay Allison—he said he herded cattle on the Brazos. Did you ever meet up with him before?"

Zeke's left eye squinted briefly into a scowl, but he answered mildly. "I reckon there was lots of fellers did what I done."

Boy's got a way of explaining things that makes them more confusing than ever. Maybe he was just trying to place the face and coming up blank, but Eliza was more inclined to believe that he would rather avoid the subject for some reason.

Zeke had already abandoned that topic in favor of one more pleasant. "So I waited just long enough for Millie to turn seventeen, and I asked her pa could I marry her, and he said yes, if she'd have me, and how could she refuse such an offer as this?" He plucked out his suspenders and waggled a rakish eyebrow before winking at the girl beside him.

Millie lashed him playfully with the now-soggy handkerchief

before tucking it back into his pocket for him, and he threw an arm across her shoulders, hugging her to his side.

Eliza crossed her arms and hugged herself. The familiar hollow feeling of loneliness even in a crowd engulfed her. *Lord, I thought this was behind me. I don't want to be bitter and jealous.* She was happy for them—really, she was—but so tired of being alone. She forced a smile and quickly excused herself to serve the pie and coffee.

"There is one thing you could do for me," Millie said as Eliza passed her plate. "I'd like you to be my maid of honor."

The request caught Eliza entirely off her guard, and the thin veneer of composure she had managed to reconstruct threatened to crumble once more. She did not trust herself to speak. Fortunately, the tears that threatened to expose her could also be explained away by the honor and gesture of friendship.

"And I'd like you to stand as best man." Zeke addressed Jake.

Eliza might not have recognized the shock and alarm that registered on his face had it not so exactly mirrored her own. For an uncomfortable moment their eyes met, and she knew that he knew it as well. An entire conversation transpired in that brief moment when neither looked away until finally Jake managed a smile—a warm, genuine, and sincere smile.

"We'd be honored, I'm sure."

ഇ൭ൽ

Eliza paused as she rolled out biscuits that night for supper. "I forgot to ask Zeke if she's got a name—the heifer, that is."

Jake merely smiled as he tallied the week's sales figures, but Uncle Rufus laughed out loud. "Child, Zeke don't name his cattle. You're from Texas. You oughta know that."

Eliza blushed but tossed her head to hide her embarrassment. "Yes, but it was Millie's cow. I'll bet she names hers." She thought for a moment. "I think I'll call her April. How would that be?"

"It's a fine name for a cow." Jake struggled to keep a straight face. "You think she'll like it? You might ought to ask her before you make it stick."

"Ask who? Millie?"

"No. That cow."

Eliza huffed at him in indignation. "I'll make this stick!" She tossed a lump of biscuit dough at the back of her tormenter's head.

He ducked, and it hit the wall with a soft splat.

"Now, now. You two behave. 'Waste not, want not. Every bit's a bite.'" Aunt Charlotte scolded and pursed her lips in disapproval, but a smile tugged at their corners.

Jake gave Eliza one last teasing smirk before returning to his books, and she returned a saucy glare before a fit of giggles ruined its effect.

"That sounds mighty fine, child."

Eliza was pleased that at least Uncle Rufus took her side. "You like the name, then?"

"Not the name. The laughter. I haven't heard you laugh since you arrived. It's an improvement."

Chapter 8

Thursday, Friday, Saturday, Sunday. Eliza counted off the days left until the wedding as she came downstairs. Stifling a yawn she pushed back the curtains, and then stopped short. Jake sat at the table, coddling a cup of coffee.

"Been waiting for you." His eyes twinkled. "Wanna help bring some good into the world?"

Suddenly Eliza was wide awake. "The calf! Is April having the calf?"

"I do believe we'll have an addition to the barn sometime this morning."

He chuckled as Eliza sprang to life, bolting to snatch a shawl from the peg above her egg basket. Her hand was on the latch before she noticed that the basket was already full. She threw him a questioning glance. "I collected them for you this morning. Figured you'd want to head right out, but I didn't think you'd leave me standing here alone."

"And I didn't reckon you'd be so slow. Get a move on!"

Jake laughed out loud as he opened the door for her.

Six quick steps later Eliza passed beneath Jake's arm and inhaled the warm, animal smell of the barn. The same warm scent clung to his jacket. Her eyelids drifted shut as she savored it. He was too close for comfort—or for propriety, anyway.

"Letting your eyes get used to the light?"

She snapped them open again. "Mmm." Let him think it was an

affirmation. She could not tell him what she was thinking.

Jake had already cleaned the box stall and spread a thick carpet of clean hay. The heifer stood against the rails. Favoring her bad leg, no doubt. She rocked back and forth, gently scratching her side against the rough wooden slats. Eliza leaned over the rail that barred the opening and reached out to stroke the heifer's muzzle.

"What do we do now?"

"We wait. She doesn't really need our help." Jake crossed his arms on top of the gatepost beside her and rested his chin on them.

His proximity was unnerving. Eliza needed an excuse to move. "Can I go in with her?"

"She might let you for just a minute."

Jake lifted the gate rails and held them for her. As she passed him she smelled again the fragrance of hay and beasts and coffee—the fragrance of a man. It made her head spin, and her thoughts, too. Eliza forced herself to think of Julia and was alarmed to realize that she didn't want to. *Traitor.*

She crossed to the far side of the stall to dip up a handful of sweet grain. Returning, she offered it to April, but the heifer was distracted. She tried to pull away and pace. She'd bust those wounds wide open if they didn't keep her calm. Eliza dropped the grain and went back to stroking her muzzle, murmuring soothing words as much for her own benefit as for April's.

She sensed Jake as he approached to check the progress of labor. Just then, the skin on the heifer's side twitched, and she arched her back awkwardly.

"See that? Shouldn't be too long." Jake walked to the gate, picked up the rail, and jerked his head in indication. "We should probably give her some room now."

Eliza rose, crossing her arms to pull her shawl close, and hastened to walk past him once more, this time trying not to inhale. She found a place to lean against the barn wall, far away from the laboring cow. When she looked up, Jake was eyeing her. She was acting oddly. She knew it. "Just cold. Didn't want to make her nervous by standing too close."

"Mmm." He came and leaned against the wall beside her.

There was no getting away from him—from the attraction. It wasn't his fault. Why couldn't she just stick to her resolve to see him as a friend?

"Want to talk about it?" His voice was low, his gaze soft with compassion.

She shook her head and looked down at her laced fingers. Jake was about the last person she could talk to about what was ailing her.

"I didn't realize until Sunday. Your reaction..." He pulled off his gloves and slapped them idly in one palm. "I had just assumed you were single."

"I am single." Ah! So, he didn't see through her completely.

"But when..." It was his turn to look awkward. "I'm sorry." He paused to search for words. "You seemed to feel just as I did. How could you know that hurt if you hadn't lost someone, too?"

She couldn't let him feel he'd blundered when he was trying so hard to be kind. "His name was Grayson, but we were never married." The sound of Grayson's name did for her what the memory of Julia had not. She sobered immediately, her intense attraction to Jake quelled. He nodded, leaving her free to go on or simply leave it there; but as his friend, she suddenly realized that she wanted him to know. "He was a chaplain. We planned to be married, but he died in the war."

"Must have come as quite a shock. Chaplains aren't usually in the line of fire. You could not have been prepared for that."

Eliza's eyes welled up with a mixture of memories, sweet and tragic. For a moment she could not speak. "He ... got hit by a sharpshooter's bullet ... pulling a wounded man from the field at Chickamauga."

Jake's brows drew close over his eyes.

"You fought?"

He nodded slowly. "It was a terrible war. I'm so sorry for your loss."

A tear traced a warm trail down Eliza's cheek. She was glad when April stirred with another contraction. Jake's gaze was too intimate, too tender. She could not bear it right now.

He glanced at the heifer only a moment. She wasn't in any trouble. Jake studied his hands, his lips pursed in thought—as if he were wondering how much it was safe to say. "In some ways, I think your loss was worse than mine."

Eliza was shocked. "How can you say that? You lost a wife and a son! Your loss was twice mine."

"Yes, but I had her. However briefly, I had her, and we were very happy. In some ways, it was harder to lose Earl than Julia. I never got to know him."

Jake held up empty arms, and Eliza's heart broke.

April hunched up again, straining longer this time. With a whoosh of breath, she lay down in the clean hay and struggled to find a comfortable position. As she rolled onto her side, a flood of water gushed forth and was quickly absorbed by the straw.

"Here we go!" Jake pulled away from the wall and went to lean against the wagon. "Come," he said, motioning with his hand. "You can see better from here, but she can't see you."

Eliza came to peek over the corner of Uncle Rufus' wagon and wasn't alarmed at all when Jake leaned against it to look over her shoulder.

"She'd probably rather do this herself, but I'm a little anxious on account of those cuts."

His breath was warm on her cheek, and a thrill coursed through her—something like the thrill of watching this new life enter a troubled world, but Eliza knew herself too well to attribute it entirely to that. She turned, eyes shining, to look up into his face. A slow smile spread across his features, forming creases at the weathered corners of his steel grey eyes, and it had the same effect it always did. She hugged her shawl to herself and turned her attention once again to the miracle unfolding in the box stall.

A tiny hoof, then two. A small brown muzzle. Then April became suddenly animated, heaving herself to a stand and dropping a little wet calf onto the hay. Eliza felt like clapping. Instead, she pressed her fingertips to her lips to keep herself quiet as the cow turned to lick her baby's face.

Jake beamed like a proud father. He walked to the stall and reached through the slats to grab a handful of straw, twisting it in his hands as he cocked his head to a better angle. "It's a heifer. That's good. Zeke and Millie will get their milk cow after all."

April licked her calf dry, and they watched as it struggled to a wobbly stand. April gave it a nudge, urging it to suck. It took a few moments of encouragement before the calf felt able to take her first steps, but soon she was eagerly butting the bag to get her first breakfast, her tail twitching.

"She's a natural mother," Jake said. "Would that it were half so easy for us, eh?"

Eliza couldn't blame him for drawing the connection to Julia's death. She'd had the same thought.

"Go on in and tell your aunt and uncle. I'll be in after I look after these two a bit."

Eliza nodded. Outside, the sky was as clear and blue as a robin's egg. She took a moment to breathe the fresh air and study the ridge before entering the kitchen.

Two sets of eyes watched her expectantly. "Well?" Aunt Charlotte finally prodded.

"It's a girl. A little red heifer with white spots. Jake will be in after a while."

Aunt Charlotte beamed with pleasure, and Uncle Rufus looked smug. "What'd you name this one?" he teased.

"May." She didn't even have to think about it, and her look challenged him to object.

Uncle Rufus raised one eyebrow. "But it's not—"

"Near enough. Besides, May always follows April," she said, throwing him a wink.

ᢒᢓ

Friday evenings were usually quiet. Most of the prospectors and cattlemen who came into town for the weekend spent their time in one of the saloons along the front streets or roamed around the prostitutes' shanties. If these men needed supplies, it was a secondary priority. They tended to that after they sobered up on Saturday. Family people stayed as far away as possible from the rowdies. By Friday evening, most of Uncle Rufus' regular customers were at home. Aunt Charlotte stepped into the back room to start supper, leaving Eliza alone to tend the store.

When the bell on the door tinkled late Friday afternoon, Eliza looked up quickly to see Clay Allison filling the doorway. She smiled. "Well, hello. I haven't seen you since Cimarron. Eliza Gentry ... from Waco ... remember? How can I help you?" Even though they were barely acquainted, she felt a certain bond to him through their shared connection to home.

Allison stepped through the doorway. Three other men followed close enough to tread on his coattails. Eliza stepped from behind the sales counter, but Allison made no move to introduce his companions. He smiled vaguely, but did not look at her. His eyes darted about the store. He seemed as anxious to distance himself from Eliza as he had in Cimarron, and she was at a loss to account for his obvious discomfort. Surely she had done nothing to offend him. Perhaps he was just shy around women. She couldn't account for that, either. Clay Allison was well-groomed and had a commanding presence. His friends would do well to follow his lead. As he walked haltingly down the aisle of shelves, Eliza realized for the first time that he had a club foot. Maybe he was just self-conscious. She didn't stare. "If you'll tell me what you need, perhaps I can help you find it," she offered, hoping to put him at ease.

"Tobacco, if you have it. Beans. Some cornmeal and jerky, and I need ammunition." He still would not look her in the eye.

"We don't have tobacco, but I can get the beans and cornmeal for you if you'll tell me how much you're wanting. Bullets and buckshot are over here." She led him to the shelves where ammunition was kept, and he stooped to study the caliber on the boxes.

The bell on the door sounded again, and Eliza straightened. It never rained but what it poured. This time it was the buffalo soldiers. "What can I do for you?"

"We come back for more of that jerky, ma'am, if you still have some."

Clay Allison snapped his head up and stared over the shelves as the soldiers casually approached the sales counter. He apparently had no qualms about making eye contact with these men. He was glaring at them, daring them to come further.

From where she stood, Eliza saw his hand drop to his gun, and her heart skipped a beat before it began to race.

The soldiers froze in their tracks. All eight men looked at Eliza, tension tangible between them. A sheen of sweat broke out on the youngest soldier's brow. His fingers inched toward the grip of his own revolver, but a warning glance from his superior stilled him.

"You want me to git this trash out of your store, ma'am?" Allison's voice was at once calm and threatening—as if he was anticipating a pleasant experience.

Dear Lord, protect us. With an effort, Eliza forced a calm she did not feel into her voice. "There's no need for that, Mr. Allison. These men just need supplies for their trip back to Fort Union." Attune to every detail, she felt the curtain move in the doorway behind her and heard the soft click of the door to the barn yard. Aunt Charlotte must have been listening. *Please, Lord, let Jake be close by.*

Allison did not seem to notice. His lip rolled into a sneer as he snorted in disgust. "I might'a known. 'Like father, like daughter.' Your old man had a soft spot for blacks and Yankees, too, now didn't he?" He drew his gun from the holster and used it to scratch his chin, as if trying to decide whom to shoot first.

Eliza could no longer hide her alarm.

Allison seemed amused. "Oh, yeah. I know who you are. Big girl like you's kinda hard to miss." His laughter was as cold as the grey steel of his revolver.

At least now Eliza understood how she had offended him. He must have been in the crowd the night of the riot. Was there no place she could escape from her past?

A boot scraped behind her, and she heard the click of a rifle hammer being thumbed back. She felt rather than saw Jake as he stepped around the curtain. "Clay Allison."

Eliza resisted the urge to turn, surprised that Jake recognized the man instantly.

"I believe you'll find what you need at another store."

"Well, speak of the devil, and up he pops! Blacks *and* Yankees! You seem to have found yourself a home at last, *Miss* Gentry." Still sneering, Allison touched his gun to the brim of his hat in mock salute before dropping it back into its holster. "I'll leave you to your chosen company." He strode from the store, and his companions ambled after him, spurs jangling.

Eliza heaved a sigh of relief and sagged against Jake for support.

The buffalo soldiers, who had remained as still as statues during the exchange, began to shuffle awkwardly. The youngest bent to put his hands on his knees, while their leader stammered an apology for causing trouble.

"Nonesense," Aunt Charlotte said as she stepped in from the stair hall. "You've done nothing wrong." She tore a sheet of butcher paper to line the scales and set a handful of jerky on it. "Now, if you don't mind, I'll help you with your order." Speaking over her shoulder, she said, "Jake, I believe Eliza could use some fresh air. Why don't you go with her?"

Jake nodded and used the business end of his rifle to hold the curtain back. With his free hand resting on her shoulder, he guided Eliza to the back porch.

She collapsed onto the log bench with her back to the barn and closed her eyes. As involuntary shaking set in, she hugged her arms tight to her chest and clamped her jaw to keep her teeth from chattering. Tears of frustration seeped from beneath her lashes. "I'm sorry," she said, swiping angrily at them. "This is the second time I've faced a gun at close range on account of ignorant prejudice."

"I gathered something of the sort." Eliza detected a note of admiration in Jake's voice as he leaned against the wall next to her. "You did well to keep your head in there. It could have been a whole lot worse." They sat in silence for several moments. "What Allison said about 'Blacks and Yankees'..."

"It's okay, Jake. I figured that out when you said you fought in the war. You don't have the right accent to have worn grey." A laugh of irony bridged the awkward silence. "Is that how you knew Allison? You called him by name as soon as you saw him."

"We've met before, and it wasn't any more pleasant the last time than it was in there."

Eliza's laugh came out as a snort, and she clapped one hand to her mouth.

Jake's laugh was genuine. "You can forgive me for that, then?"

Eliza gazed at his kind, honest face. "There were good people on both sides, Jake Craig. The war cost me dearly, but not all Yankees are cruel; I know that much. And not all Southerners were honorable. Clay Allison is an unfortunate example." His very name left a bitter taste in her mouth, but the sweet smile bestowed by the man beside her more than compensated.

ꙮ

"...nine yards of calico, and a pound of beans. Will that be all today, Mrs. Ewing?"

Eliza wrote out the sale while the lady in line behind Mrs. Ewing waved for her aunt's attention. "Charlotte, would you add a pound of cornmeal to my order? I forgot about the pounding." Aunt Charlotte began to fill a drawstring bag with meal. "That sack'll make nice quilt squares once it's empty, won't it?"

Customers had been pouring through the door all morning. In addition to the regular Saturday shoppers, everyone from ranch hands to church friends was buying an extra pound of this or that as wedding presents for Zeke and Millie.

Just before noon, the happy couple passed the store's front window. Mrs. Ewing congratulated them on her way out, and Zeke could barely restrain a grin of pride as he ducked around the corner into the barn.

Millie's ringlets bounced beneath the brim of her sunbonnet as she entered the store. "I've got my things all packed," she announced. "I'm so excited I can hardly stand it. Jake told Zeke he'd help him cart my trunks out to our ranch. If your aunt can spare you, I wondered if you'd like to help me pick some flowers for the church."

Eliza looked to her aunt.

"Run along quick, now. You mightn't get another chance." Aunt Charlotte urged her toward the door.

"If you're sure..." Eliza hesitated only a moment. "There's a heap of cooking still to be done."

"I'll close up right at five and start making pies. If you hurry, you may be back in time to help me. Sooner gone, sooner home." She all but pushed Eliza out of the store.

Millie bounced lightly, unable to contain her excitement. "'Our ranch!' Now doesn't that sound grand?"

"It does." Yearning for a home of her own was as sharp as hunger, but Eliza pushed the thought away.

Jake and Zeke already had the horses hitched to the wagon. Zeke swung Millie up into the wagon bed with ease. Eliza gathered her skirts and raised one foot to the hub of the wagon wheel.

"May I?" Jake's deep voice was inches from her ear.

She stopped short. Shocked, she nodded as if in a daze.

He placed his hands on her waist and lifted her effortlessly into the box. The warmth of his hands spread through her, lingering long after he took up the reins and drove the wagon out into the street.

Eliza made a fuss of tying her bonnet strings to hide the warmth in her cheeks. When at last she felt composed enough to look up, Millie's wink caused her to snap her head and stare with feigned interest at the passing storefronts. A soft giggle followed.

"You ladies ridin' all right back there?" Zeke twisted in his seat, his eyes barely visible over the pile of trunks.

"We're fine." Millie giggled again. "Just glad for the outing."

That seemed to satisfy him. Men could be so dense, but Eliza was glad of it. She had to put this silly infatuation out of her head, or she would ruin everything.

It would never do to repay Uncle Rufus and Aunt Charlotte's kindness to her by indulging an interest in their daughter's widower. Not while they were still in mourning. Jake had been kind to her as well—a true friend and a gentleman, but there was no reason to assume that he intended more. She would not disgrace herself by misinterpreting his thoughtfulness as any sort of ardor.

Elizabethtown ended rather abruptly after eight blocks. The horses pulled the wagon across a bridge then south along the road beside Moreno Creek. When the road curved east to Cimarron, Jake guided the buckboard over another rough bridge to continue south. They followed a wagon trail for a while before striking out over new grass. Eliza watched the dark streaks their wheels made roll from beneath her swinging feet—a path made clear in hindsight. The meadow grass spread toward the line of pines and aspen that grew on the hills to either side. The mountains rose behind the trees to their west and north and east. Soon, Elizabethtown was dwarfed against the backdrop of the mountain pass beyond. The town looked so large when she first saw it. Now it was hard to imagine that those thirty-five blocks had encompassed her life for two weeks. Her spirit soared like a bird suddenly released from its cage.

"Almost there." Jake pulled on the reins, and the wagon slowed to a halt.

"Millie, if you don't mind, I thought we'd leave you and Eliza here to find your flowers while Jake and I unload and check my livestock." Zeke looked suddenly bashful. "I don't want you to see the house yet. I got some surprises waiting."

At Millie's nod, he jumped from the buckboard and came around to lift her out of the wagon box.

Eliza's heart skipped a beat when Jake tied off the reins and came around to her side. He held up a hand to steady her as she stepped around Millie's trunks, then once again placed his hands beneath her ribs and set her gently on the ground. He lifted her easily—as if she weighed nothing at all.

She stared at her shoes. "Thank you."

"Of course."

She glanced up to see Jake touch the brim of his hat before climbing back onto the driver's seat.

Zeke gazed into Millie's shining eyes a moment longer before leaping up on the other side. "We'll be back quick," he shouted as Jake jostled the reins.

Eliza and Millie stared after them as they drove toward a log cabin set snugly into the prairie grass.

"Twice, eh?" Millie teased when the men were out of earshot. "I think Mr. Jacob Craig may be taking a fancy to you."

She could still feel his strong grasp and the touch of his hand, but

Eliza shook her head, feeling entirely miserable inside.

"Come now. Don't you like him?"

Eliza gulped, struggling mightily for composure. How could she explain her shameful attraction? She had not told Millie about Grayson and was not sure she wanted to share that chapter of her life. Hadn't she come here to start over? To make a life for herself? "I can't. Millie, he was married to my cousin. She died not eight months ago."

"I know all that. Zeke told me."

"Then you know it just isn't done. Aunt Charlotte still wears mourning colors. Jake's still grieving too, surely. He's not himself."

Millie cocked her head, squinting up to look directly into Eliza's eyes, reading what she saw in them.

Her scrutinizing gaze made Eliza want to hide.

At last, she scrunched up her face and set her hands on her hips. "Your cousin is dead, Eliza, and I'm truly sorry. But Jake is alive, and so are you."

"He was being kind, that's all." Her eyes threatened to betray her with tears. "It doesn't occur to many men to help me into a wagon or offer a chair, and it would be too easy to let that go to my head."

"Why?"

"Because I'm being stupid!" The traitorous tears spilled over at last.

"No. I mean why shouldn't a gentleman help you as readily as any other lady?"

Eliza glared down at her. "Because, if you hadn't noticed, I'm taller than most men." She nearly spat the words. Dainty and full of youth, how could Millie understand? Eliza was ashamed of the bitterness she revealed, but she could not conceal her sarcasm. "I guess they figure I'm big enough to carry my own loads. And I can, truly..." Behind her protective façade, Eliza felt small inside and less capable than she'd ever been. "...but I don't really want to have to. Jake honors me when he treats me like a lady. I will not make our friendship awkward by reading too much into that."

Millie studied her for a while without speaking then she let loose a torrent of words. "Eliza Gentry, you are a lady, and you deserve the respect and admiration of any man who calls himself a gentleman regardless of your physical stature. Jacob Craig is a gentleman to the core, and they're rare enough. Many men act the part, but I think few would set their own grief aside to show a friend such honor. It is not stupid to be impressed by thoughtfulness, but if you're not careful, that reserve of yours is going to convince him that he has overstepped his bounds—that you do not desire his courtesies. Now that would be awkward!"

Eliza was speechless. These were new thoughts.

Becoming her giddy self again, Millie nudged her elbow. "So tell me truly. Don't you like him?"

Eliza nodded solemnly a few times before she could bring herself to confess, "I do." Against her will, a timid smile confirmed her words.

Millie snatched off her sunbonnet and threw it into the air. "I knew it! 'Gather ye flowers while ye may!'" She tugged at Eliza's sleeve. "Now let's find some for my wedding."

Two hours later their bonnets were full of Pascua flower and tiny white chickweed blossoms. Though they were among the few flowers blooming, Millie was reluctant to gather any until Eliza suggested braiding them into her hair. They found shooting star at the forest's edge and were cutting blue flags near the creek when the wagon returned.

Zeke loaned them his handkerchief, and they dipped it in the cold water to wrap the stems before laying them carefully in the wagon bed.

They rode back up the valley laughing and making plans for the next day's events and pulled through the streets of Elizabethtown just as the shadows stretched to touch the buildings on the other side.

Chapter 9

Sunday dawned bright and clear. Eliza drank in the crisp morning air as she walked the four blocks to Millie's place. Like Uncle Rufus' store, Miss Anne's boarding house was deliberately located on one of the back streets of town, off the beaten path for any wild prospectors who came looking for weekend excitement of one sort or another. Miss Anne ran a respectable establishment. Eliza rapped softly at the door.

"Come in!" Anne's daughter, Rebecca, dusted the flour from her hands onto a crisp white apron. "Mama and Sarah have already started the roasts for the shivaree, and I was just about to roll out some biscuits."

Anne and her daughters had more or less adopted Millie into their family during her stay, eagerly volunteering to organize the festivities. Eliza waved to them through the kitchen door before heading upstairs to Millie's room. Sarah followed close behind with a kettle of boiling water for Millie's bath.

"I declare, I don't know if I'm nervous or just plain excited!" Millie was in such a flap that Eliza had to place a hand on her shoulders to hold her still before pouring a pitcher of rinse water over her hair. "I set a jar of spring water on the windowsill last night. Pour that on next."

Eliza hesitated when she touched the frigid container.

"No, really. It'll make it shine. Go ahead!"

She doused Millie's head, resulting in a shrill squeal, then Millie, covered in goose flesh, wrung her streaming tresses over the washtub. She shivered as Eliza hurried to wrap her head in a towel.

"You can go next, if you like," Millie offered, indicating the tepid water.

Sarah laughed at Eliza's reluctance. "I'll go put another kettle on to boil," she said and disappeared down the stairs.

Half an hour later both girls were in the kitchen, spreading their hair before the warm stove. Dinner seemed an unbearably long time away as Eliza savored the delicious aroma of roast beef. Her mouth watered, but at the same time she was too anxious to eat. Her stomach felt full of grasshoppers. The kitchen chatter was a pleasant distraction as the girls cut biscuits and Anne ironed Millie's blue flannel wedding gown.

When their hair was dry at last, Anne and her girls coached Eliza's efforts as she carefully plaited Millie's gold locks, tucking the chickweed blossoms into her curls. A crimping iron lay on the stove, ready to add the finishing touches.

"Now we'll do you!" Rebecca pressed Eliza into a slatback chair as Anne took up the brush.

"It won't be near as much fun as Millie's. I don't have her natural curls."

"No, but the white flowers will show up all the better against your dark hair."

Eliza was surprised by how much she enjoyed the pampering. It had been a long time since her mother fussed over her hair. She wondered if Millie was missing her mother, as well.

When the ministrations were finished, Anne sandwiched a slice of cold beef in a biscuit for each girl, and then sent them upstairs to change.

Eliza helped Millie step into several petticoats before holding the skirts of her wedding gown wide so as not to muss her flowery curls as she dove through the gathered fabric. At last she stepped into her own best dress—a shirtwaist of cornflower blue with fine embroidered lace at the high collar and cuffs.

As if on cue, the clop of a horse's hooves sounded in the street below, and they looked out to see the circuit rider arriving. Eliza stood behind her friend to take one last glance in the looking glass. Millie was, indeed, "all purty and pink"—just as Zeke described her the day they first met in Cimarron.

"You ready?" Eliza snatched the blue flags and shooting stars from a vase beside the bed.

"Oh, yes!" Millie took the flowers and clutched them to her heart, closing her eyes and taking a deep breath as Eliza stooped to gather her skirts.

I hope I am.

ꙮ

Uncle Rufus sat on a bench near the front of the wooden church, his bandaged legs stretched before him, his fiddle tucked beneath his whiskered chin. At the preacher's nod, he plucked gently to test the pitch, and then laid his bow to the strings. A sweet, soulful melody rose to the rafters. It seemed to spin there a while before it beckoned Eliza forward.

Forcing a smile, she took one tentative step and then another. The altar seemed a mile away. She was painfully aware of the many eyes upon her and searched frantically for something to focus her on her goal.

Aunt Charlotte looked lovely in a dark blue gown. She'd shed the black of deep mourning for this day.

Eliza longed to rejoice with them as well.

She looked for reassurance in the pastor's benevolent face, but his attention was distributed evenly among his gathered flock. Beside him, Zeke fidgeted and fretted with something in his pocket, only glancing at the door sporadically as if he were half afraid to look. She could borrow no strength there.

Her eyes found Jake's, and in them her soul found its anchor. His steadfast gaze conveyed gentle encouragement, kindling a warmth that drew her like the fiddle's plaintive tune. Her smile became genuine, and Jake rewarded her with one of his own.

Step by step she approached him.

Somewhere around the fifth row it occurred to her that in another time and place she would have approached the altar of Papa's church in just this manner, but it would have been Grayson waiting for her. Then the image became muddled, and Grayson became Jake in her mind's eye. She shook her head to clear the unwelcome thought and forced herself to re-enter the present. She was not the bride.

At last she reached the altar, as breathless as if she had swum to a distant shore. With a final smile of gratitude to Jake, she turned and took her place beside the communion rail. Then the tune changed, and the congregation rose to welcome the bride.

Millie stood in the doorway, alone but radiant with the sunlight behind her. She had eyes for Zeke only as she calmly, slowly approached her groom, drawn to him as to a magnet.

For his part, Zeke seemed mesmerized, unable to look away. A slow grin spread across his lean cheeks.

When Millie reached him at last, she laid her right hand trustingly upon his rough palm and turned, beaming, to enter into covenant.

"Dearly beloved, we are gathered here today in the sight of God and this company..."

Eliza gulped. Her eyes sought Jake's for strength again, but the warm, encouraging glow was gone from them.

"...to join this man and this woman in holy matrimony."

Visible pain. *Lord, he is hurting as badly as I am. I can see it. Please get us through this.*

Eliza clutched the stems of her bouquet, nearly crushing the tender stalks, and willed herself to keep smiling.

"Marriage is an honorable covenant instituted by God and confirmed by our Lord Jesus in Cana..."

It is not wrong to want this for myself, Lord, and I do want it. I want it so badly that it gnaws at me inside.

"Do you, Zeke, take Millie to be your wife, to have and to hold, from this day forward, for better or for worse, for richer or for poorer, in sickness and in health, to love and to cherish, till death do you part?"

Zeke swallowed hard, but his voice was firm when he said, "I do."

Millie seemed to glow with happiness. Eliza had expected her to cry, but she did not.

Father, did you create only one woman for one man? Was I made for Grayson only? And if he was my purpose, what do I do with the rest of my life now that he's gone?

The pastor turned. "Do you, Millie, take Zeke to be your husband, to have and to hold, from this day forward, for better or for worse, for richer or for poorer, in sickness and in health, to love and to honor, till death do you part?"

Without hesitation, Millie gave her affirmation. "I do." Her voice was as squeaky and childlike as ever, but it carried a tone of innocent trust and enthusiasm that was really quite endearing.

Eliza could not be envious of her friend, though it seemed

dreadfully unfair that she was half again Millie's age and still alone. *But if You knew that death would part us, then surely I am free to love again. Do I dare to hope for that?* She hazarded another glance at Jake. Were those tears? He looked away, and she saw his jaw tighten. He must be remembering Julia. How could he not? Her heart dropped like a cold stone into a stream, dashing her hopes with painful reality.

Millie was trying to hand Eliza her bouquet. Fortunately no one seemed to notice the pause before she accepted it with another forced smile. Millie turned again to Zeke and gazed into his eyes as he took her tiny hand and fumbled in his pocket for the ring.

He slipped the plain silver band onto her finger. "In token of the vows made between us, with this ring I thee wed; in the name of the Father and of the Son and of the Holy Spirit. Amen."

Millie's face shone with joy.

Zeke beamed with pride.

Jake squared his chin and smiled as he clapped Zeke's shoulder. As if he had remembered his earlier mission, he turned his attention to Eliza. She could read his thoughts plainly. *Are you all right? Not much longer now. We made it.*

Yes. We made it. And I'm glad—really glad. They're a perfect fit for each other, Lord. Bless them. Bless them and keep them safe ... she looked again at Jake and thought of Julia ... *for many long and happy years.*

The preacher was speaking again, clasping Zeke's and Millie's hands in his as he began his benediction. "I now pronounce you man and wife. That which God has joined together, let no man put asunder. Zeke, you may kiss your bride."

Someone on the back bench whooped, and several of the younger girls clapped as Zeke grasped Millie's small shoulders and pulled her into an embrace. He gazed into her eyes for a moment, savoring her, before lifting her chin with his knuckle and lowering his lips to hers. Gently, tenderly, he sealed their union as the congregation voiced their approval.

Then Uncle Rufus played a sprightly march, Eliza handed Millie her bouquet, and Zeke led his bride hand in hand down the aisle. Millie almost skipped.

The pastor raised his hands.

Oh! He's waiting for us! Eliza gathered her skirts with her right hand and reached out with her left. It was an automatic gesture, but she froze when Jake's skin touched hers. Caught off guard, she wondered if anyone in the congregation saw her stare up at his eyes and blush as he tucked her hand into the crook of his arm. Then they were on their way toward the door, and their friends folded into the aisle behind them.

Soon enough they were safely out into the bright afternoon sunshine, and Eliza was able to lose herself in the excitement of the crowd surrounding the newlyweds.

It was several minutes before she was aware of Jake's absence. Looking back over her shoulder, she found him—still standing on the doorstep of the church—and followed his somber gaze to the graveyard that lay so near yet so silent.

ꕤ

Zeke lifted Millie into the wagon as gently as if she were a china doll then climbed up beside her and kissed her again. He paused only a moment—long enough for Millie to toss her bouquet—before jostling the reins.

Millie twisted in her seat, waving madly and blowing kisses to Eliza, who stood calmly among the scrambling girls. It seemed somehow undignified and uselessly superstitious to grapple for the bride's bouquet in hopes of being next at the altar. Perhaps she, like Jake, should accept her fate. She would no longer indulge her imagination. Raised hopes had further to fall.

By the time she made her way to Aunt Charlotte beside their wagon, Jake was emerging from the church with Uncle Rufus leaning heavily on his arm. He lifted his father-in-law into the wagon bed, then helped Aunt Charlotte and, at last, Eliza into the wagon.

Eliza's heart turned toward him softly as she observed his gentle strength, but she quickly steeled her resolve. Millie was mistaken. Jake was equally considerate to everyone. The kindness he showed her meant nothing, and she would not make that mistake again. She chided herself. He was still grieving. That much was plain. For his sake, if not her own, she must make an end of this foolishness.

They stopped by the store long enough to pack up half a dozen pies and a rocker from the porch. Uncle Rufus was pale from the day's exertion, but nothing could persuade him to miss the housewarming. "The fiddler don't have to dance, but you can't dance without a fiddler," he said.

Aunt Charlotte rode in the back now to hold things steady, and Eliza was relieved that she did not have to sit as close to Jake on the buckboard. He did not smell like coffee and leather today. Today he smelled like soap, but the effect on Eliza was the same. She closed her mind, relinquishing those thoughts to the Lord.

They joined a steady stream of rigs heading south out of town, bumping and jostling along the same route they had taken the afternoon before. Once again Eliza's spirit soared to the mountaintops like a hawk that circled on the drafts above them. It was good to be alive. The sun was warm. New life was returning to the high valley, and there was cause to rejoice. Tonight there would be food and dancing and good fellowship. Yes, she could do this. She could find joy without Grayson—without any man.

Jake pulled the wagon to a halt in front of a zigzag rail fence and tied off the reins before helping the ladies out. Once the rocking chair was unloaded, a man Eliza had not met yet suggested that if Uncle Rufus would sit in it, he and Jake could carry him to the cabin that way with one on each side. Laughing, Aunt Charlotte and Eliza followed with the pies.

A table and benches were brought out of the house and set up in the yard, and additional side boards were hastily constructed out of sawbucks and planks. Miss Anne, already carving her roast, nodded her head toward the end of one bench to indicate a place reserved for desserts.

Jake made another trip to the wagon to bring Uncle Rufus' fiddle and came back with a calico bag of sugar, as well. He handed it to Eliza, who took it into the cozy cabin.

The windows were open to let in the light and breeze, and Millie stood in the middle of the main room beaming with pride. She whirled, curls flying. "Didn't my Zeke do himself proud?"

Eliza smiled her agreement. He certainly had. Every log fit tightly to the next with stones embedded in the smooth chinking between to make a pleasing pattern. Glass windows glittered as the sunshine streamed through them to form checkerboards on the sanded floor.

"And look, Eliza!" Millie grabbed her friend's hand and pulled her into a divided lean-to.

A shiny black stove took up most of one wall with a wooden drain board adjacent. The view through a glass window over the work surface stole Eliza's breath away. Hand-hewn boards fit between the logs on the back wall of the cabin to form shelves for dishes and dry goods.

Eliza added her pound bag to the growing pile of colorful gifts and set her bouquet into a jar of water before Millie pulled her through another doorway into a bedroom.

A bright quilt covered the peeled log bed. "My Mama sent this out with Zeke last year. 'Double Wedding Ring.' She pieced it out of the remnants of some of my old dresses from before the war." Millie traced the delicate lines of stitching with one gentle finger. When she turned, her eyes sparkled with joyful tears. "Oh, who could want more?"

Eliza couldn't think of a single thing that was missing. It was all she had hoped for in her own life, but now her heart was finally settled on that matter, and she set her will to leave it there.

In some ways her life was like a patchwork quilt. The dreams she had before the war lay in pieces. They could not be restored, but the fragments could be put back together to make something useful—something different but still beautiful. Like her new family here in the mountains, pieced together from the remnants of loss. Life would be what she made of it, and she was determined to make it good and full of purpose.

They rejoined the well-wishers, and Zeke and Millie ate their meals seated in a pair of willow rockers like a king and queen enthroned upon the porch. Then Uncle Rufus began to play jigs and reels, polkas and waltzes. Couples of all ages danced in the empty cabin and spilled out onto the prairie grass.

Eliza helped Aunt Charlotte and Miss Anne serve desserts and chase off children who had had too many. She did not notice the men on horseback who rode out from town late in the afternoon until she saw Zeke, Jake, and some of the other men go to meet them at the gate.

Millie naively set out to join them, but Aunt Charlotte pulled her back.

Eliza recognized Clay Allison among the gang of rough-looking riders, and from the volume of their coarse jokes, they had just left a saloon. It was a wonder they could stay mounted. She hoped they hadn't come to cause trouble.

"Zeke!" They called out drunkenly. "You didn't invite us to your shindig!"

"Hello, Clay ... John, Hoyt." Zeke doffed his hat as he greeted some of the riders by name. "It's a private party, fellas. Sorry. Just a few friends." His voice was calm and friendly, but he looked wary and ready, poised like a tight bow above fiddle strings.

"Aw, now, ain't we friends?" the one he'd called Hoyt challenged.

Jeers and raucous laughter rose from the intruders.

"Yeah, how come you didn't invite us to your party?" The man called John jumped in. "Ain't nuthin' we love more than a good time!"

Several of the men pulled out their pistols and fired them into the air, whooping and hollering as their horses reared and pawed.

Jake stepped up to stand beside Zeke. "Well, I'll tell you, Clay..." Allison glared at the man who'd singled him out, but Jake continued in a reasonable tone. "...this is a church social of sorts." The riders began to laugh and mock, but Jake raised his right hand. "I'm telling you the truth. We came here straight from church, didn't we?" The men at the gate affirmed what he said. "It isn't that we meant to exclude you, but we didn't think you were the church socializin' type." He smiled directly at Clay Allison, challenging him to respond.

Allison glared first at the wedding party and then at the men who laughed and sneered behind him. "Shut up!" he snapped. "I got no use for God; I make my own justice. And I got no time for a sweet-talk social." He slammed his hat back onto his head. "Come on, boys. If we ride hard, we can still make it to Cimarron before ol' Lucien closes his bar."

Another volley of shots echoed into the mountain air as the men wheeled and rode off across the valley toward the eastern gap.

Eliza doubted very much that they could make it out of the canyon before nightfall, but that was their problem. She was glad to see them go.

Once they were out of sight, Uncle Rufus picked out another tune to break the tension. The dancing resumed and continued for half an hour until the shadows began to lengthen. "Last dance," he called.

The final few notes seemed to hang in the cool evening air when the song was over. He tucked his fiddle back into its case. "Charlotte, I hate to take you away from the fun, but I think we ought to get home before dark. I believe I can drive this rig, but I don't want to risk running into any trouble."

Aunt Charlotte packed up her pie tins while a couple of young men helped Jake carry Rufus back to the wagon in his chair. Eliza walked with them, prepared to go, but Uncle Rufus held out his hand to stop her. "Jake, you reckon you could find a ride back to town and bring Eliza with you? Ain't no use you young people leaving before the fun's over."

Jake assured him there would be no problem with that plan and immediately received several offers for a ride.

Eliza retrieved her shawl from Uncle Rufus' wagon and swung her skirts about her, light and carefree, as she returned to the house.

The women helped Millie organize her gifts on the pantry shelves while the men helped Zeke carry the furniture back into the cabin and tend to the livestock for the night, then the guests assembled on the front lawn as the sun set behind the western ridge in a blaze of colors.

Zeke stood in the doorway of his cabin, his arm around his bride, the glow of an oil lamp behind them.

By torchlight, their friends serenaded them with love songs. Eliza sang alto an octave above Jake's rich bass.

When Zeke and Millie said goodnight and closed the cabin door, they sang one last song before heading for their horses and wagons.

The moon was dark. Against the black sky, the stars hung low and twinkling as they rode back to town

Jake was very quiet.

Eliza hugged her wrap close against the night air, remembering Jake's solemn expression as he gazed at Julia's grave. He had helped her through some hard times these last weeks. Perhaps she could return the favor. "I've never seen so many stars. Seems like they're closer here in the mountains."

Jake smiled, but did not speak.

She tried again. "It's been a long day."

"Yes."

"I'm happy for Zeke and Millie." Jake didn't seem to mind her small talk. If he wanted to talk, he would.

"I'm worried for them. Millie's very young. She doesn't look strong enough to make it out here."

"I rather think that's what Zeke likes about her, but she's tougher than she looks."

Jake smiled. "I hope so. Life can be hard. I don't think I understood that fully when I married Julia." He fell silent again.

Eliza waited, hoping he knew that she would understand if he wanted to say more or if he didn't.

"It was two years ago today—the first Sunday in May." He looked up at the stars before continuing. "It's a fine time to start married life, practically speaking, after the snow and between calving season and planting season." He tried to smile, but his face looked strained.

"Today must have been difficult for you." She was glad she had set aside her silly romantic notions so that she could help him now.

"Yes. I loved Julia very much."

"I did, too. Like a sister." Wisdom warned her to stop there, but instead she pressed gently, comforted by the openness between them. "Is that what you were doing when I saw you today? Telling her you loved her on your anniversary?"

"No, Eliza." When Jake looked into her eyes, the intensity of his gaze scattered her recent resolutions like dandelion seed.

She looked away, and the night breeze blew a loose curl across her face.

Jake reached up to pluck a chickweed blossom from the tendril. He stroked her cheek with the petals.

This cannot be happening. She hardly dared to breathe as she turned to him again, eyes wide.

Jake handed the tiny flower to her, and she accepted it, numb with shock. "I was telling her goodbye."

Chapter 10

When a rooster announced the dawn, Eliza opened her eyes at once and stared at the ceiling by the hazy light of a new day. The world seemed different—brighter, somehow, though the sun had not yet risen.

Then she remembered.

On the table beside her bed, a tiny blossom lay atop her Bible—the flower Jake gave her last night under the stars. It still seemed strange to lie in Julia's bed in Julia's room and think of Julia's husband, but she was no longer plagued with guilt about her feelings for him.

She reached for the flower and smiled, twirling its stem between her fingers before caressing the petals with one fingertip. On a sudden inspiration she plumped a feather pillow at her back and plopped her Bible onto the quilt that lay across her lap, flipping the pages until she found the verse she sought. *Psalm 37:4 Delight thyself also in the LORD: and he shall give thee the desires of thine heart.* Was it too difficult to believe that the Lord would bless her with a man like Jake? It was hard to believe that she deserved it. She'd grumbled when the way got hard, but wasn't that the point of grace? God was faithful, even when His children were not.

These last years had been full of sadness for Uncle Rufus and Aunt Charlotte, too. Would her joy in Jake be difficult for them? As she arranged the flower to press it between the pages, her eyes fell upon the next verse: 'Commit thy way unto the LORD; trust also in him; and he shall bring it to pass.' That was what they'd have to do. They'd just take things slowly.

Below the window an axe rang out as it bit wood. Must be Jake chopping fuel for the stove. A fine time to gather the eggs, she decided.

Eliza could not stop smiling with anticipation as she hurried to dress and brush her hair. With an effort she forced herself not to thunder down the stairs. She placed one hand on her ribs and took a calming breath before she entered the living quarters, trying to appear casual.

"Good morning!" Too chipper. She groaned inwardly. *Dunce.*

Uncle Rufus sat at the table reviewing the store ledgers. He returned her greeting without looking up, but Aunt Charlotte eyed her closely. Or did she imagine it?

Eliza was glad to turn away from her scrutiny as she took the basket from its peg. If her smile didn't give her away before she got out the door, her hands surely would, shaking in eagerness as she fumbled with the latch. She felt giddy and foolish and ecstatic all at once.

She wasn't sure what she would say to Jake. She was half afraid that she had dreamed last night. Now that daylight had broken the spell, perhaps things would go back to the way they were before. Ridiculous. But apprehension made her catch her breath.

Jake still stood at the chopping block, legs straddled. When he saw her he paused midswing before splitting the quarter wedge of wood that stood on end.

She returned his slow grin with a shy smile as she unlatched the hen hutch. Glancing over her shoulder as she robbed the first nest, she saw him still watching her, still smiling as he gathered an armload of kindling. By the time he stamped his boots clean and entered the house, the smile was gone, replaced by an expression that was merely pleasant. Was he, too, wondering how to proceed?

They met by the washstand when Eliza stopped to wash her hands and face.

Jake dusted the woodchips from his hands and shirt and held the towel for her.

Their hands touched as she took it.

Eliza scrubbed her face, trying to wipe away the smile she could not suppress.

"When you get those eggs inside, why don't you come help me

with April and the calf?"

She nodded. They could talk privately in the barn.

Like a naughty child anxious to hide a misdeed, Eliza carried the eggs into the store, arranged them in a crate lined with straw, and ducked back outside again without a word. This time she was sure Aunt Charlotte watched her closely, her wooden spoon hovering motionless over the porridge.

The barn was warm and dark. The sun was not yet high enough for light to reach the threshed floor. Eliza shut the door behind her and stood waiting for her eyes to adjust to the dim light.

"I'm here." Jake's voice beside her made her jump.

When he grasped her arm to steady her, she almost jumped again. She closed her eyes and blew out a breath of relief, then shook her head and sighed.

"Are you thinking what I'm thinking?" She could hear the smile in his voice.

"Not unless you were thinking that I'm an idiot. Jake, this will never work."

"Why not?"

"I can't stop smiling like a dolt. It's juvenile. Aunt Charlotte is already watching me like I'm showing signs of illness."

"And?"

"Jake, their daughter has been gone less than a year. It's unseemly. It will hurt them."

He let go of her elbow and took the pitchfork from its peg before entering the horses' stall. "Do I seem not to care?" he said, thrusting the tines into the earthen floor. "Have I in any way seemed not to grieve as deeply as they?" His look conveyed an open challenge.

She shook her head. "No. I know you do. But you and I stand to gain by going on with our lives. Rufus and Charlotte have only their loss. They can't start over. Their children are gone—both of them—and their only grandchild as well. What will it do to them to see us going on happily ever after when they cannot?" Tears stung her eyes, and she turned away. "I'm sorry. I'm a mess."

For some time Jake said nothing. There was no sound except the rustle of straw, a horse's stamping, and April chewing her cud. He finished cleaning the large pen and dropped the rail into its slot as he emerged.

"Eliza, I know it's not been a year, and I know that may go against the grain for some folks, but it doesn't dishonor Julia that I miss her and want to enjoy companionship again. I can't have her back. She and Earl are gone." He leaned against the rails of April's enclosure. "We can go slowly. I can be patient."

She nodded. "I think that's best. I'm not saying 'no,' but I think we need time—time to get to know each other and time for the idea to grow on Uncle Rufus and Aunt Charlotte."

"We'll take our time, then, but whether it's next week or next month or next year, it won't change how I feel..." his eyes locked onto hers "...or what I want."

"How can you know that?" Eliza shook her head and squinted up at him skeptically. "You only met me two weeks ago. How can you be sure?"

Jake's gaze never left her face, and his voice never wavered. "I'm sure."

ꙮ

"I'm startin' to feel plumb useless." Uncle Rufus grumbled over his breakfast.

Aunt Charlotte thought for a moment. "You reckon we could pull a chair in behind the counter for you to sit in and another to prop your legs up? Like we did for the wedding?"

"I was good like that for a couple of hours, at least." His countenance brightened.

"If Jake can stay within earshot to help out in the store, I could use Eliza's help in the garden this morning."

Eliza was glad to see Jake nod. The prospect of a morning in the sunshine, away from the normal routine, was enticing. "What needs doin'?"

"I had Jake turn the rows for me last week. We ought to be able to set some onions now and sow cabbage and such. We're past most of the frost. If we mulch the garden heavily with straw, any late snows shouldn't hurt it."

"Snow! This late in the spring?"

"Not enough to stick," Jake said. "Not likely down here. But up where I live we won't see the last of it until June."

Uncle Rufus winced as they got him settled and hoisted his legs onto a pillowed chair, but then he smiled. His chair teetered on two legs as he leaned back against the wall, surveying his store with his fingers laced across his chest. "Ready for business!"

"Only for an hour or two," Aunt Charlotte cautioned as she opened the front door.

She handed Eliza a couple of jars of saved seeds from last season, and Jake brought a crate of onion pearls from the barn, picked from last year's crop. They unlatched the gate that separated the garden from the barnyard. The soft, moist soil was rich and black and felt good underfoot. An earthy smell of humus rose as Eliza stepped between the rows, following Aunt Charlotte to the furthest corner.

"We'll set out the onions first as far as they'll go, then we'll start half a row of beets and two rows of cabbage, I think."

They worked in companionable silence, both bending over the rows, poking holes in the fresh mounds with sticks, positioning the pale green shoots, and pressing the soil around them. At the end of the row, Eliza straightened and stretched for the first time, which made her head spin. She grabbed the plank fence with one hand and pressed the other to her forehead until the world seemed still once more.

"Altitude," Aunt Charlotte said with a chuckle. "It can take some time to adjust."

"Jake referred to E-town as 'down here.' Is it really much higher on Bitter Creek?"

"Oh, yes. Quite a bit. It takes some gettin' used to. Julia had such a time just trying to draw breath as the baby grew." Her wistful expression was a poignant reminder of her loss.

Eliza tried to seem not to notice. She steered the conversation back to gardening. "And if it gets cold enough to snow again, how hard will that be on the plants?"

"Depends on how hard it freezes and when." She squatted and dragged her stick along the top of the mound to make a shallow trough. "The wildflower seeds sleep just fine under a blanket of snow all winter. If we cover these with straw, they should survive." She reached into the jar and took out a pinch of the red radish seeds, spacing them along the trough with her fingertips before brushing the loose dirt over them. Then she sat back on her heels and looked up at Eliza, squinting into the morning sun. "But if it comes a late freeze, if it catches them while they're sprouting and vulnerable..."

"What then?"

"Then we start over, best we can." Something about the way she looked at Eliza, her gaze direct and penetrating, made her understand that there was deeper meaning in the words.

"Shall we hold back, then? Just in case?" Eliza peered into the seed jars, mentally calculating whether they had enough for reserves or whether they would have to risk it all.

"I think not." Aunt Charlotte poured a mound of seeds into her palm. "Never confuse prudence with fear. Prudence tells me to use good judgment and begin when I'm reasonably certain of a good outcome. Fear would tell me never to act until circumstances are ideal." She winked. "Fear makes a poor advisor. These are hardy. We'll give it all we've got and trust God for the rest. What's meant to be will be."

They worked silently again.

ॐ

Uncle Rufus' face was ashen, and he muttered under his breath as Jake helped him back to his bed. "Useless cripple..."

"That's not true, Uncle. You just tried too much too soon." Eliza placed a folded quilt beneath his swollen legs to elevate them.

"Two hours of sitting. How difficult is that?"

She ignored his question. "You'll feel better once the swelling goes down." She offered him an encouraging smile but turned away when she saw his face. He was pouting. Eliza didn't know whether she felt amused or disgusted. Though she understood his frustration, she could not bear to see him like this.

"The longer I lay here, the weaker I git. I'm stiff and sore all over, and I'm 'bout to go stir crazy with cabin fever."

"You need to build your strength back slowly." Jake propped the crutches against the bed table. "If you can rest some this afternoon, maybe you can help me in the barn this evening."

The suggestion cheered Uncle Rufus, but Eliza's heart sank. She had hoped for a few moments alone with Jake this evening, and checking on April and her calf would have provided a perfect opportunity. But maybe Jake was taking her at her word, taking things slow. She knew she should be glad for her uncle, so she chose to smile in spite of her disappointment. "That's right, Uncle Rufus. A little today, a little more tomorrow, and you'll be good as new in no time."

Rufus snorted.

"You'd better mend quick, too, old man. I've got a claim to get back to." Jake winked first at Rufus and then at Eliza.

Her heart seemed to freeze in her chest. Jake would be leaving. As soon as Uncle Rufus was able to tend the store again, he would return to his mine and his traps. And what then? Was that why he'd been anxious to make his intentions known?

Jake seemed not to notice her dismay.

Eliza spent the afternoon in the store with Aunt Charlotte.

Jake hauled hay to mulch the new garden rows.

She could hear the squeak of the cart wheels as he traveled back and forth from the barn, but she did not see him. Eliza summoned all her will power to keep her mind on her business and scolded herself. She was the one who had wanted to take things slowly. Now she was acting like a silly schoolgirl.

The final customer left at last.

"Go on out and check on April while I get supper on." Aunt Charlotte sighed wearily as she pulled a pencil from behind her ear and tucked it between the pages of the ledger.

Uncle Rufus was waiting for her. Eliza walked close beside him as he hobbled to the barn, wincing with each step but stubbornly determined to push himself back to health. A restful afternoon had done much to mend his strength but not his foul temperament. Twice he stumbled, and Eliza reached out to support him. He shook her hand from his arm.

When they reached the door at the base of the stairs, he allowed her to hold it open. He paused on the stoop to gaze up at the ridge. Perhaps he, too, found strength and encouragement in the grandeur of God's handiwork. Or perhaps he simply needed a convenient excuse to catch his breath. He lowered his head and lunged for the barn door. His stiff fingers fumbled for the latch string, and he gave the door a vicious poke with his crutch when he finally succeeded in lifting the latch.

Jake must have heard them coming. The door nearly struck him as it banged open, and he stood staring at Rufus' dour expression for a moment. The horses, startled by the sudden noise, shied to the far side of their stall.

"We've come to help you with April," Eliza said, though no explanation was necessary and, truth be told, no help was needed. Pretending at normalcy was uncomfortable, but what could not be avoided must be endured.

Jake nodded and stood aside.

As Uncle Rufus made his way to the pen, Eliza saw that his knuckles turned white as he gripped the rails for support. He must be in such pain. He made it to the enclosure and seemed to collapse against the slats, chest heaving with effort.

Jake raised the bar and set a stool to one side, then waited patiently as Rufus inched his way toward it.

Her uncle looked old and tired as he sank onto the seat and closed his eyes. After a long moment, though, he opened them again and studied the cow and new calf. His expression softened, and a smile began to tug at the corners of his mouth. He reached into the feed trough and dipped up a handful of sweet grain.

May pressed close to her mother, and both studied the new stranger to the barn, but then curiosity got the best of the calf. She took a few cautious steps toward Rufus' outstretched palm until she could sniff of the grain. She pressed her nose into it, then quickly drew her head back and shook the chaff from her muzzle, snorting and huffing and licking at it with her tongue.

Rufus laughed.

Jake and Eliza joined him, and May cocked her head and blinked at them. With a flick of her tail, she scampered back to her mother for a drink.

"She's strong and spirited," Rufus said. "I believe she'll make it." He leaned forward, his elbow on one knee, for a better angle to study April's wounds. "How's mama healing up?"

By way of answer, Eliza squeezed into the stall and retrieved the jar of ointment from a high shelf. She twisted off the lid and dipped her fingers into the gooey balm before slapping the cow gently on her flank.

April edged over.

Rufus drew his breath in sharply. The gashes looked worse than they were now that the scabs were beginning to pull loose in the thick matt of her winter coat to reveal raw, pink flesh.

"Oh, this is so much better than it was." Eliza sought to reassure him.

April shifted her weight again and stumbled on the weak leg. The calf startled, but went back to its dinner soon enough.

Eliza began to rub ointment gently into the wounds. The cow's flesh rippled reflexively a time or two when she hit a tender spot.

"Poor thing. She'll never get full use of that leg." Rufus wagged his head. "She'll be a cripple—an easy mark."

Eliza knew he was speaking more of himself than the cow. "Yes, which is how she came to be available to us." She fixed a challenging glance upon her uncle. "So her misadventure became our blessing, wouldn't you say?"

Rufus nodded, but he twisted one side of his mouth as he looked down at his own crippled limbs. "Yup. Life changes, and God allows it for His own purposes. But sometimes those changes leave scars." He pointed toward April's mangled leg. "The wounds heal, but the scars are permanent." He looked at Eliza, then at Jake. "I look up at them mountains out there, so grand and beautiful, and I know God is powerful. Don't nothin' happen to us but what He allows it, but sometimes I gotta ask myself if He loves us, why He'd allow so much hurtin'." There was an honest question in his eyes as he looked from Jake to Eliza and back again.

The silence hung between them. Eliza's heart ached for him. She'd asked that question so recently, herself. "I don't know, Uncle Rufus. I don't." She shrugged, lifting hands as empty as her understanding. "I've got no easy answers. 'These are the times that try men's souls.'"

Jake shifted and leaned over the rails, looking thoughtful. "I'm no Bible scholar, but some of what it teaches has become clearer to me out here. I've done some thinking about how God says He refines and purifies us. That's what happens to the gold and silver that comes out of these mines, but first the rock it's trapped inside of gets pounded and crushed." He hammered his fist into his palm for effect. When Uncle Rufus laughed sardonically, he grinned. "Then it gets even worse. We pass the crushed pieces through the fire to melt the metal out of it and burn off the dross."

Uncle Rufus shook his head and snorted. "I can sympathize with the rock."

"Don't feel too sorry for it; it's shown little sympathy for me. These nuggets of insight may be the only thing I get out of it, in the end." They all laughed at that, and then Jake continued. "But the gold is precious. That's what we're after, and we don't want to lose a bit of it. So we don't just throw it into the midst of the flames." He cupped his hands. "We put it in a crucible—something to carry it through and bring it out safely on the other side."

New truth was vivid in Eliza's mind, bringing tears of wonder to her eyes—truth about the purpose of her suffering and truth about the man who shared it. There was far more to both than she had imagined.

Uncle Rufus stared at Jake. "So 'He is like a refiner's fire,' but Jesus is my crucible?"

Jake nodded. "You might say that. 'Surely he hath borne our griefs, and carried our sorrows: yet we did esteem him stricken, smitten of God, and afflicted.'"

Eliza could see the strain leave Uncle Rufus like a snowdrift melting to nourish new growth. He smiled at her as she treated the last of April's wounds. "I wish I could be as patient through the process, then, as that dumb creature."

Just then, Eliza must have touched a spot that was especially painful.

April flinched suddenly, bawled, and kicked.

The calf went one way, and Eliza went the other. Crashing into the rails, she lost her footing in the slippery straw and slid to the floor.

A loud rip told her that she had caught her dress on a splinter, and a quick look confirmed it. A jagged corner of blue calico sagged about a foot above the hem. Eliza examined it closely before patting it with disgust. She closed her eyes, sighed, and began to count slowly to herself so that she would not speak what was in her mind to say. When she opened her eyes, Uncle Rufus and Jake were both looking at her, their eyes wide, waiting.

Jake extended his hand to help her up. "Bad?"

She chewed her bottom lip and nodded. "And this was my favorite dress."

Both men did a creditable job of displaying sympathy. "Run in and show it to Charlotte. She may know a way to mend it," Uncle Rufus suggested.

Eliza obeyed quickly, but mostly because she feared she might cry over her torn skirt in front of the men. It was a small loss by comparison to those they discussed, but a disappointment nonetheless. She already knew that the tear could not be mended. It was large and frayed, nowhere near a seam, and too low to hide with a pocket—completely beyond repair.

Aunt Charlotte drew her closer to the kerosene lamp and inspected the rip carefully. "I'm sorry, dear. I can't see how we can mend it."

"I feel sick about it," Eliza lamented. "I loved this dress, and now it's ruined."

Aunt Charlotte straightened. "I only said the tear couldn't be mended. I don't think the dress is ruined. Maybe we can salvage the loss."

Eliza pursed her lips and waited for the explanation.

"We've got several lovely calicos in the store. I'm thinking of that bolt of blue with the black vine pattern. Do you know it?"

Eliza nodded.

Aunt Charlotte began to gather the fabric in her hands, folding it up from the hem in illustration. "We'll cut it here, all the way around, and then again here, just above the tear. Then we'll insert a strip of the contrasting material."

"But won't it look patched?" Hope stirred Eliza's imagination, but she wasn't convinced yet.

Aunt Charlotte shook her head. "I don't think so. What if we take off the collar and cuffs and replace them with the darker calico, as well? Then we can edge the new pieces with black crocheted lace—make it look like we planned it that way all along."

Eliza could see it in her mind. It could work. She began to smile. She might even like it better made over.

As she lay in Julia's bed that night, thinking again of Julia's husband, Eliza looked at the ruined garment awaiting the scissors' cuts in the morning. *'He has torn that He might heal.' Yes, Lord.* She could trust Him, even when she couldn't see the reason for the pain.

Chapter 11

Eliza's feelings for Jake warmed like the spring days that flew by and flourished like the wildflowers in the high valley meadows. New prospectors began to arrive with the warm weather. Days in the store and in the garden were busier than ever, but she lived for the times in between chores when she could steal a few moments with Jake. Respect grew into admiration, and admiration blossomed into a tender affection. If it was not like the youthful infatuation she had seen in Millie and Zeke, neither was it without moments that took her breath away. She still felt compelled to restraint for Uncle Rufus and Aunt Charlotte's sake, but that only served to increase her longing for a time when she could freely admit her attraction to the man who was becoming her best friend.

She could count on seeing Jake first thing every morning, at meals, and at the end of each day when they settled the livestock for the night. In between, he was attentive to every need, fetching any tools she required for the garden plot and carrying stock from the attic storeroom. She always lingered in his presence, stretching the moments as long as she dared, finding ways for their eyes to meet or their hands to touch. At least once a day she asked him, teasing, "Are you still sure?"

He always winked and gave the same answer. "I'm sure."

April's wounds continued to heal, as did Uncle Rufus's.

Eliza knew that when her uncle was well and the snow was gone, Jake would leave, too. He would return to his cabin over the ridge and his claim on Bitter Creek. She shut those thoughts out of her mind.

"Any news from the newlyweds?" Mrs. Ewing inquired when she stopped in on Saturday with her two youngest children in tow.

"Not since the shivaree." Eliza hadn't had time to miss Millie yet, but the hens were brooding on the clutches of eggs Aunt Charlotte had set aside for the couple. The chicks would hatch soon.

Mrs. Ewing selected one of the pretty calico prints and held it up to her daughter, Grace, who wrapped it around her waist for effect and dimpled with pleasure.

"Are you getting a new dress?" Eliza asked, reaching for her scissors.

"No, ma'am."

Eliza shot a questioning glance at the mother.

"Just a yard, I think. Enough to let this one out some. She's grown half a foot, but it still fits everywhere else."

The child ducked her head, and the dimples disappeared.

"Oh, then you'll have a dress like mine!" Eliza stepped from behind the counter and twirled to display the skirt she had recently patched.

Grace giggled and clapped her hands. "Did you get even taller, Miss 'Liza?"

Eliza laughed. "Actually, no. I fell down and tore mine."

More giggles.

"Thank you," the mother mouthed to Eliza before turning again to her daughter. "Grace, would you like me to get enough extra to make you a new collar like Miss Eliza's?"

The child nodded eagerly, and Eliza measured out an extra quarter yard.

Mrs. Ewing searched in her handbag for the proper coins.

Out of the corner of her eye, Eliza saw snaggle-toothed Jonathan reach a grubby finger toward a stick of horehound candy at the end of the counter. Grace scowled at her brother and slapped his hand. Jonathan shoved both fists in his pockets, but he still stared with longing at the tempting box of sweets.

Aunt Charlotte seemed to read his mind. "Jonathan, we've got a new calf out in the barn. Did you know that?"

"No, ma'am. Is she pretty?"

Aunt Charlotte smiled. "Well, we like her, but her mama is feeling sorta cooped up lately. She's got a bad leg."

"Like Mr. Rufus?"

"I'm afraid so. She'd really like to eat some meadow grass, but she'll need someone to watch her and maybe help her." She had the boy's attention. "How long until school's out?"

Jonathan looked at his mother. "About two weeks."

Aunt Charlotte nodded and looked thoughtful. "That's just about right. Do you think you might be doing any fishing this summer?" The mountain streams were full of trout, and fishing was a favorite sport for men and boys.

Jonathan brightened. "Oh, yes, ma'am. I go fishin' most every day."

"Would you be willing to take April and her calf with you? You could stake her in the meadow so she can eat grass and drink from the stream, and I'll pay you a nickel a week."

Jonathan's eyes grew as wide as the silver disk she held up. Aunt Charlotte let him hold it. He turned it over in his palm and poked at it, counting the ring of stars on the back, before handing it back to her. "Yes, ma'am. I think I'd like that," he said soberly.

"Well, then, you've got yourself a job."

A big grin fully exposed the broad gap where his front teeth had been.

഻ഀ

The moon was nearly full that night. Eliza tried to keep her mind on the quilt square she was stitching to make use of the torn dress strip, but the silvery light that streamed in through the window was enticing. She laid her needlework aside. "It's a soft night. I believe I'll step outside for a bit."

She sat on the back porch bench and gazed at the ridge in the moonlight. The moon looked just as it had her first night in Elizabethtown, reminding her inescapably that Jake's month with them was near an end.

As if drawn by her thoughts of him, Jake slipped out of the house to join her. The golden glow of a lantern silhouetted him as the door opened and closed again. He nodded a wordless greeting and leaned against a post to share the view.

"You'll be going soon."

"Not too soon." He pointed to the fish scale clouds that shingled the sky to the north and west. "See those clouds?"

Eliza nodded.

"A cold front's about twelve hours behind."

Eliza wrapped her arms about herself and shivered. Surely it wouldn't be too bad, though she almost hoped it would be if it meant that Jake could stay longer. "You think it might snow? This late?"

Jake studied the sky. "Mare's tails over the moon and a choppy sea below."

Eliza looked at the clouds again and understood his description.

"It'll snow by morning." He took a step toward the barn. "I'd better get a tarp over the chicken coop and pitch some extra straw on the garden."

Sure enough, when Eliza looked out her window next morning the rooftops were blanketed in white, and a delicate lace lay over the wildflowers on the surrounding slopes.

"How's the garden?" she asked at breakfast, but Uncle Rufus waved his hand dismissively.

"This ain't no nevermind. It'll all be gone afore noon. We'll likely even still have church. Cimarron's much lower. They prob'ly didn't git a lick. Them roads will be all clear for the preacher to pass."

She looked at Jake and tried to sound casual. "So you're still planning to leave this week?"

He shook his head as he forked up a second helping of salt pork. "No, I don't think so." If he'd looked at her at that point, Eliza was sure her expression would have revealed everything that was in her heart. Fortunately he did not, and she was able to hide her smile behind the rim of her coffee cup. "Two inches here can mean seven or more in the higher climes."

"It will stick there, then?"

"No, probably not, but I'd still rather not risk it." This time he did look at Eliza, and the twinkle in his eyes told her that he was glad of the excuse to stay.

Uncle Rufus was right. The snow sparkled radiantly as the sun rose, but was gone by mid-morning.

For the first time since Eliza's arrival, they all walked to church together. Uncle Rufus made slow progress on his crutches. Jake followed close by in case he stumbled, but he made it the full distance on his own power.

Zeke and Millie greeted them warmly as they entered.

"I was afraid I might miss you." Zeke clapped Jake on the back. "'Fraid you might already have headed back up the range."

"No. I've decided to give it another week."

Millie looked straight at Eliza and pressed her lips together to stifle an "I-told-you-so," but her arched brows made the message just as clear.

Eliza ignored the unspoken taunt. "Your chicks ought to hatch sometime this week. Have you got some place to put them when they're big enough to scratch for themselves?"

Millie looked to Zeke, who shook his head and fingered the folds of his hat.

"Nope, not yet. I gotta figure somethin' out quick."

"Why don't I organize a barn raising for next weekend?" Jake offered.

Zeke looked both pleased and relieved. "That'd be a heap o' help. I got enough deadfall for a good start, and we can cut more timbers if we need them."

"I'll bring men and axes," Jake promised.

"And I can cook up a mess of beans and cornbread." Millie was clearly excited about the opportunity to step into the role of hostess in her new home.

A weight lifted from Eliza's mind. She had one more week, one more social, one more Sunday with Jake and the opportunity to revisit the spot where he first professed his intentions toward her. It gave her something to look forward to—something to take her mind off the inevitable separation that lay just beyond.

ꕥ

The chicks began to hatch midweek. Eliza heard a muffled peep when she collected eggs on Wednesday. She was thankful that business was slow that day and seized upon every lull as an opportunity to scurry out to the coop and count the hatchlings.

"Counting your chickens before they hatch?"

Eliza jumped, startled, and made a fuss of smoothing her apron. She hadn't heard Jake behind her. "Nope. After. Look!" She stepped to one side to give him an opportunity to view the latest arrivals.

"Surely you've seen chicks hatch before."

"Of course I have. I may have grown up in town, but just about everybody kept chickens." The hen on the last nest stood to examine her brood, and one chick let out a squeak of protest when its mother stepped on it. "Aw..." Eliza reached in again and nudged it back toward the center of the nest. "It's just so captivating to watch them struggle to break into the world."

By Friday evening, she counted nineteen chicks. A fine wedding present, to be sure. Zeke and Millie would be needing that barn.

Jake was up at first light on Saturday. He gulped a mug of strong coffee and wolfed down a cold biscuit, then grabbed his axe. Shoving a second biscuit between his teeth, he held it there while he plunged his arm through the sleeve of his jacket.

"You can't work on no more food than that," Aunt Charlotte protested.

"Sorry. Gotta get going," he mumbled through the crumbs as he hurried to meet a number of other men from the church who were beginning to gather on the street in front of the store. Eliza could see Jake's horse already saddled, tied, and waiting.

Aunt Charlotte pursed her lips and stared after him. "Good thing I made some pies to send along toward lunchtime." She looked at Eliza and lifted one brow. "You reckon you could drive the wagon out?"

Eliza nodded, and her pulse quickened. She reckoned she could do just about anything if it would put her nearer to Jake.

Each hour of the morning dragged with unbearable slowness. "What time is it?" Eliza asked Aunt Charlotte for what must have been the twentieth time.

Her aunt pulled a watch from her pocket and flipped open its ornate lid. "Fifteen minutes later than it was the last time you asked." She narrowed one eye to study her niece. "You're anxious to be out there with the other young folks, eh?"

Eliza shrugged and smiled sheepishly. "I don't want to leave you with the work, though."

Just then her uncle's crutch hooked the partition aside as he came in from the barn. "Nonsense. I've just hitched up the wagon. Load up your goodies and go, girl. It's high time I made myself useful again."

Eliza could not restrain her excitement. She flew to hug her uncle, nearly knocking him off his feet. "Oh, thank you! Thank you!" She was already pulling her shopkeeper's apron over her head as she dashed toward the kitchen. In moments, a basket of dried apple tarts was nestled behind the buckboard, and Eliza was urging the horses to a trot.

The road flew beneath her wheels as she headed east over the bridge from town, then south along the main road, and then over the second bridge and out onto the alpine prairie. At a distance she could see two men pulling a cross-cut saw to fell a pine at the forest's edge and others driving a team that pulled a trimmed log on chains behind them. At the site of the new barn, just west of the house along the fence line, a larger knot of men chopped and notched the logs while others rolled them up planks to set them in place. The walls of the barn were already shoulder height on the north, east, and west sides with a broad opening framed to catch the southern sun. She could see Millie, her skirts billowing, and Zeke with his arm about her as they surveyed their new shelter.

Eliza reasoned that Jake would be with them, so she guided the horses in that direction and pulled up on the near side.

Millie, all smiles, hugged her and bussed her cheek. "We can serve right off the back of your wagon, I think," she said as she headed for the house.

"Hang on, Millie. I'll give you a hand with the bean pot." Zeke called back over his shoulder as he trotted after her. "Jake's on the other side, notchin' logs." He gestured toward the western wall.

Eliza was not sure how Jake failed to notice her arrival, but it was obvious that he had. When she rounded the barn, he was chipping a deep 'v' into a log. With one foot, he held the log to keep it from rolling as the axe arced over his head and bit deep into the cut. Sweat glistened on his bare shoulders. His shirt was flung across the rail fence, and his longhandles were peeled down to the waist.

Eliza blushed and giggled. Best to give him a chance to get covered. Thinking fast, she took a step backwards and came around the corner a second time, this time calling to him before he could raise his axe again. She didn't want him to notch his leg instead of that log.

He was quick. When she looked up, Jake had already shrugged into the sleeves of his undershirt and was hastily buttoning it up the front.

Eliza's knowing smile died on her lips before she had a need to stifle it. On Jake's chest, mere inches below his heart, she recognized the all-too-familiar wounds. Gunshot. The white, puckered skin and silvery scars that stretched across his ribs were like those her father bore. If anything, Jake's scars were more ghastly.

He saw her staring at him—he had to—but he said nothing.

"You were shot."

"Long ago."

"Where?" Pity somehow made her want to caress the wounds, even though she knew they no longer hurt.

"In the gut." A wry smirk twisted one corner of his mouth as he buttoned the last button. "Isn't it obvious?"

"That's not what I meant, and you know it." She quelled the urge now to slap him playfully instead. "I mean, where were you when it happened? Was it during the war?" Somehow Jake's scars made more real a truth she had already acknowledged. There was plenty of hurting and dying on both sides of the conflict.

"Yes."

"Was it bad?"

That quirky smile again. "Well, it wasn't good. Seemed so most particularly at the time, as I recall."

"How can you make jokes? You could have died!"

"Yes. I could have. But I didn't." His expression turned sober as he whisked his shirt from the fence. "There were lots of men who weren't so lucky—or so blessed."

It was Eliza's turn to stare silently, allowing her countenance to demand more information.

Jake looped his folded shirt behind his neck and pulled on the two ends that hung down over his chest. "The fellow who shot me must have been a late recruit right off the farm. He didn't have an issued rifle, or I'd have been numbered among the dead that day. A rifle bullet would have gone straight through, and where he hit me, I'd have bled out for sure." Jake shifted his weight, and his hand went to his ribs. He rubbed at the scar with his thumb. "Fortunately for me, a front-loading musket ball doesn't move as fast. By the time it hit me, it was falling. The ball pierced the skin, but it angled down instead of up. Broke a rib and 'bout knocked the stuffing out of me, but it missed most of the important things in there."

Eliza winced. "And is it still...?" She couldn't finish the question.

"No. A ball carries the wadding with it. If you don't clean the wound, infection sets in."

Eliza did not want to imagine the pain he'd experienced. Toward the end of the war, the South had run out of painkillers. A rag or a block of wood to bite on was about the only comfort there was to offer the wounded during surgery. She swallowed hard but did not drop her gaze. Whether she wanted to or not, she needed to know it all.

"The doctor found the lead and rag smashed against the broken fragments of my ribs. He cleaned me out good, and then cauterized the wound."

A moan of sympathy escaped Eliza's lips.

Jake shrugged. "I made it home. That's the main thing." He put on the shirt. "Let's go eat," he said, reaching out to offer Eliza a comforting embrace.

She drew back.

The simple motion caused Jake to recoil.

She stared up at him, puzzled.

"You won't let me touch you?"

She raised one eyebrow and curled her lip. "You're wringing wet!" Sniffing the air she added, "...and you don't smell very good."

"I smell just fine," he protested. "I smell beans and cornbread and apple pie, but I will allow that I stink terribly." He spread his arms and grinned.

This time Eliza didn't squelch the inclination to swat him.

He retaliated by wrapping her into a hug that nearly squeezed the wind out of her.

"I'm glad you lived," she said, though it was unnecessary, as they walked side by side to the wagon.

ꕥ

Work on the barn was finished by dusk. Jake hitched his horse to the back of Uncle Rufus' wagon and took the reins. Eliza sat more toward the middle of the buckboard than toward the end. As they crossed Moreno Creek for the first time, she looked back to see the ridge beams and rafters black against a rosy sunset. The high walls of the enclosure would provide a degree of safety until Zeke could get his crops planted. Then he would have the rest of the summer to chink the logs and nail slats to form a roof before the snows fell.

"It's pretty, isn't it?"

Jake nodded.

"Is there a valley like this over the ridge?" She had never asked him about his home before, partly because it made her think of Julia, partly because she didn't want to think of him leaving, and partly because it seemed personal somehow.

"There's a valley, but it's not like this one. Not as broad and not as long." Then, as if he feared she would be disappointed by his description, he hurried to add, "but it is wild and beautiful. The mountains and the pines nearly touch the sky. At night it's so dark, and the stars look so close, you'd swear the trees would sweep them from the heavens whenever the wind blows." Eliza sighed, and Jake smiled softly down at her. "I'd like you to see it sometime."

Warmth rushed to her cheeks at the implication. She changed the subject. "And is there gold in your valley?"

"Not that I've found by digging." He shrugged. "But in autumn the breeze shakes gold and silver from the aspens."

Eliza laughed. She'd never heard Jake wax poetic, but she liked it.

"Riches are where you find them, Eliza. If that mine never produces an ounce of metal, I'll still have claim to a piece of the most beautiful land I've ever seen."

He spoke of it longingly, and she realized that she could no longer deny the reality of his coming departure. "You're leaving soon."

It was a simple statement, but those three words felt like a knife, twisting.

"Monday, I think."

Something between a sigh and a sob spilled from deep within her. She drew a ragged breath and bit her lip, but two warm tears dropped into her hands, folded in her lap.

Jake glanced at her quickly then reined in the horse and pulled the wagon to a halt just where the road bent. Tenderly he lifted her chin with his knuckle and gazed into her face.

The light she saw in his eyes rivaled that of the first star twinkling in the evening sky.

Slowly, he leaned toward her, searching her eyes for indication of permission, until his lips pressed warm against her tear-dampened cheek. She hiccupped a laugh as he bent to kiss away the tears from the other cheek as well. Such pain and such joy. Why must those two so often come together? His eyes studied hers and found the answer he sought. Again his face drew near.

When he sat back after a long moment, it was longer still until he breathed out a contented sigh and lifted the reins from his knee.

They did not speak for the rest of their journey. If there was magic along this stretch of road, Eliza had no wish to break the spell.

When they reached home, Eliza held Jake's horse as he pulled the wagon into the barn, then she lit a lantern while he unhitched. Their eyes met as he lifted his mount's saddle from the wagon bed and heaved it over a rail. They laughed. Eliza felt almost shy now that they could see one another clearly in the lantern's glow. How long must they restrict themselves to moments stolen in the shadows? As if in answer to her unspoken question, Jake kissed her again.

As she helped him brush the horses, one further question nagged at Eliza's mind. "Why were you afraid I wouldn't let you touch me?"

"What?"

"This afternoon when you were covered in sweat. I pulled back, and it scared you."

Jake's hands slowed their rhythmic motion over the horse's withers. "I don't like to talk to you about the war."

"You mustn't feel that way, Jake. Thousands of good men fought on both sides. I know you fought for the North, and I've told you that I bear you no grudge for it. Only one man cost Grayson his life. I can't hate the entire Union. It's too much to keep up with." When Jake said nothing, she continued. "I'm glad you told me about getting shot. If we're going to learn to trust each other, then we need to know the truth about each other."

Jake's eyes searched hers. "Do you need to know everything to trust me?"

"What do you mean? Surely it can't be good to have secrets from one another."

"But could you trust me without knowing everything?"

"What would you not want to tell me?" She stared at him over the horse's back.

"There might be some information that would cause you more to distrust me than otherwise."

Eliza forgot to breathe. She felt as if all the air had left the barn. "What are you saying ... or not saying?" She watched as a storm of emotion passed over Jake's features. "Jake, where were you shot?"

He made no jests about it this time. He simply stared at her, visibly struggling with a decision that could change everything forever. "Chickamauga."

The word hit her with all the force of a musket ball, searing her insides with pain, tearing holes in her resolve.

"Say something. Please, Eliza."

She stared at him in horror. What could she say?

Jake pressed his forehead against the horse's side. When he looked up, his face was a picture of agony. He could hardly have looked worse when he had been shot. "Do you see now why I was afraid you would pull away? Why I was afraid to tell you?"

"You didn't trust me."

"I was afraid of that look—the one you're giving me now. You're wondering if I might, after all, be that 'one man' who took him from you."

"And can you assure me that you're not?"

The eyes that stared into hers now were red-rimmed, haunted. "I cannot." The barrier of truth between them was more solid than the horse. "I still feel as I always have, Eliza. I'm still sure."

I'm not. She did not say it, but she knew from his stricken expression that he had seen the doubt in her eyes.

Supper was quiet. Alone in her room, the silence was louder. It rang in her ears as silent tears soaked her pillow. She stared at the ceiling, miserable.

She knew him, or she didn't; her conscience nettled her. *'But if ye forgive not men their trespasses, neither will your Father forgive your trespasses.'* She had no option. Not before God. From the depths of her grief, she knew that this was more than a test of her love for Jake. God was testing her trust of Him, as well. She knew what she must do. *Forgive him, Father. He knew not what he did.* Tomorrow she would talk to Jake. She would tell him she was sure. They would worship together at the altar of Him who had forgiven all, reconciled.

Eliza could hardly wait for morning. She rose at first light and slipped silently out to the barn.

Jake was gone.

Chapter 12

Stunned and numb, unable to absorb the loss, Eliza climbed the stairs again and noiselessly shut the door to her room behind her. Like a child so shocked by pain that she forgets, at first, to cry, she sank onto the edge of her bed. The frame squeaked beneath her—the first sound to break the silence. As if stricken by an invisible blow, she doubled over until her face rested in her hands. Her hair fell forward like a curtain, closing her into a private chamber of grief. Then the tears began to flow and would not stop.

Agony—heartbreaking, chest-crushing, breathtaking. Eliza knew what King David meant when he wrote in the Psalms, "my heart is like wax; it is melted..." She did not know how long she wept until she ran out of tears.

At last she lay back across the quilt and stared, dry-eyed, at the ceiling. Her breath came in great hiccups. She gulped for air as if she were drowning and groped for rational thoughts just as desperately.

As badly as it had hurt to lose Grayson, losing Jake was worse. Grayson's death was not her fault. Jake chose to leave, driven away by her slowness to forgive. But who could blame her? Jake had expected her to trust him, yet he had not given her even one night to deal with her heart. Had he no idea what the war had cost her? Such forgiveness was a sacrifice—a deliberate choice not to remember things that could never be forgotten. She could not just toss off old hurts like a bad dream upon waking. After a night of wrestling with her flesh, her soul finally awakened to a new day of peace, but Jake had gone, denying her the opportunity to reap its blessings.

A soft knock at the door made her jump.

"Eliza?"

How could she face Aunt Charlotte? A glance in the mirror confirmed her suspicion. Her eyes were swollen and red from crying, and her nose seemed misshapen. No one would believe she was crying over a mere friend.

"Eliza? Are you ill, dear?"

Jake's departure would be a loss for her aunt and uncle, too, and it was all her fault. Yes, let them think she felt ill. It was not entirely a lie. She was going to have to face them eventually, but perhaps she could stall for time—

"I've brought you a bit of breakfast."

—or perhaps not. "I'm not feeling well this morning, Aunt. Please just let me sleep."

There was a moment's silence that gave her hope the ruse would work.

"Eliza, please open the door."

Of course Aunt Charlotte would not go away if she had any thought that her niece was sick. Eliza's head throbbed as she struggled to sit.

"Just a moment." The room whirled as she staggered toward the dressing table. She poured water from the pitcher onto a handkerchief and did what she could with her face. It didn't help much.

Her limbs were wooden as she crossed the room. She took a deep breath and forced herself to let it out smoothly before opening the door.

Aunt Charlotte held a plate of toast and a mug of hot tea. With eyes full of concern she studied Eliza's face. "May I come in?"

Eliza gave the door a push but didn't wait for it to swing wide before trudging back to the bed. She sank back onto the same spot she'd left, her eyes trained on the rag rug at her feet. For a long moment Aunt Charlotte said nothing. She just watched, making Eliza feel conspicuous as if her heart and soul were laid bare.

Say something, anything.

"Ah. I thought so."

Not what she was expecting. Eliza looked up.

"You do love him."

It wasn't a question; it was a statement of fact. Eliza had never put that word to it before, but if she didn't fully love Jake yet, it was something close enough. She nodded miserably.

"It's nothing to be ashamed of, dear. Jake is a wonderful man."

"You don't mind, then? I thought maybe..." She couldn't finish, but she didn't need to.

Aunt Charlotte set the tea and toast on the trunk at the foot of the bed and came to sit beside her. "We rather anticipated it. You and Julia were so much alike. It seemed natural."

"But I've heard you crying."

Her aunt drew a deep breath and smoothed the dark fabric of her skirt. She nodded slowly. "It hurt terribly to lose Julia so soon after her brother. At first grief consumed me." Agitated, she rose. "We came here to escape the painful reminders of Earl after he was gone, and now it seems there's no place left to run. Wherever you go, you take your memories with you." She offered the cup of tea to Eliza.

"I'm learning that." Eliza drank from the cup.

Aunt Charlotte looked thoughtful. "I retreated to a private world, surrounded by my memories, for a long time. It was as if I could keep my children alive by keeping their memories alive, but gradually I realized that they died in the midst of life. Did I really honor them by living in the midst of their deaths?"

That was a new thought. Was she doing that? Clinging to her losses and forgetting to live? She would have to meditate on it.

"Eliza, the ones we love and lose will always have their places in our hearts." Aunt Charlotte's hand moved to cover Eliza's. "I don't know why their time with us was so short, but I do know that our lives have purpose. Earl and Julia finished theirs. Apparently, I haven't." She shrugged. "Some things are meant to be."

Eliza's mind returned to her most recent loss. "I don't think this is one of those things."

"Did you tell Jake how you feel about him?"

Eliza gulped back fresh tears. "Oh, yes. That's why he's gone."

Aunt Charlotte looked puzzled.

"I insisted that he could trust me with any truth, but I wasn't prepared for what he told me. You know he was at Chickamauga?"

Her aunt nodded.

"Why did he not tell me sooner?"

"You'll have to ask him that."

"I did. He knew how difficult it would be for me, and it was. He was afraid it would change the way I feel about him."

"And has it?"

Eliza sighed. "I thought so at first, but knowing Jake—knowing his kindness, seeing his hurt—I could not hate him. It took me all night to lay aside that burden—to know that I could forgive him—but he didn't wait to hear it." She vented her twisted emotions on the handkerchief she still clutched. "I've ruined everything."

Aunt Charlotte straightened and drew back. "You don't have that much power, Eliza." Her voice was surprisingly stern.

Eliza scowled at her. She had hoped for more sympathy. "What do you mean?"

"Child, if something's meant to be—if it's God's sovereign will—then I just don't believe you're powerful enough to overrule God. If it's not supposed to happen, then you can't finagle to make it so; and if it is, you're just not big enough to ruin it all. I'm sorry to disappoint you." Her teasing wink brought some small measure of comfort.

The handkerchief came in handy again. "Oh, Aunt Charlotte, what can I do now?"

"You can wait on the Lord." The stern tone was back.

"I've waited on Him for twenty-eight years. I don't think I'm strong enough to wait longer."

"'They that wait upon the Lord shall renew their strength; they shall mount up with wings as eagles.'" She patted Eliza's knee. "Sometimes He helps us run without wearying. Other times we need Him desperately just to walk without fainting."

ꙮ

Eliza passed most of Sunday resting and praying, lapsing less and less frequently into tears. She looked forward to the distraction of work on Monday to alleviate her brooding mood, but when morning came the simple act of leaving her bed required an act of will. Aunt Charlotte and Uncle Rufus were considerate, but their extra care felt too much like pity. It made her feel awkward and pathetic. Her dignity would not endure for long anything that looked like coddling.

How had Jake become such a large part of her life in five short weeks? Everything reminded her of him. The barnyard was empty when she went to gather the eggs. She was keenly aware of his absence around the store, especially as she carried stock from the attic for Uncle Rufus—a chore Jake had handled seemingly without effort. At meal times Jake's place at the table was as empty as the hollow pit in her stomach, and the evening hours dragged by without his company.

Eliza tried to concentrate on her quilt but soon grew restless. She stepped out onto the porch for air, but the starlight mocked her. The silence in the barn was worse. The calf stared at her quizzically, almost as if she, too, missed the man who had cared for her with gentle strength. Eliza choked on sobs and fled back to the house. She closed the door harder than she meant to and collapsed against it, her chest heaving.

Aunt Charlotte and Uncle Rufus said nothing, but their faces expressed their compassion.

"I can't stay here." Eliza's voice sounded thin and pitiful in her own ears, but she didn't care.

"Where would you go?" Aunt Eliza asked, incredulous.

She knew without thinking. "Home."

Her aunt and uncle gaped at her.

She suspected that answer would make no sense to them as soon as the word left her mouth, and their expressions confirmed the notion. It barely seemed rational, even to her. Hadn't she come west because she was miserable in Waco? But no, she'd come here because Papa feared she'd be missing out on a chance for a life—meaning marriage and children—if she remained. So she'd followed her star, but in the end she'd found nothing she was looking for. No peace. No purpose. She'd found no remedy for trouble, and romance was obviously no guarantee of happiness.

"Aw, now, give it a bit longer, girl," Uncle Rufus coaxed. "Jake'll come down out of them mountains sooner or later for supplies, and you'll git your chance to talk to him then."

Eliza shook her head. "That's what I'm afraid of. I don't know how I'd face him. What would I say?"

"Say what you meant to tell him the morning he left," Aunt Charlotte suggested reasonably. "Tell him what's in your heart."

"He doesn't want to hear it."

"That's where you're wrong, 'Liza. I'd say that's what he wants to hear most."

She considered Uncle Rufus' words, but shook her head. "No. I can't take that chance. If he can't forgive me, doesn't want me, I cannot go back to thinking of him as a friend." A worse thought occurred to her, since Jake had decided to end his time of mourning... "I can't stay here and watch him be with someone else."

Her mind was made up. At home with Papa she hadn't known her next step, but at least she knew where she stood.

Her aunt and uncle stared at her sadly.

Uncle Rufus huffed a little. "Well, if you're sure that's what you want." He twisted one side of his mouth. "I'm afraid I ain't in a position to help you with the fare, though."

Eliza hadn't thought of that, but it stumped her only a moment. "I could finish my quilt and sell it."

He nodded, considering the idea. "You're welcome to show it in the store and keep whatever price it brings, but I gotta tell you there ain't much call for pretties out here. Most of the single men just buy necessities, and the families that's here are trying to make a go of it."

Aunt Charlotte looked thoughtful. "What about Mr. Lewis?"

Eliza shot a questioning glance at Uncle Rufus.

"The tailor," he said by way of explanation. "He makes mostly dungarees and work shirts, but he can't make them as fast as I sell them. He might have a mind to hire on help." His head bobbed as he weighed the options. "Yup, it would be worth a shot. I'll introduce you to him tomorrow if you like."

Eliza liked the idea very much. That very night, by lamplight, she wrote Papa.

I'm coming home.

ꕥ

At close of business the following day, Eliza tied on her best bonnet and walked beside Uncle Rufus to Mr. Lewis' shop. The narrow sewing room fronted on the main street of town, convenient to Moore's and Froelick's mercantiles. The treadle sewing machine and the tailor's balding crown both gleamed in the light that streamed through the shop's large front window.

"Abram." Uncle Rufus greeted the tailor as they entered, but the sewing machine hummed for several seconds before the man reached the end of a seam and looked up. "I'd like you to meet my niece."

Mr. Lewis shook hands with Uncle Rufus before clasping the hand Eliza offered. "How may I help you?"

"Actually, I was hoping to be of help to you, Mr. Lewis. My uncle tells me that you're enjoying a good deal of success. I wondered if you might have need of a seamstress." She wasn't sure where she found the boldness, but desperate times called for desperate measures.

Mr. Lewis blinked rapidly as he considered the possibility.

"She's a good worker. Meticulous," Uncle Rufus put in.

Mr. Lewis began to nod. "Yes, the notion has merit." His eyes seemed to focus on an invisible chalkboard as he did a few mental calculations. "I can cut and sew two shirts in the time it takes to hand-stitch buttonholes and sew the buttons on one. Same for the waisted overalls. They have half the buttons, but they're twice as thick, don't you see?" He leaned over his machine to grab a finished example of each from a display in the shop window.

The brown serge dungarees had a four-button fly. Eliza tested the weight of the fabric and examined the neat stitches around the buttonholes. At the waist there were six thicknesses of the bulky twill. She frowned. She would need a thimble for that.

The shirts were very fine. Eliza admired the straight line of even stitches in Mr. Lewis' flat-felled seams. Seven mother-of-pearl buttons fastened the front, and two more closed the cuffs. Eliza felt their smooth, lustrous surface with her thumb.

"Miners and cattlemen don't bother with cufflinks, mostly."

"No, I wouldn't imagine they would."

"Would you like to take two of each home with you this evening? I'll pay you ten cents apiece for the work, and you can see how you take to it."

Eliza felt like celebrating, but managed a dignified response. "Thank you, sir. That would suit me just fine."

Mr. Lewis made a bundle of the shirts and work pants and tied it with twine, and then they shook hands all around. As Uncle Rufus and Eliza emerged from the shop, she was busy figuring how many shirts it would take to earn her passage home—determined to amaze Mr. Lewis with her productivity.

The Friday evening riffraff were already swarming to bars and brothels as Eliza and her uncle made their way through the streets. Few took notice of an old man on crutches, but many took notice of the young lady who accompanied him.

Eliza was painfully aware of their lewd stares as she walked slowly so that Uncle Rufus could keep up, trying to buffer him from the jostle of the crowd. She wrinkled her nose as she stepped around tobacco-stained spittle on the boardwalk. Raucous laughter and loud voices spilled out of every open doorway, and the smell of whiskey burned her nose. Eliza wished she could take her uncle's arm, but he needed both to manage his crutches. She hugged the bundle of clothing tight to her chest and squared her chin.

A sudden volley of shouted curses erupted, and Eliza whirled just in time to see a man fly headlong through a pair of swinging doors behind them. The horses at the hitching post shied to one side as the evicted man hit the ground with a thud.

Before the doors could clatter shut, a red-faced bar keep caught them in his massive fists. "And stay out! I don't take credit, and I don't run a charity house for drunks!"

The drunkard's head bobbed for a moment then he rolled over and passed out in the street.

A dark head peeked out beneath the bartender's arm. When it was apparent that most of the onlookers were distracted, the small ragged boy ducked past them and dashed toward Eliza and Uncle Rufus, a loaf of bread in one fist and a wad of bills in the other, moccasins flying.

In less than a second the bar keep was in hot pursuit. "Come back here, you half-breed whelp!"

Eliza jumped clear, but her uncle could not move fast enough to get out of the way. The boy's dark eyes widened, and in a split second Eliza saw a half dozen emotions reflected there—resentment, desperation, fear, and determination.

Determination won out. He dropped one shoulder and launched himself at Uncle Rufus. Crutches went in both directions as the crippled man toppled like a tenpin directly in the path of the angry proprietor, who had no choice but to halt his chase.

"Sorry, Uncle," Eliza muttered as she tossed the bundle onto a bench. "Somebody help him!" she shouted, then she hiked her skirts and pummeled down the boardwalk after the miscreant.

The boy skittered under the stagecoach landing at the corner.

Eliza stooped to see where he was hiding just in time to see him scramble under the supporting structure and scamper out the other side.

He slipped in the dusty street as he dashed around the next corner and barely recovered his footing.

Eliza made it to that corner in time to see him turn the next one. She had the advantage of long legs, but he had the greater advantage of youth and practice, not to mention more suitable footwear. If he made it to the end of the street, he would have no trouble outdistancing her across the rolling meadows to the forest's edge.

Instead, he whipped around the edge of a building—their barn. That was a mistake. Nothing that way but a fenced barnyard.

Eliza caught up with the rascal as he tried to scale the stacked rail fence. She grabbed for whatever she could reach and came up with a handful of fringed breechcloth. One hard yank landed the boy at her feet where he scrabbled to sit. Panting, she examined her young captive.

The boy appeared to be Indian and about ten years old. The breechcloth hung out before and behind his deerskin leggings, and he wore a homespun shirt over all. His hair, scraggly and unkempt, gleamed as black as a raven's wing. Eyes as dark as storm clouds rode high over the pronounced ridge of his cheekbones; the look of fear and resentment had returned. He studied her, panting as well, but said nothing. Something about his expression delivered a fierce, unspoken challenge.

When she could breathe enough to speak, Eliza said the first thing that came to mind. "What were you up to?"

"I am hungry," the boy said simply, shifting his focus to the loaf of bread that had fallen to the ground in the barnyard when he landed.

"Is that yours?" If it was, it was ruined now. The chickens were pecking at it.

The boy nodded, but his eyes betrayed his lie. He eyed the loaf as if he might still consider eating it.

"Did you pay for it?"

He looked at the dirt between his feet. "No." The answer was honest, but the tone was sullen.

"Stealing is wrong."

He looked at her, uncomprehending. "Says who?"

"God says. It is wrong to take things that belong to someone else." Perhaps he wasn't raised to know any better. "What's your name?"

"Joseph. Joseph Kennedy."

Eliza's eyebrows arched high. "You're not Indian?"

"My mother is Ute. My father…my father is drunk."

Eliza put together the fragments of information. "The man in front of the bar—was that your father?"

The boy nodded.

"And that money—did you take it, too?"

The boy looked at the bills in his fist. "It was my father's..." he dropped his gaze, his voice barely audible "...but he spent it all on the whiskey." He raised his cavernous eyes then to look at her face and said again, "I was hungry," as if that explained everything.

And, after a fashion, it did. Eliza thought for only a moment, her lips a straight line. "Then come and eat."

She extended her hand. The boy stared at it then dusted his free hand on his shirt before grasping it. Eliza pulled him to his feet, and he walked beside her to the back door of their home.

Aunt Charlotte's eyes opened wide when they walked in, but she said only, "Hello."

Eliza rested her hand on the boy's shoulder. "Aunt Charlotte, this is Joseph Kennedy. He is hungry," she said, as if that would explain everything.

For now, it was the only explanation needed. Aunt Charlotte favored Joseph with a warm smile. "Then I guess we'd better feed him." She indicated a chair at the table, and Joseph sat as she turned to the stove where a stew was simmering. She filled a bowl to the brim and set it on a plate with a generous hunk of sourdough bread.

As soon as she set the plate on the table, the boy grabbed the bread and began to feast on it. When Aunt Charlotte returned with a spoon, he shoveled the stew into his mouth and swallowed without chewing, then held up his bowl. The starved look was gone from his eyes, but the edge of hunger was still there.

Aunt Charlotte refilled his bowl, and Joseph emptied it again. Eliza filled his mug with well water from a pitcher. As the boy drank, his wary gaze never left them.

Just as he finished there was the sound of horses and a wagon in the front street. Eliza peered past the curtain and watched as two men helped Uncle Rufus from the wagon's bed. He fumbled with his key ring for a moment, then limped through the store, his crutches thumping between each step.

"I declare, I am tired of bein' brung home in a wagon box!"

Eliza held the curtain for him to enter, and his eyes fell instantly on the Indian boy who sat at his table.

Joseph blinked at him anxiously and looked tensed to flee if necessary.

"Uncle, this is Joseph. He was hungry." The simple introduction had worked with Aunt Charlotte.

"Is that so?" Uncle Rufus grumbled as he dropped his battered body into the nearest chair. "Me, too." He handed Mr. Lewis's bundle of finish work to Eliza.

Eliza hurried to lay three more places at the table while Aunt Charlotte filled more bowls with the thick stew. She brought the bread to the table and filled mugs with water.

They sat, and Joseph reached for another slice of sourdough, but Uncle Rufus cleared his throat loudly. Joseph's outstretched hand froze, his gaze fixed on the older man's knit brows, but Uncle Rufus simply folded his hands.

"Bless, our Lord, these gifts that we're about to receive, and bless the hands that lovingly prepared them. Amen." He winked at his hungry guest. "Now you can git you some bread."

Joseph looked all around the room as he timidly lifted a slice of bread. He even stole a glance under the table before he noticed Eliza watching him curiously. "Who was he talking to?"

"God. He was thanking him for our food. God gives us everything we have. Don't you talk to him?"

The boy shrugged. "He hasn't given me so much. Maybe he don't like half-breeds."

His words tugged at Eliza's heart. "I'm sure God loves you, too, Joseph. He's our father in heaven."

She guessed her mistake at once when she saw the boy recoil. The only father he'd likely known lay drunk in the street.

"God is a good father, Joseph. Even if we can't see Him, He watches over us. You can talk to Him any time."

"Speakin' of fathers," Uncle Rufus put in, "yours is in the jailhouse to sleep off his drink. You got a place to stay for the night?"

The boy shook his head.

"You can sleep in the barn, if you like. We've got a comfortable loft. I'll go after supper and tell the jailer you're with us."

The boy's dark eyes were large and frightened as he stared at Uncle Rufus. He nodded as he gulped his last bite, but said nothing.

After dinner, Eliza brought a spare blanket and walked with Joseph to the barn. She lit the lantern that hung from a post by the door. April and May blinked in the sudden brightness.

"Up you go." She indicated the ladder against the wall, and Joseph quickly shinnied up to the loft. As soon as his head popped over the edge, she tossed him the blanket. He disappeared, and Eliza heard him shuffling around in the straw as she checked the livestock's feed and water. "All comfortable?"

The dark head reappeared above her. "This place is good."

"Good night, then." She reached for the lantern. "I'll see you in the morning. We'll get you a good breakfast before we take you back to your pa."

"Miss?"

She paused and in that moment almost felt the hand of God upon her shoulder, inviting her to join Him at work. "It's Eliza."

"Eliza. Do I have to go to the jail tomorrow?"

"Yes, Joseph. We need to get you back to your father."

"He will beat me."

"Why?" Eliza was horrified. "For stealing?"

"For getting caught."

"Maybe we can return the money and pay for the bread first thing. Then you can meet your father with a clear conscience."

"I got no money but what I took. That is why I took the bread. I cannot pay for it."

"Let me take care of that. I will pay for your bread."

The boy squinted at her. "Why?"

Eliza took a deep breath. "Do you remember at supper when we thanked God for our food? We believe He gives it to us, and He is good to us even when we don't deserve it. Joseph, all people do bad things. Some drink too much. Some steal. Some tell lies."

"Some kill people."

Lord, what has this child seen? "Yes, that, too. Our God had a son, Jesus, who paid for the things we do wrong so that we could stand before God with a clear conscience."

"How did he do that? Did he pay money? The judge cannot hang God for stealing."

"Well, actually, God allowed His son to be hung in our place."

The boy blinked in shock.

"'He hath made him to be sin for us, who knew no sin; that we might be made the righteousness of God in him.'"

"I do not understand."

"That means that God made His son, who never did anything wrong, to take our punishment so that we could be right before our Father in heaven."

"Would he do that for me—like you paying for my bread—so I do not get whipped?"

"All you have to do is trust Him and thank Him for it."

"That is all?"

"Well, there's a bit more, but we can talk about that in the morning."

The boy nodded, and Eliza saw him smile for the first time.

She blew out the lamp.

ဢ

Eliza worked far into the night by lamplight. By morning, she had finished both shirts and the dungarees, as well. Forty cents. It would be enough to pay Uncle Rufus and Aunt Charlotte back for the thread she'd used with plenty left over to pay for the stolen bread.

Her mouth twisted to one side as she estimated the remaining profit. Not much. If the Lord wanted her to get home before she had to see Jake again, He would take care of the cost and the timing. Some things were more important.

She fell asleep smiling.

Chapter 13

Joseph was waiting on the back porch when Eliza opened the door Saturday morning.

"Here," he said, holding out the blanket she had given him. From the looks of it, he had shaken most of the straw off and done his best to fold it neatly. "I did not steal it."

"Of course you didn't." Eliza accepted the offering.

Joseph followed her around, stroking the new chicks with one gentle finger as she gathered the eggs. When she finished they stopped at the washbowl.

Eliza handed him the soap. "Smells like Aunt Charlotte's made eggs and biscuits."

"Indians do not eat eggs," Joseph commented matter-of-factly.

"Would you rather just have biscuits? We could probably find some jam."

The boy shook his head, the gleam of a new adventure in his eyes. "No. I will try the eggs."

The boy would need time to taste and experience many things that might be different from what he'd been raised with. She didn't know if what he said about the eggs was true, but thought it would be best not to mention it once they got to the table.

Joseph did nothing to give it away. He took only one curious sniff of the eggs before tasting them then quickly devoured the rest.

After breakfast, Joseph followed Uncle Rufus out to the barn to help with the stock while Eliza helped Aunt Charlotte wash up. She took up the bundle of finished shirts and trousers and went to the barn to find her new ward petting May.

"Ready?"

Joseph nodded and came silently to join her. He tried to look like he didn't enjoy it when Uncle Rufus tousled his hair.

"I need to deliver this sewing first."

They drew a number of stares as they walked through town—the tall woman and the boy in breechcloth and moccasins. Eliza ignored them. Joseph trotted along beside her silently, head high. They reached Mr. Lewis' shop just as he was opening for business.

Joseph waited outside while Eliza went in.

Mr. Lewis untied the bundle and examined each piece closely. He looked pleased. "You do good work, and you're quick, too." He reached into his tailor's apron, withdrew four dimes, and handed them to Eliza. "If you'd like, come back this evening, and I'll give you as much more work as you can handle."

Eliza thanked him.

Returning to her small charge, she dropped a ten-cent piece into his hand.

Joseph blinked up at her.

"To pay for your bread," she explained.

He nodded again and fell in beside her as they made their way back to the saloon. Even this early in the morning, it was open, and one or two customers leaned against the bar.

The proprietor saw them as they entered. "I thought I told you to stay out, you little thief." His face was menacing as he pointed a plump finger at Joseph.

Eliza's mouth twisted in disgust. *You charge this boy with stealing, but you sell his father liquor gladly enough—taking the money that should have bought the child's food.*

Joseph's hand trembled in hers, but he stood erect beside her and showed no fear.

"Actually, it was his father you told to stay out. You told the boy to 'come back here,' and he has." She spoke calmly, but fixed the bartender with a cold, direct stare.

Joseph dropped a fistful of wadded bills onto the bar. "I took this, but now I give it back." He placed the dime beside the pile. "And this is to pay for my bread."

He looked up at Eliza with eyes full of pride and confidence, and she squeezed his hand in return.

The barkeep harrumphed as he snatched up the cash.

"Are you satisfied that the boy has paid his debt?" Eliza asked.

The man recounted the money. "Yeah, I guess so."

With a brisk nod, Eliza placed her hand on Joseph's head and ushered him back outside.

"Thank you." The boyish voice was small and earnest.

"You're very welcome, Joseph. Are you ready to meet your father now?"

He nodded soberly, and the two of them began the walk to the jailhouse.

"Eliza, if I want to tell your God thank you..."

Eliza stopped and looked into the boy's face. "You just tell Him, Joseph. He will hear you."

The boy lifted his face to the morning sky. "Thank You," he said to the wind.

ജ്ജ

The jailer looked through his ring of keys and stuck one into the lock of the barred door. Disappearing inside the cell he returned with a disheveled wreck of a man. He gripped the man's arm tightly, but whether the gesture revealed disapproval or a desire to keep him upright, Eliza could not tell.

Mr. Kennedy had the ruddy, veinous cheeks and red-rimmed eyes of a man long lost in liquor. He stumbled toward them, head down, jowls slack, staggering as if the floor rolled beneath him. His greasy hair was raked into spikes by clawing fingers, and he reeked of urine and vomit. He gripped the edge of the desk to steady himself and stared, unseeing, as the jailer dug in a drawer to retrieve his personal belongings.

Eliza covered her nose and mouth as a salty taste rose in her throat, gagging her, but Joseph broke free and ran. He wrapped his arms around his father's bulging waist then rubbed a comforting hand up and down his back.

"Pa?"

Kennedy did not respond.

"Pa? Do you still feel bad?"

Only when the boy took his hand and bent to stare up into his blank eyes did he seem to see. "That you, boy?" His voice was gruff and slurred. "Where'd you run off to? I needed you."

A surge of anger surprised Eliza. *You needed him? He needed you! He needed food, a bed to sleep in!* It was all she could do not to scream at the man and take the boy home with her, but he would not go if she offered. He loved his father.

"It's okay, Pa. I am here now. You slept. I slept. Now we can go home."

A simple nod almost knocked Kennedy off his feet.

Joseph took his arm to steady him and led him to their waiting wagon.

"You reckon he can stay on the buckboard, or should I help him into the back?" the jailer asked Eliza, as if she'd know.

She shrugged.

"Come on, Pa. Come up by me." Joseph had already scrambled up onto the bench and patted the seat beside him.

With a look back at Eliza and another exchange of shrugs, the jailer half helped, half hoisted Kennedy into his rig. "Hold on tight, now," he advised, and the man flung both arms out to grip the back of the seat.

Eliza wondered if it was the nearest thing to a hug his son was ever likely to feel.

"Can I drive, Pa? Let me help you drive."

Another half-conscious nod.

The boy eagerly took the reins. He looked at Eliza. His eyes thanked her, but he would not voice it.

Somehow she understood that to thank her publicly would be an acknowledgement that his father had neglected to provide for him and left him in need. He could not do it. He could not shame him. He loved him. She hoped that he could read "You're welcome" in her eyes.

Joseph drove with a practiced hand. He'd done this before, and more than once.

The jailer went back inside.

Eliza watched until she lost sight of the wagon.

ꕥ

"Why don't you go on over to Lewis's now? That way you can get back before evening."

This was the second time Uncle Rufus had made the same suggestion.

"I don't want to leave you to close up alone."

Business had been brisk all day, keeping all three of them hopping.

"Aw, we're about at the end of it, I think."

Eliza wished he wouldn't worry about her so, but she could see that he wasn't going to be satisfied until she left on her errand. "All right. I'll walk quickly and come straight home."

"Just be safe."

She really didn't see why he worried so. He knew what she'd left. Waco had earned its nickname, "Six-Shooter Junction." She didn't miss the violent aspect of her hometown.

As she walked to the tailor's shop, Eliza could not ignore the saloon as she had the first time she passed it. Was it just yesterday? Now the sounds and smells brought vivid memories of a boy starved for food and affection. *Bless Joseph, Lord.* The memory of his father turned her stomach but pricked her conscience. *I know You love his father, as well.* He had been young once with a future ahead of him. Who knew what caused him to drown it at the bottom of a bottle? *Bless him, too, Lord, and help me remember to be compassionate.*

Mr. Lewis had eight pieces for her to finish. It would be no trouble to complete the work if she stitched on them tomorrow, but tomorrow was a day for worship. Even if there was no scheduled church service, Eliza could not conscience working on the Lord's day. If she started after supper, she could finish at least three tonight. Perhaps if she got up early Monday she could finish a few more, and then if she worked through lunch ... Mr. Lewis had not said that he expected the work finished by Monday evening, but Eliza was anxious to earn her passage back home.

Tears sprang to her eyes. She couldn't think of Joseph's poor excuse for a father without thinking of her own, her longing and gratefulness combining to produce a poignant surge of homesickness. A dime a shirt, and stage passage would cost over two hundred dollars. Two thousand shirts! Were there so many shirts and trousers in Elizabethtown? And how long would it take her to work enough buttonholes so that she could get home again? It might be easier to strike gold.

At the very least, she knew she could not pass by the bar again. She hadn't the stomach for it. She would take the next street—the one that passed by the stage stop—and post her letter to Papa. Perhaps there would be a letter for her, as well.

Her new route took her by the assayer's office. At the end of each week a crowd gathered there, each man hoping his ore sample would be the high-quality strike that always seemed to lie just under the next rock. If Uncle Rufus was right about gold fever being a sickness, it was highly contagious. Several dozen men laughed and boasted as they waited their turn at the scales.

Once again, Eliza attracted a good deal of attention. The men's gazes were like a scorching heat as she approached, causing her cheeks to burn. She stiffened her spine, looked straight ahead, and kept walking. A shrill whistle sailed over the noise of spirited conversation, followed by ribald laughter and a few coarse jests. Eliza looked away.

"Hey, Stanton!"

The emergence of a prospector from the assayer's office provided a welcome distraction.

"What'd he say? You find a good vein?"

Eliza sneaked a peak beneath the brim of her bonnet. The young man who stood in the doorway did not answer as he tucked a folded slip of paper into his vest pocket, but the expansion of his chest and smug grin were ample indication that the news was good.

"Well? Ain't you gonna tell us?"

The boy who must be Stanton shook his head, but laughed as he threw his arms around the shoulders of the two who plied him for information. "Nope ... but I'm buying the drinks."

Amid whoops and cheers there was a surge for the door. The assayer, an official-looking little man in a business suit, held them back with one hand as he ushered the next in line through the opening.

Stanton and company made their way to the nearest bar, weaving down the boardwalk in front of Eliza as they laughed and elbowed one another, and burst through a set of swinging doors.

Eliza shook her head, but she couldn't help smiling. There was indeed something contagious about gold fever, or maybe there was just something contagious about hope.

At the stage stop, she was pleased to find a letter from Papa. She tucked it into her bundle and hurried home with a lighter step.

"What's the news in town?" Aunt Charlotte was just taking a pan from the oven. She bumped the oven door shut with one hip as she set the pan down to cool.

Eliza laid aside her bundle and untied her bonnet strings. "Mr.

Lewis gave me eight more pieces of finish work." She hung the bonnet on a peg by the door. "And I had a letter from Papa in this week's post." She pulled out the envelope and felt her hair for a hairpin to open it.

"Anything else of interest?" Uncle Rufus looked up from his ledger.

"Well, I think someone may have struck it rich—a Mr. Stanton." She slipped the letter paper from its sheath and turned just in time to see Aunt Charlotte cast a worried glance at her husband. "What's the matter? More money in town means more business, right? And more people coming in once word spreads."

"Could be," Uncle Rufus said cautiously.

"What's the problem, then?"

"Gold makes people act strange sometimes, 'Liza. Stirs up all sorts of envy and mischief. It's best if the news don't get out too quick, but sometimes the young 'uns get full of theirselves. Can't keep a lid on it, y'see? Then someone will come and steal their stash or jump their claim, and it stirs up all kinds of trouble."

"But if the claim is filed in his name—properly recorded and paid for…"

"Filed claim don't count if yer dead."

Eliza felt her throat constrict in fear for the vibrant young man she barely knew.

Her alarm must have been apparent, for Aunt Charlotte suddenly launched into a flurry of domestic activity. "There, now." She wrapped a tea towel around her hand and carried the pan of cornbread to the table. "There's no use borrowing trouble. Come and let's eat, and Eliza can read us Rutherford's letter, if she's willing."

Eliza carried a platter of meat and a pot of coffee to the table, but the unsettled feeling remained. She had lost her appetite and was glad for the excuse of reading Papa's letter.

"The letter is dated the eighteenth of April, so it's only taken six weeks to get here. He says there were over three hundred in the congregation for Easter services, and the bluebonnets were lovely this year. They're spent by now, I guess. It'll be quite warm back home."

She scanned the next few lines. It was news of church members—births and deaths, mostly. The federal officials were gone, but racial tension and atrocities continued. Papa did not go into detail. Occasionally there was mention of a local relative that would be of common interest. These bits she shared.

"And he sends his love to us all and says he is writing you separately." She folded the letter and laid it beside her plate. "That's odd. There was no post for you."

"Not so strange, really." Aunt Charlotte passed her a jar of preserves. "We'll check again next week. It'll find us eventually."

After dinner they settled in for the evening. Eliza was glad for the longer days. It meant more light to work by before the lamps were lit. A window was open to catch the evening breeze, and town noises drifted in on the wind—music and laughter and loud voices.

Eliza's needlework did not require her concentration, and she found herself listening to the sounds, edgy on account of what Uncle Rufus said. Was it louder than usual, or was she just more attentive? The muscles in her shoulders knotted, and her nerves felt as tight as her stitching. She finished one shirt. The sun set, and she started another.

Then a shot rang out, and two more answered it.

Eliza's head snapped up. She looked wide-eyed at Aunt Charlotte, but her aunt's eyes were closed. Praying?

Uncle Rufus rose to close the window, but not before there were more shots.

It had begun.

ꟷ

Much later, Eliza sat staring out her garret window. The night was full of sounds like the night of the riot. A curtain of darkness hid the actors of this murderous drama, but not their angry shouts nor the gunfire that rang out in streets and on the hills. With every shot she jumped and trembled until the pounding in her head echoed the reports of the pistols. The rush of her pulse pounded in her ears—an ominous drumbeat, ticking off the seconds of her life. *Why did you bring me here, Lord?*

Papa sent her in hopes she'd find a man to take Grayson's place in her heart. Aunt Charlotte and Uncle Rufus hoped she could bring comfort to Julia. All Eliza wanted was an escape from her grief—to find a place where men did not hate and fight and kill, a place where she could begin to rebuild some sort of life.

Now it all seemed like a mistake. A cruel jest. She'd found nothing she came for. There was no escape. The pile of unfinished sewing mocked her. Ten cents a shirt. Four dimes for an evening's labor, and one already spent for stolen bread. How many buttons and buttonholes stood between her and a ticket to … to what? Home? Safety? Love? All eluded her. She stared at her workbasket, unseeing. In her mind, thousands of shirts and trousers formed a trail that extended out of sight, littering the hillside like laundry caught in a gale, a useless squandering of effort.

She could not sleep but dared not light a lamp. A single star stood fixed above the ridge. Eliza closed her eyes and laid her brow against the window. The cool pane soothed the ache in her head until another shot rattled the glass in its frame. She bolted upright, and it was several minutes before her heart slowed.

Her faith seemed as fragile as the glass—a thin barrier, able to keep out inconvenient unpleasantness like wind and rain, but ridiculously ineffective for holding real danger at bay. A comforting deception. Just as a bullet could shatter this window, trouble and sorrow had shattered Eliza's hopes despite her many prayers.

She gazed again at the star. Was it the same one that guided their wagon to these hills? *Guide me, Lord. Show me where to go, what to do.*

Men would kill for hate and gold, but one small dime had shown Joseph a love he'd never known.

The noise of violence did not lessen. Eliza had no more answers than she had before. Nothing changed, but her trembling ceased. Everything was as it had been, yet in the moonless night it was as if someone had lit a candle. A lamp for her feet. She still had three dimes and a basket of piecework. She didn't have to see the whole road laid before her. All she had to do was take the next right step.

Weary, Eliza lay upon her bed, and when she opened her eyes, it was morning.

❧

It was Sunday, but no preacher would come today. The streets were as silent as death. When a knock rattled the front door of the store shortly after breakfast, they all jumped then laughed nervously. Uncle Rufus peered around the curtain then he went out and came back with Hiram.

The carpenter and bonesetter gave the ladies a curt nod. "'Mornin'." Eliza wondered if he left off the "good" on purpose. "There was a heap o' killin' last night. I got more work than I can handle." She remembered that Hiram also made caskets.

"How many?"

"At least ten. Seein' as you don't work in your store on Sunday, I was wonderin' if you'd help me with the buryin'."

Uncle Rufus nodded grim assent.

"It would be a ministry," Aunt Charlotte said.

Eliza thought of the young man they called Stanton—barely old enough to shave—and wondered if he was among the dead.

Uncle Rufus left with Hiram. Eliza and Aunt Charlotte said nothing as they tended to the morning chores. Last night left Eliza much to think about, and little enough to say that would make any difference.

"Shall we walk to the hill?" Aunt Charlotte suggested as they finished.

"To do what?" Eliza spoke before she thought and instantly regretted her sharp tone. She dried her hands and reached for her bonnet. "Of course, I'll go with you, but why are we going?"

Aunt Charlotte cocked her head in unspoken question.

"I mean, it does no good to pray for the dead. Wherever they're going, they're already there, and it's too late to change that now. 'While there's life, there's hope,' but for them it's too late."

"It would be a comfort to their families to know that someone marked their passing with a prayer."

The suggestion sounded futile, but Eliza had no better notion, so she merely shrugged and reached for her bonnet.

An uncomfortable silence followed them down the empty streets. Last night the valley resounded with shots; this morning the noise of hammers and the sweeping of glass were the only sounds. As they neared the cemetery hill, Eliza heard the scrape of shovels on stone, as well. She swallowed back tears. It all seemed like such a waste.

She followed her aunt through the gate and around the hill crest to where the men were digging. Nine mounds of rocky dirt were piled at the foot of nine neat holes. Two young men she did not know were working on a tenth. They did not look up.

Hesitating, Eliza looked into the first hole. A pine box looked out of place at the bottom. The wood was yellow and still carried the fresh scent of the tree it came from, but the tree was dead, and so was the poor soul in that box—both cut down in their strength. If he'd still had eyes to see, the dead man could have looked from this hillside where he now lay up to Mount Baldy. Instead of the hole he lay in, he could have seen the holes he and others had dug and scraped and blasted looking for their golden ticket to a happy life. And what had it bought him? Whiskey? A game of cards? A night here or there with a woman whose name he could not remember?

She commended his soul to God, for whatever good it would do. The opportunity to seek and be found was past. She prayed for his family, if he had any. Then she moved to the next hole and did the same.

Six holes.

Six pine boxes.

Six prayers offered a day too late.

A wagon wound its way along the path from town carrying two more caskets. As it neared the gate, the hammers stopped. Hiram and Uncle Rufus would soon be along with the last two.

The two men emerged from the last grave, heaving themselves out of the earth, and went to help carry the dead from the wagon. They returned with two others.

Eliza's breath caught in her throat as she recognized Clay Allison laboring under the weight of the crude coffin. With his club foot, it couldn't be easy going over the rocky ground, but he did not limp. In his square jaw and steely-eyed expression, Eliza thought she recognized both pride and hardened resentment.

She stood quietly by Aunt Charlotte's side as the men lowered the casket beside the hole opposite the mound of fresh dirt. The men looped ropes beneath the head and foot of the coffin and moved to lower the unfortunate soul into his final resting place. Eliza struggled not to judge, but there seemed to be no more hope for Mr. Allison than for the man he lowered into the grave. For all she knew, some of these ten were dead by his hand.

When the casket was at rest, the men freed the ropes and trudged back to the wagon with downcast eyes. But not Clay Allison. He stared directly, shamelessly, into Eliza's face as if daring her to ... to what?

She stiffened her spine and stared back. Their eyes locked and remained so, even over the top of that eighth pine box. What did he want? What did he expect her to say? She was only here to ... to what?

With a shock she realized that she and Clay Allison had at least one thing in common—neither of them knew why she was here.

The men lowered the coffin and snatched their hats from their heads. There was an awkward silence as they stood, heads bowed, looking down into those ghastly holes. Doing what? Praying? For what?

Time and tension stretched uncomfortably.

Eliza saw Uncle Rufus and Hiram as their wagon turned the corner and started out the road from town. It wasn't long before the men heard the crunch of wagon wheels and started toward the gate to meet them—all except Clay Allison. He walked carefully around the crumbling edges of the grave to where Eliza stood.

"Afternoon, ma'am." He inclined his head politely toward Aunt Charlotte. How did he do that? Menacing one moment and exuding charm the next. "Miss Gentry." He remembered her name. "Come to pray?"

Eliza nodded and swallowed, trying to get rid of the lump of reluctance that rose in her throat, but surely she should redeem this opportunity no matter what she thought of the man. "Are you a praying man, Mr. Allison?"

"I have been."

Her face betrayed her shock before she had a chance to school her features.

"That surprises you?"

She blushed. She would not mention that, other than his careful civility toward womenfolk, his actions struck her as anything but Christian. Surely he remembered that she had witnessed firsthand his hateful prejudice and wild ways. "I recall hearing you say that you had no use for God."

"Indeed." He ducked his head as he settled his hat upon it, and when he looked up again the shadow of the brim hid his eyes, but not the glint of resentment in them. "Tell me, *Miss* Gentry..." It did not escape her notice how he emphasized her unmarried title. "...have you found God's dealings fair?"

His question found its mark as surely as a blow. It punched the wind from her best intentions. "I, um..." Aunt Charlotte was watching, but Eliza gathered no help from her. She was on her own. "It rains on the just and the unjust, Mr. Allison. His ways are higher than ours."

"Did yer daddy teach you to say that?" Allison smiled—a smirking, leering, taunting grin that made Eliza want to slap him.

"My papa is a pastor—a godly man and a wise one." She barely managed to keep her words sweet. Her tone was nothing of the sort.

Allison's grin was broader than ever. "Yup. Mine, too."

A breath of a breeze swept over the hill, and Eliza half expected it to knock her over. Even Aunt Charlotte could not mask her surprise. "Your father was a minister?"

"Yes, ma'am. As good a man as you'd ever want to meet, 'cepting you can't on account of he's dead." The grin disappeared; his lips twisted with bitterness as he jerked his thumb toward the graves at their feet. "Just as dead as those men there. Consumption. I was only five, but I watched him die by inches, coughing up his life's blood and praising to the end the God who would not grant him rest. The same God that gave me this." He hitched up his pants leg to display his twisted boot. "My prayin' daddy left a widow and seven young 'uns to make do best we could ... and most times, we couldn't."

The hurt in Clay's eyes might have been merely a reflection of her own. "I am truly sorry for your loss, Mr. Allison, but we cannot blame God. We live in a fallen world."

"Oh, yes, ma'am. I got me a front row seat for that during the war."

It was almost frightening how well Eliza could understand his bitterness. She would never have thought it possible, but her heart began to warm toward Clay Allison. His life had been much like hers. *Lord, here is a man from my own hometown, another child of one of your servants. Not all the wounds of war leave scars upon the flesh.* The scars on Allison's wounded heart threatened to kill his very soul. How could she plead with him to return to the God of his youth?

She had no opportunity now.

Hiram and the other three men bore the ninth casket to its place and went back for the last one. Uncle Rufus painstakingly picked his way around the graves, rocks, and loose soil to stand beside his wife. The hill was silent except for the sound of the wind in the grasses as the last man was laid to rest.

No one moved.

It was Uncle Rufus who broke the uncomfortable silence. "Shall we pray?"

Eliza watched as Clay Allison and the others removed their hats and bowed their heads, if not in reverence, then at least in respect. She hoped that something in Uncle Rufus' prayer might reach them before it was too late for them, as well.

"Lord, our hearts are sore this day. These men were our neighbors. They were young and full of hope. They shared with us the bounty of Your provision. Their untimely deaths remind us that life is precious and fleeting. Cause us, Lord, to make our hearts right with You. Amen."

A murmur of amens went round the circle. The diggers returned to their shovels and soon a hail of stones and soil drummed upon the coffin lids. Clay's hat hid his face as he turned and walked without a word to one of the waiting wagons. Hiram helped Aunt Charlotte, Eliza, and Uncle Rufus into the other, and together they drove back to town.

Whiskey glasses clinked gaily above the tinkling music that poured from saloons and gambling halls as they passed. Now that the mess was cleaned up, it was just another Sunday. Elizabethtown had returned to life as usual, but Eliza had seen that the road through town ended on cemetery hill.

At least now she had a reason for being here.

Chapter 14

The meadow grasses were splashed with wildflowers of every hue as Eliza drove the now familiar road to Zeke and Millie's claim, and a bright summer sun beamed down on her. Beneath its warmth the calico of her dress felt freshly ironed where it stretched across her back. A pleasant starchy smell rose from the fabric. The light breeze teased a strand of hair that escaped her sunbonnet, and Eliza took her hand from the reins just long enough to arrest its flight. Behind her in the bed of Uncle Rufus' wagon, the chicks chirped beneath a gingham tablecloth she'd spread for shade.

The wagon wheels rattled over the bridge, and Millie emerged from the cabin, dusting her hands and waving as the wagon approached. "Oh, how I've missed you!" she exclaimed, welcoming her friend with open arms.

Eliza lifted the first few chicks into Millie's outstretched apron, and then gathered the rest into the tablecloth. They emptied the brood into the yard, and the impotent peeps of alarm ceased immediately as the chicks fell into the steps of a barnyard dance, bobbing and pecking in search of food.

"I guess they're old enough to scratch for themselves," Millie said after they'd watched for a few minutes. "Can you stay and have some tea?"

An afternoon's respite sounded wonderful. "I can catch you up on news. I haven't seen you in town since the wedding."

"I've been feeling a little under the weather." Millie waved off

Eliza's concern. "Nothing serious. Besides, with all the gifts from the pounding, we didn't really need anything, and Zeke's got all he can handle minding his herd now that it's calving season."

It was good to be away from E-town—away from the miners and the constant clatter of commerce. It was pleasant to sit on the porch and rock and chat and watch the chicks scratch. It would have been as near perfect a day as she could ask for this side of heaven if only Millie hadn't asked about Jake.

"He left?" Millie stopped rocking.

"Yes." Eliza really did not wish to discuss the matter.

"Why?" Millie's southern twang got worse when she was excited or upset. The word came out as two syllables.

Eliza shrugged.

"Is that all you're going to tell me?"

Eliza slanted a gaze toward her friend. Millie wasn't about to let this go. She sighed, exasperated. Best to keep it short and as sweet as possible. "We disagreed. He left before I could apologize. It may be for the best."

"Why would you say that?"

"I don't think Jake likes to deal with painful truths. Didn't he escape to the solitude of his valley cabin when Julia died? Didn't he run out here after the war?"

"Didn't you?" Ignoring Eliza's glare, Millie pursued the topic. "Didn't I?" Her gaze was direct but not accusing as she looked into Eliza's eyes, challenging her to answer.

Eliza stared at her hands. "I suppose we did, but I don't think Jake can understand the type of loss we suffered. Invaded. Attacked on our own soil. He was part of that."

"And you can't forgive him? Not even for love?"

"Of course I can, but it does make it harder to truly trust him. How can he possibly empathize with how we feel?"

Millie's face softened with understanding. "Oh, but you were so perfect together." Her voice was mournful, as if she grieved the loss of something that never was.

"Not if we couldn't trust each other. A marriage is a picture of Christ and His church. What sort of mockery is our faith without trust?" Even as she said it, Eliza's own words convicted her. She had not been able to trust Jake when he withheld from her the truth about where he'd been shot. Did she truly trust God, even when He was silent about the reasons for the evil and disappointments that had befallen her? *Perfect love casts out fear.* Uncertainties and questions troubled her like a cloud of gnats. Individually they might be small enough to ignore, but together they continually distracted and plagued her. She waved her hands as if to ward them off and signal an end to the discussion. "It doesn't matter."

"But don't you want a family? Children?" Millie pressed her hand unconsciously to her middle.

"I can have a fulfilling life with God alone. Goodness knows there's abundant need." Eliza hoped she sounded convincing, but she wasn't sure who she was trying to convince—Millie or herself.

ຯ໑ଔ

The sun was well along its trek toward the western ridge before Eliza turned the wagon back toward town. The horse walked slowly, reluctant to leave his grazing. She hated to rush him. She was in no hurry herself to leave the peace of the lower valley to return to the boisterous city, but Mr. Lewis would have finish work for her to pick up along the way. She must be home before closing.

As she neared the first river crossing, shots echoed down the valley. Eliza's head jerked up. Rifles—firing at a distance. Though she could not see the town, the shots sounded closer. She stopped the wagon short of the bridge and searched for the source.

Hooves thundered toward her, and soon she could make out three horsemen, riding like a storm cloud toward the Cimarron Pass. They did not turn or give any indication that they had seen her, but she saw them clearly enough. Clay Allison was in the lead.

Moments later, three cavalrymen galloped past in pursuit. Buffalo soldiers. Chasing the wind. They'd never overtake Allison before he reached cover in the palisades of the canyon.

Eliza waited until they had passed. Their dust settled on the road behind them, and she cautiously eased the wagon over the bridge and onto the main road.

She held the reins loosely, but inside her nerves were reined in tight. Logic told her that the trouble was over, but she sat ramrod straight upon the buckboard, and her gaze darted left and right, searching for any sign of trouble or ambush along the roadside.

She was about halfway home when a small boy darted out into the road ahead of her, eyes wide and arms flying like a crazy windmill.

"Miss 'Liza! Miss 'Liza!"

She recognized Jonathan Ewing and pulled back on the reins. The boy was pulling at her skirts before the wagon came to a stop.

"You gotta come, Miss 'Liza! There's a lady hurt." He hopped frantically in the dust of the road, pointing with one stubby finger.

Eliza looked toward a ravine he indicated.

A military conveyance, pulled off the road, was half hidden in the brush.

Extending her arm she pulled the boy up onto the seat beside her. Tears streaked his dusty face. She recognized the fear in Jonathan's eyes. Not many days had passed since her heart pounded in terror of gunfire in the streets. But she wasn't afraid today. Today she was angry.

"I was fishin' down yonder when I heard shootin'. Please hurry. There's lots of blood. I think she's hurt bad."

Eliza steered the wagon closer, tied off the reins, and clambered down.

More buffalo soldiers. A dark red puddle spread beneath one who lay sprawled on rough ground. Two others hovered over their friend.

"You've had trouble."

"Yes, ma'am."

Eliza recognized the soldier who straightened and came toward her. She had served him in the store. His insignia marked him as a ranking sergeant.

"Gunmen surprised us from that gulch there." He pointed out the spot.

"The boy said there was a lady injured?" Eliza hugged Jonathan to her side as she searched the brush for other casualties.

"Here." The wounded soldier raised a hand and laughed feebly.

Eliza heard the soft voice and looked into the beardless face. A woman! Dressed as a man!

"My cousin," the young soldier beside her explained. He tied off the yellow neckerchief he was using as a bandage and looked up. "She accompanied us when we escorted a family with several young daughters to Colorado. We were headed back to Fort Union."

The young woman motioned toward her cousin's canteen and lifted her head as he obliged her with a swallow. "We had business in Cimarron, Elizabethtown, and Taos on our return. It seemed more practical to travel like this." She winced as she lay back.

"I saw the men your friends were after. If that's who shot you, I know them." It sickened Eliza to turn in Clay Allison, but wrong was wrong. It was violence like this that brought the Freedmen's Bureau to Waco. Papa had not stood for it, and she wouldn't either.

"Allison." The sergeant repeated the name she gave him. "I know him." He kicked at a tuft of grass with his boot and exchanged a look full of meaning with the others. "I told Washington there'd be trouble, but he wanted a night off duty, and he had it coming."

The soldier who knelt beside his cousin saw Eliza's puzzled look. "Last night in Cimarron. Allison was at the bar."

Eliza cocked her head. "Was there a disagreement?" She could easily imagine Clay Allison drunk or brawling over cards, but not these men.

"Sometimes just being there is an offense."

The sergeant's dignified bearing made Eliza ashamed of her naivety. How could she forget that prejudice needed no reason? She nodded. "How can I help?"

"The others should return shortly. If they haven't caught him, we'd be wise to put distance between us and Allison before nightfall." Worry lines creased his brow as he studied the young woman on the ground. "But I don't think she's in any condition to travel."

The young soldier shook his head in confirmation of his commander's prognosis. "I got the bleeding stopped for now, but it could start up again if she moves around."

"I can take her back to Elizabethtown in my wagon," Eliza offered. "I can care for her there, and you can decide what to do about getting her back to Fort Union later."

"But Allison's seen us in your shop," the young soldier said. "He's sure to come around askin' questions. We don't want to make no trouble."

"There's no fit place for her with me, but I have a friend who would keep her."

"You sure?"

Eliza nodded. Anne would make room for anyone, and she wouldn't talk.

The men lifted the wounded woman into the wagon bed, and one brought a haversack to cushion her head. Eliza spread the tablecloth between the boxed sides just as she had to shade the chicks. Her passenger was barely visible beneath the cloth.

For the first time, she remembered Jonathan. "Did you have the cow and calf with you this afternoon?"

"Yes'm. I left them on their pickets when I came a'runnin'. Left my fish, too."

"Well, you did a good thing." The worried expression left the boy's face, replaced by a bashful grin. "Why don't you go and collect them now and take them back to town? Tell Mister Rufus and Miz Charlotte that I'll be along directly."

Satisfied that the danger was past, the boy jogged off toward the creek.

Eliza remembered her errand at the last minute. "Jonathan!"

He stopped.

"Please stop by Mr. Lewis's and pick up my stitching. And let's keep this our secret."

The freckled face scrunched up as he winked, then he was off again.

Eliza climbed into the wagon and looked back. Concern etched the faces that stared back at her.

"Don't worry about your friend. She'll be safe with me, and we'll send word of her progress." She gave them directions to Anne's boarding house before shaking the reins.

The patient in the wagon bed groaned as the wheels jolted back onto the main road.

Eliza drove slowly toward town. No need to rush and invite attention. The deepening shadows would work to her advantage.

ഗ്രൂ

Eliza passed by Anne's street and turned at the next corner so that she could enter from the rear. She saw Anne through the kitchen window, rustling up supper for her boarders. A quick tap and a wave brought her to the door of the larder.

Anne's face was wreathed in smiles, but she grew sober when Eliza glanced nervously toward the wagon bed. "Is something wrong?" Her voice was low and calm.

She could count on Anne to remain unflappable. "Not terribly, but we're going to need your help if you're able." She beckoned and led the way to the wagon, then drew back the checked cloth.

The wounded woman's brown eyes gleamed from the shadows of the wagon box. She blinked once.

"Mercy!" Anne clapped her apron to her mouth. Her wide eyes

assessed the situation. The soft, feminine face. The bloody bandage hastily tied around the uniformed leg. "Let's bring her in."

Eliza helped the woman scoot to the edge of the wagon and transfer her weight to the stoop. She was tall—nearly as tall as Eliza herself—and looked to be about the same age. She drew one of the injured woman's arms over her shoulder. Anne dragged out the haversack and helped on the other side. Together they made it the few feet to the open door, closing it swiftly and softly behind them.

The woman leaned against the jamb while Anne hurried to bring a stool from the kitchen. She collapsed onto it, panting with effort, but tried to smile. "Thank you."

"She needs a place to stay until she's well enough to travel. There's no place for her on ground level at Uncle Rufus's." Eliza kept her voice low.

"Of course she can stay here. I have plenty of room." If Anne had any reservations about how her borders might receive a wounded colored woman among them, she did not voice them.

"It would be best if I didn't stay in your rooms," the injured woman said quietly.

"I was thinking of my daughters' room. It's downstairs, and I can move them in with me so you'll have quiet."

The dark brow furrowed.

Anne patted her arm. "You're weak and wounded. You need someplace clean and quiet to heal up. Let me worry about what anyone might say."

Eliza caught the injured woman's pleading glance. "It's not that, exactly. We need to keep her out of sight. We think it was Clay Allison who shot her. It appears he did it for spite and meanness."

"He may be totin' a grudge," the woman explained. "I don't want to bring trouble to your house."

Anne grasped the difficulty in full. Her fingertips tapped her lips rhythmically as she thought, then her eyes brightened. "There's a washroom just beyond that last shelf." She indicated a narrow passageway at the far end of the storeroom. "I wash so many linens, it assures me of a dry place to hang them, but the weather's mild now. We can rig you a cot the other side of that wall. It's not much, but I dare say you'll be safe there and comfortable enough."

"I'll feel right at home in a washhouse." The woman's relief and acceptance were obvious as she struggled to stand.

Anne placed a hand on her shoulder, urging her to rest a while longer. "I'll get you a bite to eat while my girls make up a pallet." She disappeared into the kitchen and returned in moments with a tin plate and fork.

Sarah and Rebecca followed close behind her and smiled a shy welcome as they passed. Eliza heard the soft scraping of crates on the wooden floor of the washroom. By the time the patient had finished her meal, her cot was ready. The girls parted the hanging sheets like draperies as Anne and Eliza helped her to the makeshift bed, and Eliza noted with satisfaction that the drying linens would provide an extra shield from prying eyes.

The girls left and returned with the haversack, a bowl of warm water, and rags.

"Thank you, dears. If you could take over supper, Miss Eliza and I can take it from here."

The woman rummaged in her pack and drew out a clean nightshirt.

They slipped it over her head and helped her out of her flannel blouse. Then, working carefully, they slipped off her boots and eased the sticky fabric of the neckerchief bandage and light blue trousers away from her injured thigh.

Pink muscle showed clearly against the brown skin. Eliza's stomach lurched at the sight, and she swallowed hard, concentrating only on the work at hand as she wet a rag and gently cleansed the area around the wound. "How's that?" She looked up.

Tears traced wet trails in the road dust that clung to the dark cheeks.

Eliza's eyes pooled with hot tears of strain and sympathy. "Oh, have I been too rough? Are you hurting?"

The patient waved her hand in dismissal of Eliza's concerns, but it was a moment before she could speak. "You've been so kind." Her dark eyes glistened. "I feel like a real woman."

The words and the way she said them hinted at many things that Eliza could only surmise. How had this woman come to be in a military uniform, stripped of insignia? What, indeed, was she if not a "real woman"? The world had surely not always been a kind place for a woman of color.

Shot—just for being.

The leering, malevolent sneer of Clay Allison invaded Eliza's mind, and she bowed her head in shame. She had thought him so handsome when they met at the stage stop in Cimarron. She'd been so glad to see someone from home. *Pretty is as pretty does.* She found nothing attractive about him now. The tears she had forced back finally overflowed and splashed onto her skirt, unheeded. Men like Clay Allison made her ashamed to be from the South, ashamed to be white. Had he none of the traits of his Christian father?

She sniffed and caught another unbidden tear with her sleeve. She kept her head down as she gently wrapped the rag bandages around the wounded thigh. Even when she finished, she could not bring herself to look up.

A warm hand rested on her wrist. "Thank you. You've done more than enough."

Eliza looked up, directly into the soft brown eyes. "Do you have a name?"

The woman smiled. "Cathay. Cathay Williams."

ꕥ

Once Cathay was settled, Eliza left her to rest with promises to return the following day.

When she reached the store, Uncle Rufus was on the porch, watching for her. He backed the wagon into the barn, and Eliza helped him unhitch the horse and lead it to the stable beside April and her calf.

Leaving the currying to him, she washed a smudge of blood from her hands before going in to help Aunt Charlotte.

Trout sizzled in a pan atop the stove, and a bundle of shirts lay on the bench beside the door.

"I see Jonathan made it back. I hope I didn't worry you."

Aunt Charlotte's face seemed strained, but her voice was calm and controlled. "He said there was a shooting along the road."

Eliza nodded. "Clay Allison and two others ambushed a detachment of soldiers from Fort Union."

"Whatever for?"

"Buffalo soldiers."

Aunt Charlotte shook her head, but the implication was clear. "And a woman was shot?"

"A flesh wound. I took her to Anne." Eliza set a plate at each place at the table and got another for the fish.

"That was wise." The trout were golden brown. Aunt Charlotte removed them to the platter and handed it to Eliza. "Anything else?"

"I don't know much more, really. We got her cleaned up and fed, but she was tired. I hadn't the heart to bother her with too many questions today. I'll stop by and check up on her when I take the shirts back to Mr. Lewis tomorrow." Eliza placed the fish on the table. "I'm glad I have money to give Anne for the cost of her care."

Aunt Charlotte placed her hands on her hips and fixed her gaze on Eliza. She pressed her lips into a thin line, but a smile tugged at their corners. The turning fork was still in her hand, making her look rather comical.

"What?"

"I thought you were saving up your sewing money to go home. Playing the good Samaritan first to that Indian boy and now to this woman, you're not likely to get out of here anytime soon."

"Oh, that." Eliza affected a rueful expression, twisting her lips in mock regret. "I've been thinking about that." She'd turned it over in her mind all the way home. Joseph, Cathay—even Clay Allison ... they were not chance encounters. She knew it in her heart, in her spirit. They were more like the wandering stars Captain Price spoke of that long-ago night on the high plains, pointing the way to some sovereign purpose to give her life meaning.

"And?"

She had, as Papa foretold, light for the next step—some glimmer of understanding, her sign from God saying, 'Here is the way. Walk ye in it.' "I've been thinking that there isn't really any place to run from our troubles. 'Wherever you go, there you are.' If I don't deal with them here, I'd be likely to take them with me no matter where I go."

Despite her satisfaction with this philosophical epiphany, she sighed. She still had troubles aplenty, and in some ways more than she'd had when she came. The bitterness was fading, though, and that alone was a relief.

Aunt Charlotte looked amused. "And the trouble named Jacob Craig ... how will you deal with that?"

The rueful expression on Eliza's face was genuine now. She pursed her lips. "I don't know. I'd still like a chance to smooth things over with him, but at the same time I dread seeing him. It's awkward, but I think I've made an end of that."

Aunt Charlotte cocked her head to one side and raised a skeptical eyebrow. "In and out of love so soon, fickle girl? That doesn't sound like you."

Eliza shrugged. “He’s a good man, and I noticed—that’s all. But it doesn’t mean it was meant to be. I would simply like for there to be peace between us.” Her voice, even in her own ears, had taken on the same not-quite-convincing tone she had tried on Millie earlier. She took a deep breath and tried again. “I am determined to be content, and it might as well be here as anywhere.”

Chapter 15

Eliza slipped away after the lunch crowd dwindled, a bundle of finished shirts under her arm.

"I was surprised to see Jonathan Ewing come for your work yesterday." The tailor peered over his spectacles.

He was too polite to pry, but his fixed gaze held questions Eliza could not safely answer. If Clay Allison harbored a grudge against the buffalo soldiers, it wouldn't do to have Cathay's presence rumored around town.

She kept her tone light and conversational. "I took some hatchling chicks out to a friend's ranch and stayed for a visit." It didn't explain at all how she had come to send Jonathan, but Eliza hoped it would suffice. She didn't think anyone had seen Cathay with her when she returned to town, but she'd take no chances.

The tailor counted dimes into her palm. "Can you take more work?"

Eliza nodded, and he handed her another bundle. "I'll have these back tomorrow."

The bell on the door jangled as she left before Mr. Lewis could ask any more questions. She hurried to Anne's house. A satisfied smile flitted across her face as her fingers patted the tiny bulge in her pocket. The silver coins were too light to jingle, but they were hers.

She knocked on the front door as if paying a casual visit and nodded to a few boarders in the parlor as Anne led her back to the kitchen.

"Come. I'll pour you some coffee."

"How's our patient today?" Eliza asked once they were safely out of earshot.

Anne handed her a steaming cup and a slice of pie and nodded toward the back room. "See for yourself."

Eliza slipped through the larder and rapped lightly on the door frame of the laundry room. "It's me—Eliza."

"Come in."

She ducked around the hanging linens.

Cathay struggled to sit as Eliza approached and smiled when she handed her the pie.

"Dried apple, I think." She pulled the stool close and kept her voice low. "How are you feeling today?"

"Antsy." The answer brought a soft laugh. "I can't wait to get back on the road."

"We'll take a look at your leg when you're done and see how it's healing up." Eliza offered Cathay the coffee, but she declined. She took a sip herself. Any number of questions jockeyed to be first in her mind, but it would be rude to press for information that didn't concern her.

Cathay, who had been watching her silent struggle, suppressed a smile. "You're wondering how a black woman came to be traveling with buffalo soldiers, and in uniform, no less."

Eliza's cheeks warmed, but she had to nod an admission. "I guessed you borrowed it and removed the insignia for the trip back. Like you said, it's more practical for riding in rough country, and it might look inappropriate for one woman to travel alone with a company of men."

"You're close." Cathay handed her the empty plate. "But the uniform was mine."

Eliza's eyebrows shot up before she could school her features. The explanation answered her first few questions, but she had plenty of others.

The wounded woman laughed. She pulled her pack up onto the cot and set it into a corner to brace her back, then stretched out her leg and began to unwind the first layer of bandages.

Eliza braced herself for the worst, but the blood stains were minimal. "May I ask how that came about?"

Cathay leaned back and closed her eyes as Eliza gently removed the compress. "I was a house girl back in Missouri. When the war came to us, my master died."

How would it feel to call any man 'master'? "Was he good to you or cruel?"

"That don't so much matter now. He gave me my food and a roof for my head. The Yankee soldiers said we was free, but I had no one and no place to go."

Eliza nodded. She well understood the quandary that had been one of the South's objections to a hasty emancipation. Even under a harsh master one would not starve.

"My cousin and my friend signed up to go with General Sheridan."

Eliza stifled an involuntary shudder. She hated even the name of that man. Instantly she repented, but her lip curled again almost as soon as she ended her prayer. He, more than any other, embodied the cause of all she had suffered.

Cathay continued. "They said not to worry, that they'd take care of me. Send money back, you know? But I got to thinking. If I was truly free, I didn't want no man giving me my food. I wanted to make my own way. So I said no; I was going, too, and I signed on as a camp woman to cook and do for the soldiers. It was what I'd been doin' anyway, so I figured I might as well get paid to do it."

Eliza sat on the stool, a bandage in one hand, her mind a thousand miles away.

"So I just walked away from there—away from my old, sad life—and I walked all the way to Georgia. I cooked, and I washed, and I brung food to the sick, and I got paid to do it ... but not as much as my cousin, 'cause he was a man. And then we come to the end of the war."

Suddenly Eliza remembered what she was about. She gingerly peeled off the last pad to reveal the wound. They both looked. It was improved from yesterday—healing nicely. She picked up a bottle of whiskey, and Cathay winced as she applied the liquid. Here was one good use for the stuff. Eliza groped in her mind for something to say to distract the patient from the pain. "The end was likely the best thing about that awful war."

"It was. And we were free, but we still couldn't read nor write. How were we supposed to feed ourselves?

"General Sheridan said there was land out west. Folks was all going that'a'way, and they needed soldiers to protect them from the wild Indians. So my cousin and my friend signed on for that. They told me to go on home, but where's that?"

Eliza had finished her ministrations. She patted the wound dry and applied fresh rags.

The patient settled back into the corner again and resumed her story. "So I thought on it a spell, and then I says, 'I'm coming, too.'

"And they laughed—oh, my, how they laughed at that. 'You a woman,' they says, and I says, 'I know that ... and you know that, but the army don't know that.'

"'General Sheridan don't know that Cathay Williams is a woman?' they says, and I says, 'He surely does, but he don't know William Cathey.'"

The woman before Eliza grinned broadly and winked at her surprise.

"I am as tall as a man, and I been walking the same miles every day, and I been cookin' and carryin' and hauling wet bed sheets out of the wash pot at the end of a pole, so I reckoned I could tote a rifle just as easy."

They both laughed.

"So I cut my hair, and I put on men's clothes, and I signed up with them, and if that government doctor was too blind to notice a few things, I wasn't about to tell him. I walked the same miles as before, and I did the same work as before, and I got paid a sight more than before. And now they commenced to teach us how to read and work sums.

"We come west with General Sheridan to Fort Union, and for two and a half years I was proud to be William Cathey, earning my way in the world. But then I wondered if Cathay Williams could earn her way, too. So I got sick one day, and that doctor was right smart. He figured out that I was a woman, and they mustered me out." Cathay laughed, but there was irony in the laughter. "...and I went right back to the kitchen and the laundry room."

Eliza nodded her understanding. She was blessed to have a father who educated her and gave her a meaningful place in the world, but it was not a popular choice even for a white woman. She had been ostracized, but now she had experienced the deep satisfaction of working for her own wages. She still wanted all the same things any woman wants—a home and children—but she was proud of her accomplishments. Her strength. Her ministry. So here they sat—two women. One white, one black. One Yankee, one Southern. And yet they understood one another.

Eliza wound a roll of muslin strips around Cathay's leg. "So ... what will you do?"

Their eyes met. "I don't know yet." When Eliza finished, Cathay eased back and closed her eyes. "Colorado's pretty."

Eliza rose. She mustn't overtire her patient. "I'll write to your sergeant at Fort Union and tell him you're improving. Your cousin will want to know."

"Um-hmm. That's good." The eyes remained closed, and the voice was drowsy. "But don't say nothin' yet about comin' to get me."

ꟹ

Eliza's first days in E-town, when helping Aunt Charlotte mind the store was all she could manage, were forgotten in days filled with activity. Now she helped with the livestock before breakfast, tended shop, assisted with meal preparations, took her turns in the garden, sewed on enough buttons to pave a street, and still managed to stop by Anne's boarding house to check on her patient daily. Concerned that the frequency of her visits would arouse questions, she added one more project to the list. Eliza and Anne volunteered to organize a dance as part of Elizabethtown's elaborate Fourth of July celebration.

"We might prevail upon someone to give us use of one of the large halls or dining rooms in town, but if the band uses the platform at the stage stop as a bandstand, we could dance in the streets." Anne never looked up from the pan of new potatoes she was quartering.

"I like that idea. There's plenty of room at that corner for a grand march or Virginia reel. Uncle Rufus is planning on playing his fiddle. Who else plays?"

Anne patted her hand. "I know lots of folks. You leave that to me." She dumped the potatoes into a pot and returned with a pan of beans. "You can be in charge of decorations."

Eliza reached for a bean, pinched off the stem, and unzipped the stringy edge before snapping the vegetable in two. "It will be dusk—after the covered dish supper, but before nightfall."

"With any luck, we may be able to delay the revelry and inevitable debauchery."

"I never believed much in luck."

Anne nodded understanding. "I know, but I've long since lost faith in peaceful sobriety around here."

Both women laughed uncomfortably.

Eliza tossed another handful of beans into the pan. "If we do hold the dance in the streets, perhaps we can hang kerosene lanterns from cables between the upper stories."

"Yes, and we could place buckets of flowers around the bandstand. Can't you just imagine how beautiful it will be when the sun sets and the stars begin to come out?" Anne's wiggling fingers traced an arc above her.

A vivid vision was already playing out in Eliza's head.

Music, stars, and whirling dresses.

Jake extending his hand, asking her to dance.

She stopped short and swallowed hard. She must not allow her mind to wander in that direction. She diverted the topic. "I'll see how many at church would be willing to loan lanterns. Uncle Rufus can supply the kerosene."

They discussed a few other details before Anne made a suggestion. "It's been a hard year for your uncle. I hate to ask him to donate the kerosene, but would he be willing to sell it to us at cost? Maybe we can sell pie by the slice to raise money."

"That's a good idea. I'll ask him, though most folks would be willing to help."

"I still wish you'd let me help with the sick woman and not insist on paying me to board her."

"Nonsense. I'm glad to do it."

"So would I be."

"But I brought her here. Speaking of ... she's walking without a limp now and gaining strength every day on your good cooking."

"...which I should get back to." Anne's practiced hand had made short work of the pile of beans. Now she rose and dumped them into the pot with the potatoes. "We've about finished here, anyway."

Eliza took her cue. "Aunt Charlotte will need my help, and then I have buttons to sew." She picked up her bundle, hugged her friend, and left.

She walked slowly, deep in thought, until a low whistle like the call of a bird caught her attention. Eliza stopped and looked around. She had just passed the fenced entrance to the side passage leading to the barnyard. She heard it again, louder this time and off to her left. As she looked, a tan face peeped around the compost pile.

"It is me, Eliza. Joseph."

Warmth flooded her heart, and she knew it showed on her face when the boy returned her smile. "Joseph! Should you be here?"

"Pa is ... busy." Only a hint of a scowl betrayed the truth. His father must be drunk again. "He will not miss me."

Eliza decided to use the rear entrance. She let herself in through the gate and wrapped an arm around the boy's thin shoulders. "Are you hungry?"

"Yes, ma'am, please ... if your God gave you enough today."

"He did, as a matter of fact." She laughed. He hadn't forgotten their conversation. Perhaps she would have a chance to tell him more.

He followed her to the garden, carefully closing the gate behind them. "What are you going to do?"

"See if there are any beans ripe, or maybe pick some lettuce." She pulled up the leaves of one bush with an abundance of flowers on top.

Joseph put his hands on the knees of his fringed leggings and squatted to look under the leaves. "No. No beans today."

"Lettuce, then." She led the way to the next row and knelt to gather a few leaves. Joseph was on his haunches beside her. The fringe of his loincloth dragged a pattern in the dirt. He held the front flap up like an apron to hold the leaves as Eliza picked them. "You can pull a few radishes, if you like."

With one grubby brown hand, Joseph gripped a sprout near the root and pulled. Up came a radish, dumping the boy on his sitter as he overbalanced. He laughed, scrambled up, and reached for another. Soon his breechcloth held a salad.

Aunt Charlotte showed no surprise when they entered. Eliza had seen her peek out the window when she heard the boy's laughter. Now she smiled a welcome greeting. "Hello, Joseph. Would you like to stay for supper? I see you've already helped with the preparations."

The raven head nodded eagerly, then he scampered out to the porch to wash. "You have a good garden," he announced when he returned.

"Yes, we do. The rains have been good this year—just enough at just the right times." Aunt Charlotte tore the lettuce leaves into a bowl. "Do you keep a garden?"

"My mother does." Joseph grabbed a double handful of leaves and tore with gusto. "She plants corn, mostly, and pumpkins and squash. Oh! And hot red peppers to string and make soup."

There was someone at home, then, who attempted to make life good for Joseph. The same woman who wove his patterned breechcloth and made his leather leggings and moccasins. What type of woman would marry a man like Charles Kennedy? Surely there were far worse things than being single.

Aunt Charlotte handed the boy a radish. "And do you help her plant the seeds?"

Glints of blue shone as Joseph's ebony hair swished when he nodded.

Eliza longed to plant a few seeds of hope into Joseph's life—seeds that would bear fruit to nurture his soul. But if she pushed, said too much too soon ... perhaps a story would not offend. "I know a story about a man who planted seeds," she began timidly.

Joseph leaned forward in his chair and wrapped his feet around the legs, planting his chin in his hands.

"As he scattered them some fell on ready soil, but some also fell among the weeds, and some among the rocks, and some along the path. What do you think happened to the seed that fell on the road?"

Joseph looked confident and did not pause before answering. "Seed will not grow on the hard road. The birds will eat it all."

"You are exactly right. And what about the seed that fell between the rocks?"

This time the boy scrunched up his face in thought. "It may grow, if there is dirt, but it will not make it through the hot summer. Its roots cannot go down to find water."

Aunt Charlotte laughed as she sliced the radishes. "Joseph, you are a very good gardener."

The boy beamed at her praise. "Shall I tell you what will happen to the seed that fell where there are weeds? It will grow, but if the summer is hot with little rain, the other plants will steal the water it needs. It will not be a strong plant. Not much fruit." He wrapped his fingers around his neck and crossed his eyes comically, pretending to choke.

He was so close, his need so great. Did she dare to press on? Her time with him was short. Did she dare not to? "Joseph, do you remember what we talked about before?"

"About the God who paid for the things I do wrong?"

Eliza nodded. "Jesus said that the seed is like the news that God loves us. Some people hear it, but their minds are hard like the path. They don't want to listen, or they don't understand what they hear, and soon enough the evil one comes and takes any thought of it away.

"There are some people who are like the rocky ground. They are glad to hear the news, but their lives are hard. The joy springs up inside them, but they can't find the water of encouragement to grow..."

Eliza's voice trailed off with her thoughts. Rocky ground described her life as well as Joseph's. Her father's faith seemed bred into her, but when adversity put her to the test, it was hard to remember and believe that God was good—that He loved her. She thought of herself as strong, independent, ministering to others. Could it be that she served God assuming that He somehow owed her blessings in return? The thought shook her to her core.

Joseph nudged her. "Go on. Tell the story."

She didn't realize how long she'd stood there—had to shake her head to stir her memories. What was the point in trying to explain God's love to this boy unless she was convinced of it herself? But there he stood, so needy, eyes shining. What other hope had she to offer him? She had to continue. "Then there are the people who have weeds in their lives—other worries and pursuits that take all their time."

"Like gambling and getting drunk?" He made the connection quickly.

The message was reaching him, despite her limitations. The power was in the story, not her skill in the telling. "Yes, Joseph. Just like that. It chokes the joy right out of their lives."

"What about the good dirt?"

"It's soft and ready to hear good news. When belief takes root, it finds the encouragement it needs to grow strong and bear fruit. I think that means that it tells other people with ready hearts that God loves them, too." Like she was trying to do.

Joseph scrunched up his nose. "Is that the end of the story?"

"No. The end is the best part. The seeds God plants live forever."

His face blossomed into a smile, touched by the warm sun of hope.

ꕥ

Eliza carried the last supper plate out to the washboard on the porch. The plaintive call of a mourning dove drifted on a cool evening breeze. The sky above the ridge was shot through with gold. The Lord's mountain treasure—just like the leaves of gold and silver Jake described. Her stomach clenched. She longed to share the thought with him. Knowing that she could not caused a hollow ache inside her, but it did no good to dwell on such things. *Stay busy.* She drew a cleansing breath and turned to go back into the house.

"We'd better get you back to your Pa," Uncle Rufus was saying to Joseph as she entered.

"I can go alone."

"It's all right, Joseph." Eliza seized the excuse for a change of scenery. "I'd enjoy a short walk."

The three of them strode the board sidewalk. "He was in here," Joseph said as they reached the third in a row of saloons along the main street.

Uncle Rufus peered over the swinging doors that flapped as the boy entered.

Looking over his head, Eliza watched the child scan the faces at the bar and gaming tables. His father was nowhere to be seen.

Uncle Rufus beckoned for him to return.

The boy pointed across the street. "He might be in that one. He goes there sometimes."

As Eliza turned to step into the dusty road, Joseph yelped. Whirling, she saw the angry bloodshot eyes of Charles Kennedy glaring into the startled face of his son. His fist clutched a hank of the boy's hair, and he pulled it so roughly that the child's feet almost left the ground. Light glinted off unshed tears in the boy's eyes.

"I been looking all over town for you, boy." Kennedy bellowed, his speech slurred.

The ruckus drew curious stares. Eliza noticed Clay Allison in the gathering crowd of onlookers and cringed, but no one made any move to become involved.

"We invited your son to supper." Uncle Rufus offered his hand in a gesture of good will. "I'm sorry if we worried you."

The drunk did not release his son to accept the handshake. He did not acknowledge Uncle Rufus at all. His unfocused eyes found Eliza, and his face hardened. "You."

"Yes, sir. I believe we met..."

He gave her no chance to finish. "You stay away from my boy, you hear? I won't have him running off, neglecting his responsibilities, on account of you." He suddenly remembered his son and gave him a hard shake by the hair, jerking his head around. "If I catch you running off again, so help me I'll deal with you so you wish you hadn't. You hear?" He shook him again, and Joseph bit his lip to keep from crying out.

Uncle Rufus laid his hand on Charles Kennedy's arm. "Hear, now. There's no need to blame the boy. The fault is ours entirely, and it won't happen again."

To shake the calming hand free, Kennedy let go of his son. The child sprawled into the street and scrambled away, swiping at tears of pain and anger with the sleeve of his shirt, but his father had already forgotten him again. "Just stay away from me and mine," he roared.

Eliza stole a glance at Joseph. His dark eyes flashed, and he squared his chin in defiance. His fists were clenched. Almost imperceptibly she shook her head. His eyes conveyed wordless questions. She longed to hug him, to comfort him, but to do so would only invite more abuse. Beside her skirt, where his father would not see, she extended her hand in a calming gesture. *Just let it be for a while.* She tried to reassure him with a smile.

The child did not return it. He fixed his eyes on his moccasins, and a tear made its way slowly down his still-round cheek.

Kennedy lunged and grabbed his son roughly by the shoulder, hauling him to his feet. The boy winced and twisted in his grasp as he marched him away. Neither of them looked back.

Oh, Lord, let the seeds sown take root. She might not have another chance with Joseph, and his life was so like the rocky ground. Eliza's heart was heavy as Uncle Rufus took her hand and turned her toward home. Had she said enough?

Chapter 16

New pink skin covered the wound on Cathay's leg. Eliza prodded it gently with her fingertips. It was shiny, but flat and cool. No sign of swelling or infection. Eliza perched on her stool, placed both hands on her knees, and exhaled. "I don't think you'll be needing these anymore," she said, tossing the soiled bandages into a pile to be burned.

A blazing spark of determination lit Cathay's eyes. "I can go?"

"I reckon so, whenever you feel ready. Have you decided where you're going?"

The dark head bobbed once. "Pueblo, Colorado."

Eliza raised one brow. She'd obviously made up her mind. "Why there?"

Cathay was already rummaging in her haversack for a change of clothes. "That's where we come from—where we dropped that family we was escortin'. They were good people, and Pueblo was a right nice town. Gold there, too." She pulled out a clean military-cut blouse and trousers like those she wore when Eliza first met her. "Yes, ma'am! I believe I will find me a place to stay, plant a little garden, and take in laundry and sewing. I could like that."

A nagging worry plucked at Eliza's mind. "Which route will you take?"

"Raton Pass. Same way I came in." Cathay left off unbuttoning her nightshirt. "Why?"

"Through Cimarron?"

Instant understanding sobered Cathay's features. "You think he'll still be there—the man that shot me?"

"I certainly do, unless he's here in Elizabethtown. I saw him just the other day. He herds cattle on a spread north of Cimarron on the road to Raton, and he seems to divide his time and his troublemaking pretty equally along that route."

"And you think he'd still make trouble for me?"

"Could be. Clay Allison is unpredictable, but that's one skunk I'd just as soon not poke. For now, he doesn't know you're here. Can you go the other way—west through Taos?"

Cathay sank to her cot. "I could, but that way takes me south before I can go north." She rubbed her leg above the scar. "I ain't sure how many miles I'm good for just yet."

"Is there any other way?" Eliza knew there was a road north. It was the road to Jake's valley, but she had no idea where else it led.

"There is another way—the Red River Valley."

That was it. Uncle Rufus told her about the river that flowed north—the one Jake helped tap to bring water over to this valley for the mining sluices.

"They cleared a road over the ridge for the work wagons when they built the Big Ditch a couple years back. It'll be rough going after that—just hunting trails along the river until it dumps into the Rio Grande—but that should bring me out closer to the border."

Eliza slapped her knee and rose from the stool. "That's the route we ought to take, then. The Ditch and the rivers will show us the way right enough."

Cathay slanted her eyes toward her. "What you mean, 'we'?"

"You said the route was rough." Cathay didn't look persuaded. "You can't just march out of here in uniform, and you surely can't traipse out in a skirt, now can you?"

Cathay pursed her lips. "What are you suggesting?"

"I'm suggesting that folks are less likely to notice two men leaving town, and no one will make trouble for you if they think you're my servant."

The freed woman frowned.

"It's only until we get you out of E-Town. I can get the clothes we need from my uncle's store, and we can borrow his horse to spare your leg."

"Borrow?"

"Well, it will be borrowing once I return it." Eliza held up her hand to stop the objections she saw coming. "And I'll pay for the clothes. I just don't think it's wise to tell my uncle we're leaving. He'd never approve of my going. He'd take you himself, but he's lame. If we leave Sunday afternoon, he may not even miss me before I return."

Cathay's lips stayed puckered in thought as the silence stretched between them.

"We can do this." Eliza heard the pleading tone in her own voice. "Let me do this. Please."

Dark eyes stared into hers then dropped as Cathay rolled the fresh shirt again and stuffed it back into her pack. "What day is this?"

"Saturday. We can leave tomorrow after lunch."

Cathay tucked her chin and rebuttoned her nightshirt. "I'll be ready."

ꕥ

Since he left Cimarron at first light, the circuit rider came earlier in the summer. The church bell rang midmorning, calling the people of Elizabethtown to worship. As usual, a handful answered the call.

Eliza sat bolt upright on her pew, struggling to focus. A horsefly buzzed and banged against the pane of glass beside her, frantic to escape but no closer to accomplishing that end for all his efforts. She knew the feeling.

She had been up half the night, waiting until the house was quiet. Creeping through the store, she'd selected two shirts, two pairs of work pants, and a package of jerky. As an afterthought, she grabbed a pair of boots and a hat to hide her hair.

Her conscience smote her.

She was stealing.

Shoving the accusation to the back of her mind, she'd wrapped the clothing in a canvas tarp and lifted the door latch ever so slowly, praying that the hinges wouldn't squeak. Would God honor a thief's prayer for stealth? She held her breath and listened, but the comfortable sounds of deep breathing did not change. Her aunt and uncle slept soundly, suspecting nothing. Eliza felt worse than ever.

April had blinked at her as she entered the barn, but none of the livestock were alarmed by her presence. Eliza pulled the pants on under her skirt. They were long enough, but felt stiff and strange around her legs. She wriggled to settle them on her hips, then buttoned the top button. The waist gaped, but she couldn't take a smaller size and still sit a saddle. She grabbed a length of rope. If need be, she could cut a piece to use as a belt. Jamming her bare feet into the boots, she walked a few steps to test them. They felt awkward, too. Her own shoes were broken in comfortably for her right and left foot, but these were new and cobbled on the same last—identical. She pulled them off again. They'd have to do.

She'd rolled everything back into the tarp then looked for a place to stash it.

Once the bundle was safely stowed in the barn loft, Eliza slipped barefooted up the stairs. Her room was pitch dark, but sleep would not come. She reviewed the list in her head over and over and over again. A dress. Cathay would need one when she got to Colorado. Tossing back the covers, she felt her way across the room and pulled out the blue calico—the one that had been her favorite, now mended. She'd tried to feel generous, but could not enjoy it. She hated deceiving Uncle Rufus and Aunt Charlotte, but there was no remedy for that.

This morning she was exhausted, but fears and details assaulted her brain like that infernal fly in the window. They would both have their chance to escape when the sermon ended. A trickle of sweat ran down her spine, and Eliza shivered to attentiveness. The circuit rider's voice droned in the warm room. She forced her mind to hear his message.

"'If a brother or sister be naked, and destitute of daily food, and one of you say unto them, Depart in peace, be ye warmed and filled; notwithstanding ye give them not those things which are needful to the body; what doth it profit? Even so faith, if it hath not works, is dead.'"

The words were balm for Eliza's troubled conscience. Cathay had need of clothes and safe passage from this valley. Uncle Rufus would understand that ... when she could tell him. In the meantime, it was easier to ask forgiveness than permission.

She rose for the final hymn then bowed her head for the benediction. Her "Amen" was a little too hearty. Aunt Charlotte inclined her head forward to glance down the bench at her. Was that look in her eyes amusement or suspicion? Perhaps she should not seem too anxious to fly through the open doors.

Eliza slowed her steps as they made their way down the aisle. She offered the preacher her gloved hand. "A fine message."

"Yes, indeed," Uncle Rufus agreed. "I wonder, Pastor, if you're acquainted with Charles Kennedy who runs a roadhouse on the way to Taos?"

"Heard tell of him, but my route takes me to Mora from here. Why do you ask?"

"Your sermon brought him to mind. We've had occasion to feed and lodge his son a time or two when the father's been too drunk to care for him. Is there anything the church can do?"

The circuit rider looked uncomfortable as he shook his head. "I could try to visit with him—invite the family to church."

From the corner of her eye, Eliza saw the man behind them scowl. "That that Injun boy I seen you with, Rufus?"

Uncle Rufus ignored the rudeness of the interruption and simply answered the question. "Yes." He turned again to the preacher. "The boy's name is Joseph. I believe the mother is Ute."

"That could complicate the matter, but I would be glad to try. It sounds as if the family could use our help."

"It surely is a shame how some people live." The man behind them obviously now considered himself a part of the conversation. "Them Injuns was raised heathens. Ain't no tellin' if they can ever really be changed." He reached to hug his children a little closer to himself. "They just ain't like us."

For a moment Eliza had no words, and then she had entirely too many all at once. Her mouth gaped, but no sound came out. When she could finally collect her thoughts, she blurted, "And the drunken father—the white man—is he 'like us'?" She clamped her mouth shut before she could say more—something she might truly regret.

Aunt Charlotte closed her eyes, whether in mortification or prayer Eliza could not say. Uncle Rufus and the pastor exchanged glances, and both seemed to be struggling to suppress some strong emotion. She would have to apologize later, but she was not sorry now. The man behind her looked as if he'd swallowed that horsefly.

"I only meant..." He stammered, desperate to salvage his blunder. "Of course, if there's been a crime, something must be done."

Uncle Rufus eyed him levelly. "I got no desire to punish the man. I would like to help him, and his wife and son as well."

"It sounds as if your family is already reaching out to the boy. I'll commit to pray for them as well, and I'll drop by there first chance I get." The circuit rider shook Uncle Rufus' hand then reached for the hand of the man behind them.

Eliza did not trust herself to look at the man.

They walked home in silence. Eliza was fuming. When they reached the stairs behind the store, she stamped up them to return her Bible to her room and change into the blue calico before thundering down again like a brewing storm. Aunt Charlotte and Uncle Rufus looked up as she entered the living quarters, but said nothing.

She snatched an apron from its peg, wrapped the strings behind her waist, and gave them a vicious jerk.

Uncle Rufus arched his eyebrows, smirked, and raised his paper without comment.

Aunt Charlotte gazed at her with maddening forbearance.

"What?"

"Penny for your thoughts," her aunt said sweetly.

Eliza bit back an angry retort, but the gentle rebuke had done its work. She was behaving like a child—and a very tall child, at that. Covering her mouth with one hand, Eliza stifled self-conscious laughter. "I'm sorry. Sin should never be funny, but I really could have slapped him right there in front of God and everybody! I was so angry. Of all the idiotic, uncaring, hypocritical..."

"'Call not thy brother a fool,'" her aunt quoted.

"Now, Lottie, some of that might be righteous indignation. Jesus, Himself, didn't have much good to say about the self-righteous Pharisees who looked down their noses at widders and orphans and couldn't be troubled to heal cripples on the Sabbath." Uncle Rufus folded his paper and set it aside.

Now that her outrage had passed, hot tears swam before Eliza's eyes. When she lowered her head to finish tying her apron, they slipped down her cheeks. She looked up, searching the understanding faces of her aunt and uncle. "Does he not believe that Joseph and his mother deserve to be treated kindly and given the benefit of the doubt? 'Not like us'? What makes someone 'like us'? Their skin, or a heart that responds to the same Lord?"

Or where they came from? Jake serves Me, but it was difficult for you to trust him because he was not like you—not from the South. It's difficult to trust when you've been hurt.

Eliza clapped both hands over her mouth and froze, eyes wide. She had never heard the Lord more clearly in her life, and she knew it was Him because He spoke directly to the root of her sin. She was the hypocrite. She had done the very thing she despised in others.

Oh, God! Forgive me!

Her heart broke and tears washed over her like waves of water over broken shards, crushing what was once hard and sharp inside of her into harmless sand and washing it away.

Uncle Rufus half rose from his seat to comfort her, but Aunt Charlotte laid a gentle hand on his arm to still him.

Eliza looked from one to the other. It was several moments before she could speak, and when she did her voice was small and calm. "I have some thinking to do. Would you please excuse me?"

Aunt Charlotte gently untied the apron for her and hung it back on its peg. "Should I keep dinner warm for you?"

Eliza shook her head. One last sob escaped as a hiccup. She bit her lip to hold back more and swallowed hard. "I don't know when I'll be back. Please don't worry about me." Composed now, she walked out the door and closed it quietly behind her.

She paused on the back porch to gaze at the ridge that had come to represent hope and strength to her. Today it seemed closer than ever. Soon she would be there—crossing into Jake's valley. Would she see him? Her heart yearned to face him, humble herself, and be reconciled. But that would be up to God—God and Jake.

She crossed behind the barn and entered through the door to the side yard, out of view. Her conscience pinched her as she retrieved the bundle from the loft. With quick steps she left again by the same door and let herself out the gate. She looked both ways and slowed her pace. If she didn't act guilty, there was no reason for anyone to be suspicious. She often carried her bundles to the tailor's shop. Even on a Sunday she could simply be visiting Anne with needlework to pass a restful afternoon. She feigned innocence, even daring to greet a few familiar customers she passed along the way.

The act took its toll. Her confidence and her nerves were worn thin by the time she reached Anne's. To avoid the parlor full of residents, she went around to the kitchen door.

Anne welcomed her inside wordlessly. Together they entered the laundry where Cathay was waiting. Eliza dropped the bundle on the makeshift cot and flung back the layers of canvas. She drew out a pair of pants and held them up to herself. Too short. She passed them to Cathay, who lost no time stepping into them. Eliza grabbed the other pair and ducked behind a hanging sheet.

Anne picked up an empty plate. "Did you eat yet?"

Eliza peeked over the sagging clothesline. "Not hungry. Too

anxious to eat, I guess. I have jerky to take with us."

Anne scowled but did not argue as she headed back to the kitchen.

The two women changed in silence. When Eliza emerged, Cathay was stuffing the last of her belongings into her haversack.

"You want me to carry your dress for you? I got room."

"The dress is for you." Cathay just looked at her. "It'll be too long, I'm sure, but you'll be a seamstress, right? A proper businesswoman needs a proper dress to start out."

Cathay accepted the garment from her hand and laid it out on the cot. As she smoothed and folded the full skirt, her skillful hands fondled the needlework and trim. She rolled it from the hem and placed it in the top of her pack. "Thank you." Her eyes shone.

The package of jerky went in last then Cathay cinched the top and reached for her hat. Eliza set hers back on her head so that it completely covered her twist of hair. She bent the brim down in front to shadow her face and turned so the other two women could inspect her.

"You make an awfully pretty fella, but hopefully no one will look close enough to notice." Anne hugged her. "Now git along, both of you, and we'll pray for your safety."

Cathay lingered, one hand on the door. "Thank you, ma'am, for all your care of me."

Anne's eyes welled with tears, but she shooed them along. "Write when you get there, you hear?"

"Yes, ma'am. I surely can do that."

Moments later the two tall figures emerged on the street. Taking her cue from Cathay, Eliza lengthened her stride and concentrated on keeping her hips still as she walked. She did not hurry, but neither did she make eye contact with any they passed. Just two strangers passing through.

Eliza's heart skipped a beat when they rounded the corner. Leaning against the wall of the stage stop at the other end of the street, Clay Allison loitered and laughed with a few men she recognized. A glint of meanness lit his eyes, ready to touch a spark to his fiery temper. Eliza reminded herself for the dozenth time that no one would recognize her unless she gave them the opportunity. She turned her head quickly and peered into the windows of the saloon they were passing. Let him think they were looking for someone.

Cathay shot her a curious glance then dropped her gaze to the ground again.

Eliza monitored the street in the reflection of the window, ignoring the inner urge to run that would have given them away.

After a moment they ambled on. Only then did Cathay glance over her shoulder.

"That was him?"

"Mm-hmm." Eliza's heart continued to pound, but she must not show it. At the end of the street they passed Uncle Rufus' store and barn and slipped into the side yard. "Wait here."

Eliza saddled the horse and led him out. "You think you can mount?"

Cathay stared at her. "You walk out of here with your servant on a horse, and they'll stare for sure," she whispered back. "Git up."

Eliza looped the rope over the horn and put her foot into the stirrup. The last horse she mounted was a Shetland pony when she was a child, but she'd seen it done often enough to know what to do. With one hand on the horn and the other on the cantle, she stepped up—and right back down. This was harder than it looked. Good thing they were in the side yard, out of sight. She tried again, pushing off harder this time, swinging her leg wide over the horse's rump.

What a strange feeling to sit astride a horse. What a wonderfully exciting feeling of freedom. She grinned down at Cathay.

"If you done lookin' like a greenhorn, we might oughta head out. I'll tote the pack 'til we're out of sight."

Chagrinned, she wiped the smile from her face and gave her mount a nudge with the heels of her boots. The horse started smoothly, and Cathay ran to open the gate, but by the time it closed behind them, Eliza was already experiencing mild panic.

From her vantage point, Cathay must have noticed the whites of her eyes. "You never rode before?"

"Nothing this big."

"Don't let the horse know that."

Was she teasing?

Cathay's face was completely serious. "You holdin' them reins like you was drivin' a wagon."

What did she expect?

"Loop 'em through one hand, and rest your wrist on the horn."

Eliza tried that and drew a calming breath. She forced herself to relax her shoulders and breathe again. "Better?"

"Some."

"How long do you reckon we need to wait before we can switch out?"

They had made it to the meadow behind Elizabethtown. Eliza's back was stiff as a fireplace poker, and her hips and knees were already beginning to ache. She tried to relax her grip on the horse's ribs, adjusting her weight until she found a position where she could balance without pain. A grove of trees grew just ahead, but Cathay shielded her eyes to scan another grove in the distance where their path converged with the old construction road.

"Up there. Cain't nobody tell skin color that far off. We oughta be safe to change there."

The sun directly overhead was unusually warm, raising smells of horse, grass, leather, and resin. Eliza sat easier in the saddle now, the tension easing from her with every step they put between themselves and the town.

When they reached the tree line, she stood in the saddle and slid off the left side. A sharp pain shot through her hips as she landed. It took her a moment to straighten.

Cathay shook her head.

Ignoring her, Eliza arched her back to stretch out the kinks. "Your turn."

Cathay dropped the haversack and wiped the sweat from her neck before lifting it again by the strap. She shoved it into Eliza's middle. "Your turn." She grinned and mounted easily, though she winced a bit as her weight shifted to her injured thigh.

One side of Eliza's mouth twisted, and she slanted her eyes up at the woman on horseback before she hoisted the pack onto her own shoulders. "Let's go, then."

Cathay laughed. "Give me that pack. Ain't no sense carrying it when I can take it up here with me."

Why hadn't she thought of that before?

As if reading her mind, Cathay said, "You had all you could do to stay mounted without it."

The old work road curved up a ravine, and Elizabethtown was lost to sight. The slope had not seemed steep from the base, but Eliza was soon gasping for air. Her ribs expanded and her lungs burned, but she could not catch her breath. She tipped her head back to let the thin air rush in, taking in the enormous timbers that held the aqueduct—the Big Ditch—over the trees. Towering pines seemed to point to the clouds that rushed by above, making her dizzy. Drops of water seeped from the pipes and pelted her as the road zigzagged beneath the main line. She stepped wide around damp spots—puddles formed by the leakage—to spare her boots. Why hadn't she brought her own shoes to change into once they were out of sight? These were sure to rub blisters.

The way grew steeper. Eliza lost all sense of time as her footfalls matched the horse's clopping gait. The shrill of a mosquito silenced abruptly, and Eliza slapped at her neck where it stung. She wiped away the sweat. It was humid, the sun hidden now behind towering clouds.

"How far you reckon it is over this ridge?"

Cathay looked down. "You wearin' out?"

"No." She would not complain—not to a woman who had marched to Georgia and back. "I was just trying to figure the time."

"I don't rightly know how far it is."

"I thought you knew the route."

"I seen it on a survey map. Didn't look to be far, but this road don't go straight over. We been switching back and going around. It could add a fair piece." The horse tripped on a stone, breaking the plodding rhythm of their steps. Cathay stroked his neck and let him slow his pace a bit. "If you're tired, I can walk, and you can head back. You've given me a good start."

Eliza shook her head and wiped a sleeve across her brow. "I won't worry about you once you're over the ridge. I can make it that far, and it ought to be downhill from there for both of us."

She'd been foolish to strike out with nothing more than a general notion of the route, but she'd seen the way Jake took, and he made the trip within a day. She could not tell Cathay of her wish to see Jake's valley—her longing to see Jake, himself.

Eliza's shirt clung to her skin. She rolled up her sleeves then bent her head to watch her feet as she trudged on. The steady cadence of hoof beats and footsteps helped her ignore her exhaustion. She placed her feet carefully—heel, toe, heel, toe—trying to avoid the tender spots inside the new boots.

After what seemed an eternity, the Big Ditch turned south again. Eliza and Cathay looked north. A deep gorge fell away to a silver ribbon of water below.

"Is that it? The Red River?"

Cathay pushed back her hat. "I don't think so. Just a stream, likely, but it runs the right way." She dismounted and tied the horse to a pine bough. He fell to grazing even before she could open her pack and draw out the jerky. "Want to rest a spell and eat a bite? Then you can take him and head back. You oughta make it before dark."

Eliza found a rock and sat to remove her boots. She tossed her hat back on her shoulders. Golden rays streamed from the dark clouds that hung low over the valley. There was movement in them like a boiling pot. A sudden breeze struck the sheen of sweat that covered her skin, raising goose flesh. She shivered and reached for a strip of jerky Cathay offered.

A raindrop plopped onto her outstretched arm.

The two women stared at the drop, at each other, then at the clouds just as a bolt of lightning scorched a jagged path across the dark sky.

The horse reared and yanked on the lead, dancing nervously around the tree branch.

Cathay moved to pacify him. "You'd better head back before this storm breaks."

Another flash rent the air, and thunder echoed through the valley. Raindrops fell thick and fast.

"Too late," Eliza shouted as she pulled her hat back onto her head, for all the good it would do. The horse, accustomed to the shelter of a warm barn, tossed his head and nickered. "I could barely manage him before. Downhill in the rain? Not a chance." She was drenched now—a cold wetness that made her teeth chatter. Her boots squished as she shoved her feet back into them. She winced as she stood. "Come on. There's a cabin up here somewhere—a man I know." Her stiff fingers fumbled to untie the reins. She had to raise her voice to be heard above the downpour. "Mount up. We'll ride until we smell the smoke of his fire."

"You can't walk in them wet boots." Cathay mounted and extended her hand. "Ride up here with me."

Eliza mounted behind Cathay and clung to her for dear life.

Cathay wrestled with the reins as their mount pulled against them, trying to set his back to the storm. By sheer force of will she finally convinced him to trust her. They headed north and west through sheets of rain.

The horse's hooves slipped on the slick shale as they picked their way along the ridge and down into the valley. The wind howled in the trees above them, the lashing boughs alternately green and black in thc eerie flashing light. White rimmed the horse's eyes with every crashing bolt.

Cathay did not rush him but urged him forward with gentle encouragements, her voice calm and confident. "Git up, now. We'll find us a dry place soon enough."

That's when the hail started, pelting them with pellets the size of grape shot that stung like hornets when they struck.

Already numb with cold, Eliza ducked her head in an effort to shield her face. The frozen pellets assaulted her back. She reached around Cathay and held on tight as they shook in unison. There was no use trying to talk.

The stream was rushing now, hurling its water downward until it joined the river. Here the valley broadened. They rode along the bank, crossing other rivulets as they came to them.

"You know whereabouts in this valley we're heading?" Cathay shouted over her shoulder.

"Bitter Creek, but I have no idea which one that is." Eliza clenched her jaw to stop her clattering teeth. She conjured a warm fire in her mind. Her eyes drifted shut as she concentrated on the sensation of warmth. Then she smelled wood smoke—faint at first. Her eyes snapped open. A wisp of white trailed from a hollow ahead, beckoning. Mute with cold, she pointed.

"I see it!" Cathay pressed her heels to the horse's flanks.

He picked up his pace immediately.

Relief flooded Eliza as the cabin came into view. "Jake!" She shouted through the torrents. "Jake!"

The horse's pounding hooves slid to a halt in front of the cabin door just as it flew open.

Backlit by firelight, Jake stood in the doorway, rifle in hand. He stood rigid, taut, ready for action as he peered at them, then his eyes opened wide. He propped the rifle against the log wall and rushed to take the reins.

Chapter 17

Jake's appearance was like a rainbow—a promise that all would be well. Exhausted as she was, Eliza could not suppress her smile as he approached. Everything would be fine now.

The brim of his hat, pulled down low over his eyes to shed the rain, made him seem to scowl as his gaze passed from Cathay to Eliza. "Get in the house!" The command in his voice carried over a roll of thunder.

Eliza let go of Cathay's waist but was unsure what to do next. Surely Cathay could not dismount until she did, but she had no stirrup for her feet. She looked to Jake for assistance.

"Get off that horse and get in the house!" The scowl was no illusion.

Shocked, Eliza simply let go and slid off the horse's rump, landing on the soggy grass and sitting down with a plop that jarred her teeth. She waited for Jake to offer her his hand, but he reached instead to take the haversack from Cathay. Shouldering it, he turned and strode toward the cabin without a word.

Cathay looked at Eliza and shrugged before she dismounted. She offered her hand and pulled Eliza to her feet. "I thought you said he was a friend," she whispered as their heads drew close. Gathering the reins, she led the horse toward shelter.

There was nothing for Eliza to do but follow.

Jake threw open the cabin door and indicated with a sweeping gesture that they should enter. He took the reins from Cathay and led the horse around to the shed.

Alone for the moment in Jake's cabin, the two women stood dripping on the floor. Eliza shifted her weight in the awkward silence. What could she say? She could not explain Jake's angry reception.

The door whipped open shortly and slammed again as Jake entered. He stared at Cathay for only a moment, sizing her up, before glaring at Eliza.

She wrapped her arms tightly about herself but could not stop shivering. Inwardly she withered beneath his gray eyes—as cold as the rain that pounded the shake roof.

"What fool notion brings you way out here dressed like that in the middle of a storm?" He waved one arm to indicate both her attire and his disdain of it. He wasn't exactly shouting, but his tone was harsh and demanding.

Eliza stared at the puddle growing around her feet. He'd asked a question, but he didn't really want to hear her answer. His silence demanded she supply one, nonetheless. "I needed to get Cathay out of Elizabethtown without Clay Allison seeing her." She was desperate to explain. Her voice faltered at first, but then the words tumbled out. "She's going to Colorado. He shot her, and her leg's hurt, and I thought it would help if she could at least ride for the first bit. I meant to head back once we got to the ridge, but the storm caught us and..." She was babbling, so she stopped.

Jake stared at her, at Cathay, and back to Eliza. Finally he huffed and crossed the room to pull two ladder-back chairs closer to the blazing fire. "Sit."

A trail of water marked their passage across the room. Eliza sank onto the woven spline seat and tugged off her soggy boots.

Cathay's eyes grew wide as she stared at Eliza's once-white stockings. Red stains showed through in several places.

Eliza pulled up her pants legs to roll them down from the top, gingerly slipping them off her toes. Her feet were a bloody mess, covered with broken blisters.

At the sight of them, Jake softened at last. He pulled two quilts from a wall cupboard. "Get out of those wet clothes and wrap up in these." He headed for the door. "I'll sleep in the shed. There's beans and cornpone on the table. We'll talk in the morning." Lifting his hat from its peg, he raised it in a farewell salute—the first courteous gesture he'd offered—and left.

Eliza was almost too tired to eat, but the beans were well-seasoned, warming her from the inside out as she swallowed.

Cathay collected their tin cups when they finished and set them back on the table. "We can wash these in the morning. You mind sharing a bed?"

Eliza shook her head. "I'm too tired to care."

They wrung out their clothes and hung them over the chair backs to dry by the fire. The dry quilt felt good against her damp skin. Eliza didn't even pull back the covers, but lay on top, wrapped in a cocoon of warmth, and fell asleep immediately.

ᘓᘐᘑᘔ

A faint golden light suffused the square patch of sky visible through the cabin window when Eliza opened her eyes. Her first thought was of Jake. Tears sprang to her eyes. She had so longed to see him, making his anger toward her all the more painful. He didn't know she'd forgiven him, but again he hadn't given her much chance to explain.

A faint knock at the door caused Cathay to stir next to her. "Anybody awake yet?"

Eliza clutched the quilt closer to her and swung her legs over the edge of the bed. "Up, but not dressed yet. Give us a moment?" She stood.

Pain shot through both feet and up her legs, causing her entire body to recoil. She bit her lip to keep from crying out, but a deep moan escaped as she fell back onto the straw tick.

Cathay was instantly awake. "What is it?"

"My feet!"

"I'm not surprised." She came around the bed to look at them. "Can you walk?"

Eliza shook her head.

Cathay brought their dry clothes.

Eliza dressed without standing then sat as Cathay opened the door.

Jake leaned against a porch post, twirling his hat and looking out over the valley. "We need to get an early start," he said as he entered brusquely. He poked up the fire and nestled a skillet in the embers. "I can escort Cathay to the mouth of the river then bring the horse back to take you home." With exaggerated motions he slapped strips of bacon into the pan, wagging his head and muttering, "Charlotte and Rufus will be worried sick."

She'd been too exhausted to think of that last night. Her reception with them might not be any more pleasant than Jake's. Her heart sank.

An awkward silence filled the cabin until the bacon began to sizzle in the skillet

"You'll be okay here until I get back?" For the first time Jake looked at her. "How are your feet?"

Eliza tossed her hair and snatched up her socks. "I'll do fine."

The barest hint of sympathy flickered across his chiseled features but was soon replaced by annoyance. Turning back to the fire he forked the crisp bacon onto three tin plates. He set two on the table with the last of the cornpone, then cut a generous hunk of it and brought the third plate to Eliza. She was not "fine," and he knew it.

They ate quickly then Jake left to saddle the horses.

Cathay's dark eyes were sympathetic. "Can you make do for a few hours?"

"I'll crawl if I have to." Her voice cracked, and she choked back a sob. "You know he's not angry with you? It's an old matter between us." She sniffed.

Cathay nodded. "He'll come around. He seems a decent man." She opened the top of her pack and pulled out her neckerchief. "Here." She pressed it into Eliza's hand and closed her own two hands around it. "Something to remember me by."

Eliza nodded but could not speak.

Cathay patted her hand as the door opened again.

"Ready?"

She nodded and slung her haversack easily across her shoulders. Jake held the door for her as they went out. He lingered just a moment to look back at Eliza. "Please just rest and make yourself at home. I'll come back for you." Then he was gone again.

Eliza listened as their horses' hoof beats grew fainter and fainter. She didn't know how long she'd have to wait, but Jake's parting words held a glimmer of hope that his anger would not last forever.

She lay back on the bed and studied the cabin around her. Like her attic bedroom above the store, reminders of Julia were everywhere. A pink fan quilt. Delicate lace doilies beneath the coal oil lamps. A framed portrait on the mantle.

Much as it hurt to stand, the silvery tones of the daguerreotype drew Eliza to examine it more closely. Walking on the outer edges of her feet, she managed the short distance to the hearth. Julia's face smiled out at her.

She reached for the likeness to angle it into better light. As she lifted it, she noticed for the first time another portrait—a tintype pinned beneath the frame.

She gasped. Hands shaking, she set down the framed photograph and picked up the other, staring in disbelief.

Her own face stared back.

She hobbled back to the bed, taking the sepia likeness with her. She couldn't take her eyes from it. When had she ever given Julia a portrait of herself?

She hadn't.

There was only one photograph of herself in existence—one she had made for Grayson to take with him when he marched to war.

ꕥ

Eliza could imagine few explanations for how that tintype might end up here, and none of them were good. Now that she knew of it, how could she pretend not to? Her stomach twisted into a knot, and she cried until she fell asleep. When she woke to the sound of approaching hoof beats, the change in the light told her that hours had passed.

She heard Jake's footsteps cross the porch and felt ill. Then she panicked. The tintype was still beside her on the lamp table. There was no way she could return it to its place before he entered. She slipped it under the edge of the doily and hoped he would not notice. Maybe she'd have a chance to put it back on the mantle later.

Jake leaned against the door and toyed with the brim of his hat. The gesture reminded her of the first day they'd met. He was nervous. Not angry? When he finally looked at her, his eyes were soft. He pressed his lips into a line and drew a deep breath, exhaling slowly. "I'm sorry."

Eliza was sorry too ... and sorry that Jake had said it first.

"I was scared that you'd taken such a risk, but I should have let you explain."

Whatever the story behind the tintype, she was going to have to give him the same opportunity.

"And it made me angry to see you dressed as a man."

Eliza cocked her head. "Why?"

"Because you're NOT a man. You can't ride as hard or walk as far. You don't know this country. What if you'd run up on a mountain lion? Or a bear?"

She hadn't thought of that. Apparently there were a lot of things she hadn't thought about.

"You get yourself in trouble when you try to be something you're not. Why wouldn't you let someone else help you?"

"Because there WASN'T anyone!" The words spewed out of her before she could stop them. "There's never really been anyone, and I guess I just got used to doing things for myself."

Jake squinted at her and shook his head slowly. "What are you trying to tell me?"

A sudden flood of tears flowed unbidden down her cheeks. Her throat constricted, and her cheeks burned. She was making a spectacle of herself, but there was no way to hide the rush of feelings. "Jake, can you imagine what it's like to be me? Six feet tall, surrounded by dainty debutantes?" She gulped and picked at a thread on the quilt to avoid looking at him. "Daddy adores me, but he's an unusual man. Years after all my friends married I met Grayson and finally had reason to praise God for someone who loved me like I am, but he's gone. Mama's gone." She looked up at him, her eyes pleading. "It's pretty much just me and God."

Jake crossed the room and took her face in his hands. His eyes burned into hers, and his lips curved into a slow smile. "I wish you could see what I see."

Eliza tore her gaze from his and stared at her hands, clenched in her lap. Large, capable hands. "I'm not what most men want, Jake. I'm not flirtatious and fragile. I know that."

He placed the crook of his finger beneath her chin and lifted her head. "Then most men are fools. Fragility is overrated." He smiled down at her. "I understand. I've had a fragile woman, and she was a delight to me, but I saw what this country did to her—what I did to her. I didn't know." He shook his head sadly, and Eliza saw the tears that glazed his eyes, making them like polished metal mirrors that reflected her pain.

Almost instinctively, they both turned to look at the portrait of sweet Julia.

Jake's expression changed abruptly. He strode to the fireplace, lifted the framed daguerreotype and felt the mantle beneath it. He whirled to stare at Eliza, a horrified expression in his eyes.

Her cheeks burned with guilt, and her traitorous eyes flitted toward the lamp table.

Jake returned and snatched the tintype from beneath the doily where she'd hidden it. He stared at Eliza, and she stared back—calm despite her shame.

"I didn't mean to snoop."

"Of course not. I told you to make yourself at home."

She nodded.

"How many of these did you have made?"

"One."

He gulped. "Then you know where I got it?"

Tears slipped from the corners of her eyes. "I know who I gave it to."

Jake's eyes studied her face while his jaw clenched. "It's not what you think."

"I don't know what I think." Eliza smiled through her tears. "Jake, that's what I came here to tell you. I tried to tell you the morning after we quarreled, but you left before I had a chance." She reached for his hand, but her eyes never left his. "I trust you. I know your heart, and I trust you. Once I decided to forgive, I knew it wasn't your fault."

"But Eliza, I didn't leave because you doubted me." His voice broke, and he swallowed hard. "I left because I am the one who caused your pain—the one who cost you Grayson."

It took every bit of resolve Eliza could muster to force herself to speak calmly—to wait for the answer, no matter how painful it was. "Did you kill him in battle?"

"Oh, Lord!" The prayer escaped Jake's lips like a cry of pain. "I did not, but it's my fault just the same." He wiped at his nose with the back of his hand. "They told you how he died?"

Eliza nodded. "I got a letter from his commander. It arrived just before Christmas." Jake snorted. "I told you, remember? Grayson was shot while attempting to rescue a wounded soldier from the field."

Jake squared his jaw and pressed his lips tightly. His fists were balled by his sides. He looked into her eyes, and she could tell it required all of his will to do it. "I was that soldier."

"You?" Her mind whirled, trying to make the pieces fit.

"I'm sure you thought he was helping one of his own men, but it was me. I told you I was shot at Chickamauga. The rebels overran our position—swarming over the trenches like ants at a picnic. I shot my last round then swung my rifle like a club, trying to hold them back. I never even heard the shot that hit me, there was so much gunfire and yelling."

Eliza saw the battle through Jake's eyes, and tears sprang to her own.

"I fell directly in front of the Confederate line. I could see their eyes as I went down—the fear, the hate—and there was this chaplain. He didn't seem scared or angry—just sad. Next thing I knew he's pulling me to shelter, calling for a doctor."

Eliza's tears flowed freely now. "Did you see who shot him?"

Jake nodded. "Clay Allison. I recognized him when I saw him again in the store."

Eliza's heart skipped several beats.

"He was shouting, 'You traitor! Let him die!' but your chaplain just kept pulling, ducking the gunfire. Allison shot him and ran just as help arrived. They took us both to the field hospital." Jake pulled a chair beside her, turned it, and sat resting his chin on the ladder back. "I thanked him, of course—asked him why he'd done it. He said he'd had enough of hating and killing. That he'd done what he hoped I'd have done for him. I could hear the rattle in his chest when he tried to breathe—knew he wasn't going to make it. I asked him if there was anything I could do for him. That's when he gave me the picture—said if I could ever find you..."

Grayson died to save the one man she thought she could never forgive.

They were both crying now. At last Eliza rested her hand on his head like a benediction. "Grayson was right." His dark curls were soft beneath her fingers. "I forgive you."

He reached out for her, lacing his fingers through her hair, drawing her toward him, kissing her deeply.

Eliza drank in the sweetness of his lips through her tears.

"You asked me once how I could be so sure of you—of us. When I saw you Easter Sunday, I knew God was giving me another chance at a new life. I'm still sure." His eyes were filled with promise and all the love Eliza had ever hoped to find. "Give me a chance, Eliza. Give me a chance to make things right by Grayson—to show you that I see what he saw—a woman who's exactly what I want and need." He kissed her again. "You just be who you are, and I'll show you I'm man enough to handle it."

Chapter 18

Jake rocked back on his heels. "I'd better take you home. Your aunt and uncle will be beside themselves."

Home? No, Eliza didn't want to go home to Elizabethtown. She felt more at home here with Jake than anywhere she had been since she left Papa's house. Her heart was at home in this peaceful valley, but what Jake said was true. People who loved her would worry ... and others would talk.

Jake held one of Eliza's stockings open wide so that she could slip her foot in without scraping the tender skin.

She stiffened. It was a thoughtful gesture, but too intimate for comfort. Yes, it was time to go home, and quickly—before she gave the town gossips anything to talk about.

Eliza adjusted the other stocking by herself then stepped into her boots and winced. After drying overnight by the fire, the leather was tighter than ever on her swollen feet. How was she going to get home if she couldn't even stand? Tears sprang to her eyes.

Without a word Jake swept her up into his arms.

"Oh, no! Put me down. You must."

"Why must I?" Mischief twinkled in his eyes.

She'd grown up in a parsonage. For a preacher's daughter, all walls are glass. "How would this look if anyone saw?"

He laughed—a mellow sound like the rushing river. "There's no one here to see it."

"God sees it."

"Then He sees that I'm taking care of the woman I love. There's nothing wrong with that."

"I'm not sure I can say with a clear conscience that my heart is that pure."

"Oh, ho!" He chortled. "Then we'd better make this quick." He carried her out to the porch and lifted her into the saddle, shoving her new boots into his saddlebag.

They headed south, back up the valley toward the ridge. The fresh mountain air, washed by yesterday's rain, almost seemed to sparkle with newness. Now that they'd cleared the air between them, as well, conversation was easy. Jake pointed out wildlife and landmarks she had not seen in the darkness of the storm.

Jake was part of this valley, as surely as the river. His voice was as sure and steadfast as the rushing water, and Eliza drank in the sound of it. The world beyond this valley seemed full of trouble, but she had caused at least part of it without meaning to. With all her heart she longed to stay here—to be part of his world—but she could not. Not yet. She had to go back before her actions created any more worry and awkwardness for her family. And she would have to write Papa again—tell him that she no longer had any thought of returning to Waco. What would he think? What would any of them think?

As soon as they topped the ridge they saw riders—Uncle Rufus and Hiram winding their way up the eastern slope.

"Halloo!" Jake called out, lifting his rifle.

"Halloo!"

Eliza detected the joy and relief in the faint answering cry.

Jake spurred his mount to a brisk trot, and Eliza held on to her hat as her horse picked up his pace. They met the search party at a wide spot on the trail.

"'Liza-girl, we was scared we'd lost you." There was no condemnation in Uncle Rufus' voice, but the reminder that he'd loved and lost so many was a weight on Eliza's heart.

"I'm so sorry." Her tears proved her repentance. "I was terribly foolish, but..."

Uncle Rufus held up his hand. "Anne came to us when the storm broke and told us where you'd gone."

"I'll pay for the clothes..." She could not look at his eyes. The fear was still in them, and she knew her rash actions had put it there.

Her uncle rested a gnarled hand on her arm. "'Liza."

She looked up.

"It's all right now. You're safe."

She searched his eyes. "You're not angry?"

He shook his head. "Nope. Just scared you'd run into trouble on some ledge in that storm." He drew a deep breath and exhaled it. "Now let's git you home. Lottie'll be so glad to see you safe." He looked to Jake. "Thanks for bringing her back to us. You comin' back to E-Town?"

Jake shook his head. "I got unfinished business back yonder..."

Eliza's chest felt hollow.

"...but I'll be down next weekend to celebrate."

Only a week until the Fourth of July! Eliza had forgotten all she had to do next week, but Jake's wink reassured her that a reunified nation wasn't the only thing they'd be celebrating.

ꕥ

Eliza kept busy to make the week pass more quickly, but her heart was still in the valley.

Jake rode in on Saturday night, his eyes twinkling and his saddlebags bulging. "Come look what I brought you."

Eliza's curiosity only grew when he threw back the leather flap to reveal a quilt. He peeled back the folds of the quilt to uncover a layer of straw. Then he pulled out the straw. Underneath, covered with a blue tin plate, was a bucket of snow.

"I rode up to the upper valley this morning. There's a narrow canyon up there, and I was just hoping it wouldn't all be gone."

Snow! In July! Eliza clapped her hands then took the bucket and pressed her palms against its frosty side. Jake had gone to great lengths. For her? Of course, for her, though it seemed too good to be true. He was sharing his valley, inviting her to love it as he did. The sudden realization warmed her heart.

From the other side of the saddlebag, Jake removed another bucket filled with wild strawberries. "Found these growing along the sunnier slopes on the way up." He looked pleased with himself. "Come on. I'll show you how to make ice cream."

They carried the pails into the kitchen.

"Rufus, you think April can spare us a cup or two of milk?"

Eliza watched as Aunt Charlotte stirred sugar, vanilla, and fresh, creamy milk into the clean snow. She lifted a spoonful to her mouth. Icy sweetness melted and ran down her throat as the tangy berries burst on her tongue. She closed her eyes and savored the flavors of summer and winter together. "Mmmm."

"A Yankee pleasure."

Eliza opened her eyes and saw the deeper truth in Jake's actions. He was not only sharing his valley with her, but his roots and heritage as well. She smiled up at him. "I'll have to add it to the list of things I'm learning to like about the North, then."

ꕤ

On Monday horses lined the hitching posts in front of every saloon as people streamed into town to celebrate the Fourth. By noon, loud music and drunken laughter spilled through the open doorways and into the streets, but the church grounds were full of families and wagons and the happy sounds of children playing tag among the picnic blankets.

"Yoo-hoo! Eliza!" Millie edged her basket of sweet pastries into one of the few remaining spaces on the sawbuck table and waved.

Eliza smiled. Millie's shrill greeting made her want to hide that first morning in Fort Union. Now she embraced her friend with genuine affection. "How have you been?"

Millie pursed her lips in a smug smile. "Well, I've been better."

"You look mighty happy for someone who's seen better days." Eliza suspected what was coming next.

"Oh, I ought to feel much better in about seven months." Millie winked. "'Bout the same time Zeke becomes a papa."

Eliza hugged her again.

"How about you?" Millie tugged a picnic quilt from the wagon box and searched for an open area.

Eliza let her gaze wander to where Jake helped the men set up markers for the afternoon races. A flush of pleasure brought heat to her cheeks.

Millie followed her gaze. "He didn't stay gone long," she said with an I-told-you-so grin.

"No. We got everything straightened out, I think." Eliza shook the quilt out on the breeze. "Looks like I'll get to keep that quilt I started instead of selling it for stage fare home—if I ever get a chance to work on it." She made a mental note to ask the tailor for scraps of shirting.

Uncle Rufus lifted a mounded plate high and side-stepped to

avoid two youngsters as they darted past. "I found plenty of good vittles to tuck into," he said, smiling in anticipation.

Eliza shook her head. The man was a walking target for youngsters. "Where's Aunt Charlotte?"

He jerked his head toward the row of makeshift tables. "Yonder with Anne, serving up pie." Pennies clinked into a coffee tin as hungry diners contributed to the fundraiser for the day's events.

Eliza and Millie passed Zeke with a heaping platter of his own as they went to help serve. People had come from miles around for the festivities; the waiting line stretched around the corner of the church. Eliza flew back and forth behind the serving tables, whisking away empty dishes and replacing them with fresh offerings.

At last there was a lull, and she grabbed a tin plate for herself and fell into line—right behind the man who had followed them out of church the week before. She swallowed the sour words that lay ready on her tongue and forced the corners of her mouth up.

He smiled back—a relieved sort of smile, though his eyes did not meet hers. "I'm glad to see you here today, ma'am. I meant to catch up with you yesterday at church, but, well ... what I mean to say is, I behaved badly last week, and it's been on my conscience ever since." He ducked his head. "Ain't no excuse for it, 'cept maybe to explain that I was a kid in Taos when the Indians rose up back in '47. My family made a run for it, but I had kinfolks wasn't so lucky." The smile was entirely gone now, and Eliza saw the pain that replaced it. The memories were etched in his eyes. "It was a terrible thing, ma'am, and I hope you never have to see anything like it—what men can do to men." He shrugged. "It's hard to forgive—hard to remember that 'ugly' comes in all colors. But I guess 'good' does, too, and I am trying."

Eliza laid a hand on his sleeve. "I understand." It even came in blue and gray.

He took her hand, and the smile returned. "Name's Matthews. I'm a shipping agent."

"I'm glad to know you, Mr. Matthews." His hand felt amazingly human in hers. *Hurt people hurt people. Thank You, Lord, that You can heal our hurts if we'll let You.*

ꕥ

As the sun sank behind the mountains in a blaze of glory, Eliza wrapped her arms around herself, trying to contain her thankfulness. Despite the hardships, this was a good country, full of promise. Despite what it had cost her, the man who stood so close behind her was a good man. The strong hands that brushed her arms protectively were a promise of good things to come. For the first time in a long time, all seemed right with the world.

The band played a round of patriotic songs—songs that would have stirred her heart at any time—but this night, with Jake's baritone rumbling so close to her ear, his breath warm on her cheek, the words got stuck in her throat, and she could not sing.

Then someone set off fireworks, and she jumped even though she knew they were coming.

Jake chuckled as his hands steadied her.

Uncle Rufus stood up on the stage landing, tapping his foot and sawing at his fiddle, his bald head shining in the light of the hanging lanterns. After a few measures to announce the start of the dance, the band broke into a jig.

It was the strangest dance Eliza had ever seen. In a town made up mostly of men, many danced in celebration, but none had partners. Whooping and hollering, they swung each other through the steps with such vigor that no self-respecting woman would have dared join in until they'd worn themselves out a bit.

The music changed, and this time a few men picked partners—mostly bar maids dragged into the streets, squealing and blushing in protest.

By the end of the fourth dance the rowdies had worked up a thirst and headed back into the saloons for refreshment.

Now the family folks began to dance. Zeke and Millie headed out behind Mr. and Mrs. Ewing as the band struck up a march. Even little Jonathan Ewing bowed and offered his arm to his sister, Grace. His serious expression sent Eliza into a fit of giggles.

With an exaggerated bow that mocked his young mentor, Jake offered Eliza his hand. "May I have this dance?"

Charmed, she placed her hand in his, and he led her to the end of the line. Her skirt whirled as they followed the other couples in the curving promenade, ducking beneath an archway of outstretched arms. "This is perfect, you know. Just like I imagined it."

His eyebrows arched. "Surely they must have had finer balls than this back home. The South is famous for its cotillions."

The heat rushed to Eliza's face, and she suddenly felt the need to watch her feet. "I never danced at home."

"You could have fooled me. You know all the steps."

"That's from watching—so I'd be ready if anyone ever asked me."

Jake's expression softened. "It's all right. Really."

"To be passed over? Left waiting?"

"To be left waiting for me. God protected you—saved you until now." He spun her beneath his arm, his hands warm and gentle around hers as they joined the promenade. "I don't fancy the idea of sharing you, anyway."

As the music ended, Jake turned them into a shadowed area just off the main street and pressed a kiss to her forehead. Her eyelids drifted shut, and he kissed them, too. His finger traced the line of her jaw, and she held her breath. They shouldn't linger here—shouldn't embrace so publicly. Lifting her face she opened her eyes to see his only inches away—gray and luminous as the veiled moon. His lips found hers just as the music began again—a sweet waltz this time—and other couples began to move around them, but for Eliza the world stood still.

Then a scream tore through the night like a dagger.

For an instant the world around them really did stand still as everyone froze, listening.

Eliza heard it again—shrill—a woman's cry of grief and alarm, though she could not make out the words. Her eyes searched for the source.

They followed the flow of spectators as a crowd began to gather outside Pearson's Saloon. Eliza gripped Jake's hand. They edged closer to the commotion. Her mind traveled back to another dark night—a night when her life changed forever. "Can you see?" she whispered, almost afraid to look for herself.

"It's a woman—Ute, I think." Jake peered over the milling mob then tugged her hand. "Come on. We'll be able to hear better from over here."

Eliza followed him around the edge of the crowd to a place along the wall beside the door. She could not see, but she could hear the woman's story.

"My baby! He killed my baby!" The woman's wails became moans of anguish.

"Who, lady? Who killed your young 'un?"

"My husband." Her voice was barely audible.

A murmur rose around them. "Who's her husband?"

"I heard that drunk, Kennedy, had him a Ute wife."

Eliza drew in a sharp breath and strained to hear.

"Charles Kennedy? Is that your husband, lady?"

She could not hear the woman's reply, but immediately the noise of the crowd swelled in outrage. "I knew he weren't no good!"

Eliza forgot to exhale. Eyes wide with horror, she clutched Jake's arm and held on tight as the world seemed to spin wildly beneath her feet. "Joseph!" She breathed the boy's name, and her voice trailed away on a wave of emotion. She pressed her hand to her mouth to stifle a cry. "Oh, what has he done?"

Jake gently pried her hand from his arm where she gripped him, but held onto it, stroking her fingers. His actions offered small comfort.

"We take travelers in Palo Flechado Pass—the road to Taos. I cook." The woman paused, and Eliza realized someone must have brought her something to drink. Had she run the whole way? "My husband, he ... he kills them. Takes their money, and then he..."

The uproar drowned out the next bits, and it was just as well. Eliza's stomach rolled, and she thought she might be ill. *Joseph.* She could see the child's grinning face and beautiful raven hair in her mind's eye. While she had enjoyed a carefree day of celebration, he ... it was too horrible to imagine.

"Man asked what is bad smell. My son, he says there is man under floor. Why? Why say?" She paused again, and her moans voiced the despair in Eliza's heart. "Husband is crazy with anger and drink." She spat out the words. "He throws chair, and my baby falls against the fireplace stone. Husband shoots man dead, but child does not cry. No breathing." Just whimpers now. The macabre scene played out all too vividly in Eliza's mind. "Husband locks me in house. I hear him outside, loud. Then nothing. Only snores. Fire goes out. I climb out chimney and run."

The saloon doors slammed open, and Eliza jumped back to keep from being hit. In the rectangle of light that slanted out onto the boardwalk, Clay Allison stood, ominous as a gallows tree, flanked by his companions. "Who's going with me to bring him in?"

A chorus rose from scores of volunteers—most of them drunk, all of them outraged. Allison had his posse in an instant.

Jake turned Eliza to face him, his grip strong on her shoulders. "I have to go. Someone has to go along to prevent a lynching. Even a man like Kennedy deserves a fair trial—if only to give him time to make peace with the Lord."

The solemn implications of his words made Eliza's knees weak. "Joseph?" Her throat constricted in a sob.

"Is that his son? You knew him?"

She nodded.

Jake gazed into her eyes. "I'll do what I can for him." Then he was gone.

The crowd of men dispersed, mounted their horses, and regrouped in front of the saloon. Eliza saw Jake once more as he rode up, tipped his hat to her, and joined the others thundering down the road south.

Aunt Charlotte and Uncle Rufus found her then. They embraced, sharing their grief. The tears Eliza had held back came in abundance now, pouring hot and salty down her cheeks.

Aunt Charlotte held her as she cried.

"I should have done more," she sobbed, her chest heaving. "I'd only begun to share the Lord with him. I thought I had more time, but now he's gone."

"There, there." Uncle Rufus stroked her back. "It ain't never up to us, anyhow. We just plant and water. What grows in the heart is up to God."

She blinked at him through her tears.

"Jesus didn't have much time with the thief on the cross, but it was enough. You done what the Lord gave you to do. He'll take care of the rest."

His words didn't mend the ache in her heart, but they did lift some of the burden of grief.

"Now come and let's see if his mother needs a place to stay for the night."

Chapter 19

Eliza walked into the saloon like she had good sense. Of course, if she had good sense, she would not get involved. She would stay outside, whispering and speculating from a safe distance like everyone else. But she was involved already. She cared about Joseph, cared about this woman who fled to a saloon, of all places, for help. She knew there would be a price to pay, but she could no more hold back than Papa when he quelled the jailhouse riot in Waco. With a deep breath and a quick prayer, she waded into trouble.

The Ute woman sat, stoic in her chair. Unblinking eyes stared unseeing, as if the scenes of horror would not leave them.

Eliza knelt before her. "Do you have a place to sleep?"

She waited, breathing the noxious fumes of spilled whiskey, until the woman's gaze focused. The shake of her head was barely discernible.

"Would you like to stay with us?" Eliza reached a tentative finger to touch her hand.

The woman started but did not answer or even nod. She stood as if in a trance. Her feet were bloody from her flight.

Eliza winced, sharing her pain. She placed a hand at the woman's elbow to lead her away.

Aunt Charlotte came to her other side to lend support, and the grieving woman latched onto her forearm with a vice-like grip. "I'm so sorry, dear." Tears pooled in the elder woman's eyes. "We'll find you a quiet place to rest."

They did not rush as they made their way through the streets. The Indian woman's downcast eyes seemed an ironic counterpoint to the vestiges of celebration. Sympathetic gazes followed them. At last they reached the barn.

The woman stood, mute while Uncle Rufus fetched a blanket. Returning, he pressed it into her arms, and she hugged it to her chest, cradling it like a lost child. Her eyes filled with tears. She looked up to search Eliza's face. "Why do you help me?" Her words rang hollow, as if she spoke from the bottom of a dry well.

Eliza could barely speak around the lump in her throat. "For Joseph."

"My Joseph?"

"He was my friend." Eliza pressed her hand to her heart. To speak of him in past tense stabbed home the reality of her loss.

His mother's eyes conveyed confusion.

"He stayed with us sometimes when he came to town…" She'd inadvertently blundered into awkward territory, but would have to finish now. "…with his father."

A glimmer of understanding brightened the Ute woman's face. "You are Eliza?"

"He told you about us?"

She nodded. "I am Kima."

"Kima." Eliza tried the sound of it. "That's lovely."

"Means butterfly." A twitch at the corners of her mouth might have hinted at a gentle smile, but fresh tears washed it away. "But I am not. He crushes me. Like worm." She hung her head. Her hair, so like Joseph's, shone blue-black in the light of the lantern.

Eliza reached out, rubbing Kima's arm. "You are not a worm." The woman might need time, though, to cocoon herself from the pain of years of abuse before she could emerge to fly. "Come, I'll show you where Joseph slept."

༺༻

A cool night breeze carried the rush of Moreno Creek through the open window. On any other night it would provide a soothing backdrop for slumber, but tonight Eliza lay across her bed, still clothed, listening for any sound of Jake's return. How foolish she had been to come here thinking that she would find peace and security in this valley. Not finding it, she thought perhaps she could bring peace, bring change, but she couldn't even do that. *Remind me again, Lord. Why am I here?*

To offer comfort. To offer hope.

She thought of Joseph and wanted to cry but could not. She tried to pray, but words would not come. This grief was somehow too deep for tears, too profound for words. Was he in heaven tonight? The uncertainty tormented her. She would sew buttons from now until eternity if it would buy one more day to make sure of his salvation.

She closed her eyes and let the blessed numbness of exhaustion take her.

A piercing scream.

Eliza's eyes shot open. Her body stiffened.

Another scream. It came from the barn.

Kima.

Eliza's feet hit the floor. She tugged the quilt from the bed and wrapped it around her, then she was through the door, feeling her way down the stairs in the dark.

A glow emitted from the doorway at the base of the stairs. Aunt Charlotte had lit a lantern.

Eliza took it from her. "I'll see to her." She slipped into the barn.

Soft sobs from the loft diminished to a sniffle as she entered.

She held the lantern aloft.

Dark eyes, still glistening with tears, peered down at her.

"Are you all right?"

"Evil dream."

Eliza's skin tingled. She could not imagine the horrible images that must lurk in Kima's dreams. "May I stay with you?"

Kima nodded.

Eliza hung the lantern from its iron hook and climbed into the wagon bed. She propped herself into a corner of the wagon box and hugged her long legs, wrapping the quilt more snuggly around her. Her chin sank to her knees, and she listened for a while to the sounds of breathing, pondering the fragility of life. In and out, in and out, each breath sustaining life for a few precious moments, and when breath was suddenly gone—whether taken or lost—life was over. Like pennies dropped into a collection can, any one of them seemed insignificant, but taken together … how would she spend hers? She wanted desperately to trade them for something of worth—something that would last. And she wanted desperately to spend them with Jake. With tears in her eyes she realized that Grayson had spent his last few to preserve Jake's life. For her? He could not have known, but somehow she knew he would approve. She glanced up to the loft where the Indian woman lay sleeping. What was an enemy, anyway?

ꕥ

She awakened to the sounds of horses. The commotion in the streets, even though it was blocks away, was loud enough to carry through the morning air. The posse had returned.

Kima had heard them, too, and was already scrambling down the ladder.

When she turned, Eliza gasped. "Your hair!"

Kima's raven braids were gone. She pulled at the uneven ends of her hair with her fingertips. "For sadness for son." Her eyes reflected both sorrow and strength. "Now I go to husband." There was no hatred in her voice, only resignation and sadness. How could she face the man who crushed and abused her?

Everything inside Eliza shrank back from the inevitable events of this day, but she must confront them. She climbed from the wagon box, stiff from sleeping on the hard slats. Good thing the night had been a short one. She stretched, loosening her aching muscles and joints then nodded to the woman beside her. "I'll go with you."

They ran through the streets. How did Kima manage? When her own feet had been battered, the sharp pain made even walking unbearable. What drove Kima past the agony of each step? Hope that perhaps she had somehow been wrong? That it was all a horrible dream and that her child lived after all? Eliza clutched desperately to those hopes as well, but they were only a cruel mirage—a vague promise that delivered nothing.

The vigilantes filled the street in front of Pearson's Saloon where they had gathered last night. Restless horses huffed and fidgeted. Their riders occasionally let the reins go lax, allowing them to prance in tight circles.

Eliza's searching eyes found Jake at the edge of the cluster, but she did not go to him. The air crackled with tension. She groped for Kima's hand and clung to it.

At the center of the milling mob, Charles Kennedy was mounted on a broken-down nag, head down, hair and beard disheveled. Ropes bit into the flesh of his wrists, chaffing angry marks. Beside him Clay Allison held the nag's reins and those of another horse. The dead man's? Allison held his head high, glaring contempt at Kennedy from the corners of his eyes.

Eliza's heart was stirred to pity for the captured man in spite of all he'd done. If Kima did not hate him, how could she?

As the jailer approached, Kennedy lifted his gaze. There was no light in his eyes.

Kima started beside her.

Eliza placed a restraining hand on her arm.

Kennedy gave no sign that he even saw his wife.

The jailer stationed himself on the boardwalk, putting him almost at eye level with Allison. His right hand rested casually on his holster, fingering his revolver. "Is this the accused?"

Allison eyed the jailer's firearm, then shifted to sit even straighter in his saddle, his glare challenging any dispute. "He's the one that's done it. I'd 'a strung him up myself and saved you the trouble if it were up to me." His mouth twisted as he swiveled a disapproving glance toward Jake. "It seems a risk and a waste of air to let this vermin breathe any longer." With his elbow he gave the man beside him a vicious jab that nearly knocked him from his mount.

Vermin. Eliza had heard that pronouncement before. Why were men so quick to judge? To take matters into their own hands? It wasn't that she shied away from seeing justice done. The broken pieces of her heart cried out for justice against Joseph's killer, and yet she was not eager to see this man die.

The jailer snorted and jerked his head to indicate the direction of the jailhouse. "Bring him," he directed Allison, then turned and walked back down the boardwalk, brooking no discussion.

Allison passed the reins of the unridden horse to the man beside him, then spurred his own mount and jerked the reins of Kennedy's nag.

The mob parted to make way as they rode past.

Kima shook off Eliza's arm and jogged to her husband's side. "Charles?" Her upturned eyes glistened with tears, but he did not turn to see them. "Charles?"

When they reached the edge of the crowd, Jake reined in behind them.

Kima dropped back to trot along beside him. "My baby? My son? Did you see him?"

Jake's lips pressed into a grim line as he nodded. "I'm sorry."

They had reached the jail.

Kima sank to the steps.

Eliza swallowed hard and sat beside her, shoulder to shoulder. They did not speak. There was nothing to say that wasn't already clear between them. The mirage of hope was only a phantom.

A clink rang out from the back of the jailhouse.

The jailer emerged and faced the crowd of gawkers. "Go on home, now. There's nothing more we can do today." He fixed a sober eye on Allison. "You, too. Clear on out."

The vigilante did not budge. "What do you aim to do?"

"I'm going to send word to the territory marshal and wait for his instructions."

Allison snorted. "And meanwhile you'll pamper that polecat with three squares and a soft bed? Mighty high life for a killer." He looked around, inviting the mob's support.

A murmur of general agreement swelled around them.

The jailer took a stance, hands ready near his gun belt. "You've killed a man or two, yourself, from what I hear tell."

Eliza gasped. It was a dangerous thing to say.

A hush fell over the crowd. All eyes turned to Clay Allison.

The vigilante's eyes widened in surprise, but then his moustache twitched. He leaned forward in the saddle and rested his wrist across the horn, returning the lawman's steady gaze. "Well, now, Your Honor, I never killed a man that didn't need killing."

Realizing that he felt as justified in killing Grayson as he would in killing Kennedy made Eliza sick to her stomach.

"I'm not a judge, but neither are you. We got no evidence." The jailer stood his ground.

Allison threw his head back and laughed. "That, I can get." He pulled up on the reins. His horse reared as he spun up a cloud of dust. "John! David! Come with me." As his comrades joined him he looked back over his shoulder. "Anybody else wants to come along is welcome."

He had no lack of volunteers.

"We'll be back with evidence before nightfall, and then we'll be expecting swift justice." He pointed a challenging finger at the jailer then waved for his men to follow.

They pounded down the road. The sound of the horses' hooves changed pitch as they crossed the bridge.

Eliza watched as they rode south out of sight. A community effort, of a sort, but she found no encouragement in this brand of unity.

Aunt Charlotte approached with a basket. "Food. For your husband." Her aunt extended the basket to Kima. "Would you like to take it? Or shall I give it to the jailer?"

The Ute woman rose to receive it. "I will take." She disappeared into the jailhouse.

Jake, still mounted, shook his head. "How can she do that?"

Eliza squinted up at him. "Do what?"

"Face him. Care for him after what he's done."

"We're not required to like and approve of everyone, dear," Aunt Charlotte said. "We are required to love them. God, Himself, causes the rain to fall upon the just and the unjust. That young woman could teach us a thing or two about love and duty."

Eliza stared at the empty doorway that had swallowed up the grieving woman. "I hope her sacrifice has some good effect." She shook her head.

Kima emerged shortly, her face a mask.

Aunt Charlotte searched her eyes for a moment then said, "Let's go home."

Jake dismounted and lifted Kima onto his saddle, and the four of them walked through the streets.

By now Eliza was accustomed to the stares.

They settled the horse in the barn and walked through to the house.

Kima's black eyes grew large, taking in every detail of the room. "Joseph was here?"

Eliza nodded.

"It is a good place. Peace is here."

Aunt Charlotte placed a chair for her at the table and set a bowl of chicken and dumplings before her.

The Indian woman took a tentative sip from the spoon then refilled the utensil for a larger bite. An appetite was a good sign, but after a second bite, she set down her spoon and looked to Jake. "My son…"

"I buried him, ma'am." Jake's voice was full of compassion. "He was a strong boy, and handsome. I wrapped his cradleboard in a blanket I found in the cabin."

Eliza's head snapped up. She stared into the wide eyes of Aunt

Charlotte and Uncle Rufus, then all three turned to Jake. "Cradleboard?"

"Yes. Poor thing. He was strapped in snug and comfortable. Must have fallen against the fireplace when his papa threw the chair." He shook his head. "Might never have even waked up." He stared from one set of eyes to another. Only Kima seemed unsurprised. "What?"

"You buried an infant?"

"Her baby."

Aunt Charlotte found her voice first. "But, Jake, Joseph was about ten years old."

Now it was Jake's turn to be astounded.

All eyes turned to Kima.

"Husband killed baby. Joseph ran."

ꕥ

Jake ate in haste and mounted up again. With warm blankets and jerky in his saddlebag and a skin of water slung over the horn, he headed back toward the Palo Flechado Pass.

"Try not to worry." Uncle Rufus ushered the women back into the house. "The boy can't have run far. Likely he's just scared. Hiding. He won't have taken time to hide his tracks. Jake'll find him."

Eliza had no doubt of that. Her heart sang a song of praise. God had granted her ardent wish for one more chance.

The afternoon dragged as she longed for their homecoming.

Toward sunset they packed another meal for the prisoner. Eliza walked with Kima to the jail, and they were there when the posse returned.

Clay Allison spared a quick nod to the ladies as he dropped a feed sack onto the board walk.

A crowd began to gather.

The jailer emerged and stood in the doorway of the jail house. "What's this?"

"Evidence. Bones."

"Yeah. Lots of bones." The one they called Hoyt chimed in. "And there's more out there, plus the body of the man he shot yesterday and another one under the floor." He grimaced. "'Bout a dozen, I'd say."

The jailer's cool demeanor left him. His brow creased, and his lip curled. "You dug 'em up?"

"Didn't have to. Found these on a burn pile outside."

Eliza tasted bile and gulped.

Kima hung her head. The revelations obviously were not news to her.

"Looks to me like there's evidence aplenty." Allison's voice boomed, though the jailer stood only a few feet away.

The crowd began to rumble.

The murmured suggestions all amounted to the same thing. Charles Kennedy was not long for this world.

"That's for the court to decide." The jailer stood his ground. "I sent for a marshal this morning. The rider ought to return with news by tomorrow."

"We can wait that long." Allison was quick to recover the upper hand. "Couldn't hang him until dawn, on any count."

Course laughter affirmed Allison's pronouncement of sentence.

The jailer harrumphed. He stood for a moment, staring down the mob. When they did not disperse, he huffed again, walked back into the jailhouse, and shut the door.

ᘓᘐ

Back home, Eliza rocked beside the kerosene lantern, sewing squares of Cathay's neckerchief into her nine patch pattern. She bit off her thread and turned the squares. Backwards. She sighed and began to rip out the stitches.

Kima sat at the table, helping Aunt Charlotte shell beans into a bowl.

At the sound of hoof beats, their eyes met.

Uncle Rufus laid aside his pencil and ledger and headed for the barn.

The women waited, listening. Eliza's heart pounded hard enough to make the blood rush in her ears.

Footsteps approached the door.

She held her breath. Only two sets—Uncle Rufus's halting gait and Jake's, heavy and slow.

The door creaked open. Uncle Rufus entered first and held the door wide for Jake, who entered sideways, his back to the room. Then he turned. Draped across his arms a boy lay sleeping.

With a cry of joy, his mother sprang from her bench and flew to embrace him.

The boy struggled to lift his head and arms to return her embrace. "I am sorry I made father angry. I could not lie. Lies make God angry."

Weeping, Kima raked her fingers through his hair. The language that passed between the mother and son sounded strange to Eliza's ears, but her heart interpreted the words.

Aunt Charlotte hurried to the stove to prepare a plate of food.

"Don't bother," Jake said. "I fed him on the way, and he could barely hold on. He's tired tonight, but he'll be hungry as a spring bear in the morning." He smiled down at Kima. "Why don't you come with me? I'll carry him to the loft for you." He looked over their heads at Eliza and winked.

"Where will you sleep?"

"It's a soft night. I'll be fine outside."

Kima followed him to the barn.

Eliza gathered another blanket and a pillow and waited for Jake on the porch. She turned when the barn door closed softly.

"Thanks." He took the linens from her and dropped them onto the bench. Then he took her into his arms. "Long day?"

She nodded. "Worth everything in the end, though." She pressed her cheek against his shoulder and enjoyed the warmth of his hands on her back. She looked up. "I don't have to tell you how much it means, you riding with the posse and then finding the boy."

Jake's eyes shone down at her. "Seems like Allison and I keep crossing trails."

"Other than here and in the war?"

"One other time." He seemed to be measuring his words. "After the war. My unit, or what was left of it, was trying to get back home along with the Third Illinois Cavalry. A lot of those men came from farms near my family's land."

"Like Grayson."

Jake looked puzzled.

"He joined to support the boys he grew up with in Salado."

Jake nodded understanding. "Just so. One of the corporals with that unit was a cousin of mine. More than that, he was my best friend. He was like a brother to me. We'd kept up with each other—prayed for each other—all through the war, and now we were going home." He released her, sat on the bench, and patted the seat beside him. "The supply lines were in ruins, and Sherman had burned everything in his path the year before. There was no food, and we were starving. We'd been marching for days, trying to stay together. We came upon a farmhouse in Tennessee, and my cousin proposed to raid it for rations."

Eliza waited, encouraging him to continue.

"We watched as he slipped up to the cellar door. A few minutes later, he comes out with an armload of grub and heads for the bushes where we were hiding, keeping to the shadows. There were a number of us, so back he goes again." He shook his head. "He didn't make it. A man came out on the porch with a rifle. We could see him in the starlight, but we couldn't do anything. He crept around to the side of the house. I wanted to shout a warning—to make a run for him—but I couldn't give away our position. When my friend came out, he shot him at close range."

Eliza squeezed her eyes shut, as if that would take away the specter of the brutal act. It didn't.

When she opened them again, Jake's gaze met hers. "It was Allison. His face was branded into my memory even if he didn't have that club foot." He pounded his knee with his fist.

Eliza studied the lines of responsibility in his face, the torment in eyes that had seen too much killing and dying. "I'm sorry for your loss, Jake. I know it hurt, but how does this story play into your decision to ride with the posse?"

Jake was quiet for a moment as he searched for words. "My cousin was a good man, not a thief, but it was a desperate time, you understand. What we did—stealing—was wrong, but in a fallen world with so much wrong on all sides, well, a man can't just appoint himself sole judge and jury."

"I'm not sure I see the connection. Charles Kennedy doesn't seem driven by desperation. He is a drunk and a cold-blooded, calculating murderer."

"You're probably right." Jake studied his hands, stretching his fingers and turning both sides. "I've killed men, too, though. I regret it, but it got me thinking. What's the difference in killing and murder? When are you defending the law, and when are you breaking it?"

Eliza began to understand the workings of his mind.

"For me, it comes down to this. God authorizes governments—kings and armies and judges—to keep order and justice, and it's a heavy duty. We should never delight in sending a man to his judgment—especially, maybe, if hell is his destiny." His head cocked to one side. "Seems to me Clay Allison enjoys passing a hasty sentence. He may think he's upholding order and justice, but you can't keep the law by breaking it."

Eliza's heart swelled with pride. She placed her hands over his and squeezed them.

Jake lifted her fingers to his lips and brushed her knuckles with a kiss. "Go on in, now. The next few days are likely to be about like this one."

Eliza stood, but lingered a moment to look at the ridge. Her mind flew beyond it to Jake's valley. How could she ever have thought he ran there to hide from trouble.

Chapter 20

Eliza squeezed Joseph's hand, warm and alive in hers, as she and Jake walked with Kima to bring breakfast to the prisoner.

The boy had insisted on coming along. "I must see my father. I must ask him does he know about the God who takes away death."

Icy fingers closed around Eliza's mind. She doubted that the boy's words would have any effect in this world. If he meant to save his father from the gallows, that desire would surely be crushed. But there was a warming ray of hope. In the act of reaching out to offer the good news to others, Joseph demonstrated his own acceptance of the truth of salvation. Eliza would not discourage his attempts. She would find a time to talk with him later.

A crowd at the jailhouse parted to let them pass.

Eliza sensed their stares. She did not turn.

Jake placed Joseph in front of him and reached over the child's head to knock on the jailhouse door.

The jailer's face appeared at the window, and then the door opened a crack. "You bringing a meal?"

Jake nodded and rested strong hands on Joseph's small shoulders. "Boy'd like to see his pa."

The jailer nodded and opened the door for Joseph and Kima to slip through.

Jake declined. "I'll just wait here," he said, turning his back to the door and facing the crowd.

Tension, like the air before a lightning strike, made Eliza's skin prickle, but she caught Jake's casual tone and feigned her own unconcern. "I've an errand to run to the tailor's. I should be back before you're finished here." Spine straight, shoulders squared, eyes forward, her heels resonated on the boardwalk. She did not look back. If violent tempers could spread like fire, maybe a calm demeanor could slow its progress.

She hardly dared to breathe until she turned the corner. Mr. Lewis' shop was just across the street. Her skirts slapped at her ankles as she crossed in haste.

Once the door closed behind her, she leaned against it, eyes closed, gathering her scattered nerves. Three deep breaths. She opened her eyes.

Mr. Lewis and Mr. Matthews blinked at her.

"You look as if you've seen a ghost." Mr. Lewis supported her elbow and offered the chair behind his sewing machine.

"Not yet."

Mr. Matthews shook his head. "The vultures are already circling?"

She nodded. "As far as they're concerned, the trial is a formality. I hope the marshal or the judge or whoever he sends will arrive before people take matters into their own hands."

"You sure you have time for these?" Mr. Lewis said as he handed her several shirts and work pants ready to be finished.

"I'll make time." Eliza took the garments. "I'm hoping we can battle this insanity by behaving normally." She remembered to ask him about the remnants for her quilt.

He bundled a few and added them to the stack in her arms.

"Let me walk with you," Mr. Matthews offered as he held the door for her.

Eliza was touched by his kindness. They returned to the jail.

"Jake." Mr. Matthews stuck out his hand. "That was some race you ran at the picnic." *Thank you, Lord, for Mr. Matthews.* They needed more rational heads. Their pleasant chat might be a charade, but the effect was evident. The crowd quit staring and began to talk among themselves for the moment.

The door of the jailhouse opened, and Joseph stepped forth, his face as unreadable as his mother's. His talk with his father must not have gone as he hoped.

"Ready to go?" Eliza's voice almost cracked as she struggled to keep her tone light.

Kima rested her hand on her son's head and nodded.

The four fell into a formation of sorts with Jake and Eliza guarding the flanks.

ꕥ

By the time they took the noon meal, the crowd grew larger and the murmurs louder. When the jailer answered Jake's knock, the murmurs swelled to shouts.

"How long you going to protect that lowlife?"

"Long as I need to. It's a long way to Fort Union. Ain't no way that rider's gonna git back before tonight. You might as well go on about your business."

Eliza had intended to wait outside. The jailhouse was stuffy and reeked of Charles Kennedy's drunken sweat. She took no pleasure in his presence, but the rumbles of protest gave her second thoughts. Hatred and anger contorted the faces around her. She changed her mind and slipped in with Jake and Kima.

The jailer examined the contents of Kima's basket—a square of cornbread, a jar of soup, and another of buttermilk—and ushered her to her husband's cell. He returned, hung the ring of keys on a nail, and sat on the edge of his desk to wait. Lowering his voice, he spoke in confidence to Jake. "If that judge don't make it up here pretty quick, there won't be nothin' left of him to hang. That mob is ready to storm in here and tear him apart, and if they try, I don't know if I can hold 'em back."

The sound of shattered glass punctuated his warning.

Eliza jumped.

Slurred shouts and curses erupted from the holding cell.

"He's tossed that milk, I reckon. Now I got a mess to clean." The jailer shook his head. "Don't hardly seem worth the trouble."

"Would you like me to stay with you?" Jake offered.

"Would ya? I cain't deputize you or nuthin'—not until the marshal gits here."

"I don't care about that." He turned to Eliza as Kima reappeared, the ragged remains of her hair hiding her face. "Do you feel safe to take her home?"

Eliza bit her lip. She was not easily intimidated, but the angry shouts of the mob were loud enough to penetrate the thin wall that held them at bay.

"Never mind. I'll see you there safe. It'll give me a chance to fetch my rifle."

Her eyebrows rose as her eyes locked with his.

"Don't worry. It's not likely I'll need it. Sometimes just an earnest show of intent is convincing enough."

ꕥ

Jake lingered only a moment on the porch, rifle in hand. "I'll come for you when it's time to take his supper." With his free hand he toyed with Eliza's fingers. If the gesture was meant to be encouraging, it wasn't working.

"You'll be careful?"

"I reckon," he teased.

"I'm serious, Jake. I don't want to lose you."

He laughed. "I have no intention of getting lost."

Eliza bit her lip and took a swat at him.

His face became serious as he gazed into her eyes. "I haven't waited too long to find you to fall short of having you—not if I have anything to say about it." He shifted his rifle to his shoulder. "I'll be back."

Tears stung Eliza's eyes as she watched him go. She was getting mighty tired of seeing that man's back. With a deep sigh, she returned to the store. She might as well keep busy, only there weren't many customers today. Everyone was down at the jail or being careful to stay off the streets.

"Come, Joseph." Aunt Charlotte held out her hand, and small brown fingers grasped it. "Let's show your mother our garden. Bring a basket, and we'll see if we can find some fresh vegetables for your pa's supper after we pull a few weeds." She winked at Eliza over her shoulder as she parted the curtain divider.

Eliza sat on the stool behind the counter. She tapped her pencil against the countertop as she reviewed the ledger figures. She nibbled at the eraser then tucked the pencil behind her ear and closed the book. Beneath the counter she found the feather duster. Might as well tidy the shelves. When she finished she checked the pocket watch Aunt Charlotte left on the counter. The minute hand had barely moved. A long afternoon of waiting stretched before her.

She checked the front window. The street was empty, so she dashed back into the living quarters to snatch up her workbasket. She settled again on the stool, found her needle, and licked one end of her thread. The rhythm of the needle dipping in and out along the edges of the fabric usually soothed her, but today she found herself stabbing at the squares. Her stitches were small and tight. Her vision blurred.

Her breath came in desperate gasps. Peace. She yearned for peace more than all the gold in these mountains. She wanted to run away with Jake to his valley, away from the hating and hurting, the violence and the prejudice. She squeezed her eyes shut, rubbing the lids with her fingertips. If only she could make it all go away by refusing to see it. Ignorance would be such bliss.

Jake came just before sundown, and Kima hurried to meet him.

"We take food?" Her eyes looked hopeful.

He shook his head. "Better not."

The woman's countenance fell.

Eliza stared. Had she truly wanted to go? Why? There could be little love for a man such as Charles Kennedy. A man who could not be trusted. A man who had destroyed his own life and hers as well.

Jake took Kima's basket from her. "The rider came back this afternoon, and Allison was there to hear everything. Said the judge would be in on the late stage."

"And did he make it?" From the corner of her eye, Eliza saw Aunt Charlotte start to enter the room with Joseph then, hearing Jake's words, turn right around to take the boy out of earshot.

Jake nodded. "He did, and this letter came for you in the post." He palmed an envelope to Eliza.

When she saw Papa's strong handwriting, a wave of homesickness swept over her. She tucked the letter into her apron pocket to save it for a quiet moment.

Jake looked at Kima. "There'll be a hearing tomorrow morning. The judge will take testimonies. You and the boy will probably be called first. Will you come?"

Kima's eyes grew large. "I must speak against husband?"

"No." Eliza rushed to her side. "I don't think anyone can force you to do that."

Kima looked to Jake.

"There will be people, though, who will tell what they heard you say when you came to town for help, and by now they will have embellished it—made a bad story even worse."

Kima pondered this. "Boy should not come. Should not speak against father. I will not. Others will tell." She nodded once.

It was settled.

In the morning when Jonathan Ewing came for the cow and calf, Uncle Rufus sent Joseph along with him. "You two catch us some fish, y'hear? I'll git Lottie to fry 'em up for us for supper."

The boys jogged off across the meadow, and Eliza thanked God that whatever happened today, Joseph would not have to witness it. As for the rest, she did not know how to even begin to pray.

All five walked to the jail, a wall of support.

The crowd pulled back as they approached.

A short man with side whiskers and wearing an expensive suit stood eye to eye with Kima. "Are you the defendant's wife? The mother of the deceased?"

The Indian woman stared back at him.

Jake interpreted. "Kima, this is the judge. He wants to be sure that you are Charles' wife and that the baby who died was your child."

Kima nodded. "Charles Kennedy is my husband."

The judge pressed in. "And will you testify about how he killed your child?"

"No."

"Will you tell how he killed the other men?"

"No. Charles Kennedy is my husband. I must take food." She looked for the first time at the gathered mob and jerked her head in their direction. "They will tell."

A clamor broke out as various ones in the crowd jostled to speak first.

Kima walked into the jailhouse, head held high, with Eliza and Aunt Charlotte right behind her.

Jake and Uncle Rufus remained to help the jailer guard the door.

Eliza listened at the barred window as one after another of the townspeople came forward to tell their version of what they'd seen or heard. By the time they finished, Charles Kennedy was painted as the worst kind of monster. Perhaps he was, but this morning she saw little resemblance between the man they described and the waste of a man who hunched miserably in his cell. What could drag a person to such depths of depravity?

After some time the judge drew a gold watch from his vest pocket and called a recess.

"You gonna start the trial this afternoon, Your Honor?"

Eliza recognized Clay Allison's voice.

"No, sir. After lunch I intend to ride out to the scene of the crime and examine the evidence."

The grumbling rose in volume. This was an unpopular delay.

"Me and my boys will ride out there with you if it'll help speed things up."

The little judge just shrugged. If he hoped that time would cool tempers, his perceived stalling was having the opposite effect. Or perhaps he was simply following procedures. Eliza could not begin to guess at his motives, but lunch seemed to be his present priority. He strolled off in the direction of the hotel.

With nothing to watch, the crowd began to disperse.

The jailer, Jake, and Uncle Rufus stepped back inside.

Eliza hugged her arms close about her torso as if protecting herself against a siege.

They listened until the noise of the crowd faded off down the street. "This is good?" Kima's eyes searched their faces.

The jailer dropped a bar across the door. "I'm not sure."

Jake thumped the butt of his rifle against the floor, making a restless sound that caused Eliza's nerves to jitter. "That crowd is about to erupt. Allison has them stirred into a frenzy."

The afternoon passed quietly. Too quietly. The whole town seemed to be holding its breath. Jake stayed at the jailhouse, but the others went home to wait.

It was almost dark when Eliza and Kima returned with a basket of fish. A pair of mourning doves echoed each other's plaintive cries, beckoning the night. The streets were hauntingly empty.

A question burned in Eliza's mind. "Help me understand, Kima."

The Ute woman turned a serene gaze in answer.

"How can you still love him?"

Kima said nothing for the space of several steps. "I do not love Charles Kennedy—not as a woman loves a man."

"But you still serve him, honor him."

"I am bound to him. I serve him to honor my word. Whatever he does, I must do what is right. By what he does he will condemn himself." Her gaze dropped to the basket she swung in front of her. "Not many meals left to cook for Charles Kennedy."

"And can you forgive him…" They spoke of Charles Kennedy, but Eliza was thinking of Clay Allison. "…when he's hurt so many people? Is there any good at all that's come of his life?"

Kima looked up, her eyes soft. "Joseph."

True. Great pain had produced a great blessing. Without Charles, there would be no Joseph. Without Clay, she would never have met Jake. A loving God knew the hardships of the journey. A sovereign God knew the journey's end.

They were at the jailhouse when the judge returned from his sightseeing expedition.

The jailer opened the door to admit him.

Before he could enter, Allison pressed for answers on behalf of the mob. "Will the trial start tomorrow?"

The judge held up both hands, pudgy fingers splayed. "There will be a trial. I have sent for an attorney to represent Mr. Kennedy. He should arrive tomorrow. He will require a few days to examine the scene, review the evidence, question the witnesses, and prepare his defense."

The outcry was immediate and intense.

Though he tried to maintain control, the force of the protest seemed to thrust the judge through the door of the jailhouse for refuge. "They're riled," he said as the bar dropped behind him.

"They're like wolves. Now they've caught the scent of blood, I'm afraid they won't be appeased by anything less," the jailer said.

"Can you hold them off until morning?"

A terse nod was the only answer.

Jake took up his gun. "I'll escort the judge to his quarters and see the ladies home, and then I'll come back to sit watch with you."

The streets were like a swarming ant hill, kicked into a defensive frenzy by the atrocity. Eliza caught fragments of conversation as they passed.

"We got enough evidence."

"That lawyer's gonna try and git him off."

If this mob didn't storm the jail before morning, it would be a miracle.

When they reached Uncle Rufus' store, a shadow shifted by the door. Eliza sucked in her breath. She gripped Jake's arm and felt his muscles tense. He had seen it, too. A man waited in the dark.

With one hand, Jake swept Eliza and Kima behind him. He gripped his rifle near the lever and took a slow step forward.

Eliza held her breath and strained to see the shadowy figure. She could not make out his features, but she saw Jake's shoulders relax.

"Matthews." Jake stuck out his hand. "Why are you out tonight?"

"I don't like what I'm hearing in town. Thought you might be going back. I'll go with you if you like." Eliza caught the glint of his guns in the moonlight.

Jake clasped hands with Mr. Matthews before turning to Eliza. "Take Kima inside and lock the doors. No matter what you hear, do not come out."

"But—"

"I mean it, Eliza. No matter what. I need to know you'll be safe. Promise me."

Their gazes met, and it felt as if their souls joined purposes in that moment.

"Yes. I promise." Eliza's heart was pounding. *Oh, please, Lord, keep him safe. I cannot lose him.*

Eliza set her hand on the door latch. In the reflection of the glass display window she saw the men turn to go. She spun back to the street. "Jake!" It was only a whisper, but the sound carried on the night air. He turned, and she flew to him, embracing him, kissing him, and she didn't care who saw it. "Promise you'll come back."

"I promise." His hand was warm on her cheek. "Now get inside."

ᘓᘏ

When they reached the back room, Joseph flung his arms around his mother's waist. She caressed his hair.

Gunfire exploded on the street.

The boy flew to the curtain, but his mother pulled him back. "Stay. Be still." He obeyed instantly.

Eliza's heart lodged in her throat. Jake had not had time to make it back to the jail. Whatever was happening out there, he and Mr. Matthews were in the thick of it. She stared in horror at the dark curtain as she remembered the night when ten men died. The melee this night was far worse. *Oh, please, Lord.* Her terrified mind could not even formulate a prayer. She'd have to trust God to know the cry of her heart.

Uncle Rufus was suddenly beside her. They stood there, shocked into silence, for a moment that stretched into unmarked time—like a fiddle string, stretched to the breaking point. Eliza felt his hand upon her elbow, guiding her to a seat. He seated Kima, as well, in the rocker beside the lamp table. The Indian woman's face seemed chiseled of stone, her eyes fixed as on the night she fled to them in terror. Eliza was thankful that whatever horrors this night held, Kima would not have to see them.

Aunt Charlotte, seated at the table, patted the bench beside her. Joseph went to her and let himself be drawn into a warm embrace. The older woman cradled his head against her shoulder, whispering reassurances. Eliza sank to the bench beside him. A brown hand groped for hers and squeezed.

"I told him—about the God who takes away death. I told him, but father did not hear."

Eliza looked down into the face beside her. The boy's eyes were dark pools of grief. "Sometimes the seeds fall on hard ground, Joseph."

"Rocky ground. Many troubles." Even now the child gave his father grace. "Father's head is full of many evil spirits."

Eliza opened her mouth to correct him, but closed it again. The boy's words hit close to the truth. Satan had been hard at work in Charles Kennedy's mind for years. Who knew what demons drove him?

She floundered for words that might bring comfort. "As God's son, Jesus, was hung there were two men with Him. One cried out as he was dying, sorry for the bad things he had done. It was too late to change his life in this world, but Jesus promised him life after death. While there is breath, there is hope."

"Your pa heard you, Joseph." Uncle Rufus' face was soft with compassion. "You gave him that chance."

Aunt Charlotte bowed her head, and Eliza knew that she was praying. Praying for Jake. Praying for peace. And praying for Charles Kennedy's soul—before it was too late.

ꕥ

The noise in the streets roared on, unabated. If the vigilantes were storming the jail, Eliza could not imagine why it was taking so long. The jailer was only one man. Even if Jake and Mr. Matthews had managed to reach him, how long could three men hold out against an entire town gone mad?

Eliza strained to hear. The noise was changing. At first the angry shouts came from the direction of the saloons where men drank their courage. Then the words faded into a general clamor as the crowd seemed to move off toward the jailhouse. That was where the gunfire raged most violently. But now the sound came from one end of town to the other, as if men on horseback rode the length of the main street. Most disturbing, the shouting now did not sound angry. It sounded like cheering.

It went on for hours.

Joseph eventually fell asleep with his head in Aunt Charlotte's lap.

Kima just rocked.

Uncle Rufus paced. His hitch step fell into a pattern, interrupted occasionally as he stepped through the curtain to peer out the front window of the store. When he returned, he'd shake his head and begin the pattern again.

The front door rattled, and everyone froze. It rattled again—a soft knocking.

Uncle Rufus peeked into the darkness. "It's Jake." He hop-stepped down the aisle of shelves to let him in.

Eliza held her breath, but the men did not return. She heard the deep rumble of their voices, kept low. With an anxious glance at Aunt Charlotte and Kima, she slipped past the divider into the lightless shop. She blinked as her eyes became accustomed to the darkness.

"Never saw anything worse," Jake was saying.

Worse than the war? Worse than the killing fields, strewn with the bodies of men and horses?

They fell silent as Eliza approached. "They stormed the jail?"

Jake nodded, his mouth pressed into a grim line.

"The jailer?"

"Never saw him." He shook his head. "But never found his body, either. I suspect he ran." He shrugged. "Can't say I blame him."

Yes, but you didn't run.

"Matthews and I never made it back. We were behind the mob. By the time we got to the jailhouse, they were already there with the Allison brothers at the head of the pack. They dragged Kennedy out of his cell and threw a noose around his neck. John Allison tossed the other end up to Clay on horseback, and he dragged the sot up and down the street." Jake's face was pale in the darkness. He gulped and shook his head slowly, his eyes closed against the scenes in his mind.

"So the boy's father is dead," Uncle Rufus' said, his voice gravelly.

"Oh, yeah. Dead and then some." Jake's square jaw jerked to one side in a grimace. "They had a thirst for blood. Long after he was gone, they dragged that miserable soul's carcass through the streets, celebrating what they'd done." His fists clenched at his sides, and he shuddered.

Eliza shivered, too. This was not justice. It turned her stomach.

"Then they…" Jake stopped and squeezed his eyes shut.

"What?" Eliza breathed.

"They … Clay … he…" First he could not say the words, and then they all came out in a rush. "He cut off his head and stuck it on a pike."

Eliza recoiled, repulsed. She clapped her hand over her mouth and whirled toward the doorway that separated the shop from the house. The curtain hung motionless. Kima and Joseph had not heard. They did not know. Joseph must never know, if she could help it.

Uncle Rufus straightened. "Where's the rest of him?"

"They threw his body in the gulch. Matthews and I, we waited until they were gone to drag him to Hiram's. We laid him in the barn and covered him with hay in case anybody came looking."

"I'll go with you first thing tomorrow and git him buried."

"There's no way this town is going to let him be buried in the cemetery—not on holy ground."

Eliza was going to be ill. Holy? The town's actions were as barbaric as the crime committed. Surely there were any number of unholy citizens whose bodies lay on cemetery hill.

"Rufus, do you think you and Matthews can see to the burial alone?"

Eliza did not like the glint of steel in Jake's eye and the determined set of his jaw.

Uncle Rufus squinted at him. "Why? Where will you be?"

"I'm going after Clay Allison."

Eliza plucked frantically at Jake's sleeve. "Oh, no, Jake, you can't. You mustn't."

"I must."

"Why?" She was pleading now, desperate.

"Don't you see, Eliza? What he's done is every bit as heinous as Kennedy's crimes. You let that sort of self-righteous vengeance go unchecked, and this territory won't be fit for decent people to live in. His kind of hate is like gangrene. It spreads and infects the health of the whole community. He's got to be removed."

Her breath came in short gasps. She gripped his arm, imploring him to stay. "No. It doesn't have to be you. Let someone else go."

She'd seen this kind of heroic bent in Papa, and she knew well the price. "Can't you just forgive him? Love your enemy?" Her eyes searched his, beseeching. "Let him go."

Jake's strong hands closed on her shoulders. "No, Eliza." He put her away from him. "What sort of man would I be to close my eyes to such evil?"

"He has too many friends. They won't let you take him."

"I may not be able to stop him, but I can keep him from doing it here." He picked up his rifle. The argument was over. "Pray for me."

The bell tinkled as the door slammed behind him.

Chapter 21

A gaping grave on the north edge of cemetery hill devoured what remained of Charles Kennedy. Outside the fence. Out of the view of prying eyes. Out of sight and out of mind—at least she hoped so. Eliza stood with Kima and Joseph, Aunt Charlotte, and sweet Anne watching as the men pitched dirt into the hole.

"Stack stones—many stones—so evil spirits will not haunt dreams." Kima wrapped her arms about herself and shuddered.

Eliza didn't doubt that Charles Kennedy would haunt her dreams for some time to come, stones or no stones.

When it was done, Kima rode back on the buckboard between Aunt Charlotte and Uncle Rufus. Eliza climbed into the bed of the wagon next to Joseph. She swung her long legs off the back, matching the swaying rhythm of his moccasined feet.

As the horses plodded down the rutted road back to town, Eliza's imagination raced down a canyon, and fear pursued her. Allison most likely rode for Cimarron. Visions of Jake walking into an ambush of Allison's friends rose to loom over her, hemming in her every thought. Prayers, frantic and repetitious, echoed through her mind like hoof beats. Scripture poured from her heart like a river. *Oh, Lord, Your abundant mercy has begotten us again into a living hope. We are kept by Your power.* She knew Jake's eternal destiny was secure, but this trial of her own faith was like a refiner's fire that threatened to consume everything she most longed for on this earth. Men abandoned homes and comfort to fight and die for earthly riches. Jake was willing to give his life for a place where justice was done—where men loved mercy and walked humbly with God. Was she willing to sacrifice her dearest desires—for him, for a home, for peace—in exchange for a faith more precious than gold? She knew exactly what was at stake.

"Joseph, do you believe what I told you? About God sending His Son to take our punishment?"

"Yes."

Could it be so simple?

"For Him to take our death, we must also give Him our life."

The dark head snapped up. Dark eyes searched hers. "We must die to live?"

Eliza smiled. "In a way. We choose to die to who we have been—" and sometimes to what we long for "—so that He can live through us. Does that make sense?"

The boy nodded. "It is a symbol."

"Yes. We are sprinkled symbolically with the blood of his sacrifice and buried in water to wash away our old life, and when we come up, it is like being born as a new man." The wonder of this second chance with Joseph was like water to Eliza's weary soul. This—this opportunity to take hope to the places it was needed most—was why she could not retreat to a sanctuary of peace, however much her soul craved it. She must remain on the front lines of the struggle. "When you are ready to do that, will you let me know?"

"Yes." There was a sober look—a manly look—in Joseph's young eyes. He would think this through carefully.

Hiram, on the wagon behind them, did not take the route back to his shop. He followed their wagon to Uncle Rufus' store. When Eliza came from the barn with Aunt Charlotte, Kima, and Joseph, he was waiting with Mr. Matthews and Anne on the boardwalk. The burly carpenter addressed the Indian woman. "I'm awful sorry for your trouble, ma'am." He wrung his hat in his hands. "Have you thought about what you and the boy will do now?"

"I must return to my home."

Eliza started. "Kima, you cannot live there. Not after—" She couldn't say the words, but she didn't need to.

"I cannot live there. Too much death in that house. I will burn it."

Hiram nodded. "I'll be happy to take you out there in my wagon and help you, but then where will you go?"

Kima bit her lip. "I do not know."

"Back to your people?"

"I have been a white man's woman. I have no place with them."

Mr. Matthews stepped up to stand beside the carpenter. "Then perhaps you will find a place with us. I have a cabin at the back of my lot. Built it when we first came, but we don't use it now except for storage. It would be comfortable for you and your boy." He bent to Joseph's eye level. "I've got a boy just about your age."

This was a day of miracles. Eliza saw God's hand working through tragedy, softening hearts, healing wounds, shining a light in darkness.

"I cannot pay you."

"Perhaps you can." Anne joined the men. "We were talking on the way home, the three of us. I could use help in the kitchen—"

"—and I could use help in my shop, if your boy's inclined to learn a trade." Hiram smiled down at Joseph, who tugged at his mother's hand.

Kima looked from one eager face to the next.

"Say 'yes,' Mama!" The light of hope kindled in Joseph's eyes.

Kima nodded. "Yes." And then she smiled—the first smile Eliza had seen. It was beautiful.

ॐ

When Eliza tied on her apron, the rustle in her pocket reminded her of Papa's letter. She slipped up to her room to read it. The script was as familiar and as dear as his face.

Dear Daughter,

I must beg your forgiveness.

Eliza's brow furrowed until she realized that Papa had not had time to receive her latest letter—only the one in which she poured out her grief after Jake left.

I had a natural but perhaps misplaced desire to see you married. A godly home is a great blessing, and I wanted that for you. My brush with death reminded me that I would not always be there to provide one. In sending you to your aunt and uncle, though, I fear that I conveyed the idea that we must go in search of peace and purpose.

She could hear his voice in the words on the page. It was as clear as if they sat together in the parlor of the parsonage, discussing a favorite text or point of doctrine.

The Psalms admonish us to do good, to seek peace and pursue it—but, my dear, the pursuit takes place largely in our own hearts. Wherever you go, there you are, and your heart goes with you. You will not find your purpose in any duty nor your peace in any man if it does not first flourish in your own spirit, and if it is firmly rooted there, you can bloom in any garden.

I should have known that. If you still wish to return to your home, there will always be a purpose for you here, and whatever peace I can secure for you.

Your affectionate Papa

His words confirmed the lesson God had impressed on her this morning. She let the letter drop into her lap as she leaned back and closed her eyes. Barely three months ago on her first night in this very room she had felt His question, *Do you love me more than these?* And now she had a ready answer. *Yes, Lord.* More than loved ones, plans, and dreams. More than Jake. More than life itself. God was her peace, and in His presence was fullness of joy.

When the clatter of pans below called her back to her present duty, she returned to it with a heart at rest.

ÆÐ

Joseph's tears broke her heart. She had never seen the boy cry. Not when his father publicly abused him. Not at the graveside. But he cried buckets and begged to come with them as they prepared to burn the house. Eliza held him as he snuffled into her apron, his thin back heaving with sobs.

"Why would you want to come, Joseph? What is there but sadness in those walls?"

"It is my home. My mother and my brother were there. When my father was gone, there were happy times."

"You will have a new home—a better home—with the Matthews."

"Everything I have is there."

Eliza had known the same feelings of desolation when she left the home of her childhood. She knelt to look into his tear streaked face. "Tell me the things that are yours. I will find them, if I can, and bring them to you."

His chin quivered. "My bow. The blanket my mother gave me. And a very good fishing pole."

Was that all? It would be a simple matter to salvage such small things. Eliza gripped his shoulders and stroked his hair. "I will look for them. I promise."

Hiram helped Kima into the wagon, and Eliza climbed up beside her. Aunt Charlotte stood behind Joseph, her arms enfolding him as Uncle Rufus tousled his hair. She looked back until they were out of sight.

The Palo Flechado Pass was not green like the valley, but it had a rugged beauty all its own. The road skirted the slopes, winding west. When they came to the site of the cabin, Eliza would have missed it if Kima had not pointed.

Hiram pulled the wagon to a stop.

A ramshackle structure clung to the hillside. It was hard to say if it had been partially dismantled recently in the search for evidence or if it had long been in a state of disrepair.

Eliza stepped across a missing stair tread as she climbed to the dilapidated porch. Her hand froze on the door latch. She looked through a dust caked window instead. Inside was havoc and chaos—linens strewn and furniture overturned. She knew there would be blood, but the squalor obscured it. She took a deep breath to brace herself and lifted the latch.

The door squeaked on its hinges, and Eliza ducked beneath the low header to step inside. With her first breath she clapped a hand to her mouth and fled. Stumbling, she staggered to the edge of the porch, gripped the railing with white knuckles, and retched. The stench of death would not leave her nostrils. She gasped for air.

Hiram set down the barrel of coal oil he was unloading from the wagon bed and ran to her side. He held her ribcage and turned his head as she emptied her stomach, then offered his bandana.

Eliza folded it to tie over her face.

Kima stood beside her infant son's fresh grave, her eyes full of grief and shame.

"It's all right." Eliza's voice was muffled by the folds of fabric. "Is there anything you want?"

"Nothing."

Eliza understood. If it were not for Joseph's requests, she would not go in again.

She returned to the window to plan her strategy. A woven blanket in rich, earthy colors was kicked into a heap in one corner. Did the child sleep on the floor? Beside it, leaned against the wall, were a willow pole and a small bow. Must be. Eliza filled her lungs with a supply of fresh air then clamped her hand over her nose and mouth to hold the bandana in place. With quick steps, she headed directly for the pile of belongings, snatched them up, and made a hasty retreat.

Hiram waited for her. "Is that all?"

She nodded. By the time she reached the wagon with Joseph's treasures, he was already dousing oil on the roof. She joined Kima by the tiny grave.

Flint clicked and sparked onto the oily rags at Hiram's feet. When the flames caught, he used a cedar staff to spread them to the roof then pitched the rest through the open door.

The three watched as fire consumed the hovel. Kima stood dry eyed and expressionless.

Eliza took her hand. "I'm so sorry."

"Do not be. There is nothing here but death and sorrow."

The air in the canyon was still and hot. A column of smoke, black and swirling, rose higher than the trees on the cliffs above. The heat of the blaze singed their faces.

With a groan of protest the wood frame of the shack collapsed. They watched it burn to coals and ashes.

"For this Charles Kennedy killed and stole. For this he gave his life."

Kima spoke softly, plainly.

Eliza and Hiram stared at her, and then at each other. Eliza was glad the bandana hid her smile. The flames that destroyed Kima's old life freed her to live a new one. Here was another heart broken by the plow of adversity and ready for sowing.

They hauled water from the stream in buckets to douse the smoldering ashes. The red of a summer sunset tinged the sky before they left the canyon. Eliza rounded her shoulders and stretched her aching back. The smell of smoke and coal oil clung to her. Mesmerized by the creak of the wagon wheels, she let exhaustion overtake her.

Hiram helped both women clamber from the wagon when they reached Uncle Rufus' store. Aunt Charlotte and Uncle Rufus stood in the doorway.

Joseph ran to embrace his mother.

Eliza gathered his belongings from the wagon bed.

He beamed as he accepted them from her hands. "Thank you."

Eliza smiled back and stifled a yawn. She searched her aunt's and uncle's faces. "Has Jake returned?"

Their eyes told her he had not. Her stomach clenched and let out a rumble. She'd lost her lunch, and it was a long time since breakfast. Hunger was a welcome distraction, though when Aunt Charlotte set food before them, it had no taste. She picked at the meal as Kima carried a whistling teapot to add to the tub of water waiting on the porch. When she returned some time later, damp and fresh-smelling, Eliza had made scant progress.

"Try to eat, dear, while Rufus draws up a fresh tub," Aunt Charlotte admonished. "Starving won't bring him back any faster."

She forced herself to chew and swallow, but once her stomach was full and her aching body was soaking in the warm washtub, she wrestled again with her fear. Over and over she reminded herself of what she knew. God was good. He loved her. He loved Jake. His plans could not be thwarted by men, for God was sovereign. She repeated the same truths like a chant as she dressed for bed and combed out her matted hair. Only the damp tresses fanned across a towel over her pillow kept her from tossing and turning until sleep claimed her.

ഗ്ദ

On Saturday a trickle of customers grew to a steady stream by noon as people resumed their normal lives. Kima and Joseph left with Mr. Matthews to arrange their new home, so Eliza threw herself into work to occupy her mind. It did not keep her from checking the street every few minutes and praying with every breath.

Just as she stepped out to flip the "Closed for Business" sign, she saw Jake's horse at the end of the street. Flinging the sign onto a bench, she ran to meet him. The screen door slammed shut behind her.

Jake dismounted as she approached and took her into his arms.

"Oh, Jake, I was so worried." She murmured into his chest.

He shushed her, pressing kisses into her hair.

At last she raised her gaze to his. "Did you catch him?"

Jake grimaced. "No."

"How far did you chase him?"

"To Cimarron. Found him bragging in a bar."

"But you said you didn't catch him?"

"I didn't. Just caught up with him." Jake's shoulders drooped as if all the wind suddenly went out of him. "He was quite the sensation in Cimarron. I'm not a fool, Eliza."

She looked him square in the eye. "I never said you were, Jacob Craig."

"Well, I feel like one—dashing off on a fool's errand like that. Thinking I could make a difference." He shrugged, his hands palms up, empty. "What good is one man?"

"Why did you go after him?"

"To stop him. It wasn't right, what he did."

"In whose eyes?"

Jake stared at her in disbelief. "In God's eyes. Eliza, you can't mean—"

She put her fingertips to his lips. "No, of course I don't. But what I'm trying to say is that the battle belongs to the Lord. Clay's offenses are against God. All He asks of you is that you stand firm for what's right."

"I tried, but I failed."

"You did what you could."

"It wasn't good enough." His jaw clenched. "I hate to lose, Eliza."

"Be careful when you talk to a Southern girl about losing, Jacob Craig." Eliza slanted a mock glare at him. "You did all any man could do and more than most would. The results are up to God."

Jake's eyes searched hers for a long time.

"What are you looking for, Jake?"

"I wanted to keep you safe, Eliza. I wanted to earn your respect."

She flung her arms around him. "Oh, Jake, I am proud to be seen with the only man who cared enough to try." The tears in her eyes caught the light of evening lanterns so that his face sparkled as she looked up.

He wrapped a sheltering arm around her shoulders as they walked back to the barn.

She stayed to help him brush down his horse, as she did once before. That night seemed so long ago now.

Jake cleared his throat. "Eliza? Can we talk about the war again?

Just for a moment?"

At least tonight they were on the same side of the horse. She nodded and kept brushing.

"What you said about losing … how do you live with that?"

Not what she was expecting. She looked up. "Best way we can. What choice do we have?"

Jake twisted a handful of straw to rub the damp hair where the saddle had been. "When you believe something is right—care about it so much you'd die to defend it—and God takes it away … how do you…" The horse flinched as he brushed too roughly.

Eliza's eyes locked with his. "We're not talking about the war, are we, Jake? Nor Clay Allison, either."

His fists clenched as he pressed his forehead against the horse's warm flank. "No."

"Julia? Your son?"

He nodded. When he looked up, his eyes were moist. "I hate to lose, Eliza."

"It wasn't your fault."

"If I'd been here…"

"There wouldn't have been a thing you could have done to change it. Our days are numbered before we've lived a one of them."

"You can't tell me God wanted Julia and Earl to die."

"I'm only telling you that God knew they would, and He had a plan to work it into the pattern of your life and bless you in the end. He takes no pleasure in our sorrow, Jake." Her hand rested on his shoulder. "When something happens that we didn't plan, didn't want, and our life takes a new direction, it's natural to feel the pain of our loss. But if we become bitter, somewhere at the bottom of it, it's God we resent for allowing us to be hurt."

He started to protest but apparently thought better of it.

"You haven't met up with much that you couldn't whip, have you, Jake?"

His wry grin confirmed it.

"God is good, and He is just. He knows the best course for our lives. We can't spend our days making our own plans and then battling His will when it doesn't match up." She knew. She'd tried it herself for years. "It's like trying to move a river to blast away a mountainside."

Jake snorted. "That's been done."

"Not very effectively. That Big Ditch of yours is full of leaks!"

Jake's deep laugh rewarded her, and she laughed with him. She clasped his hands in hers. "The only way you can be assured of never losing, Jake, is to lose yourself in His will."

ꙮ

It was a quiet supper with just the four of them. A family again.

After the evening chores were done, Eliza stepped onto the back porch to drink in the cool mountain air. Jake was there, staring at the ridge, but somehow his gaze seemed focused beyond it. Eliza joined him. "It's pretty, isn't it?"

"Mmm-hmmm." The guttural reply was his only response for several moments, until he turned his gaze to her. "I can only think of one thing that would make it more beautiful."

She felt the heat rise in her cheeks, and Jake's hand rose slowly to caress them.

"Eliza, I couldn't stop thinking about you. I know when I go home again this time it will be the same." His thumb stroked her jaw line. "I want you to know that I would not play with your heart. We've both loved and lost—"

"—and you do hate to lose."

His chuckle was deep and husky. "I mean to win your heart, Eliza."

Eliza placed her hand over his and turned it over to kiss the calloused palm. "It will be an easy battle, Jacob Craig. In fact, it's safe to say that you could declare victory now, if you wish."

He laughed. "Not so hasty. I mean to court you properly." His eyes looked into her very soul. "I didn't come to these mountains looking for treasure, but I found it just the same."

Eliza's heart skipped several beats and caught them up again later. He wanted her—found her beautiful.

"Whom should I ask for permission to marry you? Your uncle? Your Papa?"

"Both, I suppose. You will need Papa's address—"

"I have it."

Eliza's brows peaked in surprise. "How?"

"When I carried your letter to Cimarron, I copied it down just in case." Jake laughed softly. "I carried your picture in my pocket for years before that letter joined it."

"As long ago as that?" The wonder of it.

"Since first we met. From the moment I laid eyes on you." He cupped her face in his hands and tipped her chin upward. His fingers brushed her lips. Then he lowered his face to hers. His lips were warm and soft, and she savored his breath as it mingled with hers—a symbol of their mingled lives. When it ended, his hands lingered on her face. "I'll talk to Rufus after church tomorrow, but then I must go."

"Must you?"

"I have to make ready for winter—make a place for you. I'll drop a letter to your Papa by the stage office as I leave."

"When will you return?"

"I'll come every Sabbath."

"And I'll think of you every day in between them."

Jake's gaze returned to the ridge that would separate them. The first stars were just rising. "See that one?" He pointed out a bright star that hung low in the western sky.

Eliza nodded.

"That one's ours. When it comes out each night, you'll know I'm watching for it, praying for you."

She rested her head on his shoulder and listened to the steady beat of his heart. God made all things beautiful in His time. Her heart had found its home, its place of peace.

Epilogue

Aunt Charlotte put off her mourning clothes toward the end of August. When Eliza came down to breakfast one morning, her aunt was radiant in a dress of pale blue poplin.

Uncle Rufus was just coming in from the barn. His eyes softened as they rested on her. "You look lovely, Lottie. Pretty as a new day."

Her aunt's eyes sparkled as she mimed a curtsey. "It feels good to wear color again."

"You're ready to do this?" Even though her aunt and uncle had given hearty consent, Eliza still felt a bit shy about her relationship and approaching marriage to Jake. She did not want to rush their grief.

Aunt Charlotte's eyes misted as she looked at her husband. "I will never forget them. I don't need black to remind me, but it's time to move forward. I am ready to try." She brightened. "Check your sewing basket, Eliza."

On top of the basket beside the rocker, a much worn dress of navy hue, just the color of the night sky, was folded neatly.

"For your quilt. There should be enough fabric in the skirt for the backing, if you like."

Eliza sat and spread the garment across her lap then tried the squares against it for effect. It was perfect. "I love it, Aunt Charlotte. The dark sets off the other colors." She ran her hand over the patterned blocks. Lights and darks. Bits and pieces of her life. Good times and sorrow all fitted neatly into place to make something beautiful, something useful, something good. "If I hurry, I should be able to finish it by the wedding."

Her heart fluttered as it always did when she thought of her life with Jake. The circuit-rider would be in town the second Sunday in September—two days past the end of the year of mourning. For years she had put her dreams of marriage and family aside, but God had resurrected them. If only Papa could see her wed, she could think of nothing more she could want.

ꕥ

September arrived, and Eliza saw the valley as Jake had described it. The mountains shimmered with aspen. They blazed among the pines like veins of gold. The meadows beyond Elizabethtown and the sky above were the same shade of aster blue. Here was treasure for any man's eyes.

Eliza could see her breath when she gathered eggs before breakfast, but by midmorning when she went to pick the last fresh vegetables from the garden, the warmth of the sun released the sweet aromas of earth and plants.

Saturday was especially busy as customers laid by stores for winter. Millie and Zeke dropped by for a bag of pickling salt. Before they left, Jake helped Zeke tie the calf to the back of the wagon. Eliza hated to see May go, but she was strong and leggy and able to graze on her own now. April's milk was a popular commodity with the families in town, and Aunt Charlotte's butter churn had found a permanent home beside the rocking chair.

Uncle Rufus had taken the wagon to Cimarron. "One good haul this month, and perhaps another in October if the roads stay clear. It's been a good year," he said with a shake of his head. "I'd a' never thunk it."

Aunt Charlotte hovered near the window all day, watching the street.

"I'm sure he'll be fine, Aunt Charlotte." Uncle Rufus took a good bit of money with him, but he was well armed. There had been fewer robberies in the weeks since Charles Kennedy's lynching. Elizabethtown seemed to be enjoying an epidemic of good behavior.

The shadows were long when they heard the squeak of wagon wheels. Aunt Charlotte poked her head out the door, squealed, and ran out, letting the screen door bang shut behind her. Goodness.

Eliza smiled to herself. It was good to see the affection between her aunt and uncle even after so many years of marriage.

Eliza heard Uncle Rufus back the wagon into the barn. Aunt Charlotte's voice was shrill with excitement, and her laughter carried on the breeze through the open door. Uncle Rufus must have brought back some surprises.

She closed the ledger and shut and locked the front door. They would need her help unloading. She pulled back the curtain, opened the back door, and froze. "Papa!" She found her voice after a moment of stunned silence. "Papa!" And the tears began to flow.

"I came to offer to bring you home, Eliza, but Rufus assures me there is no longer any need of that."

"Did you not receive Jake's letter, then?"

Papa laughed. "I did, indeed. Shortly before I left, but it only gave me another reason to come. I've brought your other trunk. I trust I have made the trip in time to witness your marriage?"

Eliza took both his hands in hers. "You have arrived in time to give me away—or to perform the ceremony, if you wish. I can think of nothing more fitting."

"Nor I." Papa's fingers squeezed hers. "When do I get to meet this new son of mine?"

"I am here, sir." Jake stepped onto the porch with Jonathan Ewing, who had been helping him turn the garden. He rested a pitchfork against the porch post and brushed his hands against his pants before offering one.

Papa clasped it, and they shook warmly. "You may have her only if you will treasure her as I do."

Jake's voice was warm with feeling. "More than gold, sir. More than gold." Then, "May I help you unload your trunks, sir?"

"No, thank you, just the one that is Eliza's. I believe Charlotte has made accommodations for me with your friend, Anne."

Were they all in on the surprise? "How long can you stay, Papa?" With her wedding in just a week, their time would be short and precious.

Papa's eyes twinkled. "Well, now, I hear there's soon to be a vacancy upstairs, so I was thinking I'd stay until Spring, if this town could still use a preacher."

Eliza wanted to jump for joy. Instead, she flung herself into his arms. "Oh, yes, Papa!" Looking over his shoulder, she found Jonathan taking in the scene. "Jonathan, how would you like to do a job for me?"

The boy's head bobbed eagerly.

"Papa, do you feel up to preaching tomorrow?"

"I believe I could muster the gumption." He winked.

"In that case, Jonathan, would you run to all the houses of our church members and tell them that we will have services tomorrow with a special guest speaker?"

"I will." The boy's freckles bunched up as he grinned. "And I won't even charge you a nickel." And then he was off and running, leaving them laughing together on the porch.

ꕥ

Eliza could not remember a more joyous Sunday. She sat beside Jake with Aunt Charlotte and Uncle Rufus. Joseph and Kima sat with the Matthews family, and Hiram joined them. He had begun attending since the fire, and even trimmed his beard for the occasion. In a clean suit, he looked much younger than Eliza had first guessed.

Papa preached a fine sermon on love and forgiveness. When he gave the invitation, Eliza held her breath as Joseph rose and walked to the front of the church. Papa bent to put his ear closer to the boy, but he needn't have bothered. The child's request was audible to everyone. "I want to be baptized."

Papa glanced at the boy's mother, who confirmed her approval with a nod. He sat at the edge of the altar, and man and boy conferred softly while the congregation sang a hymn. After the last verse, Papa held up his hands. "It seems as if we have a new member to welcome into our family." He paused for a moment until the noises of celebration died down. "If you'll join me after services down by the creek, we'll celebrate his new birth in Jesus."

The congregation poured through the doors and down the hillside.

Millie held back to walk with Eliza. "You're beaming," she announced with a grin.

"And you're blooming." Eliza laughed, eyeing her friend's bulging midriff. "I am very happy."

Millie pressed a hand to her waist. "You reckon this little one will have a playmate any time soon?"

"You never know." Eliza blushed and smiled through pressed lips. Best to enjoy each day as it came.

Papa removed his shoes, rolled up the legs of his trousers, and waded out into the middle of the stream. He beckoned Joseph to join him.

The boy kicked off his moccasins and stepped into the swirling water.

"With what name would you like to be baptized?"

"Joseph Ken—" He stopped short and looked up at the preacher. "If I am born again, I do not want my old name. May I choose another?"

Papa shrugged. "I don't see why not. The Bible says that in heaven, Jesus will give all of us a new name. I can't see any reason why you shouldn't have a new one now." He smiled down at the boy. "What name would you like to use?"

Joseph scanned the crowd until he found his mentor, Hiram. "May I use yours?"

"Mine?" The rugged carpenter appeared thunderstruck as he pointed to his chest.

The boy nodded eagerly.

"What's your name, sir?" Papa asked.

"Newman. Hiram Newman."

"Joseph New-man." Joseph tried the name on for size. "Yes. I like it. New man."

"Then with your permission…?"

All eyes were on Hiram as Papa waited for the go-ahead.

The carpenter's eyes filled with tears, and his whiskers twitched. He started to answer, but no sound came out, so he just nodded.

"In that case, I baptize you, Joseph Newman, in the name of the Father, and the Son, and the Holy Spirit." With a splash, Papa lowered the Indian boy into the shallow water of Moreno Creek and brought him up again, spluttering and smiling. "'If any man be in Christ, he is a new creature: old things are passed away; behold, all things are become new.'"

Papa scooped up a handful of the sparkling water. Rivulets ran down Joseph's hair and into his face. He scrunched his eyes shut and blew droplets from his mouth and nose.

"May the Lord pour out His Spirit upon you and empower you to walk in His ways."

Happy tears pooled in Eliza's eyes.

Joseph grinned broadly as he slogged up the grassy riverbank toward her. Dripping wet, he wrapped his arms around her waist.

She didn't mind a bit. Eliza enveloped him in a hug before releasing him to return to his mother. As her gaze followed him, she could not fail to notice Hiram standing beside Joseph and his mother. He was beaming, too—proud as a new father.

ꙮ

Eliza Gentry slipped her hand into the crook of Papa's arm as she waited beside him. They shared a glance that said so many things for which there were no words. Her eyes misted, and she saw that his did, too.

The church bell pealed above her, and the morning sun warmed Eliza's hair as the doors swung open. It was as if the hand of God rested upon her, confirming the rightness of this moment.

Jake waited at the altar, surrounded by their friends. The fiddle sang. Jake's eyes drew her as they had once before.

Sunlight streamed through the open doors, lighting a path before her.

Smiling, Eliza took a step. The first step of a new journey.

RESEARCH NOTES FROM THE AUTHOR

Though this story is a work of fiction, it is based on several historical characters and events.

Waco, Texas was occupied during the Reconstruction Era by agents of the Freedmen's Bureau reinforced by federal troops. Lt. Manning discovered and jailed the prominent citizens who castrated Tony McCrary, and a riot ensued.

Major General Sheridan's troops fought at the Battle of Chickamauga opposite the Third Illinois Cavalry and Hood's Texans. They were stationed at Fort Union, New Mexico during this period. "William Cathey" was among them … until Cathay Williams was revealed as a woman. Discharged immediately, she eventually settled in Pueblo, Colorado.

After being discharged from the Confederate Army for his violent outbursts, Clay Allison herded cattle along the Brazos River and spent several years in Raton, Cimarron, and Elizabethtown. An infamous gunman, his part in lynching Charles Kennedy is legend, though I took a bit of license in placing the event about three months earlier than it actually occurred.

Charles Kennedy's story is, unfortunately, also true, though it has been told so many times that it is difficult to discern the facts from the embellishments. He did keep a roadhouse where he murdered and robbed guests, his wife was Ute, and he did kill his child in a drunken rage.

The rapid growth of Elizabethtown after the discovery of gold is well documented. Many elements of this story, from the Big Ditch to the night of gunfighting, are drawn from historical accounts.

Jacob Craig, Eliza Gentry, her father, Uncle Rufus, and Aunt Charlotte as well as Zeke and Millie Pickens exist only on these pages … to the best of my knowledge.

Books in the
SANGRE DE CRISTO SERIES

More Precious Than Gold

Stronger Than Mountains

Flowing Like A River (Coming 2024)

A Preview of
STRONGER THAN MOUNTAINS

Chapter 1
Slim Pickens Ranch
Moreno Valley, New Mexico

Eyes wide, fingers rigid, Millie Pickens clutched the quilt below her chin, listening. The sound that awakened her was now lost on the other side of the boundary between sleep and consciousness. She exhaled soundlessly, her breath forming a cloud in the lean-to.

A faint pink glow tinged the frost on the windowpanes. She lay quiet, listening, drinking in the silence as her heartbeat returned to its normal rhythm. The few precious moments of peace before the late winter sunrise were almost enough to make its bitter cold worth enduring.

Zeke lay still beside her, jaw lax, mouth agape. Millie stretched her toes closer to his sleeping form, soaking in the warmth that radiated from his body. Most days he was up before the sun, but for a few weeks each year before calving season there was a blessed respite. Feathers rustled beneath her ear as she turned her head to study his profile in the pale light.

Despite the stubble he was still a handsome man, though the years had left their mark. His face had lost its boyish eagerness in exchange for a few wrinkles. The creases gave him character, but she missed the lopsided grin he always wore when they were young. One teasing glance—one wink—used to make her knees go wobbly. The twinkle in his eye explained the four young 'uns asleep in the loft … and the four young 'uns explained her gratitude for this moment of peace.

There should have been two more, but maybe the Lord knew she had all she could handle. The four she had would be up soon enough, clamoring for breakfast. Then their needs along with the duties of home and farm would claim pieces of her all day long until she collapsed onto the straw tick again tonight. She loved them, but mothering was like being nipped to death by tadpoles.

This one moment, though—this was hers alone.

With a snort Zeke stirred to life, shivered, and clawed for a larger share of the covers. "Laws a' mercy, it's cold in here!"

Just one moment—precious, brief … and over. Millie sighed. "I'll stir the fire."

She rolled to her side, but Zeke's arms pulled her back. "Come here, woman. I got a better idea for keeping us warm."

The twinkle was still there. Maybe two could share one moment…

The sudden unmistakable patter of water on the tin roof dampened any flame Zeke was trying to kindle. *Rain?*

Scuffling feet produced a downpour of dust through the boards of the ceiling that formed the floor of the loft above. "Jackson! Shut that window before we all freeze." Beau, their eldest, considered it his duty to keep order.

The moment definitely over, at least now she had a clue about the sound that woke her.

"Ew! Jackson! As if it ain't bad enough I got to share loft space with you … Ma!"

The shrill voice of her daughter shredded what remained of Millie's peace. Dixie Lee dressed like her older brothers, rode and roped—even talked like them. She'd soon be eleven, though. She'd need more privacy than a blanket hung over a rope to divide the attic. The girl needed a room of her own. Soon as the weather got fine Millie'd talk to Zeke about building one, but when would he find the time?

"If you insist upon living in the manner of beasts, I suggest you move to the barn." Forrest, her second born, weighed in with a plea for the culture and decorum he craved.

"Don't tell me what to do!" Jackson, their third, nurtured a deep resentment that he hadn't been born first. "It's too cold to run out to the outhouse every blasted time."

"Ma!"

Another shower of dirt poured through the ceiling, and boots scraped against the rungs of the ladder before the window slammed shut.

"Ma!"

Millie groaned and shrugged out of Zeke's grasp. "The fruit of your loins…" She didn't even try to conceal the undertone of accusation as she shoved her feet out from beneath the warm covers. "I'll poke the fire. You draw water."

"Aw, girl, spare me time for a kiss at least. Just one." Her husband sat up in the bed and puckered.

Millie rose to oblige him with a peck.

Her stomach lurched. Frantic, she shoved him away and gulped against familiar spasms.

Zeke stretched, rubbed his shoulder, and scratched before it dawned on him that something was wrong. His forehead furrowed. "Are you sick?"

She shook her head. Not sick … at least, not ill.

Eyes wide, she clapped a hand over her mouth and fled barefoot into the snow.

Made in the USA
Columbia, SC
11 February 2024